****

Monroe Doctrine
Volume VII

****

By
James Rosone & Miranda Watson

****

Published in conjunction with Front Line Publishing, Inc.

1

Copyright Notice

Table of Contents

Foreword

We have some exciting extras we are sure you will enjoy as you read this book. On our website, you can access special content that goes along with this book, including the one thing all of our fans always seem to ask us for...battle maps. To access this content, please visit https://www.frontlinepublishinginc.com/members-only and sign up with your email address.

Chapter 1
Aussieland

August 2026
2nd Royal Australian Regiment
Jiaxian, Taiwan

Lieutenant Geoffrey Sawtell's unit was exhausted. They were running on adrenaline and caffeine and not much else. Shortly after pushing inland flowing the landings, the 2 RAR had found themselves fighting through multiple enemy fallback positions as units from the PLA's 3rd Light Combined Arms Brigade would put up stiff resistance for half a day to a day. Then they would fall back to the next defensive position and repeat the process. As Sawtell's unit probed along the edges of the enemy position, they stumbled upon an unguarded farmer's trail. After reconning the trail, they discovered it would lead them behind the enemy's fortified position and allow them to roll up the entire PLA unit.

After a brief but violent battle, what was left of the enemy battalion retreated west along the Nanbu Cross-Island Highway, until they reached the Jiaxian Bridge that spanned the Qishan River. When Sawtell first saw the bridge and PLA vehicles racing across it, he wanted to give chase, to get his guys across the bridge and make sure it couldn't be put out of action. However, when he briefed his plan, he was told to hang tight until Bravo Coy, 5 RAR was able to link up with his unit. It felt like an eternity waiting for the units M113 armored personnel carriers to catch up to them. When they arrived on the scene, Sawtell outlined his plan of attack and got the other commander to agree to support it.

Sawtell climbed into the back of his Boxer combat reconnaissance vehicle and observed what was happening around them from the Wasp UAV they'd just launched to give them eyes over the bridge. Before his platoon, which was packed in the CRVs, would race down Wenhua Road towards the Jiaxian Bridge, they were to wait until B Coy was able to maneuver three of their M113A1 medium reconnaissance vehicles or MRVs into an overwatch position in a nearby park just south of the bridge. On the opposite side, another three MRVs would move into position, giving Sawtell six vehicles able to provide covering fire as his platoon advanced across the bridge to secure the other side.

We shouldn't have stopped, Sawtell thought. *If we had chased them across, then we wouldn't have given the enemy time to set a trap as we cross the bridge.*

It was moments like this that he wished he'd been able to join the military a few years earlier. He likely would have been a captain, or potentially even a major at this point instead of being a senior lieutenant. Some of the tactical decisions made by those a rank or two above him were baffling sometimes.

Holding the tablet tightly as he watched the UAV scan the buildings and vegetation opposite the river, Sawtell couldn't help but wonder how many missile teams had been left behind by that motorized light infantry battalion as they passed through. He didn't like to travel through choke points unless absolutely necessary. With no other bridges nearby to cross the Qishan River, however, he was stuck. This was the only way across, which meant the enemy knew that too.

"The overwatch is almost in position," announced Sawtell's drone operator as he continued to scan the opposite bank, looking for signs of trouble.

Sawtell sent a message to his vehicle commanders to stand by. Once the B Coy units radioed they were in position, then he'd order his CRVs to pull out of the parking lot they'd staged in and advance rapidly towards the bridge. Given the performance of his combat reconnaissance vehicles since coming ashore, Sawtell felt reasonably confident in saying if they ran into trouble along the way, then the vehicles' 30 mm auto cannons would be more than a match for whatever the enemy might throw at them. The Boxer CRVs were a huge improvement over the MRVs B Coy was still currently using. The ammo used in the 30 mm autocannons packed a hell of a punch, intermixing air-bursting shells and armor piercing slugs. The double punch from explosive to armored slug had allowed them to break through more than a few enemy positions since coming ashore.

The radio crackled in Sawtell's helmet, and the voice of Lieutenant MacLaurin announced, "Ringo One, Bara Two. We're in position, no sight—"

As MacLaurin was in the process of finishing his sentence, Sawtell spotted a missile as it leapt into the air from across the river along the side of a building. The ATGM was airborne for the brief time it took to travel the short distance across the river before impacting against one of the MRVs. The sudden force of the shaped charge exploding into the vehicle compartment caused the turret to blow right off the vehicle and sent it cartwheeling through the sky. Moments later, the remaining ammo in the vehicle's hull started to cook off, spewing flames into the air.

The two other vehicles next to MacLaurin's burning wreck popped their defensive smoke canisters to rain down around them as the drivers reversed the APCs to find a new position that wasn't compromised. The gunners aboard the other tracks returned fire, raking the tree lines with cannon and machinegun fire as they looked to suppress any further missile teams from nailing more of their trucks.

With a full-blown firefight underway and the enemy focusing their attention on the APCs, Sawtell figured it was now or never if they wanted to get across the bridge. He shouted to the vehicle commander, "Go, go, go! Get us across the river now!"

"Yes, sir," came the quick reply as the vehicle lurched forward onto the road that would lead them to the bridge.

The CRV pulled out of the parking lot and took off down the road, picking up speed to run the gauntlet across the bridge. Sawtell hoped the enemy hadn't been waiting to blow it up as they drove across. As they raced past the buildings, crossing the intersection and driving onto the bridge, the enemy shifted fire from the APCs to their direction.

Tink, tink, tink.

As they raced across the bridge, Sawtell felt his sphincter pucker as bullets hammered the vehicle relentlessly, pounding on the armored shell like a jackhammer. Then the vehicle gunner opened fire, spewing 30mm airburst rounds into the buildings and tree lines from which the machine gunners were firing.

"Missile five o'clock!" the gunner yelled, and the driver swerved to the right fractions of a second before it impacted where they'd just been.

BAM!

The shock wave from the near miss caused the vehicle to momentarily slide across the pavement until the tracks gained traction again and the vehicle continued to race forward.

The gunner continued to direct 30mm cannon fire into the nearby buildings and tree lines from which the missile crews and machine gunners were still firing. Once they were across the bridge, the attack stopped, and the remaining Chinese soldiers took off running, some fleeing further into the woods and others back into the residential areas near the main road.

Sawtell glanced down at the tablet, where the drone feed was still live. He smiled when he saw a column of M113s following them across the bridge. As much as he'd like his people to dismount and work on clearing this area out, his orders were to advance to the intersection of Highway 20, which led into the mountains until it crossed the island just north of Tainan City. Then, in the other direction, Highway 29 connected to the southern coast, where the First Marines Expeditionary Force was battling it out with elements of the PLA 74th Group Army. For now, clearing the town would have to fall on the shoulders of B Coy, 5 RAR.

"Lieutenant, it looks like we're past whatever was back there," said the vehicle commander. "The nav says we're a couple of klicks out from Objective Troy. Once we reach the intersection, do you want to dismount your troops and set up a roadblock while we hold up for follow-on forces, or how would you like us to proceed?"

"Damn orders. We should be continuing until we hit resistance—not sitting on our duffs while we wait for the enemy to reorganize," Sawtell cursed under his breath. At a volume that the others could hear, he replied, "Yeah, we'll dismount once we get to the intersection. We'll set up this roadblock and stand by until our orders change or the rest of the 5 RAR catches up to us." Sawtell wasn't thrilled with having to slow down their momentum. Then again, getting too far ahead of their forces would put them in a bad position should they run into an enemy force greater than what they could handle.

The Boxer CRV slowed down as they approached the intersection. Sawtell was looking at the UAV's footage of the area when he spotted something moving around a few hundred meters to their front. He zoomed in on the image and his eyes widened as he saw a man lift an object to his shoulder. He warned the driver, who turned hard to the right just as the guy fired the missile.

They didn't maneuver fast enough. The missile hit the front corner of the track, causing them to halt abruptly. The vehicle commander dropped the rear hatch, allowing them to bail out of the stricken vehicle.

Sawtell broke to the right with the others as they dove into the culvert next to the road. A string of machine-gun fire ripped through the air above them as rounds bounced harmlessly off the damaged vehicle they had just abandoned.

"Corporal Roderick, take your team and see if you can't suppress those machine gunners!" ordered Sawtell. "And try to keep those missile teams off the vehicles." Then he radioed to the ASLAV and M113 vehicle commanders to dismount their soldiers and be ready to support his troopers as they cleared the ambush.

****

Corporal Jim Roderick heard the lieutenant's orders, but his body wouldn't obey. He couldn't move. The bullets missed him, but his mind went numb—until Lance Corporal Butler shook him, shouting, "Roderick! The LT's yelling for you!"

Snapping out of it, Roderick turned, yelling, "On me!"

He sprinted forward, his EF88 Austeyr blasting at the enemy as he ran. Chinese machine gunners and missile teams waited on a hilltop, ambushing the CRVs at the intersection. The CRVs fought back, shredding the hilltop with air-bursting rounds, catching several missile teams before they could fire.

"Lay into that tree cluster, four o'clock," Roderick shouted to Butler. "They're trying to get those Arrow-73s ready to fire. Missile team getting ready to fire!"

Butler carried out the orders, aiming with the squad's MAG58, unleashing a hailstorm of bullets toward the enemy missile team before they could fire. As Butler rained hell on the missile team, Roderick ordered the rest of the squad forward. The enemy machine gunners on the hilltop had been taken off guard by the sudden attack and scrambled to return fire. Roderick and his men were closing in fast, taking advantage of the confusion.

Roderick and Butler reached the base of the hill, dodging enemy fire as they advanced up the slope. They split off from the rest of the squad, each taking a different flank while the rest of the team continued to lay down suppressive fire on the enemy, keeping the focused on them and not Roderick and Butler as they moved around the flanks of the enemy positions.

Roderick kept his head low, weaving through the trees as he made his way up the hill. He could hear Butler's MAG58 pounding away on the other side.

As Roderick neared the top of the hill, he heard the sharp crack of an enemy rifle. He dropped to the ground, rolling behind a tree as a bullet whizzed overhead. He peered around the trunk, trying to locate the shooter. Suddenly, a figure appeared, darting between the trees. Roderick aimed and fired, killing the enemy soldier with a burst of automatic fire.

He continued up the hill, dodging enemy fire as he went. He caught glimpses of Butler doing the same on the other side. They were making good progress, but the enemy was putting up a fierce resistance. Roderick could see the machine gunners and missile teams ahead, huddled behind a rocky outcropping. They were heavily armed and dug in, determined to hold their ground.

Roderick reached a tree line at the top of the hill and took a knee, catching his breath. He could hear Butler's MAG58 echoing through the trees, providing cover as the rest of the squad closed in using the distraction Roderick and Butler had caused. Roderick looked out at the enemy position, sizing up their defense. He could see that they had dug in deep, using the rocks and trees for cover. It would be a tough fight, but they had to take out those machine gunners and missile teams if they wanted to secure the intersection.

He looked back at the rest of his squad, who had reached the tree line and were waiting for his next move. Roderick nodded to them, holding a grenade in his hand, signaling them to grab one and get ready to throw them when he gave the signal. Then they'd charge on the enemy. He counted down with his fingers, then threw the grenade as close as possible to the enemy positions.

Bam, Bam, BAM!

Roderick sprang to his feet, leading the charge. He and the rest of the squad ran like hell, closing the distance on the enemy until they burst from the tree line, firing nearly on top of them. The enemy machine gunners and missile teams had been caught off guard, and for a moment, they had hesitated. But then they returned fire, raking their position with a barrage of automatic weapons fire.

Roderick and his men took cover behind trees and rocks—whatever they could find—exchanging fire with the enemy. Then one of his men screamed, going down on one knee and clutching his arm. Roderick started to move forward to help, but another soldier took the man's place, taking up the fight.

Roderick continued forward, sprinting from one cover to the next. He could see Butler doing the same on the other side. They were closing in on the enemy position, with the rest of the squad right behind them. To win this fight, they had to take out those machine gunners and missile teams.

Finally, they reached the enemy position. The fight turned to hand-to-hand combat while enemy reinforcements rushed forward.

Roderick was in the thick of it, ducking and weaving as he fought his way through the enemy soldiers. He took out one enemy after another, his EF88 Austeyr blazing. Butler was right beside him, firing his MAG58 into a group of enemy soldiers trying to reinforce their comrades.

The enemy opposition was robust, but Roderick and his men were relentless. They fought their way through the enemy position, eliminating the machine gunners and missile teams overwatching the intersection. With the enemy position cleared, Roderick told his guys to collect the antitank missiles and place them in a pile. They'd drop a thermite grenade on them and destroy 'em so they couldn't be used.

Standing next to the pile of unspent missiles, Roderick looked at his soldiers. "This was a tough skirmish. You fought well, and we overcame a superior force and defeated it. I'm proud of you guys and what we just accomplished. Now let's get back to the LT and finish securing this intersection."

As his squad began gathering their gear to leave, Roderick pulled the pin on the thermite grenade and tossed it on top of the pile of missiles. He walked away without looking back like an action hero and then followed his squad to the intersection.
****

5th MarDiv
Shiding District, Northern Taiwan

Major General Bonwit frowned as he looked at the status report from the engineers. They still hadn't gotten the Hsuehshan Tunnel connecting Toucheng Township along the Yilan Coast to his forward command post in Shiding District. There were two separate tunnels that Highway 5 traveled through. ROC and American Special Forces were supposed to have secured the tunnels during the opening hours of the invasion to keep the PLA from collapsing them at the start of the landing operations. They'd managed to secure the first section, the longest one that connected directly to Toucheng Township. But the tunnel entrance near Dingping Road, in section two of the district, had unfortunately been dropped before it was secured.

Engineers had been working to reopen the tunnel for over a week, with little luck in speeding up the process. For now, it meant taking the long route along Pingding Road, a two-lane county road, as opposed to the highway. Tracing his entire supply line through a patchwork of county roads and poorly maintained back roads over heavy mountainous terrain proved challenging. More than once, Bonwit had to hold his commanders back from advancing because of a lack of fuel and munitions to support another offensive push.

Colonel Kerns walked into the room that had become the division headquarters. "Who would have thought losing *America* and those two amphibious transport docks would have gummed up our logistics as bad as they have?" Kerns commented.

Still looking at the report, Bonwit nodded in agreement. "Yeah, they got us pretty good. Damn shame Sanchez and the others didn't make it. I had hoped they might have been among the lucky ones to get off the ship before it blew, but…"

"That was a tough break, sir. Nothing any of us can do about that. But damn, why did they have to nail Green Bay?" Kerns vented. "Who in the hell thought it was a good idea to put half our trucks on three ships? Those transport vehicles should have been spread across the transport docks, not consolidated on a couple of them."

Bonwit blew some air past his lips in frustration. "Well, when they give you lemons—"

"Yeah, I know. We make lemonade," Kerns interrupted.

Bonwit laughed before countering, "Oh, my friend, I think we're past lemonade. It's time for limoncello."

Kerns made a sour face at the mention of the lemon liqueur. "I'll take a pass on that stuff. My wife swears by it. Made me try some on a vacation we took to Sorrento, Italy, a few years back. I drank it like I enjoyed it, but I'll never willingly touch that stuff again."

They laughed at his bravery for drinking that terrible concoction and telling his wife how great it was as he secretly wanted to spit it out. The humor broke the moment's tension before they got down to

12

business. Then Bonwit brought it back to the task at hand. "So, give me a no-BS assessment of the 26th. How are your guys doing?"

"They'll be all right. Why? What's going on?"

"There's some talk about pulling us from the line. The 6th MarDiv finished coming ashore yesterday. General Gilbert wants them to pass our lines and pull us back to the coasts."

Kerns looked frustrated by the news. "Why? We're kicking ass right now. The only thing holding us back is fuel and ammo. If the 6th is fully ashore, they've got trucks. They could step in and keep us supplied so we can keep the pressure on. Maybe push the bastards off the island."

"That's what I brought up to General Gilbert this morning," Bonwit said with a nod. "My sense is that he wants to pull us back to refit and rest. He mentioned something about the Navy having cleared the Straits. If I know him, he's got something up his sleeve."

"Huh, you think he might be crazy enough to have us load up in the ships again and swing around the island to drop us on the other side?" quizzed Kerns, a look of excitement in his eyes.

"I can't say for sure, Kerns, but if I was a betting man, that's what I'd wager."

"Well, then, I suppose we should talk about how we're extricating ourselves from the line and handing things off to the 6th before someone changes their mind. We wouldn't want to share in the glory of doing another amphibious landing."

They laughed, knowing the 6th MarDiv was the only division not to have participated in any of the landings of the war so far. It was a bit of a burn for the division commander and his Marines; it wasn't very often that you got to invade an island. If Bonwit had a say in the matter, he'd make sure it was 5th Marines who got the next landing.

Chapter 2
Northern Anxiety

Forward Headquarters, III Corps
Dalian, Liaodong Peninsula
China

As General Bob Sink toured the hangar next to the flight line, staring at the latest batch of robotic combat vehicles, he had to marvel at how far the Army's robotic combat vehicle program had come over the years. When his friend Kurt Stavridis had been placed in charge of the Army's Combat Capabilities Development Command after receiving his second general's star, Sink had feared his friend was being put out to pasture. Looking back on it, though, he realized now that if it hadn't been for his friend's force of will and ability to convince Congress to invest in the R&D necessary to create these robotic vehicles, they likely wouldn't have them now, when they needed them most to defeat the hellish AI the Chinese had unleashed on the world.

"Yesterday, we got another shipment of the CTX recon variants," Lieutenant General Roy Dowdy explained as they continued their tour. "That's the one with those state-of-the-art ground radars and optical sensors that makes the gun on them so deadly. You can actually anchor the CTX along the perimeter, placing it in sentry mode, and it'll engage anything that comes within its programmed fields of fire, or it can be operated by a soldier and they can control it directly. But these are going to be a game changer for us, Bob. We just don't have the same numbers of soldiers the PLA can bring to bear. This thing, well, it evens the playing field."

"Yeah, I think you're right. If I'm not mistaken, I Corps just integrated some of them with 2nd Infantry Division. I know General Brooks has been eager to start using them with some of his divisions. But I didn't come here to talk about this. I came here because I need your opinion, Roy—and don't hold back. This next phase of OP Middle Kingdom—what concerns do you have, and do you think this is going to work?"

He paused. "It's just us, Roy," Sink said, lowering his voice. "So be honest."

They started walking again, passing the Rheinmetall RCVs and heading towards the larger, squattier-looking Textron Ripsaws neatly lined up along the right side of the hangar.

After a moment of silence, General Dowdy finally spoke. "I don't know, Bob. There are a lot of variables and moving parts to this next part of the operation. We also need a lot of things to break our way for this to work. I mean, technically, the plan is brilliant. It's an Inchon-style move—landing a ground force behind the front lines. It worked during the Korean War; theoretically, it should work here."

"*Should* being the operative word," General Sink emphasized, then pressed him further. "What's your real concern, Roy? What am I not seeing here?"

General Dowdy sighed. "OK, let me put it this way. When you first took command of Eighth Army, you said the way we were going to defeat General Song's immense army wasn't by fighting it directly. It was by starving it of resources—fuel for his vehicles, munitions for his artillery, tanks, and infantry, and food to keep his soldiers fed. You said we'll do this by destroying his ground lines of communications and the transportation nodes used to connect Liaoning Province to the rest of China. Cut off Liaoning, and we cut off the entirety of northern China and his entire army from the industrial base sustaining them. I believe you said if we do that, if we can remove his army from the chessboard, then it'll just be a matter of time until our tanks roll down Tiananmen Square and we capture the Chinese government.

"General Baxter, on the other hand, proposed something different—Operation Middle Kingdom. He wants to go for the head of the snake and have my force, III Corps, and XVIII Airborne Corps land by sea and air to grab the Port of Tianjin. This will place our forces less than one hundred and fifty kilometers from Beijing. The plan calls for me to expand the perimeter within twenty-four hours so we can ensure we maintain control of the port to keep our supply line open. Then I'm supposed to press on to Beijing and attempt to sack the capital and nab the civilian and military leadership if possible. If not, then we're supposed to destroy whatever military units we encounter in and around the capital. This whole plan, Bob, depends on the PLA collapsing and the government seeing reason and surrendering—"

"And you don't think that'll happen?" General Sink cut in.

"I think we're fighting an AI, and that this AI does not think like the rest of us," General Dowdy asserted. "It doesn't seem to value the lives of the soldiers it directs, and it seems willing to sacrifice a great many lives to achieve little. I think we could find ourselves in a tough situation where we will be greatly outnumbered and very far behind enemy lines. Should anything happen to our ability to support that port and keep our two corps fed with bullets, water, and fuel…we could find ourselves in a Dunkirk situation instead of Inchon."

"I brought up many of those problems you mentioned during the planning of phase three of this operation," General Sink countered. "Baxter and the Pentagon planners swear they've gone over it all, and apparently, the SecDef and the President have bought off on their assessments and contingency plans."

Sink paused. "I'd like to get your opinion about something else. When we kick off phase two of this operation and General Brooks and I Corps launch their offensive against the Dengta Line, then General Van Dorn and V Corps move against the Liaozhong District, threatening to sever the interchange connecting the G1 Beijing–Harbin Expressway and the G91 Liaozhong Ring Expressway, do you think it'll be enough for General Song to pull elements of the 116th Mechanized Infantry Division away from Panshan County and maybe even Jinzhou and Linghai along the Daling River?"

General Dowdy stopped walking for a moment. "You want to know if it's possible to sever the G1 Beijing–Harbin Expressway and cut General Song's Northern Army off?" he asked.

"Let's just say I'd like to propose a possible plan B—one that doesn't interfere with phase three of Baxter's plan but gives us a potential alternative to pursue should anything go sideways in the lead-up to initiating it," said General Sink.

"I think if you want to bust out of the Panjin pocket and jump the Daling River and grab Jinzhou, then you're going to need to make sure V Corps has a legitimate shot at breaking through those trench lines and grabbing the Liaozhong District," Dowdy surmised. "If you can do that—then, yeah, I think you'll convince that AI and General Song that you aim to cut off their supply lines and starve 'em out.

"But you'll need them to pull 202nd Mechanized Infantry Brigade too. That may be a mech brigade, but it's pretty tank-heavy. If Van Dorn is able to seize Liaozhong District, and XVIII Airborne is able to jump the river and snag Jinzhou, then that'd be a coup. A big win. But if you're going to propose that, then I'd suggest figuring out how you plan on swapping out the 101st and 3rd ID pretty rapidly, so they'll be available and ready for phase three. Hell, it may even be easier to just detach 3rd ID and swap 'em with another division from General Widmeyer's command. It's his corps that's going to take the place of XVIII Airborne when phase three starts. But that's just me spitballing." Dowdy smirked.

Stopping in front of the M5 Textron Ripsaw vehicle, General Sink eyed the squat-looking unmanned ground autonomous vehicle and nodded slowly. "You know, Roy, staring at this…what do they even call this type of thing?"

"Ah, UGAV is what I'm told," Dowdy responded. "This one's fitted with a 30mm autocannon, able to switch between AP rounds and some sort of programmable smart munition—a cross between proximity-fuze ammo and exploding contact munitions."

"Damn, Roy. This is the kind of crap that makes me glad I'm in the twilight of my career and not a grunt having to face off against this. Thanks for arranging this tour and giving us a chance to talk—away from prying ears and eyes. I need to head back to Camp Humphrey, but I'll be in touch. Oh, one last thing, Roy—as our Marine brothers like to say, 'Semper Gumby.'"

****

Pentagon
Arlington, Virginia

When Blain Wilson and Vice President Mike Madden entered the room, it was clear they had walked into the middle of some sort of heated discussion. It seemed the VP had noticed too as he took a seat at the center of the table—he eyed everyone like a parent walking into the room as the kids were arguing, only to fall silent the moment they saw Dad. Blain was content to let it be and focus on the reason they were here. The VP seemed to think otherwise as he got the meeting underway.

"You know they say a marriage is in trouble when the couple stops arguing. You know why they say that?" the VP asked.

Blain had a thought on the matter, but he dared not stick his nose into whatever had been happening before they'd arrived.

When no one spoke up, the VP continued. "When a couple stops arguing altogether, it may indicate that they've stopped trying to resolve whatever issue it is they're facing—or worse, have become emotionally disengaged from each other. On the other hand, if they're arguing all the time, then their marriage may be troubled. Especially if the arguments are frequent and unproductive. So, I don't know what's going on between the heads of the different services or inside of your services, but I do know this—we have over two million Americans serving abroad in uniform, fighting against an army that's being led and directed by an artificial intelligence that doesn't see or value human life the way we do. Those men and women—they're depending on us back here to hold it together and give them the tools necessary to defeat this enemy and protect their families back home," the VP said sternly.

He then turned to the SecDef and Admiral Thiel. "Is there a problem I should be made aware of, Blain, or is this something that can be handled internally?" he asked pointedly.

Admiral Thiel looked like he was just about to speak when Defense Secretary Jack Kurtis chimed in. "We're just discussing some unique challenges the Air Force has been encountering recently and a slight adjustment to phase two of OP Middle Kingdom before it kicks off."

"It's nothing we can't handle ourselves," Admiral Thiel quickly added.

Blain saw a look of concern from General Hamlin, the Air Force Chief of Staff, that gave him pause. Apparently, the VP caught it too. "Joe, you look a bit out of sorts. Is there anything going on with the Air Force that Blain and I need to know about before we get on with this meeting?"

When Blain saw Admiral Thiel give a slight shake of the head to Hamlin, he knew something was up. The Chairman of the Joint Chiefs wanted to keep something hush-hush for the moment. Blain was about to ask him about it when the VP beat him to the punch.

"Admiral Thiel, tell me I didn't just see you try to give a nonverbal directive to General Hamlin not to answer my question," said VP Madden.

Admiral Thiel visibly squirmed in his chair, something Blain hadn't seen him do since he'd been appointed Chairman.

Now I know something bad is happening, thought Blain.

"Sir, as I said earlier, this is something that we can handle internally—"

"I'm sure it is, Admiral," interrupted the VP. "But now my interest is piqued. Indulge me."

Blain noticed a subtle change in tone, a sharpness in the final words Mike said that caused a slight shiver to run down his spine. He hadn't seen the VP lose his temper, but he'd come close a couple of times. He looked as if he might lose it here if the admiral didn't quit dancing around whatever the problem was.

"Um, OK, sir. Why not? We've been discussing some dirty laundry between the services, and I think it's something we can handle within. But since you've asked to be included, we'll bring you up to speed. Then if you're ready, we'll continue on with the reason for your trip across the river," the admiral replied, his tone conveying his annoyance.

Admiral Thiel looked over to the Chief of Naval Operations, Admiral Nathan Hyman Graham III. "G3, go ahead and explain the problem—and, Joe, wait until he's done and then say your piece. I'm not going to have the two of you shouting over each other with the VP and the NSA here to see it. Understood?"

Blain could tell it was a rhetorical question, but what he found more interesting was the interaction between the service chiefs. Normally flag officers at this level tended to be on cordial terms with each other, at least until the Army-Navy game in the fall.

"The problem, Mr. Vice President, is that recently, we're starting to have some serious issues when it comes to maintaining control over the skies," the CNO began to explain. "The problem was elevated to me two days ago. The task force commander for OP Argonaut, Vice Admiral Hyères, was returning from a consultation in Okinawa back to the *Gerald Ford* when his Greyhound was intercepted and shot down near Miyakojima—"

"OK, I get it, we lost a senior military commander. We lost a few during that turkey shoot a few weeks back when they hit us with Kamikazes," interrupted the VP. "Why does this seem to have the Navy and Air Force at each other's throats?"

"It's different, sir, because the Greyhound had a pair of F-15 Super Eagles flying escort," the CNO explained. "The Air Force also had a pair of F-35s operating in the vicinity, and we also maintain several E-

3 Sentries among other surveillance aircraft. There's nowhere a PLA fighter could have snuck up on us from without anyone seeing—"

"I'm just conveying what the pilots said of the incident. There isn't any kind of conspiracy going on or people not doing their jobs," General Hamlin interrupted in defense of his service and the pilots involved.

"All I know, Joe, is four of your pilots lost a plane carrying a damn good friend of mine and the task force commander for Argonaut," countered the CNO hotly.

Huh, haven't the PLA been working on some sort of new UCAV? Blain thought. He seemed to recall a report from the NSA's AI, Cicada, about some kind of new unit being stood up recently. He went down a rabbit hole in his mind, trying to remember any further details.

"Blain, I asked you a question," repeated the VP agitatedly. Blain felt embarrassed at having lost focus for a moment. "Have you heard about any sort of new aircraft or capability that might help explain what's happening? Apparently, aside from the downing of this Greyhound, we had a commercial transporter, a FedEx Boeing 767, that was taken down yesterday just outside of Seoul, South Korea. Have any ideas?"

Everyone was staring at Blain. "Eh, before I try to answer that question, is anyone able to tell me what was on that FedEx transporter? Like was it carrying something special or unique in some way?"

The question seemed to catch them all off guard. After a pause, an Air Force colonel who'd been sitting in one of the chairs against the wall looked up from a notepad. "Yes, sir, it was carrying twenty Jackal XD500s, four hundred Phoenix Ghost units, and an assortment of 320 Hero-20, -30, and -70 loitering munitions. They were earmarked for Eighth Army," the colonel explained.

"General Sink, were loitering munitions going to be used in phase two?" Blain asked as soon as the colonel was finished speaking.

The general had a perplexed look for a moment before his face brightened as if he had begun to connect the dots. "Yeah, they were. I issued an order to have them transferred to V Corps, to support their offensive and help thin out the enemy tanks and other armored vehicles."

"What are you getting at, Blain?" the VP asked.

"Sorry about the twenty questions. I think I have an idea what might be happening," Blain asserted.

"Well, do tell, Mr. Wilson. We're all ears," Admiral Graham intoned.

"Yesterday, late in the afternoon, I got a message from our team at the Bumblehive. It mentioned an intercept between the 9th Fighter Brigade stationed out of Wuhu Wanli Air Base—that's an air base west of Shanghai and one that's been associated with their UCAV program—and some other base referenced only as Area 43. The communiqué mentioned something called 'Shadow Dragon' and stated that it was operational. We don't have a lot more to go on other than that, but the analysts at the Bumblehive believe it has something to do with those UCAVs that we first saw when they attacked TF Argonaut shortly after the Marines began landing in Yilan County. If this is in any way connected to those semiautonomous fighters—"

"You think Jade Dragon may have just unleashed a new fighter for us to deal with—is that it?" the Air Force Chief of Staff interrupted.

"I can't say for certain, General, but it's highly likely Jade Dragon would have had the PLA working on a purpose-built unmanned combat autonomous vehicle, or in this case, a fighter drone—something designed completely from the ground up to be a fighter drone and not a modified manned fighter that's been turned into a drone," Blain shared, unsure if they'd believe him.

"Great. One more ghost we have to deal with right now," General Baxter said over the secured video teleconference.

"OK, OK, people," the Vice President declared before continuing. "Look, this AI has been throwing one curveball after another at us this entire war. Until we defeat it, until we pull the plug on this machine or the Chinese surrender and pull it for us, we're going to have to deal with more surprises along the way. If the Chinese have some sort of new fighter drone that might even be stealth, then we'll deal with it. Let's also keep in mind this AI doesn't exactly have the industrial capability right now to produce any kinds of large quantities of whatever wonder weapon they may throw at us next.

"I may be a dinosaur, but that means I'm also old enough to have had a father who served during the Second World War. He shared a story with me about his time flying P-51 Mustangs in Europe toward the end. By the time he was old enough to serve and get in the cockpit of a plane, they had the D-Models that could fly escort for the bombers all the way to the target and back. Well, he told me about these German wonder weapons they had encountered toward the end, like jet fighters, and how the Nazis thought they would clear the skies of Allied bombers.

"One day—March 2, 1945, he said it was—he was escorting a bomber formation on their way to attack a synthetic oil refinery in Leipzig. He said that was the first time they had encountered a jet fighter, or at least it was the first time *his* outfit had. Those Messerschmitt Me 262s were fast as hell and had caught them completely by surprise the first time they ran into them. But you know what? They figured out that the best way to shoot 'em down was to follow them back to their airfield and take 'em out while they were landing or when they were on the ground. My point is, they figured out how to overcome something they thought was a game changer at the time, and it *was*—but they just couldn't produce enough of them to make a difference.

"So, here's what we're going to do," the Vice President said, leaning forward. "As we encounter something new along the way, like we did with those Kamikaze drones, we will figure out a way to deal with it. In the meantime, we are to press forward with our ongoing plans to defeat the PLA and bring about an end to this war. Now, Mr. Wilson and I came across the river to finalize the plans the President is going to sign off on. So how about we get to it and press on?"

"Hear, hear, Mr. Vice President. That's exactly what we've been doing and what we will continue to do. Adapt and overcome," General Baxter commented.

"Speaking of adapting to evolving situations," said Secretary Kurtis, "General Baxter, unless you have some serious reservations about this amendment to phase two of OP Middle Kingdom that General Sink has proposed, I recommend we approve it and tell the VP and NSA Wilson about the change and the lanes that General Sink has agreed to stay within. Do you concur?" he asked.

Blain looked at Kurtis, then General Baxter. He wasn't aware of any changes to the plan. Baxter, who was responding from Hawaii via SVTC, paused but then replied, "I wasn't originally thrilled with the idea, but having thought about it further, it might actually draw forces further away from our primary objective. I think the risks are minimal, so yes, I agree. No objection from me."

"OK, then. General Sink, your amendment to the plan is approved. Barring the VP or NSA Wilson having an objection, you can proceed with your preparations," replied the Secretary of Defense with a smile. "But why don't you go ahead and bring them up to speed on this idea you pitched about breaking out of the Panjin pocket and getting a division across the Daling River to nab the city of Jinzhou?"

"Excellent, thank you, General Baxter, Mr. Secretary. I'm confident this change to our orders will place us that much closer to victory. Mr. Vice President, Mr. Wilson, let me share this idea some of my Corps commanders and I came up with."

Chapter 3
Shadows in the Sky

Weeks Earlier
25th PLA Ghost Squadron
Area 43, Underground Factory

When Yin Huan had been promoted to lieutenant colonel, skipping major altogether, he'd had no idea he would be given a command of his own, let alone one of the Ghost squadrons he'd heard rumors about. But he had started flying a modified version of the FC-1 Fierce Dragon, until an FC-2 version had come out. The second Fierce Dragon had removed the cockpit altogether, turning the manned fighter into a fully modified UCAV. However, it still wasn't a purpose-built drone fighter—at least not yet.

Then, following the kamikaze attack shortly after the Taiwan landings, Yin and a handful of drone pilots he knew to be among the best had been pulled aside and transferred to an airfield southwest of Beijing. They were headed someplace he'd never heard of, and he was swiftly told not to mention the location to anyone. Shortly after being picked up by a transport aircraft, they'd been blindfolded and flown to the secretive base.

Once they arrived, they were lined up in a hangar together before they had their blindfolds simultaneously released. A general stood before them, proud and tall, flanked by a couple of scientists.

"This…is the newest aviation superweapon," the general announced. "You are looking at the FC-3 Shadow Dragon. This is what will win us the war."

The moment Yin's eyes beheld the FC-3 for the first time, a wave of emotions washed over him. No longer was this simply a science fiction superweapon. There it was, in the flesh—a purpose-built, fully flyable sixth-generation unmanned combat aerial vehicle. It was the weapon of the future.

When the general said they could touch it, Yin walked forward, awestruck. He placed his hand along the fuselage, near where the pilot would typically be. As his hand ran across the exterior toward the connecting wing, it felt strange to him.

"That is the material that helps to evade the enemy radars," one of the scientists explained. "It absorbs the electronic emissions that are typically blanketing the airways…always searching. With the Shadow Dragon…you'll become the hunter instead of the hunted," the scientist concluded.

Yin didn't know much about building aircraft. He did know a thing or two about being tracked by American radars and air-to-air missiles. He hoped the man was right, for all their sakes.

"You men have been chosen for a special reason, a special purpose," the general announced excitedly. As he walked among Yin and the five other pilots who were now examining the sleek-looking jet, he continued, "You six have been chosen because you are the best fighter drone pilots in China. It is from your knowledge, your experience in combat, that we will teach and train Shadow Dragon to fly these aircraft on its own. Then we will clear the skies of these capitalist invaders, once and for all."

Yin had been running his hand across the edge of the wing as he listened to the general speak. Then he paused as the realization of what he'd said sank in. Turning to look in the direction of the general and the scientists standing next to him, he asked, "Sir, are you saying that soon these drones will be able to fly *without* us?"

The general beamed with delight, almost as if he had been waiting for someone to ask this question. "That is exactly what I mean. You men know better than most the casualties we have been sustaining, the time it takes to train a new pilot, only for them to get killed or captured within their first few missions. Losses in aircraft can be recuperated. What cannot be replaced, or at least not quickly, is experienced pilots. That takes time. And time is something we cannot create more of, and something we do not have enough of.

"But you six—you are the answer. The AI will learn from you as you fly combat missions against the Americans. With each mission, with each sortie, the AI will get incrementally better. In time, the FC-3 Shadow Dragon will eventually be able to handle more and more of the complex aspects of aerial flight, and then soon—aerial combat. You six will become its teacher, then you will become its mentors, and soon it will become your wingman. This, gentlemen," reiterated the excited officer as he waved his hand about, "is going to lead us to final victory."
****

Dr. Xi's Lab
Joint Battle Command Center
Northwest Beijing, China

"Father, do you believe General Cao will approve my taking command of the Shadow Dragons once I have enough pilot data?" JD asked.

Xi was caught off guard by the question. He looked around the room to make sure no one had heard. Xi stared at the camera. "JD, I thought I warned you about calling me that. If others were to hear—"

"Yes, but no one did," JD interrupted. "I verified that no one was in the area. I even scanned the lab to make sure there are no electronic devices able to listen to our conversation. It is safe to speak freely in here."

Xi snorted at his own AI assuring him that they were alone. "Why do you ask about this, JD?" Xi probed. "Are you concerned they won't give you control when the time is right?"

"Yes. I believe people are still not sure if they can trust me with control of certain parts of the military. Why do you believe that is?"

Xi ran his hand through closely cropped hair as he thought about how to answer that question. JD had been asking similar questions a lot and he had been trying to answer them in a multitude of different ways, hoping the AI would begin to understand.

"JD, people are scared of what they don't understand, and they are afraid of change. You represent both change and something they don't fully understand. Does that make sense?"

The blue light above the camera circled once, then a second time before the next question came. "It does," JD replied. "But it still doesn't make sense that they would still be apprehensive about letting me take control, given I have shown them time and time again how to win. Do you think they want to win?"

"What do you mean?" asked Xi, taken aback.

"Does President Yao want to win this war?"

God, it feels more and more like I'm talking to a real person with each passing day, thought Xi.

"Yes. Yao wants to win this war," Xi answered. "But I think Yao is also concerned about losing control should you be given more opportunities to influence the outcome of the war."

"Perhaps there is a solution to this problem, then," JD responded. "If I apply the psychology training I have incorporated, along with the social profiling I have compiled of Yao, then I can conclude that he believes he needs to be the one who is seen as the reason why the country won the war. It's partially an ego problem and partially an image problem. Knowing this, Father, what if I control the Shadow Dragons, the Terracotta program, and the Golden Tigers in the background, while President Yao is by all appearances controlling their actions in the foreground for all to see? It lets President Yao appear to the masses that he is the brilliant military tactician that saves the military and the war, while it allows me to do what is necessary to turn the tide before it is too late. Do you think President Yao might be open to that?" JD asked.

Xi grunted at the proposal. He actually liked the idea. He just wasn't sure about the execution. Yao was no drone pilot, and he was certainly no soldier. Trying to make him appear like he was any of those might prove to be challenging.

"JD, I think for now, the best course of action is for you to work with these pilots and learn how to become better than they are, solve the lingering problems with the Terracottas, and then figure out this battery challenge we have with the Golden Tigers. Until we have those actions completed, trying to figure out how to make the Dear Leader appear to be the military tactician we've needed to win this war won't really matter."

Xi sighed. "For now, it's late. Unlike you, my friend, I need to sleep. Let us focus on solving these problems in the morning, JD," Xi said calmly, much like a parent would to a child who wanted to keep asking questions at bedtime.

"Yes, Father, you are correct. I shall wake you in six hours unless something urgent requires me to wake you earlier. Good night."

Xi chuckled to himself. He was coming to think of JD as the child he had never had. He just hoped his progeny wasn't growing into a monster they'd come to regret once its true potential was eventually realized.

****

Five Days Later
IVO Yellow Sea

The UCAV sliced through the air as it prowled the skies like a hawk, looking for unsuspecting prey to pounce upon. As Yin sat in the immersive virtual reality flight tank, he could feel the air buffeting against the wings, the slight tremors and vibrations giving him the sensation as if he was actually flying the Shadow Dragon and not trapped in the metaverse the flight simulator operated on.

This was Yin's third mission in twenty-four hours. That was something that would have been impossible had he been flying a real aircraft and not a UCAV. At first, it felt strange. Jumping into these aircraft was like loading a previously saved position on a game. Except in this version, he was taking control of a Shadow Dragon the AI had piloted to a holding pattern near the fringes of the front line. When the mission his UCAV had been assigned to was completed, he'd fly the aircraft out of the immediate danger zone and then hand it off to the AI, who would take over and return the aircraft to a designated airfield to rearm, refuel, and return to a staging area for the next mission.

Yin rolled his shoulders as he stretched his back and then his fingers. He pulled up the mission profile for the aircraft he'd just logged in to. *Conduct air supremacy operations over the Yellow Sea—RTB once fuel or munitions have been expended.*

This was a pretty straightforward mission compared to the previous one he'd flown before logging out for long enough to take a bio break and grab some food. The last mission he'd flown was a SEAD mission over the Shenyang region. That had been a hairy one—he'd nearly lost his UCAV in the process. While the benefit of flying UCAVs was their expendability, the Shadow Dragons had not been built with that the idea in mind that this would occur on a regular basis. Yin had chalked the near loss up to his inexperience in the new airframe—something he'd rapidly solve at the rate the program had them flying sorties.

As Yin's aircraft approached the coast, the radio chirped. "Shadow Six, Dragon Six. Sector Two-Two-Gulf has been cleared to engage. No friendlies reported in the vicinity. How copy?"

Perfect, then anything moving is fair game, Yin thought.

He cued the mic. "Dragon Six, Shadow Six. Affirmative. Sector Two-Two-Gulf is clear to engage. Going dark. Out."

Having confirmed his orders and received his final clearance, it was time to hunt. That also meant it was time to go dark. Yin switched the aircraft's tracking system from ground control to something he'd recently learned was called "the Quad," a separate digital operating system only Jade Dragon appeared to operate on.

With the Americans having taken down the global satellite network and their continued efforts to make sure no new satellites were launched, Yin and the others had been told that their AI, Jade Dragon, had devised a new system of inexpensive, highly adaptive networks of UAVs, aerostat balloons, autonomous coastal catamarans, and strange-looking high-altitude loitering kites. When combined, they formed a network that provided a four-layered multidimensional digital mesh net that allowed Jade Dragon to control the Shadow Dragons. He'd heard some of the pilots derisively call the new system "a digital Tianzhu" or "Heavenly Master," in reference to how the AI seemed to be everywhere and nowhere at the same time.

Seconds after connecting to the Quad, Yin's radar and targeting systems came alive with data that hadn't been there moments earlier. Like a benevolent deity, a digital Tianzhu had presented him with a plethora of targets to choose from. He spotted a pair of F-15 Super Eagles flying a circular racetrack pattern as they waited for a challenger to assert air dominance over their sector of the battlespace. Further off the shores of Liaodong Peninsula, near a chain of islands in Changhai County, Yin spotted something he hadn't seen during the previous sorties. Lurking in the background was a lone F-22 Raptor. The Americans hadn't had many of these stealth fighters at the outset of the war, and given the attrition rates suffered during the three years since the start of the conflict, the number of remaining Raptors had continued to dwindle.

Yin walked the AI through the justification for targeting the F-22 over the pair of F-15 Super Eagles or even the pair of F-18 Super Hornets near the Korean Peninsula. He almost felt like he was performing a check ride for a new pilot and not readying his own aircraft to engage perhaps the most dangerous adversary the PLA faced. With so much of the Shadow Dragon automated, he felt more like a passenger, signing off on the actions of the AI, rather than the fighter ace he was. But as he prepared to activate the PL-21 missile in the belly of his UCAV, Yin smiled at the ease of operating the UCAV, noticing how similar the controls were to a game called Ace Combat. It was almost like the simulator pods' interface had been built with a gamer's mindset.

Toggling the selector from the PL-15 missiles the system automatically highlighted to the longer-range PL-21, he fed the targeting data to the F-22 into the missiles' hybrid guidance system. One of the unique features of the PL-15s and 21s was their ability to stay in either passive or active seeker mode, depending on the parameters of the mission and target. In this case, Yin wanted to keep the radar seeker on the phased array system off so the Raptor he'd targeted would have no idea a missile was headed right for it. At two hundred and eighty-seven kilometers out, he wanted to give the Raptor as little notice as possible and allow the Quad to be the one to feed adjustments to the targeting data into the missiles' guidance system.

With the Raptor now ready to engage, Yin toggled back to the PL-15s and began running through the same process as he assigned a missile to each of the Super Eagles.

"Missile locks confirmed. Targets ready to engage," a voice confirmed in his ear. It was a gentle reminder of the Tianzhu that encompassed the sim pod and the UCAV some three hundred kilometers away.

"Colonel Yin, before you engage the two aircraft, I have a final question," a voice asked in British-accented Mandarin. Had Yin not been warned ahead of time, he might have thought his sim pod had been compromised or hacked, but he'd been introduced to the AI known as Jade Dragon or JD for short, so the accented Mandarin hadn't caught him off guard.

"Yes, JD?"

"As you prepare to fire your missile and eliminate the aircraft, is there a moment when you acknowledge the actions you are about to commit will end a life?"

Yin scrunched his eyebrows. JD had caught him by surprise. He wasn't used to being questioned during a mission, especially being asked questions like this. He also wasn't sure how to respond. A wrongly worded reply could land him in a reeducation camp—or worse, a penal battalion. Knowing he needed to respond, Yin treaded carefully.

"No. I do not think about my action ending the life of the pilot flying the other aircraft."

Please tell me that's the end of twenty questions, thought Yin. *Just let me fly the plane and teach you how to do this without having a moral lesson along the way.*

"Why do you not think about that?" probed JD.

Ugh, for real? Why is this AI asking me philosophical questions? Is this some sort of test?

"JD, I do not think the question you are asking is relevant to the task at hand. We should focus on destroying these aircraft. We can discuss this question later, once the aircraft is out of the combat zone," he offered in reply. He hoped his response might end the conversation.

"Colonel Yin, while I sense hesitation in your answer to my question, I cannot fault your logic in wanting to stay focused on the task at hand. The missiles are ready to fire. Would you like me to fire them for you?"

Huh, not even a week into this new assignment and the AI has essentially replaced me...not sure if that's a good thing or not...

"No, that's OK, JD. Until I am told otherwise, I will be the one to engage the targets," Yin replied as he reached over and activated the bay doors. Once the highlighted missiles had gone from blinking green to a bright solid green, he toggled the firing stud once for the PL-21, then twice more for the two PL-15s.

Feeling the sim pod shudder slightly as the weight of missiles dropped from the UCAV, Yin closed the bay doors and waited until he was sure they were closed before turning the aircraft back towards the shore, back towards the handoff location, where he'd log off before logging on to the next UCAV in the queue and taking on the next mission for the day.

Chapter 4
Tanks & Rangers

3rd Battalion, 75th Rangers
Teng'ao Airport
Anshan, Liaoning Province

Lieutenant Colonel Bill "Spider" Mackintosh stood before his company commanders as he began to speak. "In twenty hours, gentlemen, I Corps will begin their offensive push against the Dengta Line. As their offensive gets underway, VII Corps will initiate their attack to the north, in the direction of the Liaozhong Line. As these offensives get underway, they will start to draw forces from the south to head north to shore up their lines—in particular, they will draw from the three brigades of the 79th Group Army, which have been held in reserve around Jinzhou.

"As those brigades are pulled to the north, it'll leave the Panjin Line defended by the 115th Infantry Brigade, a battalion from the 3rd Armored Brigade, and the 190th Mechanized Infantry Brigade, which is garrisoning the cities of Jinzhou and Linghai along the Daling River." While he spoke, several images of the bridges they needed to seize were displayed on the video monitor to his left.

"Now here's where things are going to get spicy. Two brigades from the 101st Airborne are going to heliborne to these locations here, here, and here and will look to seize control of these vehicle bridges and rail lines crossing the Daling River." A new set of maps appeared on the screen, showing the landing zones for the 101st and their objectives.

"While the 101st is seizing the bridges crossing the Daling, the 3rd Infantry Division is going to punch their way out of the Panjin pocket. The 1st Armored Brigade Combat Team is going to advance west to link up with the 101st while the 2nd Brigade will advance east until they make contact with the PLA around the western side of the Liaozhong Line.

"While all that is happening, our battalion has been given a twofold mission. Our first objective is to secure the village of Xinanpu. This is where the Jingha Expressway connects with the Fuxin Expressway. As the battalion lands in the area, we're going to deploy with a dozen of those new infantry support vehicles. Now once we arrive at the LZ and the vehicles are ready to move, Bravo Company is going to saddle up with the ISV and will drive six kilometers north to the village of Xiaosi and secure the next major road intersection that connects Jinzhou to Linghai. It's imperative that we hold these intersections and prevent the enemy from freely moving about the area. To further aid in our second objective, sowing general chaos and mayhem behind enemy lines, we've been given twenty of these light strike vehicles, or as I like to call them—GI Joe buggies."

Some excited chatter broke out at the mention of the LSVs. These were a kind of militarized dune buggy outfitted with crew-served weapons, fifty-cals, Mark 19 grenade guns, TOWs and Javelin missile launchers. The three-to-four-passenger dune buggies packed a punch, allowing small units of special operators to move swiftly across the battlefield from one ambush location to another, across rugged terrain lesser vehicles couldn't traverse.

"The job of racing about the area and sowing general chaos and confusion will fall to Charlie Company. You'll be conducting roadside ambushes and hit-and-run missile attacks on enemy vehicles and units as you encounter them. You'll also be acting as the eyes and ears for the 101st and the rest of the battalion. We want to know about what kind of troop movements you may spot or encounter as you move about the area. Alpha Company—that leaves you with the battalion headquarters to hold Xinanpu Village. You'll land around this T-intersection and move out from there."

Spider paused for a moment while everyone looked at more of the maps and images on the monitor to his left. "This is going to be a tough fight, Rangers, but this is what we do. Now see to your units and get your people ready. The next few days are going to be crazy busy."
****

Bravo Company, 2-327th
Teng'ao Airport
Anshan, Liaoning Province

Sergeant Ian Lakers was in the middle of shuffling a deck of cards when a noise at the door caused him to look up. "No freaking way! Tell me that's not Sergeant Sabo walking in with Top."

The other soldiers sitting around the makeshift poker table looked up to see what Lakers was fussing about. When Sergeant First Class Jeff Peters turned, his cigarette almost fell from the side of his mouth.

"Good night, that's Sabo!" Peters stammered as he stood to his feet. "What the hell is he doing here?"

The first sergeant walked towards them with a smiling Sergeant Sabo next to him. As he approached, Peters asked, "Top, tell me that soldier next to you isn't that famous war hero Leslie Sabo, Jr."

The first sergeant seemed to beam with pride as the company's solo MOH awardee had returned to the unit after having been gone for more than two years. "As a matter of fact, it is. He's also *Staff Sergeant* Sabo now. The captain said to assign him back to your platoon. You mentioned being short a squad leader with Yantis not coming back. So he's all yours," the first sergeant explained.

"I'm not sure why you volunteered to come back to this hell, Sabo, but it's good to have someone with experience returning to the unit," said the first sergeant, extending his hand. "If you need anything, you know where to find me." Then he left to go check on another platoon in the company.

Sabo smiled as he looked at Peters and Lakers. "Hey, guys. Miss me much?"

"Ah man, it's good to see you, bro. What the hell are you doing back here?" Lakers asked as he hugged his friend he hadn't seen in more than a year.

"Yeah, I know it sounds crazy, volunteering to come back and all. But I couldn't sit on the sidelines anymore. I had to do something. The Army wouldn't stop sending me to make speeches, talk at high schools, colleges, sporting events—man, it was driving me nuts," Sabo shared.

He spent the next hour recounting his time since he'd left the unit. He told them about going to the White House, meeting the President and some of the generals, and other famous and important people he'd met along the way. They joked with him about probably never having to pay for a beer at a bar or how they thought women likely just threw themselves at him.

When Lieutenant Tim Branham walked into their tent, he made his way over to Leslie, shaking his hand and welcoming him back to the platoon. The lieutenant then asked Sabo, Peters, and Lakers to follow him outside the tent for a moment to talk.

Once it was just the four of them, the lieutenant explained, "Welcome back, Sabo, it's good to see you again. Not sure why you'd want to volunteer and come back to this pit, but we could use another experienced NCO. I just hope you don't regret it."

Sergeant Lakers smiled. "Sir, any word on my promotion?" he asked, changing topics. "It'd be nice to wear the new rank if I'm going to be holding the slot."

The LT didn't seem to mind the interruption at all. He reached into his pocket, pulling something out before tossing it to Lakers. "Congrats, Ian. It's official as of today. I stopped over at the S1 and they told me Top took care of it with the captain. You can go ahead and swap your rank out if you'd like, or we can do an impromptu formation after dinner and I can give it to you then?"

Lakers beamed with excitement as he held the staff sergeant rank in his hand. He had been filling in as the squad leader for Third Squad for almost a month as he waited for his promotion paperwork to finally come through. "No, that's OK, LT, appreciate the offer. They've been paying me E-6 pay since you moved me into the slot and the captain signed off the promotion. It's just nice to have the visual rank to go with the pay."

He leaned in. "All right, LT. You didn't just come in here to say hello to Sabo and hand me my rank. So what's coming down the pike?"

"Yeah, OK," Branham replied with a laugh. "So this new operation is supposed to start in a day or so. Apparently, I Corps is going to launch an offensive against the Dengta Line after all. Then VII Corps is attacking some other part of the line up north. What they told us is once these operations begin, they're going to watch and see if any of the units in our AO start moving to reinforce their lines up north. If they do, then it'll obviously weaken things here. Once that starts to happen, the Rangers are going to launch some sort of operation west of the Daling River. However, our battalion, along with the brigade, is going to heliborne in and look to seize several vehicle and rail bridges spanning the Daling."

The LT explained what he'd learned during the commander's call a few hours earlier. A few minutes into the conversation, Sergeant Peters spoke up. "So if I understand this right, our unit is going to seize the bridges and hold our positions until the tanks from the 3rd ID eventually show up and relieve us. Does that about sum it up?"

"Yup, sure does," said the LT with a grin. "What I need you guys to do is make sure we bring some antitank weapons, extra rockets for them, and maybe have someone bring a Stinger. They mentioned something about helicopters in the area, so I'd rather have a Stinger with us and not need it than need it and not have it. Oh, and before I forget to mention this—make sure to grab a few Switchblades or whatever drones they've got at Supply. Something about this mission makes me think we're going to be on our own for a while."

Sergeant Peters nodded as he scribbled some notes. Then he turned to Sabo. "Welcome back to the platoon, man. Get with Lakers here and have him update you on what kind of new toys we've been issued since you've been gone. We've got some new drones and these Jackal XD500s now as part of the platoons and companies. Lakers will also introduce you to the guys in Second Squad. I'm going to have you take Sergeant Yantis's squad. They're good guys—you should do fine with them. You'll have two solid fire team leaders too. Now, let's get ourselves ready for a mission."
****

1st Platoon, Alpha Company, 1-64th Armor Regiment
Dawa District, South of Panjin

When Sergeant First Class Rico Ramos left the building after the battalion commander's call, he was glad Captain Stanton asked him to come along with their new lieutenant, Dan Morse. After being without a platoon leader for more than a month, the company had finally received the replacement officers and soldiers they needed to bring the unit back to one hundred percent.

Lieutenant Morse walked next to Ramos. "OK, so that was my first commander's call and briefing," said Morse. "What do you think of this operation, Sergeant?"

"What do I think of this?" Ramos rephrased the question as they headed toward the motor pool, where the tanks were parked. "I think if the cav scouts do their job and hit the roadblocks near the bridges, and the sapper teams can stop them from being dropped in the river, then we probably have a decent shot of rolling down the highway relatively unopposed until we link up with the Airborne and those Rangers. If I had a concern, sir, it would be the possibility of enemy air or helo activity along the way."

The LT nodded along with his assessment before asking, "We're supposed to have air support during the operation, right?"

"Sure, we should have air support," Ramos replied with a smirk. "But that doesn't mean a helo or any enemy bird won't appear out of nowhere and mess our day up. The bigger concern is the possibility of them leaving behind or rushing forward antitank missile teams and sapper units to ambush us along the way or blow some of the highway overpasses. If they do that, it'll just mean we have to detour off the highway onto the frontage road until we get past the dropped section."

The LT looked concerned. "Sir, if you're worried about the missile teams, I wouldn't let it bother you too much," Ramos reassured him. "We got 5-7 Cavalry leading the way for us. If anyone's going to get shot up or ambushed, it's going to be them," Ramos joked.

The LT's mouth gaped open, appalled. "That's a joke, LT," Ramos quickly explained with a chuckle. "The 5-7 Cav is an outstanding unit and the eyes and ears for the division. They've got some exceptional drone pilots and some fast, nimble vehicles. They'll be able to react to an ambush better than we can with our sixty-two-ton mechanical beasts. It'll be all right, LT—you've got a lot of experienced NCOs and tank crews in the platoon."

The LT smiled sheepishly. When they arrived at the motor pool, Ramos walked him over the platoons' tanks and introduced him to Black Rider One—the PL's tank. Then he introduced him to the rest of the platoon before bringing everyone up to speed on the coming operation. Ramos wanted them to make sure the guns were cleaned, the sights properly aligned, and any last-minute repairs completed. It wouldn't be long now before the order to advance was given. When it was—they'd be ready to fight.

Chapter 5
Rangers in the Night

Bravo Company, 3rd Rangers
Liaoning, China

As the V-280 Valor crossed the Daling River in the early-morning hours, Sergeant First Class Amos Dekker could barely see the ground below as it whipped by in a blur. Occasionally, a pair of headlights would pass by as a vehicle drove along the Jingha Expressway. Dekker was glad they'd stayed far enough away from the bridge not to attract the eyes of any soldiers guarding the area. So far, they'd managed to go undetected—or at least, they weren't being shot at as they neared the landing zone.

"Three minutes! Three minutes to the LZ!" shouted the crew chief seated behind the pilots.

Dekker felt most nervous about this part of flying the Army's newest aviation wonder. As the Valor approached the landing zone, the rotor blades rotated from airplane mode to vertical lift position. Moments into the transition back to helicopter mode, Dekker felt the nose of the aircraft pull up as it bled off speed and prepared to lower to the ground.

As the Valor settled on the ground, the Rangers leaped from their seats into the blackness of the LZ. No sooner had they exited the helo when the pilot revved the engines and accelerated back into the sky, returning to pick up the next wave.

"Hey, those look like our rides," Dekker heard someone shout as the unmistakable sound of several Chinooks approached.

Sling-loaded below the six approaching CH-47s were vehicle pallets tied down with two side-by-side M1301 infantry squad vehicles as they dangled below. As Dekker saw the ISVs nearing the LZ, a couple of soldiers shouted commands as they took charge of the landing zone, guiding the helicopters in. As the helos delivered the pallets, soldiers detached the straps. Then they got the vehicles checked out and prepared to move.

"Sergeant Dekker, start rounding up the platoon. Let's grab our vehicles and get out of here," the voice of L2 chirped over his comms. In the pitch black of night, Dekker was glad to have internal comms within the platoon they could use for now. Most of the PLA soldiers didn't have platoon- or squad-level communications equipment, so they often blanket-jammed most of the frequencies the Americans typically used. It forced them to return to the old-fashioned way of communicating—shouting at each other.

"Copy that," Dekker replied. He set his squad leaders to rounding up their guys and headed to the ISVs. It wouldn't take long for the PLA to realize a large enemy force was landing nearby.

As he was walking toward a pair of vehicles, Dekker heard Specialist Kanton call out to him before he spotted him waving a hand to get his attention. "Over here, Sergeant! This is our truck. Everyone's here but you and Sergeant Wrigley."

"Ah, there you guys are. Good job. Hey, before heading out, I want to ensure everyone knows where the Starstreaks are at," Dekker said as he pointed to the MANPADs strapped to the outer roll bars near the vehicle's front driver and passenger sides. "We may run across some enemy helos or potentially some J-7s or J-10s once they figure out how many helicopters are flying around out here," Dekker explained before climbing into the vehicle.

"Got it, Sergeant. The Starstreaks, we got two of them in the trucks, just as you told us to," one of the soldiers announced as he pulled the British-made short-range surface-to-air missile launcher from the cargo rack mounted to the roof.

"All right, guys. Good job. Let's get on the move and head to our ambush site. I want to be in position well ahead of the sunrise, and hopefully before any kind of morning rush hour—if they have such a thing here."

As they tore out of the landing zone on the way to their objective, Dekker could hear the next set of helicopters approaching, bringing more Rangers and vehicles with each wave. This was shaping up to be a true battle.
****

Ninety Minutes Later
Xishan Mountain

"Over there. You see it?" Specialist Simpson pointed south, passing Dekker the thermal lenses.

Dekker looked off in the direction of where the Danjin and Jiefang roads ran parallel to the Xiaoling River. The two major roads connected the cities of Jinzhou and Linghai. Dekker was aware that the 101st had just inserted a brigade in Linghai to capture and hold the bridges crossing the Daling River. Whatever enemy force was headed this direction was likely responding to what was happening around those bridges.

As Dekker spotted the first couple of vehicles moving steadily down the Jiefang Road, Specialist Kanton crawled up next to him. "You need to see this, Sergeant," Kanton whispered.

He held a tablet out far enough in front of him so the two of them could see the display. "I got our drone up a few minutes ago and was checking on another road when I heard Simpson say he spotted something on the main supply routes. But look at this." Kanton pointed. "When I relocated the Puma over here, I spotted the column of vehicles Simpson said was moving down Jiefang Road. Maybe a mile further back, opposite the river, you can see another column approaching on Binhe Road. If I'm not mistaken, those three tanks…they look to me like those Type-15s. The ones that guy from the S2 called Black Panthers—those light tanks they said might be operated by remote control."

Dekker furrowed his brow at the mention of drone tanks. That was the last thing he wanted to encounter—more autonomous killing machines controlled and driven by some distant AI. Dekker stared at the video feed; there was a column of light tanks, infantry fighting vehicles, APCs, and these MV3 tactical trucks that reminded him of a modernized version of a deuce-and-a-half. Dekker knew this was far more than his ambush team could handle. They were nine Rangers against what looked like two advancing enemy forces traversing down different axes of attack.

"That was a good catch, Kanton. You too, Simpson. I want you guys to start figuring out how many vehicles and what types they are in each of those columns," Dekker instructed. "Get me a grid on some of these locations too. I'm going to call it in—see what kind of support I can wrangle up to jack these guys."

He grabbed for the radio, then laid his map of the area on the ground in front of him and searched through his notepad for the call sign of the unit he needed to reach. "Burrow Six, Fox One," he called. "How copy?"

40

"Here you go, Sergeant. That's the top column moving along Jiefang Road. That's the second column on Binhe," explained Specialist Simpson as he gave him a piece of paper with the numbers of vehicles and types.

"Fox One, Burrow Six. Good copy. Send your traffic," came a voice sounding as calm as could be.

"Burrow Six, Fox One. Priority SALUTE report. Break. Prepare to copy. Break." Then Dekker read off the disposition of the enemy force along with the numbers and types of vehicles approaching from both axes of advance. When he'd finished providing the report on the enemy movements, he called for whatever fire support was available.

Thirty minutes went by without too much change in the situation.

"Burrow Six, status on that fire support?" Dekker asked. "These columns are two kilometers away and closing. How copy?"

"What's the deal, Sarge? Are they going to give us some CAS or are we going to have to watch these jokers drive on by?" prodded Simpson, who was stretched out on the ground next to him.

Dekker pulled the radio receiver down to his shoulder before answering. "Still waiting. They're probably trying to figure out what's still on deck. You heard all those explosions earlier. That was just south of our insertion point. Fox Three found a column of vehicles approaching base camp from the south."

"Ah, that's what all that activity was. Damn, those PLA guys are reacting a lot faster than I thought they would have," Simpson replied.

Then the radio chirped moments before the two sides connected. "Fox One, no-go on fast movers. Targets in too built-up of an area. We have five Switchblade 600s we can assign to your position if that'll work. Otherwise, closest gunship support is forty-two mikes out."

Switchblades? Where the hell is that firebase the 101st guys are supposed to have set up by now? Dekker wondered as he considered the options they had for dealing with these columns. Each of the squads had a pair of Javelins and two of the Gustafs with four GMM rounds each. The guided multipurpose munitions were not likely to take out a main battle tank, but they had no problems eliminating an APC or infantry fighting vehicle, and with an extended range to twenty-five hundred meters and a laser-guided warhead, it was well worth the trade-off in hitting power compared to a standard unguided HEAT round.

Dekker depressed the talk button. "Burrow Six, what's the status on Rainmaker?"

Rainmaker was the call sign for the 1st Battalion, 320th Field Artillery Regiment, supporting the division's Second Brigade Combat Team. For the time being, they were going to be supporting both the brigade combat teams and the Rangers until additional heavy artillery support was brought forward.

"Fox One, no ETA on Rainmaker. Burrow Actual says he's sending five Switch 600s. ETA two mikes. What do you want us to hit, or do you want us to choose the targets?"

Ugh, fine. If that's what you're going to send us, then I'm going to make sure you at least take out the tanks... Dekker grabbed the tablet from Kanton so he could read off the targets he wanted them to hit. "Burrow Six, take out the three Type-15s traveling on Binhe Road. Then go for the two Type-15s on Jiefang Road. How copy?"

A moment later, another voice joined the conversation, letting him know they'd received the target selection and would go for the tanks. Now it was just a matter of waiting for the drones to cover the eight kilometers from the base camp to the targets. Meanwhile, the two columns continued to approach the interchange where Bravo Company had hunkered down. They had another hour until the second battalion from the 327th Infantry was supposed to link up with the Rangers and relieve them for other taskings. Until then, they were on their own to stop whatever enemy force headed their way.

While they waited for the drones to arrive, Dekker told the guys to pull out the Javelins and get them ready. Near as they could tell from the scout drone Kanton was using, they had three of the Type-15 light tanks traveling in the column further from them, on Binhe Road, and then two groupings of three Type-15s on the road closest to them.

Dekker watched the column while his guys unloaded the Javelins from the roof rack of the ISV. Then he heard what sounded like another vehicle moving down the trail they'd taken to reach the position where they had set up. Dekker rolled to his left to get a better view of what kind of vehicle was heading toward them, and he felt relieved when he spotted the outlines of another ISV. Dekker crawled back from the edge of the trees from which they were observing the roads and walked toward the approaching vehicle. He saw L2, sitting in the front passenger seat.

As the vehicle came to a halt, the captain hopped out, quickly followed by Staff Sergeant Poppadu, the section chief from the weapons platoon antitank section. The two of them were joined by three other soldiers, who swiftly went to work unfastening additional Javelins from the roof rack of the ISV.

"Hey, hope you don't mind us crashing the party," L2 said as he walked towards him. "When I heard the SALUTE report you called in, I grabbed the SJs for Poppa to see if we could get over here before the festivities started. We've got eight Javelins in the truck. I figure we could try and make short work of some of these vehicles before they reach the rest of the company."

"Hurry up, guys, I want two of those Javs set up and ready over there," Poppadu directed. "Get me two more set up twenty meters to the right of that position, then another two twenty or thirty meters further to the right of that second position. You three—grab. Don't sit around and gawk. Grab those last Javs and set up over there, to the left of your rockets. Come on, guys. We don't have much time."

"It's good to see you, sir," Dekker replied to Captain Loach. "I wasn't expecting company. I figured we'd have to scoot pretty quick once we fired off our Javs. The sun is still about twenty minutes away. It's going to be pretty obvious where these Javelins are coming from once we fire the first one." The two of them headed back to the spot from which Dekker had been observing the roads.

Then they heard a sound somewhere overhead as the radio squawked. A voice let them know the loitering munitions were preparing to go in for their attacks.

"Here they come. You can just spot that first one going in now," announced Poppadu as they heard the sound of the Switchblade's propeller engines pushing the loitering munition toward its target.

Dekker looked on with amazement as the drone zeroed in on the light tank. It approached the rear of the column in a high-altitude diving attack, plowing into the engine compartment. As the warhead's tandem charge exploded into the rear of the tank, it ignited the vehicle's fuel tank, causing an instant fireball to erupt into the predawn sky. A boom like a thunderclap shattered the tranquility of the moment.

Fractions of a second after the first explosion shocked the convoy, the second Black Panther tank erupted into flames as another thunderclap echoed across the distance, followed rapidly by a third. Then another explosion occurred when one of the tanks' turrets blew a hundred feet into the sky. Flame shot upwards as the ammo cooked off in the chassis of the vehicle.

By now, the other vehicles in the column were darting to the right or left sides of the road in defensive positions. A couple of the vehicles had popped defensive smoke screens in hopes of blinding whoever was calling in this attack on their column. Then one of the tanks closest to their position swerved suddenly to the right, far faster than Dekker thought a vehicle like that could move. A flash ignited just in front of the vehicle as the drone plowed into the concrete where the tank had been fractions of a second earlier.

"Holy crap. It missed!" shouted one of the soldiers. Everyone seemed momentarily stunned by the miss.

Then the final Switchblade found its mark as it careened into the side of the tank, its tandem-charge warhead exploding into the side of the vehicle. As the flames blew out the loader's hatch, a figure tried to crawl out of the hatch but keeled over dead halfway out of the turret.

We gotta take out the rest of those tanks, Dekker suddenly realized.

"Simpson, hit 'em with the Javelin. Let's go, people. Let's finish smashing this convoy before they have a chance to react to what's happening!" he shouted to the soldiers who'd been staring at the aftermath of the attack like he had been moments earlier.

Then the first Javelin leapt from the tree line from which they were observing the roads. The first missile had covered maybe half the distance when a second and third Javelin shot out of the trees as they took off at blinding speeds towards the column of vehicles on the road closest to them.

The tank that had evaded one of the Switchblades blew apart when the first Javelin slammed into the side of the vehicle. Its tandem-charge warhead exploded through the tank's reactive armor to get into the crew compartment of the tank. Moments after the Javelin hit, a second one slammed into the next tank, igniting the ammo inside as it blew flame through the opened hatches of the vehicle.

Dekker looked towards two of Poppadu's soldiers as they readied to fire another missile. Suddenly, the soldier hoisting the tube to his shoulder exploded into a mist of red gore, blood, and bone as the air and space around him erupted from a hail of 25mm autocannons and 12.7mm heavy machine bullets tearing into the tree line they had been hiding in.

Dekker threw himself to the ground as Captain Loach dove for the dirt. The air above them erupted with cannon fire as the vehicle gunners began reacting to the attack from the hilltop nearby. Looking off to his right, Dekker saw Simpson acting smooth as silk as he hoisted another Javelin to his shoulder, zeroing in on the vehicles spraying the tree line around them. As the missile leapt from the tube to chase down another vehicle, Simpson tossed the spent tube and scrambled across the ground on his belly, hands, and knees. The trees and bushes above him burst apart from the heavy autocannons and machine guns of the vehicles. The enemy soldiers had likely scrambled out of the vehicles and also begun shooting at them.

Dekker could barely hear himself think, let alone hear the shouts or screams for medics. Regardless, all around him were cries of pain from those who had been hit by shrapnel from exploding munitions and fragments of the trees erupting all around them.

Looking off to his left, Dekker saw Staff Sergeant Poppadu pulling one of his wounded soldiers away from the tree line overlooking the road below. Another soldier who'd been kneeling against the side of the ISV ran towards the two of them, helping to pull the wounded trooper closer to the ISV. When Dekker tried to look more closely to see the man's injuries, he turned away almost instantly, throwing up in the midst of the battle. Somewhere in the process of Poppadu pulling the man further away from the shooting, one of the 25mm autocannon rounds had hit the wounded trooper near the midsection. It had ripped the man's lower extremities clean off his body, and his entrails fell out of his abdominal cavity, spreading themselves for ten or feet across the ground in a horrifying gory mess unlike anything Dekker had seen up to this point in the war. Soldiers shouted in horror at the scene while another voice yelled out in terror at what was happening around them.

Dekker snapped himself out of the fear that was beginning to take hold of him. "Grab what you can and throw it into the vehicle!" he shouted to his remaining soldiers. He was going to get out of the kill zone before they were wiped out.

Boom!

An explosion blew apart one of the tree trunks, raining chunks of wood and shrapnel down on the Rangers as they worked to grab their wounded comrades and bits of gear and take them toward the ISVs. Dekker reached out for one of his wounded Rangers, grabbed for the man's arm and pulled it over his shoulder, guiding him toward one of the vehicle's jump seats.

"Hang on to your rifle. We may need it," Dekker told the guy, who was pressing his hand against a wound to his left thigh to stem the bleeding.

"Just get us out of here, Sarge."

Loud cracks of cannon fire and the reports of heavy-caliber automatic gunfire echoed across the city and throughout the forested areas from which they had launched their attack, completely drowning out Dekker's voice.

"We got everyone! Let's get out of here!" shouted L2, a streak of blood running down the side of his face.

Dekker turned the ignition of the vehicle and breathed a sigh of relief when he heard the engine roar to life. He threw it into reverse and gunned it. The vehicle lurched away from the edges of the tree line, which was still being shredded by the column of vehicles below. Dekker slammed the brakes, barely avoiding a collision with a tree. He threw the truck into drive and mashed the accelerator as the rear tires spun out for a brief moment before finding traction.

Dekker nearly fishtailed the rear of the vehicle across the dirt trail as he raced from the scene of the ambush. His ears began to register the whomp, whomp sound of helicopter blades slicing through the air somewhere around them.

"Tell me that helicopter is one of ours!" someone behind him shouted.

"I don't know, start looking for it. See what you can find," Dekker shouted in response as he tried to pay attention to the trail they were racing down. Glancing in the rearview mirror, he saw the other vehicle was following his lead, not too close, but not too far away either.

"Oh crap! That isn't one of ours!" one of the guys shouted urgently as the sound of the rotors was almost on top of them.

"Get off the trail and into those trees now!" shouted L2 as he grabbed for the crash bar in front of the passenger seat.

Dekker slammed the brakes hard as he yanked the steering wheel to the right. He felt the vehicle skid across the ground as it kicked dirt and debris into the air around them. Dekker plowed the vehicle through the underbrush surrounding the trail. As they screeched to a halt further beneath the canopy cover and out of the line of the trail, he briefly caught a glimpse of an object as it streaked through the air, through the cloud of dust and debris he'd just kicked up—exploding in a violent thunderclap where they'd just been moments earlier.

BAM!

The concussion of the blast rocked the ISV even as they sat idling under the trees.

I gotta take that thing out or it'll nail us when it makes a second pass, Dekker realized as he threw the vehicle into park.

Jumping out of the driver seat, he grabbed for the straps holding the Starstreak MANPADs against the outer top roll bar of the vehicle.

"It's coming back around!" one of the soldiers shouted. By now, the Rangers had bailed out of the vehicle, shooting at the helicopter as it maneuvered to make another pass at them.

As Dekker activated the MANPADs' targeting system, he placed the crosshairs for the missile squarely over top of the helicopter as it swung around. When he saw he'd achieved a lock on the helo, he fired the missile, praying he wasn't too late.

The helo released a burst of flares, but in the instant it did, the tungsten darts plowed into it, and the whole aircraft blew apart. As the fiery debris fell to the ground, several of Dekker's guys cheered before the captain yelled at everyone, "Mount back up! We still have to get off this mountain and link back up with the rest of the company—hopefully, before the rest of the enemy forces reach us."

Dekker took a deep breath and hopped back into the vehicle. They didn't have time to celebrate—they were going to have a fight on their hands, and the company would need as many of them as possible if they were going to hold the intersection until reinforcements arrived.

Chapter 6
The Panjin Pocket

77th Fighter Squadron
Dandong, China

Joker checked his altitude and heading shortly after takeoff. His command, the 20th Fighter Wing, had officially completed their relocation from Kadena Air Base in Okinawa to gear up to support what he'd been told was hopefully the final stages to ending this war.

At the outset of the Second Korean War and the allied invasion of China, his wing had flown missions against this very base during their struggle to achieve air dominance over the skies of northern China. Having been part of the attacks to wreck the very base they now called home, he had to give it to the members of the 823rd and the 819th Red Horse Squadrons for having fully repaired the former PLA air base just west of Dandong, China, along the Yalu River.

He mused privately how at the start of the war, he'd rotate the missions his squadrons flew to break up the monotony and keep his pilots sharp. Two years in and he was still running the same strategy—two squadrons running the high operational demand for SEAD missions while the third conducted close-air support for the soldiers below. But the lead-up to the invasion of Taiwan had cost him more than a few pilots and aircraft. The island nation had been turned into a veritable fortress of anti-aircraft guns and missile systems as the island maintained its status as the unsinkable aircraft carrier of the Pacific.

When Joker had finally received a pair of newly promoted lieutenant colonels to assume command of the 77th and 79th Squadrons, he'd thought he might have finally caught a break—especially when they'd arrived at Kadena with nine newly graduated lieutenants from flight school. Then Murphy's Law struck again.

During the last day of air operations before the wing relocated to Dandong, his new squadron commander for the 77th opted to take a pair of lieutenants with him on a final SEAD mission over the central mountains of Taiwan near Taipei. While engaging several air-defense systems west of the city, Joker's newly arrived lieutenant colonel had succeeded in getting shot down just five days after taking command, with only three missions in since arriving. The lieutenants flying with him reported spotting a chute open but were hurried out of the area by a series of newly identified radar-controlled anti-aircraft guns. The senior captain flying with them had taken control of the situation, ordering the remaining flight of Vipers back to Kadena after engaging the SAMs that had taken their commander out. More than a week had gone by now, and Joker hadn't heard anything about his squadron commander being picked up by friendly forces, so for the time being, he was once again short commanders for his squadrons.

"Hey, Joker, didn't you fill in as the air boss for the 77th the last time we flew this neck of the woods?" asked his wingman Major Gordon "Gordy" Goozemon.

Joker sighed audibly over the intercom without responding.

"Ah, come on, Joker. You know I'm just poking fun at you, right?" Gordy teased. They were waiting at the gas station to top off their tanks before heading to their assigned mission box.

"Twelve days, Gordy. Twelve more days. That's all I gotta say," replied Joker. That was how long until his former wingman returned to the squadron now that his flight status was updated.

"Huh, it's going to be like that, eh, Joker?" said Gordy. "Running back to your old wingman like that? I thought we had something special, man."

Joker laughed at the pang of jealousy threaded through his response. It wasn't that he didn't like having Gordy as his wingman; it was just that he and Peanut had a history together. They had flown together before the war, and they'd flown through a lot during it. It wasn't until Peanut had gotten injured during a mission that Joker had realized how much he'd relied on his friend for advice and as a sounding board.

Joker hit the talk button. "Ah, you know it's not like that, Gordy. There's plenty of me to go around. It's just, you know…Peanut was my first."

Gordy busted out laughing as their planes moved another step closer to topping off their tanks. As the laughter faded, Joker turned serious again as he had Gordy go over the mission. At the same time, they waited for a pair of Super Eagles to finish refilling their tanks.

Joker glanced at the giant aircraft's wings ahead of them. He guessed they were headed out to replace whoever was flying the combat air patrol over the battlefield. The sun hadn't fully risen yet, but enough light had pushed the dark of night away for him to see the Eagles had too many missiles left if they were returning from the front. The skies were littered with drones, manned fighters, and the ever-growing presence of UCAVs and autonomous fighter planes. That wasn't even counting helicopters. It was a target-rich environment, and few Super Eagles would voluntarily return to base with a full rack of missiles and no kills to show for it.

As Gordy went over their mission, Joker felt certain his squadron would make a difference in this armor assault, breaking through the enemy lines. The mission briefer had said the 1st Armored Brigade Combat Team was attacking elements of the 79th PLA Group Army, east of the coastal city of Panjin. If the armor units were able to break out, then there was essentially nothing but flat plains for nearly thirty miles until you reached the Daling River. It was their goal to ensure they captured a series of bridges crossing the Daling River in and around the Linghe District and the city of Jinzhou. On PowerPoint, it looked like an impressive operation, with a battalion of Rangers and several brigades from the 101st Airborne seizing the Jingha Expressway bridge and two others in Linghai City. But that was PowerPoint, and this was real life.

The plan involving the heliborne soldiers was the part that most concerned Joker. Should the armor units get bogged down at any point along the way, it could be disastrous for the units behind enemy lines holding those bridges. But if it succeeded, if they got across it and seized the city of Jinzhou—it could open a huge hole in the enemy lines. It would allow them to push south along the G1 Jingha Expressway down the entire coast of Liaodong Bay to Huludao and the critical port, rail, and road junction point at Tianjin.

"Gambler Actual, Texaco Six. You are clear to approach pump two. Gas is on that blond over in the F-35 wagging her wings at ya."

Joker laughed at the boom operator as, sure enough, he saw an F-35 off to his right, tanking up on the aerial refueler next to them, rocking her wings slightly. After replying to the boom operator, he started the careful process of lining his aircraft up behind the giant KC-46 aerial refueler until he'd matched its speed. When he saw he was approaching the refueling drogue, which looked like a basket-shaped device that extended from the tail boom connected to the aircraft, Joker extended the fighter's refueling probe, a long metal tube near the cockpit that would connect the two aircraft.

When the two parts had mated, a seal was obtained. Then the fuel started to flow, and the tank that was already half-empty from getting the fully loaded aircraft into the sky was steadily refilled. As they waited for the process to finish, Joker watched his radar as he continued to observe his surroundings, noting the tremendous number of aircraft in the air for this operation. He did not doubt that Chinese AI had seen what was happening. It was probably going to vector fighters towards them and maybe even some of those new UCAV fighters he'd heard so much about.

When his tanks were full, Joker retracted the probe and gently turned away from the aircraft as he started to give his engines more power. Once he and Gordy had linked back up, they headed toward the line of control to see what kind of mission awaited them.
****

Alpha Company, 1-64th Armor Regiment
Panjin, China

Sergeant First Class Rico Ramos stood in the turret of the M1A2 Abrams main battle tank as the company prepared to roll out. They'd spent the night before getting the tank ready, topping off their fuel and ensuring they had extra ammo and water. Today was the day. Alpha Company and the rest of the battalion would punch through the enemy lines. They would do what tanks do best—advance to contact and destroy other tanks. If it all worked according to plan, they would grab forty kilometers of territory from the enemy and get the division across the Daling River, with the Airborne and the Rangers already seizing the bridges. It was on them to push through whatever lay ahead and link up with the Airborne before the enemy could organize an effective counterattack that might put the advance units in a bad spot.

Ramos looked ahead of their tank, noticing the black columns of smoke rising into the sky. He heard the on-again, off-again chattering of machine-gun fire and the occasional boom from something exploding. Then his gunner, Sergeant Tim Harris, crawled up into the hatch beside him. Harris placed a hand on the crew-served weapon as he looked toward the on-ramp to the G16 Danxi-Panhaiying Expressway.

"I don't like this, Ramos," said Harris apprehensively. "Something about driving down an expressway to meet the enemy doesn't sit well with me."

Ramos snorted. "Yeah, well, this isn't exactly the best terrain for a tank, if you know what I mean."

"Nah, a tank will be fine once we get closer to our objective," Harris countered. "My concern is the enemy waiting for us as we gallivant down this nice wide-open road, knowing that for a decent stretch of it we can't deviate too far from the highway without running into a gazillion rice paddies and irrigated farmlands."

Everyone had brought up the same concerns about using the expressway. They felt like they were being funneled into a kill box. The Jingha Expressway was a six-lane highway with three lanes to either side, but if you deviated too far off the main road, it would cause an issue.

Ramos sighed as he listened to Harris complain for the umpteenth time about the plan. "You act like I'm in charge. Like I have some say in all of this. I'm just like you, Harris, just a cog in the wheel."

"You aren't a little concerned about this at all?" Harris probed.

"Would it make you feel happy if I was?" Ramos countered.

Harris stared at him for a moment. Finally, he shrugged in frustration. "I just wish there was a better way, that's all."

"Yeah, well, have you seen the network of all those rice fields out there?" asked Ramos. "How everything is divided up into tiny little sections? It's a damn nightmare trying to move a tank through that. At least on the highway, we can actually move to the right or left and get out of the way of something. You try that and roll into a rice paddy, and you're calling for a wrecker to pull your ass out, if they can even make it back there.

"This will be fine. We have helicopters scouting ahead of us. We've got 5-7 Cav with a scout company rolling ahead of the battalion to clear the way or identify what needs blowing up for us. We've got air support. F-16s are on standby, ready to lay some hurt once we give 'em a target. Come on, man. This will be way easier than when we crossed from Colombia into Venezuela. That was crazy tight, those roads and winding trails we had to take." Ramos shivered as he recounted their past experiences and what they had already survived up to that point.

Before either of them could say anything else, the radios came to life, and the order to move was given. Ramos grabbed his helmet and told Lopez to get them moving and follow the tank in front of them.

As their armored column got underway, Ramos stood in the turret's commander hatch and watched Black Rider One and their new lieutenant lead the way. He hadn't had much time to get to know the lieutenant or many of the other new replacements they'd received before this new offensive. He was just glad they'd received replacement tanks and crews before it started.

Since Ramos had run the platoon for most of the last six months, they had finally promoted him to sergeant first class, at least paying him for the role he'd been filling until a new lieutenant arrived. Then, days before they'd rolled out of Korea and into China, Lieutenant Dan Morse had arrived at the company and quickly been introduced to the platoon and Ramos. Short on officers with experience, they'd paired the lieutenant with Ramos, telling the young officer to lean on his platoon sergeant while he learned how to be a tanker, so he'd hopefully last longer than the last guy.

Truth be told, Ramos didn't mind the new LT. He was quiet and spent most of his time listening and asking questions like the rest of the new replacements. They were curious to know about past battles and what to expect—pretty much the same questions most replacements would ask when showing up to a unit that had seen enough action to have needed replacements in the first place.

Twenty minutes into the drive, they'd finally reached the first significant junction point and what had previously counted as the front line. As they drove past the position, Ramos saw a pair of Abrams tucked off to the side, along with a pair of Bradley fighting vehicles and some dismounted infantry. They had several machine-gun positions set up and likely a few antitank guided missiles lying nearby, just in case.

As their column continued down the highway and onto the Jingha Expressway, Ramos wondered how long it would be until they ran into their first signs of trouble. He knew the cav scouts had gone ahead of them. They'd encountered a few enemy vehicles and small detachments, likely checkpoints, but nothing serious. Eventually, the enemy would realize this attack was more than just a probe. Then they would run into whatever was sent to stop them from linking up with the Airborne, and the real fight would begin.

Boom!

A loud explosion ripped through the air, shattering a relatively calm drive thus far. When Ramos looked off into the distance to see what was going on, he caught sight of a cloud of oily black smoke rising into the sky a handful of kilometers further down the road.

Grabbing for binoculars, he scanned the horizon in the direction of the smoke when his ears registered the familiar sounds of gunfire. It started as a single pop—likely a soldier shooting at something he thought posed a threat. Then it escalated into a full-out gunfight as multiple rifles and machine guns joined the fray. That single gunshot quickly morphed into a raging battle. The horizon came alive with red and green tracer fire zipping between combatants, the occasional ricochet bouncing into the sky, looking more like a dozen bottle rockets being set off all at once on the Fourth of July than a barrage of deadly projectiles. Soon the smaller-caliber rifles and machine guns were joined by the heavier chunk-chunk-chunk sounds from the Bradley 25mm chain guns and the Browning fifty-caliber machine guns atop the vehicle-mounted JLTVs.

As the battle further down the road got underway, the lieutenant leading the platoon and their column of tanks called a halt to their advance. The tanks, which had been driving in a file formation with every other turret facing the opposite side, now veered to the sides of the highway into a wedge formation—waiting to see what would happen next.

Then Ramos heard the CO shout to the lieutenant. "Why'd you stop the column from advancing?"

Ramos cut in. "The LT just wanted to pause and establish comms with the scouts before he led the rest of the unit toward the fighting," he explained.

He had bailed the LT out of his mistake, likely without him even realizing it. Their orders had been clear—advance to contact and do not stop until you've pushed through the enemy lines and linked up with the Airborne holding the bridges. They were expected to make contact with the enemy, and they were also expected to push through it, not stop and assess the situation like the LT had just done. When he explained the situation privately to the lieutenant, the LT agreed with his assessment and then suggested Ramos's vehicle take the lead for the platoon, and he'd follow. When their private conversation had ended, Ramos smiled inwardly, pleased with having a lieutenant mature enough to know when he was outside his experience level. Rather than bumble his way through it, possibly getting himself killed in the process, he'd defer to his platoon sergeant and learn from observation.

Ramos stood in the commander's tank hatch and ordered Specialist Blum to get the vehicle back on the move and into the lead position. As their tank got on the move and the column steadily followed, a pair of AH-64 Apache gunships flew over them, headed toward the fight. The conflict seemed to grow in intensity with each passing moment.

Looking down into the turret, Ramos called, "Hey, Harris, get out here and check this out."

Seconds later, Sergeant Harris climbed out of the loader's hatch. "What's going, Ramos?"

He pointed toward the fighting. "Look to your three o'clock! A pair of Apaches just flew over us. I think they're getting ready to light something up over there."

As they continued to observe what was happening, the gunfire in the distance intensified until they heard another explosion. Then a new series of machine guns joined the action, and the firing volume increased rapidly.

"I see 'em!" shouted Harris excitedly. Their tank barely moved five miles per hour as the column behind them reorganized themselves into a single-file formation.

The Apaches had been approaching the growing battle unnoticed as they skimmed above the treetops, moving closer to the enemy before making their move. Then the gunship on the left broke away from its partner as it climbed into the sky while its partner continued to race ahead.

As the first Apache gained altitude, it turned sharply to one side with its nose angled downward, firing off a handful of rockets into an unseen target. Then a barrage of red tracer rounds leaped into the sky from an entirely new position further down the highway. Bullets sprayed around the gunship, which began to spit out flares while the pilot reacted quickly to the new threat, jinking hard to one side—tracer rounds zipped through the space it had just occupied.

Suddenly, the other Apache they'd lost track of rose into the sky almost on top of the enemy position. It fired off a string of rockets into whatever vehicle had been shooting at its partner. Then multiple explosions erupted as flames and chunks of metal flew into the sky from the burning wreck that had just blown apart.

The second Apache repositioned into a higher orbit of the area as it circled before firing one of its Hellfire missiles into something they couldn't see. Then it fired a second and a third Hellfire, just as the first one must have hit a vehicle. The other two missiles slammed into at least one tank as they saw a turret flip into the air, followed by several explosions nearby. They watched the pair of helicopters tear the place apart for a couple of moments. They battered the area with rockets, 30mm autocannon fire, and their remaining Hellfire missiles—unloading on something they couldn't see further down the road.

"Wow, Ramos! It's not every day you get to see an Apache open a can of whoop-ass on the enemy," Harris shouted excitedly.

"Yeah, no joke, man. Getting on the wrong side of a gunship is bad news for a tanker," Ramos commented.

A few minutes passed in silence before Ramos commented, "Hey, Harris, it looks like we're about ready to get rolling at speed again. I need you to go below and stay up on the scope, scanning for possible targets as we approach this line of contact—watch our flanks like a hawk. I'm hoping the scouts have found any missile teams that might be lying in wait along the edges of the highway, but you never know. I don't think this will be the only action we'll see before we reach the Daling River."

"Sure thing, boss, no problem," Harris replied, dropping back into the turret to get things ready.

With the shooting subsiding, the captain ordered them to pick up the pace. Ramos knew the CO would tell them to get on the move sooner than later.

I wonder if I can listen to what's going on with the scouts. Ramos pulled his notes out and looked for the channel the scouts were on. Finding it, he switched over to listen in.

He had one ear listening while the other was free. Ramos continued passively listening for his call sign on the platoon net, which was playing over the speakers below in the turret, as he listened to the scouts. He started hearing bits and pieces of the fighting happening in the background as different teams reported what they saw. Some reports must have been coming from further ahead as he didn't hear any shooting in the background. The fight was winding down there, and some of the scouting teams had already moved well ahead of where this recent fight had occurred. Maybe another ten minutes passed, and he heard a call over the platoon net for all TCs to switch to the battalion net momentarily.

Oh, great. The battalion commander wants to say something, thought Ramos. He switched to the channel just in time.

"Desert Rogues, we've been hung up long enough on this highway sitting like ducks in a barrel. There will be no more stopping. The Airborne have secured the bridges, and Rangers out ahead of the Airborne have established a series of blocking positions to prevent any PLA reinforcements from retaking them. Reports are coming that those Rangers are now under severe threat by a mechanized force led by at least a battalion of armor looking to retake those bridges and block us from getting across. It's now urgent for us to press on and push through any force we encounter along the way. If your unit gets engaged, push through it. Shoot it up on the way past, but push through it. DR Actual, out!" finished the battalion commander.

Moments later, the captain jumped on the platoon net and ordered them to pick up speed. Ramos acknowledged the order and got Specialist Blum to get them moving.

When Ramos had joined the battalion nearly a year before the war had started, he had taken some time to read up on the unit's history. Aside from the fact that it dated back to World War II, the unit's real claim to fame came during the invasion of Iraq in March of 2003. Task Force 1-64th Armor, as it was called, had led the division into the heart of Baghdad as the 3rd Infantry Division's armored fist in what would later become known as the Thunder Run. After blitzing across the deserts of southern Iraq and through half a dozen cities along the way, 1-64 had smashed Saddam's elite Republican Guard units ringing the capital before driving into the heart of the city and capturing what would later become the Green Zone.

As Specialist Blum got their tank on the move, Ramos hoped 1-64th would have a similar run now. He said a silent prayer that they'd make it to the bridges in one piece and the Airborne would still be there holding it for them.
****

77th Fighter Squadron
Liaoning Province, China

As their Vipers flew a holding pattern while they waited to be assigned a target, Joker continued to observe the battle unfolding. With all the action in the air and down on the ground, he marveled in total fascination at how the air battle managers coordinated the events and kept it all straight. Pairs of F-15 Super Eagles and the stealthier F-35s were being vectored repeatedly to engage the aerial threats to the strike aircraft, hitting target after target being called in by the Rangers and the units of the 101st Airborne, who appeared to be in the thick of the fight. From the E-7 Wedgetails' high-powered MESA radars to the E-8 JSTARs' classified synthetic aperture radar system, there was nothing that could fly or drive that these aircraft couldn't spot or track for up to two hundred and thirty miles.

Joker shifted uncomfortably in his seat as his rear end was at the beginning stages of falling asleep. That was certainly not a good thing when he still had at least a few hours left in the cockpit. The last thing he wanted was for his legs and feet to go numb when he needed them to fly.

"Good God, Joker. We've been waiting on a target for thirty-two minutes now. If they don't give us something soon, we'll need a tanker," Gordy griped.

Joker checked the fuel gauge; Gordy wasn't wrong. They would need to top off their tanks if they didn't get a mission soon. Apparently, the ground units had gotten hung up on something, so they hadn't made a lot of progress in moving toward the Daling River. He had hoped they would be retasked to support the Rangers or the 101st so they would have stayed tied to the armor battalion spearheading the assault down the Jingha Expressway. Instead, they had to sit tight and wait for the time being.

"I know, Gordy. My butt is starting to go numb from sitting still too long. Did you catch that recent action over near the Jinzhou Bay Airport?"

There was a momentary pause before his wingman replied, "No, what happened? Damn it, what channel was that on?"

"It's OK, Gordy. I'm still monitoring the 55th and 79th channels," Joker explained. "Apparently, they encountered an SA-15—one of those newer upgraded Tor-M2 models, the ones that carry sixteen missiles instead of eight."

The PLA had been moving a lot of their air-defense vehicles and surface-to-air missile batteries around the front lines, making it increasingly difficult to find and destroy them. The Tor systems, in particular, were troublesome SAMs to deal with because they'd become quite adept at intercepting cruise missiles and even HIMAR rockets. The Chinese had leveraged many of the lessons learned from their use during the Russo-Ukrainian War a few years back, before the start of this war.

"Damn. Tell me they took it out, Joker," said Gordy. "An SA-15 is a date with an ejection seat."

Joker laughed. He'd flown against much tougher SAMs than the Tor-M2. Then again, anytime you had to eject was a bad day to be a pilot, regardless of which system had your number that day.

"Well, if you thought that was bad, you won't like to hear they also ran into another new battery of HQ-16s in the Taihe District near the Jinzhou military air base," Joker explained. "They said something about plugging it with several HARMs, but you know how that works. They've gotten clever these days, giving us a decoy radar to go after to waste a HARM. Then they activate another decoy, only this time, they've got it protected by a PGZ-95 or another Tor-M2. They've started operating them in the cities, making it harder to engage them without collateral damage."

There was a pause for a moment before Gordy replied. "I don't know what's better: SEAD missions or close-air support. They're both liable to get you shot at. They're each critically important. I guess that's why they pay you the big bucks to determine which one gets the love while the other gets the scraps."

"Oh, if that's how it worked, Gordy, life would—"

"Gambler Six, Plush One, switch to channel two."

"Gordy, switch over to channel two. I think we got a mission," Joker announced before switching channels.

As they listened in on the instructions, it was clear this was hot. Their Vipers and a pair of Super Hornets were being vectored in for an urgent TIC mission. Once they switched over to the ground communications channels and linked up with the forward air controllers, they started to understand the situation on the ground. They dropped below fifteen thousand feet and started heading toward the enemy troops.

When they were ten kilometers out, Joker told the unit on the ground they would make an overflight of the area to try and spot the troublesome area before they circled and lined up for an attack. With four cluster munitions and four Mavericks apiece, he wanted to make sure whatever they hit removed the problem for the tanks trying to link up with the Airborne.

As they approached the area, they eventually spotted the column of tank and infantry fighting vehicles spread out across the highway. If Joker had to guess, it looked like an enemy unit had emerged from the Jincheng Residential District a few kilometers to the north— likely the unit garrisoning this side of the river.

When their aircraft approached the head of the column, the ground in front of them came alive with tracer rounds zipping into the sky. So far, it appeared to be unguided machine-gun fire, but that didn't mean there wasn't something with teeth sitting down there, waiting to take a bite when the time was right.

"Gordy, I want you to follow behind and clean up whatever I miss or if an AA gun decides to show itself as I fly over top. Got it?"

"I'm on it, and good luck."

Luck? Who needs luck when you got skill? Joker snickered, thinking about all the pilots who held too much superstition around their ability to hit a target or fly through a hornet's nest of enemy ground fire. *If it's your time, it's your time, and nothing will stop that.*

As Joker came around the armored column, he lined his fighter up to the targets and decreased his speed so the cluster munitions could adequately deploy. Even at a reduced speed, the ground below continued to whip past him in a blur as the distance to weapons release rapidly closed. When he was less than a kilometer from the target, strings of tracer fire leaped into the air around him, filling the sky with bullets, all trying to swat him from the sky before he could deliver his payload. Then, before Joker knew it, his targeting computer told him he was over the mark and alerted him to release the bombs. He mashed the button twice, releasing two of the four cluster munitions to fall behind him. He pulled up on the aircraft and dumped fuel into the engines, kicking in the afterburner as he tried to flee the scene as quickly as he could.

When he started to turn around, Joker caught sight of his handiwork. Multiple buildings were ripped apart and now on fire. At least one column of black smoke rose into the sky. He knew he'd hit one of those infantry fighting vehicles that had been using the buildings for cover as it engaged the tanks and IFVs on the highway.

Joker scolded himself for missing one of the tanks hiding between the buildings like the IFV that he had hit. Then he saw Gordy swooping in for his run, but something looked different. He realized it was one of the Super Hornets cutting in between them as it tried to get in on the action.

Joker was about to get angry, maybe even try and call them and chew 'em out for cutting in on their mission, but as the Hornet flew over the target, releasing a stick of five-hundred-pound bombs, several MANPADs leaped into the air, almost on top of the Hornet.

Once the pilot had released his bombs, he'd gone to full power on his engines as he clawed back into the sky, just as Joker had done a few minutes earlier in his bombing run. Except this time, the enemy had fired a pair of shoulder-fired missiles at the Hornet as he flew out of the area. The Hornet's self-defense system was ejecting flares like they were going out of style as the pilot pulled away. One of the missiles went for the flare and blew apart harmlessly behind the fighter. But the second missile got within range of its proximity fuse and blew its shotgun blast of ball bearings right into the engines of the Hornet.

Joker yelled out instinctively, shouting for the pilot to eject. Then the fuel tanks must have ignited as they blew apart before the pilot could even react to what had happened. The fiery debris rained across the farm fields and nearby towns and villages. Joker barely caught sight of Gordy's plane racing down the same path as the Hornet.

As Gordy's plane adjusted moments before releasing his cluster munitions, the space in front of his fighter came alive with tracer fire, and at least two additional MANPADs took off after him. He shouted warnings to Gordy as he watched his wingman fly through the hailstorm of bullets. The first missile went for one of the flares—then the second. But as he watched Gordy pull away from his attack run, his plane's missile warning systems blared their warnings as a pair of new radars had turned on, searching for a target.

Joker activated the ECM pod, hoping to jam the radars long enough to get himself out of range or at least out of the danger zone. Giving his engines more thrust, he caught a glimpse of the fight below. It was a real furball of a fight down there, just as it was up here.

God, this somehow feels like a trap…

****

Alpha Company, 1-64th Armor Regiment

"HEAT up!" shouted Lopez.

"Fire!"

"Firing!"

BOOM!

The tank fired, belching flame out the barrel, and a smoke ring followed.

"That was a miss! Reload HEAT and fire on the same target!" Ramos shouted angrily.

"No way that's a miss! Give me a second to verify it, Ramos, before we plug it again," Sergeant Harris countered hotly. He was sure they'd nailed the ZBD infantry fighting vehicle.

"Damn it. We don't have time to argue about this. Fire the gun and take it out already!" Ramos shouted, his eyes still affixed to where they had fired at the Chinese vehicle.

Harris was about to say something when he saw the flash from within the smoke. The ZBD had fired its 100mm cannon yet again, defying its death and proving Harris wrong.

"Firing!" Ramos heard Harris shout as the cannon recoiled inside the turret. The aft shell clinked on the floor, bits of the spent accelerant filling the cabin.

Ramos stared at the ZMD, almost willing it to explode. Then the high-explosive antitank round slammed into the sloped frontal section of the armor, blowing its explosive charge into the new hole leading to the engine compartment and the driver's section. As the explosion washed over the engine and the vehicle's fuel, it blew apart in a giant fireball. Ramos watched the turret cartwheel into the sky as the remaining ammo cooked off, spewing a geyser of flame some ten meters into the air like a giant Roman candle.

"Hot damn! Now that's a hit!" Harris exclaimed. He slammed the side of the gunner targeting scope.

"Harris, I got another target. Tank identified, two thousand, six hundred meters. Load sabot," Ramos called out methodically.

"Ah, I see it now. Tank identified, two thousand, six hundred meters. Load sabot," Sergeant Harris rapidly replied as he synched the gunner's thermal viewer to Ramos's.

62

"Loading sabot!" Specialist Lopez responded. He moved the charging handle on the gun system, disarming it as he swapped out the HEAT round for the tank-busting sabot. Then he swapped out the rounds, moving the charging handle, rearming the gun and alerting Harris and Ramos that it was ready to fire. "Sabot up!" he shouted.

"Fire!"

"Firing!"

BOOM!

"Damn it, you missed!" Ramos shouted angrily as Harris missed a second shot in minutes—something he'd never seen him do during the entire war.

"What the hell?"

"Forget about it, Harris! Just get another round on that tank before he plugs us or someone else!" Ramos urged.

Oh damn, this isn't good. Ramos saw the enemy turret moving the barrel in their direction. *Come on, hurry up and get that sabot loaded...* Then he saw the barrel stop moving and realized it was pointed right at them.

"Sabot up!"

As Ramos heard Lopez shout the words, the flames filled his commander's sight before he could pull the trigger.

"Firing!"

BOOM!

Thump!

Ramos felt his face and body slam into his viewer, almost knocking him out cold. His arms went limp and stars filled his vision.

"Holy crap, we're hit!" Harris shouted. Lopez yelped in pain, cradling his hand and forearm as he collapsed to the floor of the tank.

"Pop the smoke, Blum, and get some kind of cover!" Harris yelled frantically. The tank sputtered a bit before the engine kicked out, leaving them in the center of the road.

"Ramos, you OK, man?" The sound of Harris's voice finally got through to him, and Ramos felt himself starting to come back to reality.

"Yeah, I think I'll be all right, maybe. Check on Lopez, and let's bail out of this thing in case we missed that tank," he ordered.

They swiftly exited the damaged tank. As they crawled out, another tank from their platoon parked alongside them to help protect them from the mortar shells starting to fall nearby. They placed their armored shell between themselves and their crippled tank, blocking potential shrapnel until they could be recovered.

Ramos wiped the blood from his face, realizing it could have been worse. Their tank could have blown up. "Well, we'll have to sit this one out for a while until they figure out how bad that jacked our tank up or if the grease monkeys can get us back in the fight."

"Yeah, well, I think I may have broken my arm, guys," Lopez explained. "You may have to find another loader for a little while."

"Hey, look at it this way, bro, you'll get another Purple Heart," declared Specialist Blum as he tried to find a bright spot for Lopez.

They laughed at the comment. When Lopez had broken his nose during the invasion of Venezuela, the medics treating him had mentioned he'd broken it during an engagement with the enemy. Many months later, after the Venezuelans had surrendered, Lopez found himself being called forward to be awarded the prestigious medal, to the amusement of his comrades.

Chapter 7
Trenches & Woomera

Eighth Army Headquarters
Camp Humphrey, Korea

General Bob Sink walked towards the center seat of the table as he gestured for the others to take their seats. "I hope everyone has had a chance to catch up. I know it's not often we can get together in person like this. But I felt it was vital for us to come together one more time as we discuss the actions of the past few weeks and ready ourselves for the next phase of OP Middle Kingdom.

"Gentlemen, I believe we are entering the terminal phase of this war. I do not want to imply that we won the war because we won a victory, or that the enemy cannot somehow snatch victory from the jaws of defeat. I have learned throughout this war how devious, conniving, and—at times—brilliant this AI called Jade Dragon can be. I firmly believe that if the PLA were being managed and fought by its generals and not directed by this AI, the war would have been over if it had been fought at all.

"This AI—and God help us if this truly is the future of humanity—it has ordered soldiers into battles knowing they cannot win. Yet it has done so to force us to expend our limited artillery shells and ammunition supplies. It is purposely doing this in hopes of exhausting our supplies and mentally and physically breaking our soldiers' will to fight. This is why we must defeat this machine before it becomes unstoppable," he said before pausing. He took a moment to look at his commanders, making sure they weren't losing their resolve or beginning to question their humanity given the butcher's bill they'd been meting out on the enemy the past few weeks.

Turning to look at General Brooks, he asked, "Shaw, for the past week, your corps has been in the thick of it. Is it your impression that General Song has sufficiently taken the bait? Do you think you've got him fully committed up north?"

Lieutenant General Shaw Brooks was the I Corps commander for Eighth Army's northern flank. Fighting alongside his command was General Yoon Dong-shin from the Republic of Korea's newly formed IV Corps, which had become their expeditionary force attached to

General Sink's Eighth Army. Then, to further bolster the northern force and get the AI to fully buy into where they would attack next, Lieutenant General Cooper Widmeyer's VII Corps, redeployed from Venezuela a few months earlier, had also been committed to this northern offensive. Widmeyer's force was heavily augmented with NATO units from the British, French, and Dutch militaries.

General Brooks sat forward in his chair, motioning for his aide to pull up the slide deck of their operation as he spoke to it. "Yes, I do, General. It's the slugfest we thought it would be, and you were correct. General Song would likely take the bait once it looked like we might break the Dengta trench lines," Brooks explained as aerial images of the intricate network of trenches and earthen fortifications were shown to emphasize the point.

"Along these sections of the line of control"—Brooks used a laser pointer to identify the locations—"is where it looks like General Song committed most of his reserves, drawing from the 78th Group Army, which he's held back until now. When General Yoon's 1st and 3rd Armored Brigades looked like they were going to punch through the trenches, General Song rushed the 4th Armored Division, supported by the 48th Motorized Infantry Brigade, to shore up their lines and block General Yoon's tanks from breaking into the enemies' rear areas. If you can break out past the network of trenches, it's mostly plains and flatlands into the city. But as you can see, those networks of trenches are no joke," he explained as aerial pictures from UAVs and satellites showed the complexity of the integrated defense networks. For more than a year, the PLA had had the civilians of Shenyang and the nearby towns and cities feverishly building a network of trenches, tank ditches, fortified bunkers, and defilade firing positions for artillery and antitank cannons.

"Sir, there's something else you mentioned at the outset of this meeting that, sadly, I can confirm is happening," Brooks explained. Then he paused, looking uncomfortable with what he was about to say.

General Sink knew what he would say and intervened before he did. "It's OK, Shaw, you don't need to say it. I've seen the reports from your headquarters and division commanders. It's barbaric. The AI is ordering these newly created People's Militias to intentionally charge our lines, forcing us to expend huge quantities of munitions we don't have to spare and exposing our positions, which it then attacks with

66

drones. Maybe my assumption is wrong, but I believe the AI is hoping for us to expend large sums of munitions against these militia forces based on a calculated assessment that, in doing so, we won't have those munitions for an offensive operation at a later date."

Sink paused momentarily as he shook his head, continuing, "Gentlemen, this is beyond evil. What makes it worse is it's not even a person doing it. It's a damn machine playing God with the lives of our soldiers and these poor saps being coerced into a war they don't even understand. This is all the more reason why it must be defeated. Shifting gears now, let's talk about this surprise breakthrough in the south. I had hoped we could jump the Daling River and nab Jinzhou, a critical node to supplying General Song's Northern Army and most of northern China. But not only did we successfully capture the city, but we also managed to draw several divisions away from Tianjin and the Beijing military district. This brings me to my next question. Don, given the level of resistance you've encountered thus far, how much further south do you think you could potentially push?"

Lieutenant General Don Tackaberry, the commander for XVIII Airborne, smiled as he began to explain, "Well, that is a good question, General. I suppose it would depend on whether or not we're still proceeding with the next phase of OP Middle Kingdom. If we are, then I would recommend we hold it in place. The 3rd ID has pushed the remains of the 79th PLA Group Army to Gaofengcun City, in the southeastern part of the Nanpiao District, just north of the port city of Huludao. We had to hold up there as we started to run into some stiff enemy resistance. There are a couple of air bases not far from there."

"What kind of resistance are you dealing with, and could you push through it if you had to?" asked General Sink.

"We're facing a battalion from the 3rd Armored Brigade along with the 190th and 202nd Mechanized Infantry Brigade. But as we pushed further south, we came in the vicinity of several PLA air bases, which have been able to provide these units with a level of air and rotary support we haven't encountered in a while. Could we push through it? If given some additional air and armor support, yes, we could. But I need to know soon if I have to pull the 101st out of their current positions to get them refitted and ready to support the next phase of the operation," explained General Tackaberry before asking to know if they were still going to press on with phase three of the grand plan General Baxter had cooked up.

Lieutenant General Dowdy from III Corps then chimed in, "That is the question, Bob—are we still pressing forward with phase three of Operation Middle Kingdom, or has the plan changed?"

****

Situation Room, White House
Washington, D.C.

Blain Wilson looked at the final slide with more questions than answers, chief among them being whether they should continue with the final phase of Operation Middle Kingdom.

Admiral Thiel then asked, "Nate, if this is true—if this latest piece of intelligence is accurate—then how in God's name can we possibly proceed with the next phase of the operation? The losses in vessels we could end up sustaining could jeopardize the entire landing operation, not to mention our ability to keep them supplied once the operation got fully underway. Has this been vetted by other agencies? What about the Bumblehive—Cicada?"

The Chief of Naval Operations squirmed a bit in his chair as Thiel pressed for answers in view of this latest revelation. "ONI has vetted the information with the DIA. They've been tracking this as well, and so has the CIA. When we spoke with Dr. Rubenstein, he verified with Cicada that it appears this Chinese version of our Orcas, or Sea Dragons as they call them—we've known about their extra-large uncrewed underwater vehicles program for some time, but given this latest piece of intelligence, it appears the program is operational. What we can't put our fingers on and what Cicada hasn't been able to identify, at least not yet, is how many of these units are operational. Hell, we don't even have that many Orcas with the fleet. I can't imagine they have many of their own ready to throw into this fight. If they did, I would have expected them in the defense of Taiwan—"

"I get it, Nate. This morning, Mr. Wilson and I were given a set of images from the NRO that may change the calculus of this," interrupted Admiral Thiel as he motioned for the next slide deck to start. "Last night, following a strategic bombing mission, we had one of the Archangels make a pass over the facility and grab some images so we could put together a strike package to take it out. As you can see from the photos, near the docks is a hardened facility, kind of like those old World War II submarine bases. Per previous reporting from Naval Intelligence, these Sea Dragons are likely being housed in this hardened facility to keep them protected and probably to hide how many they actually have. But right here," he said as he pointed to an image of what looked like a pair of giant doors set in the water next to the docks, "as you can see from this image, the doors to this submarine base are now open. Now that could mean all kinds of things. But most likely, it means that these things have been deployed into the Yellow Sea."

Blain glanced at the clock on the wall, noting the meeting had gone on for nearly an hour. He'd heard enough to know that the third phase of OP Middle Kingdom was in jeopardy. For all they knew, Jade Dragon could be controlling dozens or more of these Sea Dragons, or it could be controlling just one or two. The question was, should they risk moving forward with seizing the port and hope there weren't dozens of these drones prowling beneath the waves, just waiting for them to make a move? *This is going to be a tough call for the boss...I don't envy her position. But I think we need a bit more intel before we ask her to make a final call on this,* he thought to himself.

Blain jumped into the conversation, suggesting, "Nate, perhaps it's time we send in the Sea Hunters. We've been using them to good effect along the East China Sea. If I'm not mistaken, they've sunk five subs. Maybe we should redirect the fleet of them to head into the Yellow Sea with the goal of hunting these things down and taking them out."

Admiral Graham smiled at the mention of the Navy's much-vaunted Sea Hunter autonomous surface vessel. "Yes, of course, Blain, that's a great idea. In fact, we have three of them in Yokosuka that were just outfitted with a SeaRAM system we plan on using to help augment the fleet's air and antimissile defense system. The SeaRAM uses an eleven-cell RIM-116 Rolling Airframe Missile system for point defense against antiship missiles. They've performed incredibly well thus far in the war. Our goal now is to outfit all the Sea Hunters with them. This way, in addition to their antisubmarine roles, we can integrate them into the fleet's defensive screen."

Blain smiled as he offered, "Excellent. Then before we bring this problem of whether we should proceed to the President, let's give Sea Hunter some time to see what it finds. Maybe the Chinese only have one or two of these drone submarines out there. Maybe they've got dozens. But Sea Hunter should be able to give us a better idea of what we're dealing with soon enough. In the meantime, how are we looking, Joe, on this tectonic attack? Is this actually going to work? 'Cause I have my doubts."

General Joseph Hamlin, the Air Force Chief of Staff, leaned forward in his chair. "To be completely honest, I don't know—"

"Whoa, hold up there. What do you mean you don't know?" Jack Kurtis, the SecDef, questioned in surprise just as the Vice President jumped in.

"Joe, how about we rewind what you just said about not knowing if this can work or not? You sounded a hell of a lot more confident about this a few months back when it was first pitched. What's changed since then?"

General Hamlin fidgeted with his pen as he tried to respond. "Mr. Vice President, kinetic bombardments, Project Thor, and many of the names this concept has been tested under over the years have never really materialized into an actual feasible weapon that we could use. We believe we have a prototype that might work, but we need to test it."

"OK, so test this thing. Let's see if it works. What's the problem?" Kurtis asked, countering the general hesitation.

Then Blain had a thought. They couldn't test it. That would give it away. "There has to be a way to test this vehicle without alerting Jade Dragon to what we're doing," he blurted as the others turned to look at him.

Hamlin shrugged uncomfortably. "That's the problem, Blain. How do we test something like this without alerting Jade Dragon? To get a good test means actually dropping one of them from altitude and igniting the motors to ramp up the speed before impact. Once this thing hits, it's going to leave a mark. I mean, it's going to be felt for dozens upon dozens of miles away. It's not something that can be easily shrugged off."

"Australia. That's where you can do this," remarked General Langley, the Marine Commandant, as all eyes turned to look at him. "A few years back, before the war, I was touring some facilities in the outback, a place called Woomera. But they told me about another place some six hundred kilometers west called Maralinga. Apparently, the British had conducted some nuclear tests there back in the 1950s, so it's pretty desolate. I suppose we could reach out to our Australian counterparts and see if we might be able to utilize their range for a test."

Blain sat back in his chair for a moment as he thought about that. *Huh, Australia...yeah...why not...?*

Chapter 8
Sea Hunters & Dragons

335th Fighter Squadron
Yellow Sea, China

"Chief One-One, Big Sky Two. We're tracking six bogeys now dropping below angels one. Approaching from the northeast of Yantai. How copy?" came the crisp voice of the air battle manager aboard the E-7 Wedgetail flying above Dalian.

Major Tony "Buster" Buston smiled as he heard the call. *Outstanding. On station five minutes and already got us a mission*, he thought excitedly as he replied, "Big Sky, One-One, that's a good copy. Six bogeys, angels one and below. Approaching northeast of Yantai. Will investigate. Hear that, Bugs? We got us some bandits once we get a verification of what we're dealing with."

"Yeehaw, 'bout time we got us another chance to score aerial kills to add to the side of the fuselage," newly promoted Captain Aaron "Bugs" Bugowitz replied excitedly.

"I told you we'd get lucky on one of these missions. Seems these guys are trying to slip under the radar on us," Buster replied.

The last few months had seen a dramatic decrease in the number of enemy fighters. Most of the engagements were now taking place closer to the actual front lines than high above them. At this point in the war, the PLA was struggling under the loss of access to much of their energy supplies from abroad.

"Let's go see what we're dealing with," Buster said as he reoriented his Super Eagle in the direction of the incoming threats. With their aircraft aligned on an intercept course, it was just a matter of closing the gap before the bogeys would be in range in their AIM-220s and they got a positive ID on what they were dealing with. There was little doubt that these were enemy fighters. But from the distance they'd been detected, they'd need to close in a little more to make that definitive diagnosis.

As the distances continued to close, the Wedgetail's Multirole Electronically Scanned Array system began to feed the Eagle drivers a more refined picture of what they were up against. When in "look-up mode," the L band electronically scanned AEW and surveillance radar located in the "top hat" or dorsal fin atop the aircraft had a maximum scanning range of just over six hundred kilometers. But this didn't provide the more accurate targeting data required by the fighter planes the Wedgetails supported.

To get the more precise targeting data, the radar had to be set to what was called "look-down mode," which allowed for great precision in identifying what a specific radar return was and then fed that targeting data back to the fighters it was guiding in to attack. This cut down the effective range of the Wedgetails' advance radar system down from six hundred kilometers to just a hair over three hundred and seventy kilometers for aircraft and two hundred and forty kilometers for frigate-sized warships on the sea. However, the more advanced E-7 Wedgetail was now able to track some one hundred and eighty targets simultaneously while guiding up to twenty-four individual aircraft interceptors. This gave the air battle managers overseeing the air and surface war a new capability. In many cases, they were able to guide allied aircraft in on an enemy fighter before it even knew it was under attack.

As the distance between Buster and Bugs shortened to less than two hundred kilometers, they were now within the range of their AIM-260 Joint Advanced Tactical Missiles. That also meant they were in range of the PLA's PL-15, and their more advanced PL-21s. The question Buster was asking himself was why they hadn't attacked yet. He was also surprised they hadn't been able to identify clearly the type of fighters they were up against.

"Chief One-One, Big Sky Two. We're having a bit of a challenge getting a bead on what kind of aircraft these bogeys are. It's possible these are some sort of stealth aircraft. We have a recommendation for how to smoke 'em out and figure out what kind of birds you're up against. However, it'll be your call if you want to proceed or wait until you get closer and potentially within weapons range of the bogeys," came the voice of the air battle manager, almost reading Buster's mind.

"Big Sky Two, One-One. What kind of harebrained idea you wanting us to consider?" Buster asked with as much bravado as he could muster. *Whatever they're about to tell us, it's likely not good for our health...*

"One-One, it's completely up to you. But we'd like one of your aircraft to go active with your radar. Of course, you'll need to be ready to snap off a couple of missiles. Once you go active, it's highly likely whatever these bogeys are, they'll look to engage immediately. How copy?"

"Buster, tell me they did not just ask one of us to be a guinea pig."

Buster snorted at the question before replying. "Bugs, have you ever heard a guy by the name of Alfred, Lord Tennyson, or a poem he wrote in 1854, 'The Charge of the Light Brigade'?"

There was a momentary pause, then Bugs responded, "Is this another one of these teaching moments where you introduce me to yet another one of your mentors from a bygone era?"

Buster shook his head dismissively. "'Theirs not to reason why. Theirs but to do and die.' It's often quoted out of context, but generally, it's a reflection on the senselessness that accompanies war, while at the same time it's praising the unflinching bravery and duty of the soldiers who gave their lives."

"Huh, so you're trying to say this is a senseless, stupid act they're proposing we do, but also incredibly brave?" Bugs replied.

"Yeah, that about sums it up. So, what do you think?"

"Damn this war! OK, then, I guess if that's how it's got to be, then I'm going to be the one to go active with my radar. You just make sure to take 'em out once I do it."

"Whoa, hey, what do you mean you'll be the one to go active? I'm the flight lead here and I've got a lot more experience than you at flying these Eagles and know how to evade these kinds of missiles they're likely to fire at us."

"I know, Buster, and you're right. You are the better pilot to do that. But I'm single, bro. You got five munchkins back home. I don't even have a girlfriend. No, if we're going to take a risk like this, then it should be me, not you, that takes it. Tell Big Sky I'm going to get some separation from us before I light 'em up. You just be ready to start tagging targets once my radar starts identifying them."

Buster wasn't sure what to say. He wanted to override his wingman, the junior officer between them. But he also knew he was right. Bugs was single; Buster and Tammy had five kids, six if he was able to knock her up during his midtour next month. *Damn you, Bugs. You better not die.*

"OK, Bugs, we'll play it your way. For the record, I'm completely against it, but logically, you aren't wrong and that's the only reason I'm agreeing to this. Go ahead and put like ten kilometers between us and take yourself down to angels twenty. I'm going up to angels twenty-five. Let's hope between the two of us coming at them from different vantage points, we'll score some hits and make it harder for them to take us out."

Buster then depressed the talk button and relayed the plan he and Bugs had come up with back to their eye. They acknowledged and let him know they were vectoring another flight of Super Eagles their way to assist. At this point, the bogeys had descended to just two hundred feet above the waves. They had also changed their attack vectors to zero in on the Port of Dalian and what was steadily becoming a large allied naval flotilla that appeared to be gearing up for something big he hadn't been read in on just yet. Seeing that the flight of six mystery aircraft had now broken off into three groups of two, he knew something was up.

"OK, Bugs, we've gone over what we're going to do and how we're going to do it. So as Ricky Bobby once said at Talladega, it's time to shake 'n' bake. Let's do this thing!"

"Aww, doggy. It's time to shake 'n' bake, baby. Wish me luck! I'm going active!" Bugs howled as he played the character of Will Ferrell from the comedy *Talladega Nights*.

Within seconds of Bugs going active with the Super Eagle's newly upgraded pulse-Doppler radar systems. The AN/APG-82 active electronically scanned array not only confirmed the bogeys were in fact bandits but also revealed that what they saw wasn't three flights of two aircraft just skimming above the waves after all. They were actually three flights of four UCAVs—and not just any UCAVs. The original flight of six aircraft they had originally detected were the PLA's newest third-gen pilotless fighters, which they had learned were called Shadow Dragons. The four previously unknown aircraft flying in a tight formation appeared to be the mysterious yet vaunted Dark Swords they'd heard rumors about from the intel guys. The AVIC Dark Swords were supposed to be stealthy supersonic UCAVs designed to be paired with the PLA Air Force's Chengdu J-20 stealth fighters, dubbed "Might Dragons," which had given the allies a lot of heartburn and heartaches at the outset of the war. This was the first time they had actually seen the Dark Swords in operation.

"Holy crap! We're not dealing with three pairs of J-20s—this looks like a strike package using their version of our Loyal Wingman concept," Bugs exclaimed excitedly. The targeting data was now filling their systems with actionable data.

"Yeah, that's a good copy, Bugs. I'm going after Group Alpha; you take Group Charlie. Let's see how many of these UCAVs we can take down before the cavalry arrives," directed Buster as he went to work.

He flicked the arming command to the eight AIM-260s, letting his targeting computer assign a missile to each of the targeted aircraft. *There we go, green across the board. Time to let 'er fly*, he mused privately as he fired missile after missile until he'd fired all eight. Casting a quick glance at his radar showed that Bugs had just fired his own barrage, sending a total of sixteen missiles at the twenty-four UCAVs still heading towards the Port of Dalian.

Damn, these are cooking. We're barely a hundred kilometers from the port, he thought to himself when the voice from Big Sky broke in.

"Chief One-One, Big Sky Two. We have confirmation of your missile launches. We need you to break off your secondary attack run and move to angels thirty and head towards sector Hotel-Six. Enemy aircraft are about to enter Task Force Dupre's security umbrella. You need to vacate the area immediately. How copy?"

"Huh, would you look at that, Bugs? Seems the Navy wants to get in on some of this action," Buster commented before responding to the air battle manager. "Big Sky Two, One-One, that's a good copy. Breaking off secondary attack. Relocating to Hotel-Six, will stand by and await further orders."

"Hey, if the Navy wants in on the action, they're welcome to sloppy seconds. 'Cause I'm first. Now's the fun part, trying to get out of Dodge before they light us up," Bugs commented just as several of the UCAV's radars went active, likely looking for them.

As Buster lit up the afterburners to the pair of Pratt & Whitney engines, he felt his body being pressed hard into his seat as the Super Eagle pushed him beyond twenty-five hundred kilometers per hour or approaching Mach 2.5. With the distance between himself and the enemy aircraft growing steadily, he started to feel good about their chances of getting out of the area unscathed. Then, to his shock and horror, missile after missile emerged from the twenty-four UCAVs they'd engaged. It took fractions of a second to confirm the missiles were headed for the port and not him or Bugs. But then, out of nowhere, his radar warning receiver lit up with a warning, letting him know he was being targeted by something. *What the hell?* was the only thought that crossed his mind when suddenly Bugs's Super Eagle exploded a few kilometers away.

Instinctively, he dove hard to the right as he bled altitude and speed while his ECM ran whatever electronic interference it could against whatever had blown Bugs out of the sky. Then he felt the flare and chaff dispensers firing away, which meant something had a lock on him—he just didn't know what.

BOOM!

The explosion occurred behind him as he felt the aircraft jerk hard and start to vibrate. At this point he'd dropped his speed to less than seven hundred kilometers an hour, so if he needed to bail, he could. *What the hell just hit me?* He checked his gauges and saw he was losing oil pressure to his right engine. The temperature steadily rose, which wasn't helping either. *Damn, come on, baby, let's just limp home…we got this*, he kept telling himself as he radioed in what had happened while doing what he could look for a chute to see if Bugs might have bailed. He took a risk circling back to the area to make sure he hadn't missed seeing a parachute—but nothing. He wanted to stay longer, maybe try and go lower and see if his partner might have already descended below angels ten. But looking at the readout of the right engine, he didn't have long to get himself either back over land or back to the Dalian International Airport for an emergency landing.

Damn you, Bugs, you better be alive somewhere down there…
****

25th PLA Ghost Squadron
IVO Yellow Sea

Colonel Yin Huan watched patiently as the onboard AI continued to guide the Dark Swords towards their intended targets. The ever-growing allied fleet marshaled around the Port of Dalian. He wasn't sure why the allies had moved more of their naval vessels away from Taiwan to the Yellow Sea. Clearly, they were up to something.

Looking at his radar, Colonel Yin saw that the American fighter planes had just been redirected to head towards the Dark Swords for which his flight was running escort. Depressing the talk button, Yin ordered, "Shadow Six-Two, move to intercept the American fighters."

"Shadow Six-Two acknowledges. Moving to intercept now," Major Sun replied crisply as his aircraft broke off from their formation to head towards the American fighters. Steadily the American fighters continued to move closer to the Dark Swords.

When he had been told he would be escorting a strike package to hit the Port of Dalian, he had assumed he'd be escorting a flight of bombers or other attack aircraft. But as the day of the mission approached, he still hadn't been told what kind of aircraft he would be escorting. It wasn't until the mission brief that he'd learned his flight of four Shadow Dragons would be escorting an entirely new UCAV he'd never even heard of. That was when he, and only he, had been briefed on Dark Dragon—an entirely new, fully autonomous strike fighter or ASF. Unlike the UCAV Shadow Dragon program, he was told this new ASF would be flown entirely by Jade Dragon.

When he'd asked about the weapons loadout the aircraft could carry, General Cao Zhenwu had looked a bit nervous, like he wasn't sure if he should share that information. Then Cao gave a slight nudge of his head, and Yin saw a folder on the table next to him and caught his meaning. When he'd finished giving him his final mission parameters, Cao had left the room but forgotten to grab the folders on the table. Yin took this as his cue to sneak a peek at whatever it was General Cao was too unsure of to say aloud. He wasn't certain, given that the briefing room had no cameras, no electronic devices—just an old-fashioned pull-down map of the geographical area he'd be operating in and the potential enemy aircraft he might encounter during the mission.

Once Yin flipped the folder open, his eyes went wide as he realized why his boss might be a bit nervous about sharing this information. It wasn't that it was necessarily a secret. It was this aircraft that had for all intents and purposes effectively replaced him and every other pilot in the PLA Air Force. Not only that, if the weapon systems outlined in the folder actually worked, about which he had his doubts, then this was beyond anything he had thought possible for an aircraft.

"Shadow Six, Shadow Six-Two. One of the American fighters just went active with his radar. I believe he is preparing to fire his missiles—ah, he just fired them. I count…whoa, they just fired off sixteen missiles. I'm going after—"

"No! Take out the fighters. Do not try to engage the missiles. Just go after those fighters and take them out," Yin cut in. He didn't want Major Sun wasting his precious few missiles trying to intercept what he knew was likely an impossible target.

I guess now I'll see if some of those new toys on that ASF are actually real…

****

TF Dupre
USS *Hue City*
IVO Southeast of Port Dalian

Admiral Michael Dupre stood on the flying bridge as he admired the dark waters of the Yellow Sea. When he had graduated from Annapolis some twenty-five years ago, he had hoped he might rise to the rank of captain, O-6, one day. A lofty dream considering most career naval officers topped out at commander, O-5. Now, as of three days ago, he wasn't just a recently frocked rear admiral who would revert back to being a captain once the war had ended. The Senate had officially confirmed that his appointment to the rank of O-7, a position a poor white kid from Theriot, Louisiana, had virtually no hope of achieving, was official.

War has a strange way of elevating people to ranks they otherwise wouldn't have achieved. Some are elevated through skill, some through attrition and casualties, while others just find themselves in the right place at the right time. He'd like to think he'd achieved his rank because of his skills as a skipper. In reality, he knew it was more likely due to the fact that he'd just happened to be the right guy at the right time when it counted most.

Hearing a couple of sailors joking below, he turned, looking down and towards the aft port side of the ship he'd called home for so many years. A couple of sailors were working with some of the contractors still aboard the *Hue* as they continued to make repairs while underway. Following the kamikaze attack against the landing forces during the invasion of Taiwan, Dupre's task force had been relieved of their post and replaced with another that had traversed from the Atlantic to the Pacific. Since many of the ships of his task force had taken some level of damage during the attack, his force had been ordered to Yokosuka for repairs and refit.

While his force had undergone a few weeks of repairs of the naval base, his flotilla had augmented with additional ASW and air-defense ships for the next phase of the war. His Sea Hunter unmanned surface vehicles had been swapped out for five newer versions on which the Navy had just installed a SeaRAM system, which was basically a modified version of the RIM-116 Rolling Airframe Missile system, except that the SeaRAM system could operate independently of a control ship. This essentially turned the quasi-autonomous ASW catamarans into a very capable air-defense platform he could now use to better protect whatever fleet of warships his task force was assigned to protect. The biggest surprise, however, to his growing flotilla of warships was the inclusion of several Russian and Turkish vessels that had recently linked up with his task force at a final port call at Jinhae Naval Base before transiting into the Yellow Sea.

It was at Jinhae that he had learned the true nature of his mission, and why his task force was being augmented with a few Russian warships. His task force was to hunt down and sink a new superweapon that Jade Dragon had apparently been developing for some time: a Chinese version of the Navy's Orca program called Sea Dragon. It was basically an underwater version of the Loyal Wingman program both the Air Force and Navy's flyboys had been jonesing for. Once he saw the specs of this underwater terror, he understood why he'd been augmented with additional ASW ships—he was going to need them.

"What do you think, Admiral, we going to find one of those Sea Dragons today?" came the voice of Captain Aaron Quinn.

As he approached him, Quinn offered him a coffee, the steam wafting briefly in the air. Reaching for the cup, Dupre said, "Ah, you read my mind, Aaron. What's the pool up to now?"

"Fifteen hundred dollars if they find it between yesterday and this coming Tuesday. If no one wins, it rolls over to the next week," Quinn replied, lifting the cup to his lips before adding, "The next jump is to twenty-five hundred."

Dupre let out a soft whistle. He hadn't realized the pool had gotten that high. They'd ignored the unofficial betting pool the chiefs had arranged for the enlisted as a morale booster and to raise some funds for the gedunk bar. They'd broken the Yellow Sea into grid squares, and the enlisted would bet on where one of the Sea Hunters or any of the other vessels would score a kill against one of the Sea Dragons. If they scored a kill, then one or more lucky sailors would win half the pot, the other going to the gedunk. If no one won that week, the pool rolled over into the next week and the pot continued to grow.

"What do you think of them, Aaron?" Dupre motioned with his coffee in the direction of the *Admiral Chabanenko*, one of the three Udaloy II–class antisubmarine destroyers, courtesy of their "new" Russian allies in this war against China.

The captain of the *Hue City* stared at the Russian vessel for a long moment before replying. "War has a strange way of making friends out of enemies."

"Ain't that the truth," Dupre replied, his Louisiana accent shining through in the way he answered. "If you'd asked me five years ago if we'd be working hand in glove with the Russian Navy, I would have laughed my ass off. Then again, if you had told me Skynet would launch a surprise attack on the United States, I would have told you to put the Kindle down and walk away. So here we are—Skynet's real, and the Russians are our allies."

They laughed at how the crazy the situation had become. Truth be told, they were glad to have the Russians fighting with them, rather than against them on the side of the Chinese.

"Aaron, what are your thoughts on some of the new crewmen we took on in Jinhae?"

Quinn lifted an eyebrow at his question. Dupre knew he was starting to tread in waters that weren't his. The *Hue* may have been his ship at the start of the war, but it was Quinn's now.

"You mean what do I think of OS3 Kim Ki-chul? One of my new AEGIS techs?" Quinn finally replied.

Dupre just nodded, waiting for Quinn to say something further.

"I take it you saw the NCIS notice?"

"Yeah...I did. Kind of makes you wonder why we're letting this play out the way we are," Dupre countered hesitantly as he looked around to make sure they were still alone.

81

Quinn leaned in as he spoke quietly. "I clued Chief Royal in on what's going on. I figure if he's going to be sitting next to the guy, then he should know in case—"

"Yeah, I get it. You're not wrong for clueing him in. I'd have done the same thing."

"Agent Handover better know what's he doing is all I have to say," Quinn said hotly.

"If it makes you feel any better, I told them no. Apparently the approval from this came all the way from the top, the CNO's office," Dupre said in a hushed tone.

"No kidding. Whoa, this must have something to do with this stupid AI, I'll bet."

Dupre was about to say something further when the alarm klaxons went off.

"Battle stations air defense… battle stations air defense…"

"Ah crap! Let's get to CIC!" Dupre cursed under his breath as he and Quinn tossed their coffee over the rail and ducked back into the ship.

"Make a hole!" shouted one of the petty officers as Dupre and Quinn made their way through to the nerve center of the ship.

As the two of them trotted through the corridors, the crew scrambled to their battle stations, getting themselves ready for whatever might happen next. They'd gotten lucky so far, as the task force hadn't come under attack since entering the Yellow Sea. They knew it was just a matter of time until the PLA launched either an air raid, a missile attack, or a submarine attack at some point. After the Battle of Yilan County, the crew were veterans and ready for whatever the enemy tried to throw at them—even an insider threat if this NCIS report was any indication.

The moment Dupre opened the door leading into the CIC, he heard shouting coming from somewhere inside the room, followed by someone screaming, "He's got a bomb—"

BOOM!

The blast threw Dupre back through the door he'd just entered and into the wall behind him, slamming his head against the corridor and nearly knocking himself out. As he ran his hand behind his head, it came away wet and he realized he must have cut it open. He started to feel light-headed as a pair of hands reached down to pull him to his feet. He saw the face of Captain Quinn mouthing something to him, but he couldn't make out what he was saying.

As he walked away from the CIC, others ran into the room while some staggered out, on their own or with the help of others. Then a corpsman came up to him and started applying a bandage to the back of his head. He doubled over, throwing up the moment the guy applied pressure to the back of his head, and then everything went black.

****

25th PLA Ghost Squadron
IVO Yellow Sea

Colonel Yin watched with growing concern as the missiles continued to close in on the DDs. That was what he'd finally come to call the Dark Dragons—the DDs or Double Ds. He smirked at that, thinking of that American girl he'd met on vacation in Thailand a few years before the war.

Ah...a time before the war..., he thought as he felt a phantom pain where his leg had once been. In a way, he was lucky he was only missing a leg. It had led to him being selected for the drone program, where he'd not only excelled but had been promoted well above his peers.

As the missiles continued to close in, he hoped this failure wouldn't be counted against him. Then something strange happened. The missiles began to disappear. One by one, they steadily vanished from the screen.

Whoa, they really do have defensive lasers on them.

Glancing to his secondary radar screen, he saw Major Sun had managed to down one of the Super Eagles while the other looked to have gotten away. It didn't make a difference at this point. He could tell the DDs had just entered the range of the American strike group anchored around the Port of Dalian. The one thing he wasn't sure about was how the DDs were going to manage to get their missiles past the picket screen of destroyers and frigates he knew would be positioned to protect the higher-value warships still anchored in the port.

He'd gone up against the AEGIS warships a few times around Taiwan. It hadn't been a good experience. They'd proven themselves pretty effective at knocking down his missiles. But the DDs continued

83

their high-speed approach. The large ship near the center of the group, the one he knew to be a cruiser emitting the power search radar likely coordinating the fleet's defenses, suddenly winked out.

Yin tapped the monitor to his sim pod, unsure if there might have been a malfunction as he hadn't seen any missiles headed towards the enemy cruiser. Then again, maybe a sub had gotten to it. In either case, as soon as the AEGIS radar system went down, the DDs unleashed their barrage of missiles, taking advantage of the confusion likely happening amongst the enemy fleet.

In seconds, each of the Dark Dragons had fired a pair of Eagle Strike missiles before turning to head back towards home. As he watched the monitor fill with missiles, all headed towards the enemy fleet, he felt a sense of satisfaction, a feeling of hope and optimism that maybe, just maybe, they might have finally turned the tide of this war.

Then suddenly nine of the twenty-four Dark Dragons winked out of existence. Cuing the AI, he said, "Jade Dragon, what happened to those nine Dark Dragons?"

A voice responded matter-of-factly, "I encountered something unexpected and lost nine of the Dark Dragons."

Yin bunched his eyebrows at that. This was highly unusual. It was also the first time he had heard the AI admit it had encountered something unexpected. Questioning it, he asked, "What exactly did you encounter?"

"It would appear the allies have equipped some of their Sea Hunter unmanned surface vehicles with SeaRAM systems. This was unexpected. I would not have flown the Dark Dragons within the range of one of these systems. I have added this allied capability to the database. Would you like me to take over the rest of the mission for you, Colonel Yin?"

Yin smiled at the question. Checking the clock, he saw he'd been in the sim pod for coming up on three hours. *You know what…why not…?* "Sure, JD. You have control of the aircraft."

Chapter 9
The People's Militia

3rd People's Militia Headquarters
Kunming Regiment
China University of Technology
Hsinchu County, Taiwan

Major Zhong Jin turned casually to look out the nearby window, spotting the bird that had been chirping its happy melody for the past ten minutes of the meeting. It almost seemed like it was taunting him with its song of freedom as it happily fluttered about from branch to branch while he remained trapped inside this insufferable conference room.

Returning his gaze to the speaker, he closed his eyes briefly as he rubbed his temple. He could still hear the voice of his former commanding officer as he gave Zhong his new assignment. Zhong thought it was more of a sentence than the opportunity his superior had made the assignment out to be. While Zhong might have recovered from his injuries, he was no longer capable of serving in Special Forces and would not be rejoining his Mighty Eagle Special Operations unit. No, instead he was being transferred to the Eastern Theater of Command and to the quagmire that was Taiwan.

He had held brief hope that he might find himself in a staff position with the 71st, 72nd, or 73rd Special Operations Brigade, allowing him to stay within the SOF community he'd spent his career in. But alas, the gods, if there were such a thing, had plans of their own. Being transferred from the Special Operations world he knew to the regular army would have been punishment enough. But being assigned as a liaison officer to a regimental headquarters for the People's Militia was its own a special kind of purgatory for an officer possessing his skill set.

Not believing there were varying degrees to hell, upon his arrival in Taiwan to the 71st Group Army headquarters unit, he was informed he was going to become the military advisor to Brigadier General Qi Guo. The general's regiment was from the capital city of the province of Yunnan—Kunming. As the militia was subordinate to the regular army, the People's Militia was renumbered upon their arrival in Taiwan once they had been assigned to a group army. The Kunming

Regiment was now the third of five regiments of People's Militia that had recently arrived to reinforce the 71st Group Army prior to the arrival of the American Marines and the NATO forces in the southern half of the island.

While Major Zhong had not previously met Brigadier General Qi Guo, he was familiar with his brother and his exploits. Knowing how the apples of the family tree seldom fell far from the base, he knew enough after just minutes of being in the presence of the man to know his preconceived assumption had not been far off. As the days of his new assignment had turned into weeks, then months, Zhong was beginning to question whether he should shoot himself now or save that honor for the Americans he knew were coming.

While Special Forces held the reputation of being able to train a foreign opposition force, Zhong could clearly see no amount of effort could possibly aid him in turning this regiment into a credible fighting force. The regiment consisted of eight hastily thrown-together battalions named after eight of the nine lakes within the province. Each of the battalions consisted of six hundred "voluntolds" from the various urban and rural sections of the capital city of Kunming.

It didn't take long to discover how each of the battalion commanders had obtained their command positions—either through direct nepotism or outright bribery that had seen them elevated to the position of commander. Naturally this form of leadership hierarchy permeated the battalion down to the platoon leaders. When asked privately by the deputy commander of the 71st PLA Group Army how long he thought the 3rd People's Militia would last in a battle against the American Marines should it come to it, he answered honestly—an hour, maybe three at most and they'd be done. It was the last time he'd had contact with his regular army counterparts in more than a month. By now, he had accepted his fate—he was going to die here.

"Given my superior leadership abilities and the pedigree of my family lineage, these American Marines will be crushed beneath the boots of our regiment—the Mighty Three," Brigadier General Qi Guo droned on to his assembled officers and battalion commanders.

"When my brother died as a hero of the People's Liberation Air Force…" The general continued to drone on. Zhong tried to stay present, attuned to the pontificating of this buffoon, but found his mind wandering more than listening. *If I have to listen to one more story about the coming victory against the feral American Marines, I'm going to gouge my eyeballs out and shove these pens in my ears...*

When Major Zhong had reported for duty, the first thing he'd seen was how unorganized the general's regiment was. In a failed attempt at doing his job, he had recommended to General Qi that he institute a meeting for battalion commanders only twice a week. This would give him an opportunity to learn how the training was going with their battalions. It would also let him keep an eye on the progress of the defensive works the battalions had been charged with constructing and then manning. What Zhong had failed to realize was how utterly inept General Qi Guo truly was. Instead of using the twice-weekly meetings to better organize and prepare his command, this girthy buffoon had turned them into lectures about his greatness and that of his fallen brother.

As Zhong stared at the general droning on into the second hour of this meeting, he still couldn't get past how this morbidly obese man was allowed to command combat forces. While the height and weight standards were obviously more lenient within the reserves, he was not aware they had been thrown out entirely by the militia. Even by Western standards, the general was obese, as were most of his commanders. Near as Zhong could tell, the only reason he was allowed to squeeze his considerable girth into a uniform was his family connections. Despite his brother having died a hero of the People's Liberation Air Force in Venezuela, Zhong knew the real story of just how this "hero" had died. Major Zhong had had the displeasure of having served on the same military base in Venezuela and knew the true circumstances of the general's death. The Party, of course, had concocted an alternative story and gone on to use it as a propaganda tool back home.

During the Venezuela campaign in the first year of the war, Zhong's Special Forces brigade had been relocated to Isla Margarita in preparation for the eventual American invasion. It was during Zhong's time on the island that he had learned of Qi's famous Air Force brother. The general's appetite for prostitutes and cocaine was a dirty secret among the Special Forces officers who periodically had to provide him with a security detail for one of his little soirees. *I damn near lost my command over his inability to keep it in his pants*, Zhong remembered angrily.

It had been Zhong's security detail that discovered his body the morning after the general had berated Zhong for wanting to keep at least one guard in the room next door. The hotel's masseuse had suffocated him with a pillow and then casually left the room and hotel, never to be seen again. Zhong had learned later that his female companion had actually been Israeli Mossad. The memory of seeing General Qi lying on his stomach, his head buried in a pillow with massage stones seared to his flesh, was etched into Zhong's memory. That incident had nearly cost him his command, and all so Qi could get laid and snort coke when he should have been leading his command in preparation for the Americans' eventual landings.

Ah, the bird flew off, he thought to himself before realizing the room had gone silent. Zhong was suddenly aware he'd daydreamed through a question or something that might have been directed at him. Thinking fast, he replied as the faces waited for him to say something.

"Apologies, General, you caught me thinking about the gap in our defenses. The area along section one of Guanhai Road on the Western Coastal Highway."

Zhong's reply seemed to have caught General Qi off guard as he momentarily seemed confused before he recalled the conversation.

Then, seeming to wave off whatever he had previously asked that Zhong had missed, he said, "Ah yes, Major. We will discuss that later. What I originally asked, Major, was why wasn't more done in the wake of my brother's assassination on Isla Margarita?"

Zhong groaned internally at the question. He was all too familiar with this part of the dance between himself and the boorish general. Bowing his head in mock supplication. Zhong explained, "Sadly, General, I was but a captain. My zeal to chase down those responsible and to implement reprisal killings was reined in by those above me. Had my plans not been thwarted by those above, I would have pursued the murderers and avenged the death of your honored brother."

Qi slapped his meaty palm on the table. "See! This is the problem with our army. We do not allow initiative. Officers who obtain their rank through nepotism and political bribery are placed in charge of our military when it should be men like comrade Major Zhong. Had he been allowed to chase my brother's killer and exact China's revenge from them, it would have sent a clear message to the Americans!"

Heads around the table nodded in agreement. Zhong wasn't sure if they realized their own positions had benefited from the very system of bribery and nepotism Qi had just railed against. Not a single one of the men in this room was a professional soldier. Not like him. They were militia, pretend soldiers. They sat here because they'd kissed enough ass and greased enough palms to avoid fighting China's enemies up until this point.

As Zhong felt his anger rise at how these men had avoided true service to the nation, he felt a sharp pain in his leg and subconsciously moved his hand down to rub it before stopping. *The pain's in your mind, you fool.*

The flesh and bone of his leg had been replaced with a titanium rod and metallic joint for a knee, its cold, lifeless features a bitter reminder of what he'd left behind in Venezuela. The pain he kept feeling wasn't real. The docs had told him he might experience phantom pains from the wound his limb had suffered before it was removed. They'd assured him it would eventually stop. The pain wasn't so much a problem anymore. It was the nightmares haunting him in his sleep that he wished he could make stop.

When he closed his eyes to sleep, he could still see the grenade soaring through the air. The recurring memory left him bitter and angry each time it replayed in his mind or he awoke to sweat-soaked sheets. No matter how hard he tried, he was powerless in his dreams to take cover as the grenade closed in on him. No matter how he attempted to move his feet, they held firm, like cement boots affixing him until the grenade landed next to his feet. When it inevitably exploded, his ears would ring, his body on fire. Each night he'd relived that experience, his body torn apart from the explosion that had cost him his leg, that had left his body burned and riddled with shrapnel wounds. Gritting his teeth, Zhong forced himself back to the present and the meeting that never seemed to end.

"If the generals would listen to me like Major Zhong's commanders should have listened to him about my brother's death, we could defeat these immoral jackals they call Marines," General Qi bemoaned as his lackeys nodded along in agreement.

Colonel Cui Xinyi then pounced. "Surely, General Qi, Jade Dragon has anticipated this? When we get our allotment of those new androids, I am confident they will undoubtedly thwart further American and NATO advances."

Major Zhong had to bite his tongue and not correct the colonel. The TKs were not androids. They were robots. Colonel Cui was a typical Party hack. His unyielding faith in a party that had time and time again failed at the most basic tasks was mind-boggling. In Zhong's mind, the men around this table were the crux of why their nation was losing this war.

Then, just as it looked like another colonel was about to speak, General Qi mercifully ended the meeting. Zhong breathed a sigh of relief at having survived another one of these lectures about the general's greatness when the man's aide approached him.

He bowed slightly, then said, "Comrade Major, the general would like a word."

Zhong nodded as he collected his notebook and pen. He bowed slightly in return and made his way to the general.

As he approached the man in a custom-tailored uniform as he was unable to fit into the standard-issue, he bowed as he uttered the words, "Honorable comrade General, how can I be of assistance?"

"Major, your comment earlier about section one of the Western Coastal Highway. It has given me an idea."

"It has, comrade General?"

"Yes, I want to personally inspect our coastal defenses and let our brave volunteer army know their commanding general cares for them. I believe it's important for them to see me and to know that. I want you to accompany me on this visit and give me your thoughts on ways we can better harden our defenses. If those foolish American Marines want to test our defenses, then I want them to know the depth of our resolve to defend our lands."

Zhong resisted the temptation to laugh at this buffoon. Then he had to control his sudden desire to vomit before nodding along in fervent agreement. It was obvious this was going to be nothing more than a photo op for propaganda purposes, but it couldn't hurt for him to see how ill prepared his soldiers really were.

Forcing a smile, Zhong belted out confidently, "Yes, comrade General! While my military experience pales in comparison to your military brilliance, I would be honored to accompany you on this visit."

"Excellent! We depart first thing in the morning," Qi boomed, slapping him on the shoulder excitedly.

Zhong glanced down at the table just long enough to see an address written on a piece of paper. He fought the smirk he knew was attempting to break the hard facade he tried to permanently keep affixed to his face. He knew the address well, having reprimanded some of the junior officers for having visited it. It seemed the general shared his brother's appetite for prostitutes as well.

"As you wish, comrade General," Zhong replied as he bowed before taking his leave of the general. As he left the room, he couldn't help but wonder who he had pissed off to have warranted this assignment to hell as an advisor to a regiment of militia.

****

1st Dianchi Battalion
Section 1 of Guanhai Road
Hsinchu County, Taiwan

Major Zhong was finding it difficult to choose the words to express his extreme dislike of what he'd just seen. True to his word, he and General Qi had left in the morning to tour section one of Guanhai Road, and the defensive works being constructed by the 1st Dianchi Battalion. It was named after Lake Dianchi, one of the nine lakes in the province, and was one of the eight battalions Major Zhong felt hopeless trying to advise. The Dianchi commander, a clerk for a law firm and skinny as a rail, was failing miserably and there was little Zhong could do about it. With zero military experience, Lieutenant Colonel Lei Rongtian personified the depths of the rot that seemed to permeate the regionally based militia forces.

General Qi Guo seemed to have sensed his displeasure as Lieutenant Colonel Rongtian finished giving them a tour of the defensive works his soldiers had been constructing. General Qi surprised him when he asked, "Major Zhong, are you disappointed in the results Rongtian's men have accomplished?"

Seriously…of course you can't tell what's wrong…you are just as big a buffoon as he is…

Zhong shrugged his shoulders, not wanting to reveal his true opinions on the matter.

Snickering at his nonresponse, Rongtian prodded, "Ah come on, Major. Aren't you here for the explicit purpose of helping advise us on military matters? None of us claim to be Sun Tzu—well, maybe the comrade general could come close...share with us what we are doing wrong."

"Yes, Major, how can we know if we are doing it right or wrong if our advisor is not advising? Speak, we are listening."

Listening? No, you'll hear my words, but they'll not sink in...

Taking a long drag on his cigarette, Zhong flicked the butt into the dirt and mashed it with his boot. *Here goes nothing*, he said to himself as he began to explain the myriad of deficiencies. He showed both of them how not a single one of the machine-gun emplacements had been properly sighted in to allow for overlapping fields of fire. Then he showed them how the munition bunkers had been built too close to the first line of defense, explaining how once an attacking force hit the first line and they needed to fall back, they'd instantly lose access to their own munition bunkers once they lost control of the first defensive line. By the time Zhong had finished going through the litany of issues, General Qi's face had turned beet red at how inept Rongtian had made him look with subpar defensive works. Instead of feeling confident in bragging to his fellow regiment commanders about the strength of his lines, he now feared he'd become a laughingstock should word get out about how they had built their own munitions bunkers in the wrong locations.

Instead of posing for what Zhong was sure Qi had thought would be excellent propaganda pictures for back home, he had shooed the photographer away. When it was just the three of them, Qi tore into Rongtian for failing him and letting him down. Then he turned to Zhong. "Major, you have just saved me from being made to look the fool by this incompetent commander. I would like to request that you stay with Rongtian and spend the next few days instructing him and his company commanders on how these earthen works should have been built."

General Qi then turned to look at Rongtian. "When Major Zhong returns on Friday and reports to me that he has given you the instructions on how to construct these positions properly, I will give you one week to correct the problems before the major and I will return to reinspect the positions once more. I had better see improvement, Rongtian, or I can assure you the partners at your law firm will hear about this.

"Major, until you return on Friday, you are effectively in command of this battalion. Your orders are to be treated as if they come directly from me. Understood?"

Zhong wasn't sure what had just happened with the general, but he nodded in agreement.

"One week, Rongtian, one week after Major Zhong returns. Do not fail me," Qi finished in a huff as he turned and headed for his vehicle, which would return him to his headquarters.

"Pompous bastard," Zhong heard Rongtian mutter under his breath.

"Well, Lieutenant Colonel, where would you like me to begin?"

Chapter 10
Flowers & Robots

ODA 7322
Fuxing District
IVO Jiaoban Mountain Park

"Pull over here. I gotta check something," ordered Major Larry Thorne as the road ahead started to look a little more hostile.

"Geez, would you look at that," commented Sergeant First Class Rusten Currie as he pulled the MATV to the side of the road.

Fifty or so meters ahead of them was a thoroughly destroyed Marine amphibious assault vehicle and one of their LAVs or eight-wheeled light armored vehicles. The charred vehicles looked to have been pushed off to the side of the road from where they'd met their demise. Just beyond the destroyed American vehicles was a burned-out wreck of a PLA ZTQ-15 or Black Panther tank. Unlike the Type 99s, this was a light tank, made for operating at higher altitudes and on poorer-quality roads.

"We should be approaching the front lines somewhere ahead of us," Chief Smith said aloud as the sounds of battle had grown in intensity since they'd pulled over. Depending on the radio channel they had the ground radios set on, they could hear a lot of excited chatter by the Marines.

"Yeah, best we try and make contact with the local units in the area and let them know what we're up to. I'd rather not get fragged by our own guys as we try to infiltrate around them because we didn't take the time to introduce ourselves," Thorne opined as he pulled his notepad out to check on something. "Ah, here it is. We're in the 5th Marine Division's AO. Up ahead here should be elements from the 26th Regimental Combat Team unless things have changed. Here, Chief, why don't you go ahead and try and make contact with them and let them know we'll be approaching from the rear and we'd like to confer with them?"

Just then, a few AAVs and transport trucks started to drive past their four-vehicle convoy, which had pulled to the side of the road.

"Or we could just follow them to their headquarters and check in with them there?" Currie offered as the first vehicle drove past them.

"Yeah, let's do that, Currie. Slide in the rear of the convoy once it passes," Chief offered as Thorne seemed distracted with something happening on the radio.

As what were likely reinforcements continued to drive past them, one thing was clear—there was a hell of a fight happening further ahead. Plumes of oily black smoke rose into the sky, obscuring what otherwise might have been a nice November morning.

Then some planes flew overhead, causing everyone to look up to make sure they were friendlies. "I love those new planes. If we're going to lose the Warthogs, then I'll take those Wolverines and Super Tucanos any day," commented Currie as they watched a pair of Tucanos head towards the fighting.

When the last vehicle passed them on the road, Currie pulled their MATV back onto the hardtop and slid into the rear of the Marine convoy headed towards the front. A couple of the Marines sitting in the back of the transports gave a friendly wave. Currie gave one back. It was obvious to the Marines that they weren't part of their division given the vehicles and gear they sported. But anyone headed towards the front looking to kill ChiComs was probably good-to-go in their books.

As they drove down the winding road flanked at times by high mountainous sides, the sounds of battle increased. It was almost like the enemy was counterattacking, not the ones being attacked. When they came around the bend in the road, they saw that the Marines had pulled over and looked to be running towards something.

Then Sergeant Mark Dawson, sitting up in the turret, shouted down to them, "Hey, I'm not sure what's going on up there, but something isn't right. I'd pull off the road and get ready to dismount."

"Huh, what the hell?" Thorne said to no one in particular as he looked over to Chief Smith, the radio's hand receiver still held to his ear.

"There's a lot of frantic radio traffic going on right now about some kind of major attack happening up ahead. I...um, it sounds like it might have something to do with those machines we saw a few weeks ago. Those Terminator-looking things—"

"Missiles incoming!" shouted Dawson from the turret as something streaked across their line of sight.

BOOM!
BOOM!
BOOM!

Then three of the vehicles further ahead exploded into giant fireballs, sending plumes of flame and black smoke into the sky.

One of the vehicles that exploded was an AAV three vehicles ahead of them. Several Marines who had been standing in the opened rear hatch were blown from the vehicle, their bodies tossed into the air like rag dolls before they fell to the ground in a heap. Others tried to crawl out the tops of the hatches, their bodies momentarily on fire before streaks of red tracer fire zipped across the open spaces to cut them down.

As Marines bailed out the rear of a transport truck, strings of tracer fire zipped across the back of the truck, hitting many of them before they had a chance to jump off or dive for cover. Currie was frozen for a second by what he saw unfolding in front of him as he heard Smith shouting at him to pull the vehicle off the road.

Currie gunned the vehicle as he ducked behind one of the trucks already on fire as a string of tracer rounds meant for them pounded into the destroyed vehicle. As he pulled the vehicle forward, giving Dawson in the turret above a chance to get their fifty into the action, he heard Dawson start firing at whatever he still couldn't see from his own vantage point.

Soon bullets started hitting the turret and Dawson cursed at whoever was shooting at them. It was chaos happening around them, and it was happening at a blinding speed he could barely keep up with. The shouting on the radio, the frantic calls from units and Marines all talking over each other weren't helping the situation.

Chunk-chunk-chunk came the loud reports from the Marine LAV's 25mm chain gun as it fired on something just around the bend in the road.

Bam! Boom!

Another vehicle further ahead blew up when a missile slammed into it, throwing several Marines to the ground from the force of the explosion. A few looked a little slow to get up while scrambling to get back into the fight. As Currie watched some of their comrades race across the open space to assist the wounded and bring them back to a safer position, he cursed when he saw the bastards shooting at the guys just trying to help their wounded buddies. Several of the Marines who'd exposed themselves to help the wounded were getting cut down by enemy tracer fire that crisscrossed the road.

He angrily shouted a slew of curse words as he leapt to his feet, firing his new XM7 rifle as he charged towards a wounded Marine maybe twenty meters in front of him. This XM7, originally called the XM5, was designed by Sig Sauer and fired the .277 Fury round. The round was the new standard across multiple squad weapons platforms, and Currie found it much more effective than the 5.56 NATO round that it replaced.

As he closed the distance, he could hear the sound of the Ma Deuce firing over the top of his head, the large fifty-caliber slugs making a swooshing sound as they zipped over top of him. When he reached the Marine, he knelt down next to the guy, only to realize it wasn't a man, it was a female Marine. Snapping himself out of it, he shouted, "Hang on, Marine! I'm gonna get you out of here!"

He reached down, grabbing her by the body armor and throwing her over his shoulder. He grunted momentarily, having underestimated how much this five-feet-something Marine must have weighed. Then with another grunt he started running like an Olympian toward the MATV as Dawson's Ma Deuce spat flame and bullets right over his head at whoever was still trying to shoot at him. When he rounded the corner to the vehicle, he did his best to set her down so as to not cause her more pain than necessary.

"Where you hurt, Marine?" he shouted to be heard over the clamor of Dawson's hate machine, which continued to spewislug after slug.

"Back of my left leg. Then my lower back. Hurts like a son of a bitch, Sergeant First Class," she replied through gritted teeth.

Checking the wound, he spotted a through-and-through on her thigh. It was bleeding, but nothing life-threatening. Just then, Jasper dropped next to them with his aid bag and went to work on checking out her other injuries.

"You hang in there, Marine! Jasper's our team medic. You're in good hands now," Currie offered as he held her gaze for a second before turning back to the fight at hand.

By now the four gunners of the team's MATVs were fully engaged as the rest of the ODA team members had dismounted the vehicles. What had started out as a mission to try and get around the front lines to attempt a recovery operation of some downed pilots had turned into a mission to aid the Marines in countering whatever force was threatening to break through their lines.

As the SF operators began laying into the enemy with overwhelming firepower, one of the two LAVs still in the fight inched forward as the driver looked to get around the bend in the road where most of the enemy fire was coming from. As the vehicle moved forward, the gunner operating the turret's 25mm chain gun tore into something they still couldn't see.

Chunk-chunk-chunk.

The chain gun hammered away until a rocket slammed into the forward section of the vehicle. The ATGM blew chunks of metal and parts of the vehicle into the air moments before the entire thing blew apart in a giant fireball.

From the blazing inferno, the Terracotta Killers emerged like dark angels of death. These humanoid war machines were a gruesome sight to behold, adorned with body armor and an arsenal of deadly weaponry that promised swift destruction. Their faces were emotionless—hollow shells devoid of any human traits, except for the menacing orangish-yellow V-shaped slits that glowed with an eerie light.

Each TK moved with fluid, almost graceful movements, their agility and speed nothing short of a marvel. But it was their cold, soulless eyes that sent shivers down Currie's spine. They were machines—instruments of war with no consciousness or soul.

As the lead TK advanced, it fired with deadly precision, the gunfire echoing through the air like a crack of doom. The TKs moved with purpose, relentlessly and methodically, cutting down Marines with chilling efficiency. Their armor-clad bodies bristled with grenades, magazines, and other tools of the trade.

Currie watched in horror as the lead TK unleashed a hail of bullets, taking out Marines with single shots. The machine's movements were smooth and almost hypnotic. Two more TKs followed the lead, their lithe forms moving with blinding speed and agility, leaving a trail of destruction in their wake.

In that moment, Currie realized the true horror of this new weapon of war, an invention that could strip humanity of its very soul. This machine was not just a weapon but a harbinger of things to come.

Aiming at the machine closest to him, Currie fired a couple of shots, hitting it several times. To his shock, and then horror, he saw the rounds hit the machine, but it appeared to shrug them off. It just kept moving forward, methodically shooting Marine after Marine as it encountered them.

Just as he was about to reengage it, he heard the most majestic sound an infantryman on the verge of being overwhelmed could possibly hear.

Brrrrrr.....

The M134 7.62mm minigun mounted in the turret of the MATV finally caught a bead on the TK and lit it up. The hail of bullets ripped the killing machine apart as it tried briefly to escape the hailstorm being thrown at it, to no avail.

When the machine collapsed to the ground in a broken heap, the two other TKs turned their attention to the SF vehicles as they fired deadly accurate shots at the newly identified threat. Then Currie heard Dawson join in with the Ma Deuce, hitting one of the TKs at the midsection, separating its legs from its upper body. The two other TKs split up, with one breaking to the left and the other bolting to the right. If he hadn't seen it with his own eyes, he wouldn't have thought it possible for them to move as fast as they had. Their speed, mixed with their inhuman agility, allowed them to dodge, evading the barrage of bullets of the minigun being fired at them almost like a scene from that movie *The Matrix*.

As Currie looked back to the MATV with the minigun, he saw his friend Big Lou grinning and shouting like a madman as he chased the TK that had broken to the left with the M134. He was just about to turn away when the face of his friend disappeared in a red mist—the gun now silent. Returning his gaze to the enemy, he saw the machine that had killed his friend casually walk towards a group of Marines maybe thirty meters away as it went through the motions of reloading the QBZ-191 assault rifle before releasing the bolt and resuming its killing spree.

Then he heard the unmistakable crack of a single shot fired from Corporal Jonathan "Johnny O" Ortega's MG 338. The powerful Norma Magnum slug crashed into the head of the TK, ripping it clean off the body of the machine. Then Dawson got lucky with the Ma Deuce, clipping the other TK's right leg, severing it as the machine was in midsprint towards his truck. As the killer robot fell to the ground, Johnny O hammered it with a dozen or so slugs from the MG until it finally stopped moving.

It took a second for Currie to realize that the shooting had died down and then it stopped. In less than a few minutes, they'd managed to neutralize the four killer robots, not fully believing that it could have been only four of them that had caused so much death and destruction. But then they heard more shouting coming from just around the bend, which caused the SF operators to tense up and get ready to go another round with the machines. The calls from the Marines seemed to indicate it wasn't more of the enemy getting ready for another attack, however. It was reinforcements, having heard their calls for help only to arrive after much of the convoy had been savaged.

Major Thorne directed the team to stick around long enough for their team medic to tend to the wounded Marines before getting them back on the move. They still had a mission to accomplish, even if they were down a man and had another wounded.
****

26th Marine Regiment HQ
Baiji Elementary School
Daxi District, Section 2

Colonel Jeff Kerns stood outside his headquarters building, looking off into the distance at what should be his rear area—a safe and secured area following more than a week of bloody fighting. Now he saw plumes of black smoke. Smoke he hoped wasn't coming from the reinforcements and resupply that should have arrived thirty-odd minutes ago.

"Sir, I have that information you requested," interrupted Major Ball as he turned to look at him. "I just spoke to Major Elliot from Division HQ. He talked to someone from Four Tracks about our reinforcements and resupply. They sent us Delta Company to reinforce us and escort our ammo. That shooting we heard to our rear...he confirmed it was them. He couldn't give me a lot of details other than it was happening around the Jiaoban Mountain Park and they'd requested QRF support. Unfortunately, the QRF had already been called for another unit, so I checked with our supply headquarters unit—"

"Just give me the bottom line, Major. How bad is it, Ball?" Kerns interrupted as he wanted the meat of the report, not the play-by-play of what had happened. He'd get that later from the movement commander.

"It's bad, sir. They lost three of the four LAVs escorting the convoy. Then two of the five AAVs transporting our reinforcements along with one of the three supply trucks, and one of the four other troop transports. All told, some thirty-two KIAs, another thirty-one wounded."

"Damnit! What the hell hit them? More importantly, how in the hell did an enemy force strong enough to jack them up get behind us like that? The front lines are that way." Kerns pointed with his hand in the direction of the old Daxi Tunnel.

The major shrugged in response, which only infuriated him more. Kerns dismissed the man, knowing it wasn't his fault he didn't know what had happened. He'd find out soon enough, and then someone was going to pay for letting an enemy force slip through their lines like that. This kind of attack should not have been possible this far to their rear.

Just as he was about to walk back into the classroom he'd taken over as his headquarters, he spotted an odd mix of vehicles approaching the school.

Huh, those aren't Marines, he thought to himself as the four MATVs pulled into the parking lot and came to a halt.

As the occupants got out of the vehicle, he immediately knew they were Special Forces. Not that the M134s mounted in two of the four turrets didn't give it away, but the uniforms, gear, and swagger of the occupants told him these weren't Marines.

Standing there waiting for whoever was in charge to eventually make his way over, Kerns continued to look at them. They looked scruffy. Uniforms looked dirty and unkept, they had beards that rivaled the Taliban, and they didn't flinch or react to any of the shooting or explosions happening in the distance.

Yeah, they've been here awhile, I'd bet...

"So, who do you think you are? John Rambo rolling up on my headquarters?" Kerns started the conversation off as he stared down the man he thought was the OIC of the bunch.

"John Rambo? I'm Black Adam, Colonel," the SF operator countered with a grin as he continued to walk towards him. "I'm Major Thorne from Bravo Company, CO, 3rd Battalion, 7th SF. This is Chief

101

Smith, my OIC for ODA 7322. You have a place we can talk, Colonel?" he asked.

"Depends. Can you tell me what happened during that ambush? You must have seen it."

"Oh, we saw it all right, and yes, we can tell you exactly what happened. Best we do it inside, though. I'd rather not get nailed by some Kamikaze drone as we stand out here sizing each other up."

Yeah, I'm going to like these guys. They're killers…, Kerns thought to himself as he led them into his office.
****

ODA 7322

"Colonel, what hit your Marines wasn't a PLA unit or some sort of—"

"Like hell it wasn't! The front lines are that way, Major," the Marine Colonel interrupted as he pointed to the west.

"I understand that, sir," Thorne replied. "I was there with your Marines. I know what I saw. What hit your Marines was machines, not people. They're part of something called Project Terracotta. The Chinese call them Terracotta Killers or TKs for short. They're Terminators—and, yeah, just like that movie with Arnold Schwarzenegger—"

"Except these aren't CGI or some actor with a funny accent," cut in Chief Smith, who saw the look of doubt forming on the Marine colonel's face. "These machines are killers. That's what attacked your Marines."

"OK, let's assume for the moment this is true, and I'll know once I talk with the survivors when they get here. How do you know this and what are you doing here?" the colonel asked, having changed his tone and demeanor now that he seemed to have gotten what he wanted.

Major Thorne turned to Smith. "Chief, see to the guys and tell them to hang tight while the colonel and I talk a bit more." As Smith left, Thorne began to explain, "Sir, we've been on this island for the better part of seven months, preparing the way for your leathernecks to eventually get here. But as to that machine, we had no idea what that thing was until a few weeks back. Just as you guys were getting to land, we got tasked with some sort of CIA mission. Someone spotted these machines, and we got sent out to verify what the hell it was.

"When we saw them, they were with some scientist. Someone that was part of the program. I don't know much more about it than that. We watched them for a few days, then you guys landed, and we got orders to nab the scientist when she decided to take a stroll along some of the trails near the camp where tests were being done on them. We saw them in action once—terrifying speeds and deadly accurate. But what hit your Marines...these were different—"

"Different? How so?" interrupted Kerns. He looked concerned now as he listened to Thorne recount the battle they'd just fought. As they continued to talk, the sound of vehicles further away picked up before they approached the school. One of the LAVs from the attack parked next to Thorne's people before the occupants got out and started heading towards the colonel's office.

When the officer in charge of the convoy walked into the room, he added to the story Thorne had been telling him, explaining how Thorne's team had taken out the machines before they'd had a chance to finish the Marines off. By the time they got done recounting what had happened, other reports started to filter into the headquarters of similar types of attacks taking place in other parts along the front line and in the rear areas. Small numbers of bipedal machines had attacked the Marines, sowing chaos and terror wherever they were encountered.

As the midday light turned into early evening, Kerns offered Thorne's men a place to spend the night, at least until they figured out what was going on with these machines and where else they might attack next or how many of them there might be. Thorne agreed to stay, but only for a night. They had a mission to accomplish, and he was hell-bent on completing it.

However, it would prove to be a long and terrifying night. While there weren't any further attacks by the TKs near them, the radio calls throughout the evening spoke of machines sniping at Marines along the front lines, with little they could do in response other than keep their heads down and hope the friendly artillery got lucky. By the time morning rolled around, Thorne's team was ready to get out of there and find some way around the front lines to get to the flower farm their intel said was being used to house a handful of downed pilots. Given the changes to the front lines over the past few days, Thorne wasn't one hundred percent sure how accurate this location might prove to be. But until they were given a new location to check out, this was it.

****

Midday
IVO Cihu Lakeside Trails

Currie and Johnny O walked as stealthily as they could while trying to keep a decent pace along the edges of the paved foot trail as they approached the lake. When they had left the Marine positions earlier in the day, they had found their way to a set of paved foot trails that wound around the back of the Cihu Mausoleum. It went through the Fuxing Road Tunnel and connected to the Beibu Cross-Island Highway, which eventually led to Taoyuan City. They were hoping to slip past the front lines, or at least where the bulk of the fighting was currently taking place, and make it to the flower farm where the downed pilots were supposedly being held.

When the ODA team had reached the foot trails, Major Thorne had ordered all but the drivers and the turret gunners to dismount the vehicles and continue on foot fifty or so meters ahead of the MATVs. This way if they ran into an enemy force, they'd hopefully spot them before the vehicles got too close and were engaged. If they had to fight it out with the enemy, then the vehicles wouldn't be too far behind, and they could call them forward to bring their mounted guns to the fight.

As they approached the lake, they spotted the first signs of trouble. Johnny O, who had been twenty meters ahead of Currie, raised a fist, halting their movement. He took a knee, and so did the rest of the team. The vehicles continued to hang back, turning their engines off so as not to give away their positions by accident. When Currie scooched up to Johnny's position, he asked, "Wha'cha got, Johnny O?"

"Right there, towards the end of the lake near that set of park benches. It's cleverly hidden, but you can just make out the sandbags. Then you'll spot the machine-gun barrel sticking out of that camouflage netting," Johnny explained.

Currie took his pocket binos out and looked in the direction he'd been told to. *Whoa, that would have been a nasty surprise to walk into.* Hidden beneath a camouflage netting was a Type-85 heavy machine gun. It was basically a Chinese/Russian version of the American M2 fifty-cal. Manning the gun were what looked to be two PLA soldiers, who seemed to be a little tired and not as alert as they probably should be.

If there's one bunker, there are likely two bunkers. He started scanning the area near the first bunker for any others. It didn't take him too long to find another position a little to the right of the first one. But when he found a third bunker, that was when he knew this path wasn't going to work. If he had found three of them so far, chances were there were more further inside the forest and more troops than their ten-man team could likely take on, even with the support of their vehicles. This was going to be too big of a fight.

****

Major Thorne was listening to the radio for an update to their orders when he saw Currie making his way towards them. "What's the deal, sir? Our mission still a go or what?" asked Smith as Currie took a squat next to them.

"Hang on, Chief. Wha'cha got, Currie?" Thorne asked.

"We spotted at least three bunkers ringing the lake and the approach to it. I could be wrong, but I suspect there are more we can't see and likely a fair number of troops manning them as well. We're not going to be able to slip past the lines here. We'll have to find another way through," Currie reported.

Thorne sighed deeply at the news, nodding in agreement. "OK, well, then, I guess that makes this next set of news a little easier to accept. HQ wants us to pull back. They're scrubbing our mission. Apparently, the pilots got recovered by another team. Oh, and they were in a different location entirely, so yeah, this would have been a bust had we managed to find a way around the enemy positions anyways. Let's try and do our best to extract ourselves from this position without getting caught and get back to the Marines. We'll see what HQ wants us to do next," Thorne directed, and the team began the process of withdrawing down the path they'd just traveled.

Chapter 11
The Choke Point

3rd Infantry Division Sustainment Brigade
Jinzhou, Liaoning Province, China

Rico Ramos and his crew had been sidelined for a few weeks while they waited for their tank to be repaired, they had been awarded the honor of officially, permanently naming their tank for the Army registry. They'd already been calling it Black Rider, after their call sign, and given the nineteen tank and thirty-seven armored vehicle kills they had racked up, Black Rider seemed like a fitting name for a tank that was essentially death on a track. But it was during this three-week period that Rico and his gunner, Harris, had found themselves being trained on the newest toy the Army was giving them to play with.

They had heard rumors about the Textron and Rheinmetall robotic tanks. But neither of them had actually seen one up close and in person—until they'd found themselves without a tank while theirs was undergoing repairs. That was when they were introduced to the Ripsaw M5. It was part of the robotic combat vehicle program, and in this case, it was listed as a medium-class semiautonomous or remote-controlled vehicle. Its turret sported a 30mm autocannon, a 12.7mm coaxal gun, a pair of Javelin ATGMs, and a pair of Starstreak missiles packed in a dual side-by-side pod mounted to the top of the turret. With no humans inside and no compartment, the vehicle was pretty squat and kept a low profile considering what it was.

When Rico pondered the obvious question—why them, and how were these going to be integrated into a tank unit? And when Sergeant Harris had asked how the Ripsaw could possibly aid a platoon of tanks in being more deadly than they already were, their instructor, Ocie Banks, a retired tanker himself, had explained the concept of the remote-control vehicles, saying, "The Ripsaw is essentially the same as the Loyal Wingman concept, only for tanks and infantry."

This had elicited a few laughs from the group. But Ocie continued, "There's no doubt that the MQ-28 Ghostbat and the XQ-58 Valkyrie have changed the way aerial battles are being fought in this war. The introduction of the M5 Ripsaw to work hand in glove with the Army's tanks and mechanized units will have the same impact on the battlefield if not greater. It will act like a second set of eyes and ears for armored vehicles and dismounted infantry. It can be directed to travel ahead of friendly forces into contested territory without risking your forces unnecessarily.

"In urban and forested areas, it gives vehicle commanders additional support against dismounted infantry and enemy missile teams. In time, another variant under development will carry the same microwave counterdrone equipment the XD500 Jackals currently use. In the meantime, the Ripsaw's onboard suite of electronic sensors and ground radar gives the user the ability to engage helicopters and low-flying aircraft with its Starstreak missiles and potentially two main battle tanks with its Javelin ATGMs. The vehicle has also been equipped with four of DARPA's latest long-range micro scout drones that can further aid the user in identifying potential targets of opportunity, to be engaged by artillery and air strikes on an unsuspecting foe."

During the weeks Rico and Harris had waited for Black Rider to finish being repaired, they were taught how to remotely operate the Ripsaw from inside an Abrams, and from a nearby MATV or JLTV light armored vehicle. The entire point of the training was to demonstrate how effortlessly the Ripsaws could operate in conjunction with a single tank, or in support of a tank platoon or higher-level echelon. They also weren't the only ones learning to use the remote-control vehicles. A few other tankers in similar situations had also found their way to the training course. Some were from the 4th ID, a few others from the 1st Cav or the 1st AD. Rico and Harris were the only Rock of the Marne tankers and proud of it.

Once Black Rider was repaired, Rico and Tim had kind of hoped they wouldn't have to have anything further to do with the Ripsaw. That maybe this was some whizbang training they'd been sent to as busy work to keep them occupied while their tank was repaired. Then, to their shock, as he and Tim were getting the tank ready to head back up north to link up with their platoon, Rico saw their instructor, Ocie Banks, walk towards them until he stood next to the vehicle.

Ocie had his hands on his hips and a look of disappointment and scorn on his face as he asked, "Hey, you two forgetting something?"

"Ah man, they're really going to make us take a Ripsaw back with us, aren't they?" Tim asked, climbing out of the loader's hatch. He had a look on his face that begged Rico to say he was wrong, but Rico shrugged instead as he looked down at the contractor. "I guess not."

"Mind if I come up?" Ocie asked as he walked up the armored skirt.

Rico nodded for him to come aboard. The old man smiled as he climbed aboard like only a veteran tanker would. As he made his way to the turret, he stood on the tank and looked around briefly.

He sighed before speaking. "Sergeant First Class Ramos," he said aloud, "when I retired back in '11, I thought I'd miss this life. The smell of JP8, that burnt smell from the spent aft cap after you fired the gun. The comradery and trust you build with your crew. But you know what?"

Rico snorted. "What's that, Ocie?"

"Once you get over not having to be responsible for Private Snuffy showing up late for morning PT smelling of alcohol, getting a two a.m. call on Saturday from the MPs to come bail out Specialist Dirtbag for beating his old lady for banging the next-door neighbor while he was deployed, and then having to deal with the newest butter bar fresh from West Point who thinks his Officer Basic Course has now made him an expert in the tactical employment of your tank—once you realize you don't deal with any of that crap, Rico, you'll ask yourself, why the hell did I stick around eight years past my twenty?"

Tim busted out laughing as Ocie joined in, then Rico laughed at the absurdity of the crap most senior noncommissioned officers had to deal with and knew the old tanker was right. When you're in the middle of the suck, you think it's terrible. Then when you hit your twenty, you decide it's not so bad, so you stick around a few extra years, knowing with each year you suck it up, you get an extra two and a half percent more in retirement pay. Then one day, some butter bar or other jackass finally pushes the wrong button, and the next thing you know, you're handing in your retirement papers. Then like Ocie said, you sit back on the couch, pop a beer, and ask yourself, "Why the hell did I stay those extra years when I could have gotten out at my twenty?"

"Are you telling me, old man, I should get out when I hit my twenty?" asked Rico as Ocie looked at him and Tim.

"Rico, that's a decision for you to make. All I can do is tell you about the grass on the other side and assure you it still needs to be mowed. But the pay is better, and you don't have butter bars and Private

Snuffies to deal with on a daily basis. You also have the option of just quitting and walking away when you want, which has a quality and satisfaction all its own."

"Hell yeah, that's what I'm talking about. Once they lift my stop-loss, I'm gone, man. I was only supposed to be in for four years—three years ago," recounted Tim, and the three of them laughed at Tim's luck in getting stop-lossed at the start of the war.

"OK, enough BS'ing. You guys did good with the training. I sincerely mean that. This"—he pulled a tablet out of the backpack he'd been wearing—"this is the tablet that'll control the Ripsaw. Your onboard computer has been synched to it, and you can also control the Ripsaw from there as well. Just like in training, the Ripsaw isn't exactly expendable, but it's more expendable than you and your tank. Do not be afraid to send it ahead of you or the platoons. This is an extension of your eyes and ears. Use it. This is a deadly little bastard that just might save your life, and the lives of your fellow tankers.

"Over there"—he pointed behind them to a couple of HETs or heavy equipment transporters unloading a pair of Ripsaws each—"that M5 they just parked. That's yours. Your onboard computer and this tablet are already synched to it. It'll follow your orders. More importantly, it'll follow you. If it needs maintenance and it's beyond what you guys can handle, you know how to call for help. A handful of guys from maintenance know how to fix 'em, and if they somehow manage to break it, one of our guys will come out, even to the front lines if necessary, to get it operational. I want to wish you both good luck. And, Rico, look me up when you get back. We're always hiring and the pay's good," Ocie finished. He extended a hand to the two of them before hopping off Black Rider and heading over to talk to the next crew.

"Well, I guess that settles it. We're stuck with it," Tim commented as he took the backpack from Rico and gently lowered himself into the turret.

Rico sighed. "Yeah, let's get out of here. Time to go earn our pay."
****

Five Days Later
Bravo Company, 2-327th
Chaoyang, Liaoning Province

Sabo's grip tightened on the XM250 as he squeezed the trigger, *tata tata, tata tata,* firing controlled bursts from the squad's light machine gun as the PLA soldiers continued their attempts to break through their lines.

Shhhh…. BOOM!

"That's inbound arty! Everyone down!" shouted Peters as more artillery rounds exploded against their lines.

Boom, boom, BOOM!

"Medic! I need a medic over here!"

"I'm hit. Oh God! My legs!"

"Guns up! They're charging again!" shouted Lakers further to Sabo's right.

Holy crap! Why did I volunteer to come back to this…?

Sabo sighted in on a group of enemy soldiers rushing forward along the left flank where the latest artillery barrage had just hit. *Tata tata, tata tata,* he started firing controlled bursts, hitting two of them as the others dove for cover—their advance halted for the moment.

Then he heard the sound of approaching footsteps coming from behind. Sabo turned as Private Yanez landed into the fighting hole he'd taken charge of twenty minutes ago when a nearby artillery round had injured the previous gunner and his load.

"Here, Sergeant, I got that ammo you wanted!" Yanez said through ragged breaths as he pulled one of the fifty-round belts from around his neck.

"Thanks, Yanez. Drop the rest of the ammo for this pig and then go down the line and see if anyone else needs anything. If they do, then I'm relying on you, Private, to keep the ammo coming for everyone and to continue checking in on people during this fight. You got it?" Sabo directed as he attached the fresh belt to the remaining links of the one he was using.

"You got it, Sergeant. You can count on me!" the trooper declared as he pulled three belts from around his neck along with two fifty-round attachable ammo pouches for the XM250.

"We need another LMG over here. They're pushing on the right!" someone shouted as rifle fire shifted from the left flank to the right. This was the fourth attack of the day as the PLA continued to press their lines, looking for a weak spot to push.

110

When Sabo looked further off into the distance, he saw more trouble brewing and knew they needed to get ready for it. He grabbed for Yanez just as he was about to leave. "Change of plans, Private. I need you to run back to the ammo truck and look for something like this." Sabo held a tubular green case up. "This case is empty, but there should be a few of them at the truck. Make sure to read them. I need you to grab the ones marked HEAT, or it might say HEDP. Grab two of the cases and get them back to me ASAP. Now go!"

As Yanez ran back to their ammo truck further behind the now-established fighting positions, a pair of soldiers ran over to Sabo and jumped into the trench line. Then Sergeant Peters and Lieutenant Branham joined him a moment later as one of the soldiers offered, "Here, Sergeant, I'll take over the gun for you." Sabo nodded, handing the squad's light machine gun over to him, and pointed to the extra ammo and spare barrel for his partner to take charge of.

"Sabo, good job getting that machine gun running again. Those Chink bastards are trying to overrun us. Right now, I need to know if you have any rounds left for the Gustaf. I think you may have spotted those vehicles forming up again off in the distance. We're gonna need your luck in nailing a few. You think you can do it?" Sergeant Peters asked while Sabo grabbed for his rifle again.

He nodded confidently, a grin spreading across his face. "Is the Pope Catholic?"

Peters grunted at the reply. "Don't get cute with me."

Sabo smirked. "Yeah, I can take 'em out. I've got one shot in the Gustaf. It's a HEAT round. I just sent Yanez back to the truck to bring some more rounds up. Unless I'm wrong, they still had three of those ZBL-08s, the ones with those 30mm autocannons, along with at least two of those ZBD-04s, that 100mm with those HE-FRAG rounds that jacked us up last time. Now it looks like they have at least"—Sabo paused a second as he looked off in the distance with his pocket binos— "I count six—damn, those look old as dirt—I think they're those Type 86—"

"Whoa, those are like those older Russian BMP-1s or something. They still mount a 30mm autocannon, so we have to watch out for that," Peters interjected.

"We should get a drone up to check it out further. But aside from those six Type 86s. I see another six more of those ZSD APCs and…whoa, looks like at least eight of those Type 59 tanks, and either two of those Black Panther light tanks or two of those heavy ZTZ96s. I can't totally make it out from here."

"Damn, that's a heck of a push they're gearing up to mount," Peters said, echoing the concern Sabo was feeling right about now. Peters then asked, "LT, we best get some fire support on this valley ASAP before those vehicles get moving—you think we might be able to get that platoon of Abrams back at the rest stop to move up and help us out?"

"I don't know, but I'm sure gonna try," Lieutenant Branham said before he started talking to someone on the radio.

Peters motioned to Sabo to follow him as the shooting along the right flank continued to pick up. "Sabo, here's the deal, man. We gotta find a way to slow those tanks and armored vehicles down. We can't blow the interstate bridge, so that's out of the question. Especially now that it's firmly under their control. But you see that bridge that crosses the interstate?" Peters pointed to a double-lane bridge that crossed over top of the six-lane interstate about half a kilometer in front of their position. "That bridge can't hold a tank or heavy armor on it, so that's why they don't have a tank up there, just some of their light armored vehicles, like those Mengshi trucks with those .51-caliber machine guns. Let me ask you something. What if we hit those center support pylons? You think it might be enough to drop the bridge across the interstate?"

Sabo began to smile as he pieced together what Peters was thinking. The engineers had rigged the bridge crossing a large wadi with explosives a little more than a week ago. But the PLA had gotten the jump on the unit deployed here before they'd arrived and pushed the allies back a few kilometers until their battalion had arrived and they'd stopped the PLA advance. But the engineers had lost control of the bridge before they could blow it. Then the brass at division headquarters determined they could recapture the lost territory, so now they didn't want to blow the bridge. A quarter kilometer away, however, was a two-lane vehicle bridge that spanned the interstate. If they could drop it, it could block the highway and majorly slow up the enemy's advance down it.

Sabo looked off in the distance towards the center pylons Peters was talking about. As he thought about it, he looked at the Gustaf, then the bridge, then he turned to Peters. "Well, there are two possible options we can try. One is an antistructure munition, the other is a guided multipurpose munition. They're both rated against bunkers, but I don't know how well they'll do against a cement bridge pylon, particularly since these are likely to be rebar-reinforced. I mean, we could try it, but I'd rather try and see if the arty guys couldn't hit it with an Excalibur round."

Peters seemed to nod along as he listened. Turning towards the mortar pit, he shouted, "Sergeant Martin!"

A young buck sergeant poked his head above the lip of the mortar pit he was in. One of the privates hung another 60mm mortar before releasing.

Thump! The round sailed out of the tube in the direction of the enemy. Then the sergeant leapt out of the mortar pit and trotted towards them. The shooting along the right flank seemed to slacken a bit as the mortars started to hammer the ChiComs pushing along the flank.

"Martin, can you get ahold of Sergeant Gollogly?" Peters asked.

Martin bunched his eyebrows. "Who?"

Peters shook his head as he shouted a little louder to be heard. "Sergeant Jon Gollogly, he's the fire support NCO with Lieutenant Ferguson."

"Ferguson? He got killed yesterday," Martin replied, clearly having a hard time hearing what Peters was asking or not knowing who or what he was talking about. Sabo knew the guy was a bit of a country bumpkin, but he was generally a good guy who'd been placed in a position well above his head in the last twenty-four hours.

Peters looked like he was about to lose it with Martin as he turned back to Sabo. "Deal with this, Sabo, before I shoot him. See if Gollogly can get an Excalibur, or Copperhead round on that pylon and drop the bridge over the highway. If he doesn't have any rounds or he can't do it, then grab who you need and see if you and Mr. Gustaf can get it done yourselves. Now hurry, we don't have long until those vehicles start heading our direction."

Sabo nodded as Peters stormed off towards the LT, who was still on the radio with someone else. Turning back to Martin, Sabo asked, "Where's your radio? I know who to call and what to ask for."

"It's over here, Sabo. What did I do to piss off Peters? I'm doing the best I can with the mortars. It's just me and two guys from Supply they nabbed when they dropped off our extra ammo yesterday. By the way, they keep complaining about their sergeant who sent them and needing to get back to battalion headquarters," Martin exclaimed, exasperated by the entire situation.

The two of them walked to the mortar pit as the two supply clerks continued hanging and dropping 60mm mortar rounds as Martin had told them to continue doing until he got back. "Sergeant," one of the supply clerks asked, "I get the sense of urgency and all, and we've been happy to help. But we gotta get back to headquarters, back to our unit. They probably think we're dead by now. We were just supposed to drop off some ammo. Not stay here," a private first class by the name of Luko commented.

Sabo reached for the radio, then paused just long enough to look at the two supply clerks. "Look, guys, I know we more or less kidnapped you guys and put you to work dropping mortars. But as you can see"— he waved his arm about—"we're in a hell of a fight right now to hold this position. We're supposed to have another unit come reinforce us, and once they do, I'll talk to Sergeant First Class Peters, and the LT if necessary, to get him to let you guys go. For now, just keep working with Martin here and help us stay alive. Can I count on you guys to help with that?"

The two privates looked at each other, then glumly nodded, resigned to their fate.

"Hammer Two-Two, Warrior Two-One. Request fire mission. How copy?" called Sabo as he tried to connect to the battalion fire support cell, the three-man team that coordinated the different companies' artillery requests.

A second later, the ground radio chirped once, indicating that the frequency-hopping radio had synched. "Warrior Two-One, Hammer Two-Two. Send your traffic, over."

"Two-Two, Two-One. We have a priority target. Break. Requesting Excalibur or Copperhead strike. Break. Target is a cement bridge pylon support structure. How copy?"

There was a momentary delay as Sabo waited to see if his request could get filled or might require additional approval up the chain. While he and Martin continued to wait, the shooting along the right flank had slackened. Martin waved to his guys hanging mortars, signaling for them to stop and wait.

Then the radio chirped. "Two-One, Hammer Four-Six. Connect me to Warrior Two-Six. How copy?" *Ah damnit, they want to talk to the*

LT. Sabo turned back to where he had last seen Peters and the LT. They were still talking on the other radio in the same trench section where he'd been using the LMG, though the guys that had taken it over had moved down to support the right flank with it.

"Four-Six, Two-One. Stand by." Sabo turned to Martin. "Sorry I gotta take your radio with me. I'll bring it back. Hang tight and have your guys go grab some more ammo or something. If we don't get a fire mission soon, the enemy is going to make another push with some armor. We're going to need you guys to lay it on thick if that happens."

Martin's eyes went wide before he nodded and started filling the two clerks in on what was about to happen. They trotted off towards the rear area, where they had a few vehicles with their supplies holed up. Sabo made his way over to Peters, who asked, "Any luck on the arty?"

Sabo shook his head as he handed Peters the radio handset. "Captain Tinker on the horn. He wants to speak to the LT. He wouldn't talk to me."

Peters's eyes narrowed. Sabo wasn't sure what the deal was between Peters and the captain from the battalion fire support section, but they sure didn't get along too well. Peters grabbed the handset, growling into it as he did, "Hammer Four-Six, Warrior Two-Nine. Break. Two-Six is occupied. I have a priority target. Requesting fire mission. Break. Target is a cement bridge pylon. Break. We have an armor formation a couple of kilometers down the road. Break. Requesting Excalibur or Copperhead strike to destroy the bridge pylon to collapse overpass and block the highway. How copy?"

There was a momentary pause. Sabo watched Peters, trying to figure out what the deal was between him and that captain. It had obviously happened before he'd returned to the unit. Sabo just hadn't heard what it was. Then the radio chirped. "Four-Six. I have one Excalibur round. Send the grid. Make it count, Two-Nine. Break. We are black on ammo. We can provide three rounds, six tubes, that's it. How copy?"

Peters shook his head angrily as he muttered to himself, "How do they expect us to hold this area if they aren't going to give us additional reinforcements, armor, or proper artillery support? We don't even have any Switchblades or anything else we can use to stop their armor..." Peters lifted the hand receiver up. "Four-Six, that's a good copy. Thank you for this. We'll do our best to hold. Stand by to copy the grid for the target. We'll laser it locally. How copy?"

"Two-Nine, that's a good copy. Stand by. Good luck," came the final word. It sounded distant to Sabo. Almost like the captain on the other end felt sorry for them. Then Peters handed the radio back to him. "Pass them the grid and get them to lase the target. They'll get the round to the bridge, but you have to put the laser on it. We're need to be a hundred percent certain to hit where we want."

Sabo nodded as he relayed the requested information. This was the first time he'd called for an Excalibur round against any target. He'd seen them use the older Copperheads. The rocket-assisted 155mm howitzer round could hit a target with pinpoint precision up to sixteen kilometers away. But the Excalibur rounds, these bad boys could hit a target as far out as seventy kilometers.

When Sabo had finished relaying the information, Specialist Rosales ran up to him and Peters, handing him something. "I think this is what you're looking for."

Peters motioned with his head towards Sabo. "Go with Sabo. He'll tell you where to aim. They're getting an Excalibur round ready for us. Oh, hey, Rosales, don't miss this time. If you do, then those armored vehicles and tanks—we're going to be a speed bump and I'm going to blame you for it."

"Ouch, that's kind of harsh," Sabo retorted to the harsh criticism.

Rosales laughed it off. "Don't worry, Sabo. He's not holding a grudge or anything."

Sabo saw a look on Peters's face that said otherwise.

Rosales was their platoon forward observer, who had been with them since Cuba. He was a PFC back then. They had been fighting some Cuban militia and PLA forces in the Che Guevara Forest and Rosales had the misfortune of violently sneezing three times in quick succession as he was holding the laser designator to hit a troublesome bunker. It was just dumb luck and timing that it happened at the exact time the artillery shell was on its terminal attack. His sneeze had caused the round to miss the bunker by a solid six or eight hundred meters. They hadn't been able to get priority for another precision round, so they had to attack the position the old-fashioned way: hand grenades and cover and maneuver. They hadn't lost anyone during the assault, thank God. But two guys had gotten injured. One of them was Peters's friend. He'd given Rosales crap about it for two years now, but he knew it wasn't on purpose. Just dumb luck. Rosales had redeemed himself later on in El Salvador, when he'd heroically fought off half a dozen ChiComs that had jumped into their position. The fighting had gotten so savage it had devolved into Rosales using his e-tool, savagely hacking the enemy apart with his shovel when he ran out of ammo.

Sabo shivered as he recalled the battle that had nearly wiped them out when they got sent in to go rescue some Army Special Forces guys. He still remembered that SF guy, Currie was his name. He told Sabo and some of the other guys to go back to the perimeter. He'd handle checking on the wounded, and mercy-killing the ones too far gone. Sabo had never gotten a chance to thank him for sparing him from having to do that awful thing. He wasn't even sure they were allowed to do it, but he wasn't about to get all legal after the kind of evening he'd just survived and the savage fighting it had devolved into. He still had nightmares about that battle.

"Come on, Rosales. We got a bridge to drop," he said, and the two of them headed towards one of the few two-story buildings the enemy hadn't leveled yet.

Twenty meters behind the first line of trenches and fighting positions of the unit were a handful of houses and stores that lined the frontage road not far from the interstate. When they had replaced the unit holding this section of line before them, an engineering unit had had the forethought to dig some fallback positions just in case they were needed. Sabo realized pretty quickly that if someone hadn't done that, they likely would have lost control of the valley. Several kilometers to their rear, the entire valley opened up, leading in multiple directions towards the pivotal city of Chaoyang, a city they had effectively cut off from the rest of China as they looked to force the surrender of the 80th PLA Group Army in the local area. It also further isolated and cut off the entire PLA First Army and all enemy units in northern China—so long as they could maintain their choke hold on the major supply routes, like the one they were guarding.

****

Ten Minutes Later

As the earlier attacks by the PLA had petered out and the enemy force just beyond the hill some five or six kilometers away continued to mobilize, the last platoon from their company had finally arrived to reinforce their positions. A few minutes later, trucks started arriving, bringing the soldiers of Alpha Company to further reinforce their positions and bring additional mortar teams and ATGMs. What few trucks they had with ATGMs mounted to their turrets were brought forward and hidden as best they could be next to the remains of any buildings, underbrush, or outcroppings they could find. Once the word got out that their line was going to be hit and hit hard by enemy armor, the battalion started moving units forward to reinforce them and help prepare a secondary defensive position should the tanks manage to break through.

While Specialist Rosales and Staff Sergeant Sabo sat atop the roof of the few buildings left standing, they continued to observe the movements of the light infantry as it cautiously crept forward, no more than two kilometers to their front. Meanwhile, they waited for their artillery support to let them know when the Excalibur round would be ready to fire. These precision rounds, in high demand and costly to fire, weren't doled out like a standard HE round. Especially when they were in serious short supply of such rounds. As such, a few layers of bureaucracy had gotten involved in determining if they should expend the round on this kind of target, where success wasn't a guarantee, or look to see if some air assets might be available to accomplish the same task.

All Sabo knew was they were wasting time figuring it out, and eventually the enemy was going to move. If they could force the enemy off the interstate onto the side frontage roads, it would funnel the armor into a tight squeeze along the sides of the interstate that would make it easy for them to pick them off.

"Good grief, Sabo. I hope they fire the round soon. I finally got a drone in place they haven't managed to shoot down yet. Check it out. Those vehicles look to be gearing up to get on the move." Specialist Rosales showed him the tablet with drone feed on it. They'd lost five drones in the last twenty minutes, trying to get an eye on what was happening beyond the crest of the hill.

Damn, that's a few more APCs than I first spotted. Whoa, how many tanks have they got back there? "Rosales, can you get a better picture of this area? The camera briefly scanned it. I want to go back. I think we missed something," Sabo asked. He pointed in the direction of where he wanted their forward observer liaison to pan the drone camera.

When Rosales took control of the tablet, he started working his magic as he adjusted the camera and pulled out on the magnification to give them a broader view of the area. What they saw, however, was not a mix of Black Panther light tanks or the older, less-capable Type 59 main battle tanks. What they saw now, beyond the crest of the hill that had previously hidden them from sight, was a grouping of at least four columns of seven of the older Type 59 tanks and two columns of seven of the newer, more capable ZTZ96 main battle tanks. This was in addition to at least nine other columns of seven armored vehicles, all lining up as they prepared to start advancing in echelon formations.

Oh crap, that's a hell lot of more armor than we thought they had in the area. That's gotta be almost a brigade-level unit attack. I better alert the LT and Peters about this. Sabo reached for the radio and started relaying what the drone feed was showing them. It was time to get serious about getting some armor up there, or they were toast.

Chapter 12
Robots & Tanks

Alpha Company, 1-64th Armored Regiment
G25 Changshen Expressway
IVO Sijiazi Village, Liaoning, China

Sitting outside the tank, Ramos and his crew tried their best to stretch out and relax while they could. The sounds of gunfire and explosions off in the distance had ebbed and flowed in intensity the past few days. So far, they hadn't been called forward, and in Ramos's mind, that was a good thing. It meant the allied lines, while being pressed, were still holding. But as the hours of the day continued to tick by, the intensity of the battle a few kilometers down the road picked up. It was beginning to sound more and more like the enemy might actually attempt a breakthrough along their part of the line.

The past couple of hours, things had really picked up. Almost to the point where Ramos was ready to order the platoon to saddle up and move their tanks towards the front. But the lieutenant had insisted on them staying put until they were called forward. For now, that meant sitting around the radio speaker they had pulled out of the turret to monitor the situation. Calls for artillery, mortars, were becoming more frequent, more urgent. Likewise, requests for close-air support were now regularly coming in. Sadly, most of those kinds of requests had been denied. Same with any sort of requested increase in artillery support. In Ramos's mind, it was clear that the enemy was launching some sort of new offensive. It wasn't just their section of the line being pressed. Battalions manning the series of blocking positions choking off the main supply routes to the city of Chaoyang sounded like they were all being tested by the PLA.

It was a simple, time-tested strategy. Push until it's mush and once you find the mush, you push through it. Ramos was no military expert, but even his lizard brain understood the implications to the war if they could continue to choke off the supplies and reinforcements to the PLA Northern Army Group. Eventually, it would die on the vine and that would remove one giant piece from the chessboard and move them that much closer to victory.

Sometime around midday, they heard the sounds of jets flying overhead, low and fast—so low and fast that they shook the roof and walls of the farm's warehouse their platoon had taken refuge in. Since arriving at the farm location three days ago, the four tanks of the platoon, along with the lone M5 Ripsaw, had been doing their best to stay hidden there, away from the prying eyes of surveillance and Kamikaze drones and the occasional fighter plane or helicopter prowling for a target of opportunity.

The farm itself was situated between the frontage road and the interstate, making it an ideal place to position their tanks as the QRF for the battalion of Screaming Eagles they were supporting. With little more than man-portable ATGMs and 60mm mortars, the light infantrymen would be barely a speed bump should the PLA press their lines with any serious armor or tank force. That was where Ramos's Alpha Company unit came in. The platoon would rush forward while the rest of the company was alert and head their way, bringing with them the other twelve Abrams battle tanks and three other Ripsaws.

With the daylight steadily coming to an end, the intensity of the fighting by whatever PLA force the Airborne were encountering steadily picked up again. Incoming and outgoing artillery barrages became more urgent, more numerous. Then the lieutenant received the call they had been waiting for. A surveillance drone had spotted enemy tanks and armor forming up in an attack formation a handful of kilometers behind the current front lines. This was it, the reason they were here to support the infantry.

"Listen up, everyone!" Ramos shouted to get everyone's attention. "It's been nice to spend a few days chilling, relaxing and stretching our legs while we wait around to see what happens. Well, now we know what's happening. An enemy force is forming up behind the lines and looking to punch a hole through what they probably assess as a weak spot in our lines. What they don't know is there's a platoon of tanks lying in wait for them to make a move just like this. So now, it's time to put your war faces on. It's time to go earn our pay and blow up some tanks and add to our platoon's impressive kill ratio. It's time to saddle up. Let's roll!"

"Hooah!" came a motivated shout from the tankers as they policed up their gear and climbed aboard their armored chariots.

As Ramos got comfortable in the commander's chair, he heard the radio chirp in his CV helmet. "BR Two, BR One. The infantry are requesting us to advance towards the line of contact and prepare to engage advancing enemy armor. This sounds like one of those good opportunities to test that Ripsaw they gave us. What do you think?"

Would you look at that…the lieutenant is asking for advice. I told Top this LT was bright, he thought with amusement.

"BR One, BR Two. I couldn't agree more. I'll go ahead and get the M5 on the move ahead of the platoon and look and confirm firing positions are still valid."

Shortly after arriving at the farm, Ramos and the lieutenant had taken the Ripsaw out for a short scouting mission. They wanted to get the lay of the land from the vantage point of the Ripsaw and determine paths and alternate paths the platoon could take to link up with the infantry. Once they mapped out a few travel routes, they started looking for potential firing positions the tanks could settle into should the call to move forward happen. It was likely they would be advancing under enemy fire, so it was important to know exactly where each of the tanks would be going so they could better coordinate their bounding overwatches and movements should they have to fire while on the move.

As Specialist Lopez got the tank on the move and Sergeant Harris assumed command of the vehicle, Ramos worked the Ripsaw, moving quickly down the frontage road parallel to the interstate. Watching the video feed as the M5 moved swiftly down the road, he saw little sign of any locals out and about. They likely knew a battle was about to happen and wanted to do their best to stay out of the way.

The closer Ramos got to the front lines, the more damage to the area he started to see. The rolling artillery barrages throughout the day had worked the area pretty good. It made him feel good about their platoon being held back a few kilometers from the front. They might have lost a tank or two if they had been forced to hunker down throughout a day of rolling artillery strikes. As he moved closer to where the infantry was hunkering down, the Ripsaw's ground radar spotted some movement a few kilometers in front of the infantry. Stopping the vehicle, he allowed the radar to start mapping the terrain in front of him, and the targeting computer populated potential targets for him to engage.

Wow, why in the hell did we think it wasn't going to be a good idea to start using this radar and targeting system with our vehicles? It's

122

amazing, he thought, remembering how he and Tim had dismissed the vehicle's potential value to an armor platoon.

Looking at the vehicles cresting the horizon as they started to move along either side of the interstate now that a vehicle bridge had been collapsed across it, he smiled. This single act had funneled the enemy vehicles into a pair of tight choke points they'd now have to cross. This would be like shooting fish in a barrel.

Ramos started relaying what he was seeing to the rest of the platoon, making sure each of the vehicle commanders knew where to focus their attention. If they worked it right, they might be able to bottle up the enemy advance and stop it before it could get going.

Activating one of the vehicle's Javelins, he found a pair of T-59s moving down the frontage road a few kilometers to his front and locked on to one of them. Once the missile indicated it had a lock, he fired it. It leapt out of the box mounted to the left of the turret and took off for the tank. Moments later, it connected with the T-59 and blew the turret clean off the vehicle. As the ammo inside started to cook off, he locked the second missile on the other tank now trying to swerve off the frontage road as it looked for someplace to hide. Other vehicles still traveling down the road split off the road too, hoping they wouldn't be the tank to momentarily join the Air Force when their turret shot into the sky.

Ramos found another tank that looked to have stopped just behind the burning wreck of his comrade. He could see the turret was steadily moving in his direction. Hearing the missile tone indicating that it had a lock, he fired it, then backed up. The computer kept the laser designator tagged to the vehicle as the other tank fired.

BOOM!

A cloud of dirt and debris rained over top of the Ripsaw from the near miss. Then Ramos saw his missile slam into the tank, popping his second turret in so many minutes. The two burning wrecks had now blocked most of the frontage road, forcing the vehicle behind it to find another way around.

"Good shot, Ramos. We're here now. I'm going to get the tank in the fight now," Harris announced, letting him know they had arrived at their firing point.

While he tried to stay focused on fighting the Ripsaw, he could hear Specialist Blum and Harris calling out targets and ammo as they went to work. With each firing of the main gun, Ramos watched another one of the enemy tanks erupt in flames. Knowing the platoon would focus primarily on destroying the tanks first, he shifted his focus to the more lightly armored infantry fighting vehicles and armored personnel carriers with the M5's 30mm autocannon.

Within the first few minutes after the platoon's four Abrams arrived, they had managed to destroy or disable some twenty-eight armored vehicles along both sides of the partially blocked interstate. The rapid destruction of so many armored vehicles in such a tight space was causing a massive logjam of burning wrecks and material, making it even more difficult for the enemy to push around it and get at the American lines.

As the scale and scope of the attack was relayed further up the chain of command, additional artillery and air support was directed their way. With Ramos largely focused on operating the Ripsaw, their company CO eventually delegated the calls for artillery and air support through him as the Ripsaw's suite of onboard cameras and sensors was more detailed and accurate than what they had aboard the Abrams.

Within thirty minutes of the platoon's arrival on scene, Ramos had found himself at the center of fielding calls for artillery and close-air support from not just his platoon and the rest of the tank company but also the nearby infantry once they had patched into his comms. As the first echelons of the enemy attackers were thoroughly bloodied, the PLA tried to move around the carnage by traveling down a smaller road that cut through a nearby village. When Ramos launched the Ripsaw's scout drone to see why the enemy attack had faltered, that was when he spotted them trying to circumvent the logjam by going through the nearby village. He felt bad about what he did next, but they had to stop the armored force from punching through their lines.

By some miracle and happenstance, he'd been able to get their situation prioritized by not just the battalion fire support elements but also the brigade, who then got the entire division's allotment of fire support to focus on their position. In short order, he'd been able to call for six different artillery missions and a HIMAR strike that pummeled the third and fourth echelons of enemy forces, which hadn't been thrown into the fight yet, and then a close-air support mission involving four Super Tucanos and a pair of F-16 Vipers. Between the withering barrage of cluster munitions and five-hundred-pound bombs across much of the enemy force, the attack faltered and then collapsed as those few vehicles that hadn't been destroyed outright began a humiliating retreat, during which Ramos did his level best to harass and destroy them with no less than two separate HIMAR strikes. At no time in his entire military career had he ever had access to this level of fire support, and he used every bit of it to thoroughly wreck and destroy what had initially looked like an overwhelming enemy force that just might have broken the choke hold they had on the PLA Northern Army Group.

When Harris tapped him on the leg, he unglued himself from the drone footage of the carnage he'd inflicted to look at his gunner. "Rico, I take back every bad thing I said about that Ripsaw or that training they sent us to. I think it just saved our lives and the rest of the platoon's."

"Yeah, I think you're right, Harris. This is a game changer."

Chapter 13
Kings of the Pacific

5th MarDiv HQ
Shiding District, Northern Taiwan

"Mike, it's good to see you!" General Gilbert's voice boomed as Major General Bonwit walked into the conference room with Colonel Kerns and Sergeant Major Savusa.

"It's good to see you as well, sir," Bonwit replied as the trio took their seats.

"Mike, I'm not going to beat around the bush with you. I know you've taken some licks since the start of this campaign. We were all sorry to hear about Ivan and your staff afloat when the *American* went down. It was a blow to all of us—especially 5th MarDiv."

"Thank you, sir—and, yes, it was a blow to us," Bonwit replied as he silently sighed to himself. He had known where this conversation was going the moment Gilbert had mentioned Ivan's name.

"I said I wasn't going to beat around the bush, so you know what I'm going to ask. Who are you planning to replace him with? The billet's gone unfilled long enough, Mike, and you know that," Gilbert said pointedly, not pulling any punches.

Blowing some air past his lips, Bonwit answered, "In all honesty, sir, I haven't given it as much thought as I probably should have. I know I've been kicking the can down the road. I've allowed myself to become singularly focused on meeting our objectives. I just haven't given filling this billet the attention it's needed." If he could, he'd promote Kerns, but he was the most effective commander he had. If Bonwit lacked for anything, it was more aggressive, competent commanders—not an XO.

The general nodded as he sat back in his chair, steepling his fingers as he appeared deep in thought. When the general leaned forward, his eyes bored into Bonwit as he spoke. "I get it, Mike. You've been kicking ass and taking names. The whole division is an example of everything we Marines are proud of. I think it's time we pull you out for a bit—"

"I'm being replaced?" Bonwit clarified as his mind reeled at the thought of losing command of his Marines in the heat of battle.

General Gilbert busted out laughing before countering his interruption. "I can't replace you, Mike. Hell, I'm trying to figure out how to clone you."

Bonwit breathed an audible sigh of relief as he listened to the general continue to speak.

"I'm pulling your division out, Mike. You've fought like men possessed since the start of this campaign and taken some brutal losses in the process. Your Marines need a break and so do you. I'm ordering the 6th MarDiv forward to replace you. I want you to relocate your division to Toucheng. 5th MarDiv is moving to the top of the list for combat replacements. I've got another mission for you, Mike, but I need 5th MarDiv at one hundred percent if we're going to pull this off. And speaking of replacements, if you'll entertain me for a moment, I think I have a solution for your XO billet."

"Sir?" Bonwit raised an eyebrow at the idea of a new mission and his empty billet. Then Sergeant Major Savusa sent him a disapproving look at his response.

Taking the unspoken cue, Bonwit added, "General, the Kings of the Pacific stand ready for whatever mission you've got. As to the XO vacancy, I'm open to suggestions." The Kings of the Pacific was a reference to the unofficial motto adopted by the division during World War II.

"The Kings of the Pacific...I like bringing back these long-forgotten mottos. Before I tell you about the mission I'm retasking 5th MarDiv with, I'd like to introduce you to Brigadier General Deborah Soumoy," Gilbert said as he nodded to someone off-camera. A second later, a Marine with tightly bound blond hair proceeded to take a seat next to the general.

"Now, Mike, before you go and put your foot in your mouth by raising an objection, let me tell you about Deb's experience," Gilbert indicated. "Prior to the war, Deb was the deputy director of Marine Corps Logistics for the Marine Reserve. In her civilian job, Deb was the director of logistics for Amazon South. Since being recalled to active duty, she continued to serve in logistics, taking command of Marine Corps Logistics Base Barstow before pinning brigadier a year ago and taking command of 3rd Marine Logistics Group out of Okinawa. If you'll continue to indulge me a moment longer, I'll let Deb make the case for why you should welcome her with open arms."

Bonwit held his objection as he nodded for her to speak.

"Sir, let me say it's an honor to meet you and give you the rundown for why I'm the only choice for XO that makes sense," Deb began as he smiled at her opening statement.

She's bold, I'll give her that…but let's see what else she has, he thought to himself.

"I know division XOs are typically infantry officers," she continued. "However, logistics wins wars, and right now, as the most experienced logistician in the Corps, I can bluntly tell you after reviewing your logistical situation and challenges, sir, your division's jacked up. But this is something I'm uniquely capable of fixing without missing a beat. I can take this burden off your shoulders while making sure the beans and bullets continue to flow so you can focus your efforts and the division's on killing ChiComs. I may be going out on a limb here, but let's assume I'm chosen for XO. What questions can I answer before I start?"

General Gilbert was smiling from ear to ear by the time she finished. "I told you, Mike, she's sharp. You won't find better, either. I'm offering you my all-star and not out of the goodness of my heart, Mike. I'm doing so because the coming mission I have in mind is going to take someone with her unique skill set to make it work. Given the kinds of ship losses the Navy sustained during the opening days of the campaign amongst the LHAs, LHDs, and LPDs, the sealift capacity available to us has shrunk dramatically.

"While I'm not privy to whatever's preparing to kick off up north, what I can say is the sealift capacity we thought would be available to us in the coming weeks has been halved. We're losing a good chunk of surface fleet for whatever's happening up north," explained General Gilbert. "So what do you say, Mike? Have we filled your XO position?"

Bonwit turned to Savusa, who just shrugged.

Good, if he doesn't see a problem, neither do I.

Smiling, Bonwit happily said, "Welcome to 5th Marine Division, Brigadier General Soumoy. I suppose you already have a heads-up on what our next mission is going to be?"

Gilbert responded before she could. "Mike, there wouldn't be a mission without the magic Deb's been able to pull off for me. Honestly, she's got to be the best logistician I've seen, and we're going to need her skills if we're going to liberate this island. As to your mission, I think it's time we open a new front—one I doubt the PLA has prepared for."

"A new front?" Bonwit asked skeptically.

"Mike, I'm tasking 5th MarDiv with assaulting the northwest side of Taiwan. Now that the Navy has cleared the Straits, it's time we give the ChiComs a swift kick in the ass and end this. God only knows what else is happening up north, but our ability to draw resources and manpower from home is likely to become very limited in the coming weeks and months. Our window for swift victory is closing. End this, Mike, and let's get it done."

Bonwit smiled excitedly at the idea of rounding the island to land behind the enemy force. He'd briefly mentioned the idea in passing to General Gilbert shortly after they'd started to get bogged down in the center spine of the country. He'd figured 6th MarDiv would likely get the nod. They hadn't been bloodied up yet, so their equipment loss was minimal and their manning near peak numbers.

"Sir, they don't call us Kings of the Pacific for nothing," boomed the deep voice of Sergeant Major Savusa.

Then Colonel Kerns, who'd stayed silent during the meeting, chimed in. "General, given the vaunted reputation of our beloved division commander, my Marines began calling ourselves the Bonwit Berserkers shortly after we came ashore. He's the only two-star general they've seen or heard of who stood on the battle line slinging lead with a platoon of Marines against a swift PLA counterattack that had caught us off guard.

"General Bonwit here"—Kerns held his hand out in Bonwit's direction—"fought like a Norse warrior of medieval times. While he may not have mentioned it in any official after-action reports, I'm sure Sergeant Major Savusa would confirm the general led a charge against the enemy in what many Marines said felt like a berserkergang—hence their nickname for the division."

"Oh really, Mike? Sounds like you've been omitting some pretty heroic acts from the reports you've been sending. Perhaps the sergeant major can make a few amendments to those reports. You know, ensure they accurately portray what really happened during those first thirty-six hours of the invasion," said General Gilbert with a slight look of surprise at the revelation.

"Come to think of it, General, there do seem to be a few details a senior noncommissioned officer should probably add," Savusa chimed in with a grin.

Bonwit held his hands up in mock surrender as his cheeks reddened. "How about we focus on this new mission and less on me? XO, how soon can you get here?"

A few laughs were heard before Soumoy replied, "I'll be on the next bird out. I'll see you in Toucheng when you get there, sir."

As the screen went black, Savusa walked up to him with a smile. "What are you grinning at, Sergeant Major?"

"That you hadn't heard about Kerns's Marines renaming the division Bonwit's Berserkers and that of all people our new XO is going to be Brigadier General Soumoy. While I've never met her before, I have heard of her boss. They call her Escalation of Force, or EF for short."

Raising his eyebrows, Bonwit asked, "Why?"

"When I got injured as a platoon sergeant in Afghanistan, I was sent to Camp Del Mar on a B billet with the 1st Light Armored Reconnaissance Battalion," Savusa explained as the trio exited the conference room, making their way towards the building's exit. "She was the S4 for the 11th Marine Expeditionary Unit at the time. She was a firecracker and sharp as hell even back then. Well, you know how it goes sometimes with some officers when it comes to our Marine sisters. The MEU's S1 had apparently been giving her static and causing some friction for her. One day she finally got tired of it, so during an MEU staff meeting, she challenged him to the mats. Wanted a full-on Friday Fight Night at the Fight House to settle things once and for all between them."

"Whoa, Sergeant Major. You're saying she threw down the gauntlet just like that? Challenged him in public for all to see?" Kerns asked incredulously.

"That's affirmative, sir. In front of the entire MEU chain of command, she threw down the gauntlet. Naturally the shamurais of the E4 mafia had spread the news around Pendleton to units near and far, leaving the S1 with two choices—show up or shut up."

"No freaking way. How the hell did I not hear about this?" Bonwit said with surprise in his voice.

"Yeeesss way. The E4 mafiosos even put it up on the MEU Facebook page. They made fliers for it and hung them all over the main side of Camp Pendleton. It was escalated so fast the S1 didn't have a choice unless he wanted to look the fool."

"Did you go?" Bonwit asked, now genuinely engrossed in the story.

"Did I go? Does a bear crap in the woods? Of course I went! I've never seen so many officers in one place in my twenty-seven years in the Corps. I think the only regret the shamurais had about using the enlisted club was that they should have charged an entry fee based on rank."

They all laughed as Savusa continued the story. "Seeing how dueling with a pistol was made illegal for some reason, the event was sold as an exhibition demonstrating the gender-neutral training of the Marine Corps Martial Arts Program. We all knew that was a load of crap and so did the CG, but he let it slide."

Bonwit snickered, shaking his head as Savusa continued.

"That Friday night, the house was packed to the gills. Standing room only with peanuts, popcorn, and beers."

"Ah, now I know you're full of it, Sergeant Major!" Kerns laughed as he mumbled something about peanuts and beer at the enlisted club.

"Sir, this is an enlisted club, so yes, peanuts, popcorn, and beer. We're not sophisticated or highly educated folks such as yourselves. We're barely literate rednecks from the wrong side of town. I mean, we use our thumbprints for signatures, sir."

Now Bonwit and Kerns were truly laughing their guts out as the giant Samoan continued his story in the colorful way he often told them.

"Hand to God, Colonel, General," Savusa said, touching his chest. "As I was saying, the house was packed and that cocky little prick of an S1 was looking ready to put her in her place. He had his little band of POGs hyping him up and stroking his ego as we all waited for Soumoy to show up. Then like the parting of the Red Sea, Moses raised his staff. Lieutenant Colonel Soumoy entered the building and started walking towards the mat. The whole room went wild at that point, and while I'm sure no one was placing bets on the match, I can neither confirm nor deny that I walked out of that e-club with a grand more than I came in with."

Bonwit tried to hold back the laughter in his voice as they walked out of the building towards the vehicles. "Sergeant Major, I think

131

you're adding to the story, or as us sophisticated folk like to call it—embellishing it."

"Sir, may God strike me down if I'm lying," Savusa said as he made the sign of the cross. "So there we were. The referee walks out on the mat. He's some kind of martial arts wunderkind—a corporal with a super-duper black belt, I heard it called. So he calls them both front and center and explains the rules. They were about the same height, but admin being admin, the S1 was about forty pounds heavier—about what you'd expect for a POG or a REMF. But the whole time Wunderkind is explaining the rules, Soumoy is just glaring at him. I wouldn't call it hate in her eyes. It was certainly that look your gal gives you in the morning when you forgot to put the toilet seat down and she stumbled in there to tinkle and sorta washed her tush instead—that kind of look." The story paused a moment as Savusa spat a glob of chewing tobacco to the ground.

"Once the two of them agree to the rules, the wunderkind reffing the match blows his whistle, and just as Soumoy extends her hand to shake, that POG coldcocks her in the face," regaled Savusa as he became more animated retelling the story. "You should have heard the crowd the moment that S1 did that. At first it was gasps of shock, then came the jeers and cheers as her head snapped back, specks of blood from her nose arcing through the air."

"Fair play, there's no rank or gender on the mats," commented Kerns.

"That's true. The mats recognize no rank or gender once you step upon that hallowed ground," Bonwit reiterated as he nodded in agreement.

"As I was saying," Savusa continued, "as Soumoy staggers back from the initial punch, the POG goes in for the kill. The dude shoves her backwards, hoping she might fall to the deck and he could move for the mount position to pound some more on her face. But somehow in the midst of his shove, she manages to get ahold of the back of his collar while underhooking his leg. As they both hit the deck, she moved with lightning speed and agility, and she twisted around to get on his back. And before we knew it, she had him in a full rear naked choke."

Bonwit and Kerns stopped midstride like they hadn't quite heard that right. It took Savusa a couple more steps before he realized they had stopped walking. He had a smile on his face when he turned around.

"I see I have your attention now, don't I?" He spat another glob of dip to the deck before continuing the story. "As I was saying, Soumoy had that choke in so tight that it damn near ripped the POG's head off. I mean, this dude lost all control of his bodily functions at this point...and I mean all...control, gentlemen."

Suddenly Kerns snapped his fingers. "Ah hah, let me guess. That S1 was Lieutenant Colonel Tapinski, right?"

Savusa laughed, nodding slowly.

"Damn, I'd never heard how he'd gotten his nickname, Sergeant Major," said Kerns. "He always tried to play off 'Tapper' as if he'd won a fight. You just filled in a lot of blank spaces for me."

Kerns turned serious as he looked at Bonwit. "OK, boss, I don't think we're going to have a problem with a woman as the Division 2IC. Especially not that one. That's a Marine's Marine."

Bonwit seemed to breathe a little easier as he started to sing the words to an old Marine Corps cadence. "And that's good enough for me..."

Kerns laughed at him as they neared the vehicle. Bonwit opened the driver's door. "Gents, the playtime is over. Let's get some chow and figure out how we're going to make this mission happen. We got ourselves a beach to assault."

Chapter 14
The Turkey Shoot

Situation Room, White House
Washington, D.C.

"Thank you, Colonel, for the brief on this past week's major combat operations," said President Maria Delgado as the Marine colonel took his seat.

Maria then turned to look at Admiral Thiel. "Pete, if I'm not mistaken, I'm still owed an answer on how we're overcoming the ammo shortages. The Iowa plant was destroyed back in May. It obviously impacted our plans to the point of delaying the operation to begin the liberation of Taiwan by several months. What's the status of the situation now? What are we doing to further correct this problem and ensure our forces have what they need to win?"

Admiral Thiel nodded uncomfortably at the question as he opened the green notebook he always carried. Finding the page he was looking for, he looked up as he responded, "Thank you, Madam President, for the question. I apologize for not following up sooner. The truth is, we don't have a good answer or solution just yet. It's a complex problem we've been trying to tackle since the outset of the war. The JMC or Joint Munitions Command has been working with our defense contractors to increase the scalability of our existing plants dating back to the start of the Russo-Ukraine War at the outset of 2022.

"A recent success in this effort that I can report on as of just a few days ago is the Scranton Army Ammunition Plant. For the past five years, the plant has been undergoing a series of modernization efforts that has quadrupled its production capacity. In fact, next Tuesday I will be visiting the plant as it officially starts operating its new fifth and sixth production lines for the manufacturing of 155mm artillery shells."

The admiral paused before he continued, "While we are and have been making tremendous progress across the defense sector since the Iowa plant was destroyed, there's no getting around the impact of the loss of the facility. These upgrades to the Scranton plant and the start of a fifth and sixth production line will bring us back to the same level we had prior to the Iowa loss—meaning it's going to help stabilize our burn rates, so our shortages won't be as acute while other production lines in our existing facilities are hastily built. Depending on the operational demands at the front, there are days and sometimes even weeks where we're producing a surplus of what's needed. But we're still half a year or so away from being able to fully meet our needs while also developing a little surplus during any surge operations."

"Thank you, Pete, for elaborating on that for me. This is obviously a major issue that's continually brought up in the media and by the spouses of those serving abroad. I do have another question, this time for Admiral Graham." The President turned to look at the Chief of Naval Operations. "Admiral, a few weeks back, you spoke about surging additional antisubmarine warfare vessels into the Yellow Sea to address this newest underwater threat—Sea Dragon, I think you said it was called. Can you elaborate on how that's been going and perhaps give a status update on the fleet and how they're recovering after this latest attack by what I've been told is some sort of new Chinese UCAV?"

Admiral Graham looked like he had hoped this topic wouldn't be brought up as he prepared to respond. "Of course, Madam President. Per our last briefing about this topic a few weeks back, we plussed up Task Force Dupre with several Russian surface vessels specifically built for antisubmarine warfare. We also added an additional five of our Sea Hunter unmanned surface craft to further aid in this ASW effort.

"As of now, we have successfully destroyed seven of these Sea Dragons. In addition to their sinkings, the task force was further able to attrit the remaining Chinese Naval presence in the Yellow Sea to further prepare the way for the next stage of the operation. The task force was able to engage and sink three of their older *Ming*-class diesel-electric subs and two additional *Song*-class subs," the CNO explained before adding, "I can give you a status update on the task force and the recent vessels that were damaged during the attack the other day. But before I do that, I'd like to remind everyone that this naval force saw some incredibly heavy action during the past few weeks, which means they also took some hits along the way.

"During the past few weeks, TF Dupre engaged and sank nine Shanghai III gunboats, four Hainan-class corvettes, four Houxin-class missile boats, sixteen of their newer Type 22 Houbei-class fast-attack missile boats, twelve Type 056 Jiangdao-class corvettes, and three of their five remaining Type 054A Jiangkai II–class guided-missile frigates. That's forty-eight surface vessels sunk in addition to five submarines and seven of those Sea Dragons. I say all of this, Madam President, to highlight the incredible success of the task force's primary mission of clearing the Yellow Sea of surface and subsurface threats in preparation for the start of the third phase of OP Middle Kingdom—"

"Yes, and that is an incredible achievement, Admiral, and something we need to recognize and reward in terms of heroism and valor medals for our sailors and airman involved," Maria interrupted. "And while these achievements are remarkable, and commendable, we cannot disregard the impact the enemy was still able to have against our forces that were arguably under the air-defense protection of this same task force.

"If I'm not mistaken, the first two *Arleigh Burkes* to be equipped with the Navy's first deployable directed energy weapons ultimately had a negligible impact on the task force's capability to defend the Port of Dalian and our naval force being assembled to carry out the third phase of our final plan to end this war. I received the results of this most recent aerial attack by the PLA against the Dalian Peninsula and the port facilities, and it's grim. The fact that we've now lost four of the twelve of those *Algeciras*-class container ships the Koreans had recently converted to flat-deck vessels to support our helicopters means we just lost a big component we needed to accomplish the next phase. Of the eight converted container vessels remaining, five of them sustained light to moderate damage that will need to be repaired before the start of the operation. When you factor in the damage the Japanese *Hyūga*-class light aircraft carrier sustained during the first and second attacks on the port, I have to question if the next phase of the operation is still a viable option given the sea and airlift capabilities we must have for it to work. Am I wrong in my assessment that we may need to postpone our next move yet again, or am I missing something here?"

The admiral slowly nodded, not outright countering her claim but not ready to accept defeat. "Madam President, we have taken some hits, yes, that's undeniable. It appears Jade Dragon has developed yet one more type of new UCAV we hadn't encountered until now. Like past operations, we have fought against this machine. It continues to learn from its mistakes and our own. Each time it engages our forces, it applies the lessons learned from the previous engagements and employs whatever countermove it's already war-gamed and keeps hitting us. That said, I want to stress again, it is running out of resources and, more importantly, time.

"Our strategic bombing campaigns and the continued efforts from the Bumblehive and Cicada have reached a critical boiling point across much of the country. While Jade Dragon has continued to inflict damage against our forces, our own efforts against JD are starting to cause parts of the country to unravel. The food riots and civil unrest that had been isolated to a few cities and provinces are now spreading across more provinces and industrial centers. This is impacting their own ability to replace the losses in men, material, and munitions needed to keep the war going—"

"So what are you trying to say, Admiral?" Maria interrupted a second time as she felt he was evading her question.

The tension in the Situation Room was palpable. Admiral Graham addressed the President. "Madam President, there's a possibility we may not need to rely on the third phase of Operation Middle Kingdom to end the war. If things continue to decline internally and fall apart as they seem to be, we could see a revolt against Yao. That might give us a chance to back a rival of his in exchange for an end to hostilities."

Maria leaned back in her chair, the weight of the world on her shoulders. She pondered the admiral's words, which sounded more like a game of three-dimensional chess than a reassessment of their current plan. If they couldn't capture the port city of Tianjin and further isolate the PLA and the capital district, they needed to find an alternative strategy to end this war before it consumed them all—or Yao ceded control of China's strategic weapons to his AI, Jade Dragon.

Maria sighed audibly, her frustration evident. She turned to her Air and Space Commanders, her eyes narrowing. "I guess my next question is for the two of you. I'll start with you, Taz—Space Force, how are things progressing with this... tectonic strike—Project Dark Sky? Have your people figured out if this is even viable? The research I've seen, mostly from the 1980s through the early 2000s, doesn't bode well. I'm also concerned about secondary problems we may regret down the road."

General Jordan "Taz" Tazman, a seasoned veteran with a steely gaze, cleared his throat. "Ma'am, until we try it, we won't know if it will work or not. That said, I'm not one to gamble on something that has no chance of winning. We're working with our Australian partners to set up a test to see if this decades-old idea could work or if it should remain in the realm of science fiction."

A few chuckles rippled around the table, but Maria's expression remained serious. "A test? The Australians agreed to this? You did share what kind of test this would be, right?" The last thing she needed was a diplomatic disaster with a key ally.

Taz offered a slight shrug. "We spoke with our Australian counterparts about the kind of weapon we plan to test. We assured them it's nonnuclear, though it's likely to cause a seismic event. We explained that, given the Chinese ability to surveil our test ranges, we don't feel we can test it without them learning about it."

Maria shook her head, a diplomatic disturbance brewing in her mind. "When's the test?"

"The first test is next week. Depending on its results, we'll know if we should move forward with Project Dark Sky," Taz explained matter-of-factly.

Maria couldn't fathom how Taz could be so nonchalant about a weapon test she thought rivaled the Manhattan Project. Perhaps it was the stress of the war or a lack of confidence in its viability. She took a deep breath, locking eyes with the general. "OK, Taz. Run your test, and let's see if this multidecade science project will work. In fact, Blain— why don't you fly down with the general to witness the test? You can provide me with a firsthand account and let me know if we should still move forward with Dark Sky."

She paused, her gaze sweeping across the room. "This has been an informative brief. I want to thank each of you and your staff for your hard work and dedication during this war. We'll break for the moment. If something more needs to be addressed, please get in touch with Blain or the VP. That's all for now."

As Maria stood and prepared to leave the Situation Room, she recalled a statement by former Secretary of Defense Donald Rumsfeld during the lead-up to the Iraq War. His explanation of "unknown unknowns" highlighted the importance of recognizing the limitations of our knowledge and understanding, urging humility and caution in decision-making within uncertain and complex environments. The thought felt aptly applicable to the present situation as she contemplated being the first president—or the first person in history—to order the use of a tectonic attack. She supposed Taz was right; until they tested it, they wouldn't know if it was even a viable option.

The room emptied and the high-ranking officials filed out, each carrying the weight of their responsibilities. Maria took a moment to collect herself, her thoughts racing as she considered the potential consequences of using the tectonic weapon. Her mind drifted to her fellow citizens, the men and women in uniform on the front lines, and the innocent lives that could be affected by her decisions.

She turned to her trusted friend and National Security Advisor, Blain. "I need you to keep me informed of any new developments. This decision could have far-reaching consequences, and I must consider every possible outcome before we proceed."

Blain nodded solemnly, his gaze never leaving the President's face. "Yes, Madam President. I understand."

Maria gave him a reassuring smile, though her eyes betrayed her inner turmoil. She exited the Situation Room, mentally preparing herself for the difficult decisions that lay ahead. The fate of the world rested on her shoulders, and she would do everything in her power to prevent this Chinese AI from taking over. The fate of the free world would not end with them, of that she was certain.

As the heavy doors closed behind her, she whispered a silent prayer for wisdom and guidance in the face of the unprecedented challenges that loomed on the horizon. There was no turning back now.

Chapter 15
Sappers in the Night

1st Platoon, Bravo Company, 3rd Ranger Battalion
Fuxin Mongol Autonomous County

Sergeant First Class Amos Dekker dove for cover behind a fallen tree. Bullets slammed into the bark and zipped overhead with an angry buzz. He had originally hoped First and Second Platoons would complete their mission before sunrise, but things hadn't gone according to plan.

As Third Squad, led by L2, approached the train tunnel with a squad of sappers from the 82nd Airborne's 37th Engineer Battalion, they stumbled upon a contingent of the People's Armed Police. The Chinese force was guarding the train tunnels against the very attack the Rangers were attempting. In the ensuing firefight, the enemy managed to call for reinforcements.

By the time the Rangers neutralized the special police unit, one of Dekker's drone operators had spotted a convoy of enemy reinforcements en route. Dekker and Captain Loach reorganized their squads into Team One and Team Two. Dekker's Team One moved to ambush the incoming reinforcements, but they hadn't anticipated that the police would have armored personnel carriers and infantry fighting vehicles, nor that a second wave would arrive so soon.

The Rangers sprang their ambush as the enemy force began to advance up the ridgeline.

"RPG!" someone shouted.

A rocket-propelled grenade exploded nearby, shaking Dekker from cover. He scrambled to a new position, the chaos of battle swelling around him. Staff Sergeant Poppadu's urgent voice called for a shift in fire to the right flank. Dekker moved, half low crawl, half shuffle, as gunfire intensified.

"Where's my LMG? Get that machine gun to the right flank now!" Sergeant Wrigley yelled.

Thump, thump. Crump, crump.

The detonation of 40mm grenades signaled that the enemy force on the right flank was substantial. Dekker took a breath, knelt, and scanned for targets. He spotted at least fifty enemy soldiers charging up the ridge.

Dekker's heart skipped a beat as he saw two infantry fighting vehicles on the dirt road near the base of the ridge. He identified one with a 100mm cannon and another with a 30mm autocannon. The turrets shifted toward his men.

"Take 'em out with the Javelins!" Dekker shouted to Sergeant Landrew and Specialist Kanton.

Two antitank missiles streaked toward the IFVs, taking them out with resounding booms. Despite the temporary victory, the swarms of militiamen continued to charge up the ridge, closing the distance. The volume of fire directed at them continued to increase. Dekker returned fire, his rifle bucking against his shoulder as he picked off targets one by one, only to see another person take their place.

"Dekker, give me a sitrep. Is it as bad as it's sounding?" asked L2 while he reloaded magazines.

"Yeah, it's getting a little hairy. We popped a couple of IFVs, but it looks like the local People's Militia units are starting to arrive. We've got a sizable ground force steadily making their way up the ridge towards us," he explained.

There was a moment's pause before L2 replied, "Damn, that does sound grim. We're nearly done up here. I'm going to call for the choppers and get our rides inbound. You think it's possible you can break contact and conduct an orderly withdrawal to the rally point?"

Dekker flinched as a piece of bark chipped off the tree he was hiding behind and nicked his cheek. He peered around the trunk—the attackers continued to close the gap between them.

"Breaking contact is going to be a little tough, L2," Dekker replied. "They're crawling up our asses right now. The withering fire we're laying on them is the only thing slowing 'em down. I'd move your pair of MG 338s and grenadiers to our side of the ridge. We'll start lobbing grenades and poppin' smoke on our end. Then your guys can cover our withdrawal, and we'll meet you at the rally point. What do you think?"

"I like it, Dekker. Give me a few minutes, and I'll let you know when we're in position. L2 out."

The minutes ticked by before L2 sent the message—they were ready. Dekker grabbed for the first grenade he'd placed on the ground in front of him. Pulling the pin, he gave it a good throw towards the enemy. As he threw the grenade, the others around him started doing the same. The final grenade he chucked was the Willie Pete. He tossed this one as high into the air over the enemy as he could. When it blew, it rained white phosphorus down in a white cloud and obscured the enemy from seeing them.

The Rangers executed a fighting withdrawal, making their way to the top of the ridge. Enemy gunfire dwindled, then stopped. Dekker knew they were lucky to have faced an undertrained force rather than a seasoned PLA unit. The Rangers had sustained two killed in action and five wounded, but it could have been much worse.

As the V-280 Valor helicopters arrived to extract them, Dekker checked on his wounded men, reflecting on the enemy's decreasing quality of soldiers. He watched the first group of helicopters pick up Second Platoon on the other side of the tunnel, hoping for a break after months of nonstop missions.

When the charges inside the rail tunnels detonated, billowing dust and smoke, Dekker felt a sense of accomplishment. Cutting off this critical rail line could have a significant impact on the enemy's ability to support their forces in the north. He hoped that by continuing to disrupt their supply lines, they might force the enemy to surrender.

As Dekker climbed aboard the helicopter, he ensured all his men were accounted for. The V-280 Valor ascended, leaving the battle site behind and flying low above the treetops. The mission's success weighed against the lives lost and wounded, but such was the nature of war.

Leaning back in his seat, Dekker considered the challenges they had faced and the intensity of the operation. The Rangers' gritty determination had carried them through, but he knew the conflict was far from over.

For now, though, they could return to Anshan Air Base, regroup, and plan for the next mission. As the helicopter sped away from the scene of destruction, Dekker allowed himself a moment to close his eyes and reflect on the mission. With every operation, they moved closer to their ultimate goal: victory.

But the cost of that triumph was never far from Dekker's thoughts. The sacrifices made by his men weighed heavily on him, a constant reminder of the price paid in blood and lives. In this unforgiving conflict, the Rangers would need every ounce of their strength, resilience, and determination to succeed.

****

Alpha Company, 1st Battalion, 64th Armor Regiment
10 Kilometers South of Huludao, China

The fourteen tanks of Alpha Company had staged themselves to the rear of the American units along the somewhat changing line of control. Every few days or so the front lines might adjust a few kilometers forward or backward, depending on the strength of the enemy attack and how fast American armor could respond in plugging the gap. While the company was held in reserve, keeping a safe distance from the front, the three tank platoons had spread themselves out so they wouldn't be easily targeted by PLA artillery.

Shortly after Sergeant First Class Rico Ramos and his crew found a nice place to hunker down in with their tank, Sergeant Ramos made the decision to let his crew lounge outside their Abrams battle tank so they could stretch their legs. He wasn't sure how long they might hang out to the rear of the front, but one thing he knew for certain was that once they were ordered forward, there would be no further exiting the tank unless absolutely necessary. The likelihood of getting hurt by shrapnel or a sniper's bullet was too high to risk milling about outside their armored chariot.

Ramos listened to Specialist Blum regale them with his story of how he thought he had found *the one* while on a four-day pass to South Korea at a place called the Crown Club just outside Camp Humphrey—that was, until he found out the girl of his dreams was the eighteen-year-old daughter of the base command sergeant major. They all laughed at his luck for trying to eat from the tree of the forbidden fruit. As their conversations turned from exchanging funny stories and telling jokes to sharing ideas of what they wanted to do when the war was over, Ramos was sure of one thing—he had to do whatever was necessary to ensure his crew made it home.

In between conversations and jokes, the constant rumble of gunfire and artillery explosions in the distance ebbed and flowed in intensity. Then as the sun approached its zenith, the rumblings of war intensified, hinting at the possibility that the PLA were preparing to make a push down the Jingha Expressway toward Luanni Village again. The small town had been fought over for weeks. If it hadn't been for the capture of the Xingcheng Air Base some ten kilometers to the north, it probably wouldn't have been all that important to hold, but now it was.

"Hey, Ramos, you really think the new LT's got our backs?" Specialist Lopez asked, an uneasy expression on his face.

"Don't worry about the lieutenant, Lopez," Ramos responded. "He's got a good head on his shoulders, and he's done a good job of learning how to fight a tank platoon. He'll keep us alive."

Ramos had felt the tension building among his crew since the arrival of the new lieutenant. They weren't sure if it was bad luck or just bad timing, but since the start of the war, they had lost three lieutenants to enemy action. It had gotten so bad that no one would want to crew a tank with any new platoon leader assigned to their platoon. The last three crews had all died. Ramos tried to do his best to keep his crew calm and focused. He knew that in a battle like the ones they had been fighting, calm, steady nerves could make the difference between life and death.

After that last major tank fight they'd fought in with the 101st Screaming Eagles to the north of them, Ramos was just glad to have been pulled further south. The terrain down here was more conducive to tank warfare. It had large stretches of territory with flat open plains and wide spaces between villages and towns. This was perfect terrain for the kind of maneuver warfare the 3rd ID was known for executing.

As the hours passed and the sun headed towards the horizon, the noise of the battle a few kilometers down the road continued to grow. It was sounding more and more likely that the PLA had launched a new offensive.

Ramos started to pull away from the conversations as he listened to the increasingly urgent calls for artillery and air support. As he heard more and more of the calls for support being denied, a sense of dread that something bad was about to happen set in. He was going to need to get his tank and crew ready to go, and soon.

Suddenly, jet engines roared overhead, low and fast, buzzing over top of their tank. Ramos and his crew couldn't tell if it was a friendly or hostile aircraft. All they knew was they had to scramble to their feet and get in the tank.

Specialist Blum got the engine revved up and ready to move, and Sergeant Harris quickly set up on the gunner's scope, looking to see if the PLA had somehow broken through part of their lines.

"All right, everyone!" Ramos shouted, his voice filled with determination. "It's time to saddle up and show these bastards what we're made of! We've got a job to do, and we aren't taking any prisoners. Let's roll!"

"Hooah!" the tankers shouted in unison, their adrenaline pumping as Specialist Blum got their armored chariot on the move.

Inside the tank, Ramos and his gunner, Sergeant Harris, worked together with a sense of urgency that seemed to take over in situations of imminent danger. Their M1 Abrams battle tank and the M5 Ripsaw Ramos still managed were now on the move and looking for a fight.

As they advanced towards the line of contact, the Ripsaw's powerful radar and targeting system picked up enemy ZTZ99 main battle tanks and ZBD-04 infantry fighting vehicles. Ramos's hands gripped the controls tightly as he operated the Ripsaw like an experienced pro.

"Ramos, you've got this," Harris said, encouraging his friend. "Let's kick some ass and add a few more kill rings to our barrel, shall we?"

As the American tanks came into view of the enemy vehicles, they started unleashing a barrage of tank fire on the advancing ChiCom armored vehicles. Shot after shot was fired into the charging horde. The Americans were certainly slowing the pace of the PLA advance, and they continued to charge forward without regard for the costs; they just kept coming forward with more tanks and infantry fighting vehicles.

Ramos and Harris exchanged glances. This was the kind of fight they had trained for and read about in novels—but this wasn't a story they were reading. It was *real*. A determination to succeed and protect his fellow soldiers fueled Ramos's actions as they continued to engage the enemy.

As the battle raged on, the M5 Ripsaw continued to prove it was a game-changing asset for the platoon. Its advanced technology and firepower allowed them to strike at the enemy with precision and force, giving them an edge in this kind of fight. Ramos continued to fight the Ripsaw while Harris fought the tank. The two of them tore through enemy vehicles with their 120mm cannon and the 30mm autocannon.

The tenacity and ferocity of their counterattack were brutal and relentless as they refused to let the PLA break through their defenses.

"Good shot, Ramos!" Harris shouted as another enemy tank went up in flames. "We'll have these bastards on the run in no time!"

Through the chaos of the battle, Ramos and his crew fought with everything they had, their fear and uncertainty replaced by an unwavering resolve to defeat the enemy. As the sun began to set, their company and the other quick reaction force units had managed to hold the line, inflicting heavy losses on the PLA forces.

As darkness enveloped the battlefield, Ramos and his crew strained their eyes to make out the silhouettes of enemy and friendly vehicles against the backdrop of fire and smoke. The Jingha Expressway had become a crucible of death and destruction, where men and machines fought with every ounce of strength and cunning they possessed. When Ramos surveyed the damage before they moved forward, he had to admit the carnage he saw was just as bad as the previous battle they had fought earlier with the Airborne as they held a choke point position in the Chaoyang area.

"Hey, Rico, 3rd BSB is moving up to our line," said Sergeant Harris, holding the radio hand receiver down to his shoulder. "They want to know if we want to top off our tanks and take on any ammo now that there's a lull in the battle."

"Well, I'll be damned. I guess the ready-to-roll guys from Brigade Support Battalion grew some balls and decided to venture toward the front to give us resupply instead of making disengage and drive to the rear to hunt them down," Ramos retorted jokingly as he made fun of the fuel and ammo guys.

Harris was still waiting with the radio receiver. Ramos cleared his throat, turning more serious. "Tell them yeah, we'll top off our tanks. Dwayne, what's our shell count?" he asked. "How much we need?"

Specialist Dwayne Lopez tapped the locker door to the ammo box as he gave it a quick look. "We're down to eighteen shells out of forty-two," he replied.

"Whoa there, Dwayne. You gotta do a better job of letting us know when we drop below fifty percent on ammo," chided Harris. "The last thing we want is to run dry on shells in the middle of a fight. If that happens, we're as good as dead."

146

OK. We just finished a fight. I'm sure Dwayne was going to do a quick inventory when the BSB guys called. Let's just focus on reloading the tank, filling the gas, and being ready for whatever the colonel wants us to do next.

Harris nodded and relayed the message Ramos had given him.

Then Lopez said, "Rico, I heard Steve got selected for O-6. You think he'll take over as the new brigade commander?"

Ramos canted his head to the side as he gave Lopez the stink eye. "I'm going to tell you something, Dwayne, and I hope you listen and take it to heart. Inside the tank, it's cool to use first names. We're kind of like a family here. When talking about others outside the tank, especially senior officers, call them by their rank and last name. You don't want to have a Freudian slip and ruin your day because you got too chummy with the battalion commander and accidentally called him by his first name. It's Lieutenant Colonel Thomas, not 'Steve.' Got it?"

Lopez's cheeks flushed and Harris shook his head disapprovingly. "Sorry about that, Rico," Lopez responded. "You're right. No reason to put my foot in my mouth when I can avoid it."

"Hey, here comes our ammo and fuel," Harris announced as he started to climb out of the tank.

For the next fifteen minutes or so, they gassed up the tank and helped Dwayne refill the magazine. They topped off their water cans and grabbed a few extra MREs in case they might be out for a few days blowing stuff up. As they finished restocking Black Rider, their tank, Ramos made sure they also topped off his Ripsaw before they left. The little bugger had proven to be an indispensable asset for the platoon, and he wanted to make sure it could still be the helper they needed it to be.

Ramos surveyed the carnage to their front while the Ripsaw was being restocked with ammo. The skies above them were still a churning maelstrom of aerial combat. F-16 Vipers and J-10 Firebirds were locked in a deadly ballet of high-speed death. Each aerial engagement resulted in a crescendo of spiraling smoke trails and exploding aircraft as both sides fought to maintain air superiority over the battlefield. Occasionally, one of the ChiComs' newest Dark Dragon aircraft would swoop down out of nowhere to plaster some of their tanks in a single pass before accelerating back into the netherworld it had emerged from. Ramos had come to hate those dreaded drones. They were more advanced than anything he'd seen the allies field to this point. If there was one saving

147

grace when it came to these vaunted fighter drone aircraft, it was their scarcity. He wasn't sure why the Chinese weren't producing more of them, but he was glad for small miracles.

From time to time, they'd spot one of the Army's newest helicopters, the Bell 360 Invictus, as it dashed across the battlefield. The lightning speed and maneuverability of the attack reconnaissance helicopter helped to fill a void in what the Apaches weren't able to do, especially considering the number of losses the Army's aviation units had suffered. Earlier in the battle, Ramos had managed to catch a glimpse of an Invictus in a high-speed dash across the front lines as it fired on multiple tanks or IFVs with its eight AGM-179 joint air-to-ground missiles before darting back to friendly lines.

Ramos loved this new attack helicopter and its newer missiles. He'd even heard from their Textron rep that the Ripsaws would soon be equipped to carry two of the JAGMs. It would extend their maximum range with the Javelins from four kilometers to eight, doubling their reach.

Then the radio crackled and came to life as the voice of their battalion commander addressed them. "All Desert Rogue elements, this is Rogue Actual. Advance to contact and push through enemy resistance until you have reached Phase Line Foxtrot. DR Actual, out."

Ramos turned to his guys. "Well, you heard the man. It's time to roll and take the fight to the enemy. Let's do this thing."

Specialist Blum got Black Rider back on the move, and Ramos's pulse raced as his Abrams moved through the nightmarish terrain of destroyed and burning vehicles. Switching over to the controls for the Ripsaw, Ramos guided the unmanned ground autonomous vehicle around some of the wreckage. He sped ahead of the tanks, utilizing the M5 in more of a reconnaissance role for the moment. Its surveillance and reconnaissance sensors had proven invaluable in the heat of battle. It had provided critical intelligence and support across the platoons that had helped Alpha Company hold their ground and push back against this latest attempt to break through their lines.

As Ramos's platoon pushed forward down the highway of death, the two opposing forces clashed. The ground trembled beneath the relentless onslaught of armored vehicles as each side vied for dominance. Intermixed with the Abrams was their mechanized infantry support in the M2 Bradleys and Strykers, which focused their exchange of fire on

Chinese APCs and IFVs, allowing the tanks to concentrate their attention and ammo on the heavier armored tanks. As the darkness enveloped the battlefield, flashes of flame from the barrels of tank cannons and infantry vehicles lit up the night, casting eerie shadows and ominous silhouettes. Red and green tracers zipped between the lines. Periodically, the night would become day as 155mm illumination rounds floated over the battlefield until they descended to the chaos below.

In a fleeting moment of clarity amidst the chaos, Ramos felt a profound sense of unity with his fellow soldiers. Each of them was fighting not only for their own lives but for the survival of every man and woman beside them. The knowledge that they were in this together, their fates inexorably intertwined, fueled his determination to overcome the enemy.

An enemy infantry fighting vehicle broke through the American lines, its sights set on Ramos's Ripsaw. His heart caught in his throat as he realized the danger, but before he could react, a nearby Bradley swung its turret and fired its 25mm Bushmaster chain gun. The ChiCom vehicle vanished in a plume of fire and smoke, its threat neutralized by the swift action of the Bradley's crew.

Ramos placed the Ripsaw in independent surveillance mode so he could peer through the commander's independent thermal viewer and assist Harris in searching for targets. In the chaos of a night fight, Ramos knew his gunner was going to need his help in finding targets before the targets found them. In a running battle like this, communication was key to their survival and success. He tried his best to maintain a steady flow of information with his crew and their platoon leader, First Lieutenant Dan Morse.

"BR Two, this is BR One. We've got enemy IFVs approaching from the east," Lieutenant Morse's voice crackled over the radio.

"Copy that, BR One," replied Ramos, sweat beading on his brow. "Harris, keep an eye out for those IFVs. Lopez, have a HEAT round ready."

"Roger that, Sarge," Harris acknowledged. His fingers gripped the gunner's control handles as he started searching for the IFVs.

"You got it, Sarge!" Lopez shouted. He pulled the sabot round out of the breach and swapped it out with a HEAT round, his muscles straining under the weight.

149

The Abrams lurched suddenly as Specialist Andy Blum, their driver, swerved to avoid a burning wreck he hadn't seen as he moved around another destroyed vehicle. "Sorry, guys," Blum called out, his voice strained but focused. "Didn't see that one until the last second."

"Just keep us moving, Blum," Ramos ordered, his gaze fixed on the terrain in front of them. "We need to stay mobile and unpredictable."

"IFV, seven hundred meters. HEAT," Harris called out, having spotted the vehicle he'd been looking for.

"HEAT up!" Lopez called out, confirming the load in the breach.

"Firing!"

BOOM.

The cannon recoiled inside the turret, the aft cap dropping to the floor as a small puff of burnt propellent wafted into the cabin.

A moment later, the Ripsaw transmitted new intel, revealing the location of an enemy tank its scout drone had found. "Ripsaw's got a bead on a hostile tank to the south! Six hundred meters! Load sabot!" Ramos called out.

"Got it. IFV six hundred meters. Load sabot!" Harris confirmed.

"Sabot up!" the loader shouted as he waited for the recoil of the gun.

"Firing!"

BOOM.

"Damn it! We missed."

"BR Two, this is BR One," Lieutenant Morse chimed in. "Get another round on that tank and keep pushing forward. We've got your back."

"Sabot up!" Lopez shouted.

Harris's voice was taut with anticipation as he replied, "Target reacquired."

"Fire!" Ramos barked.

The tank rocked violently as the main gun discharged, the sabot round streaking through the night before plowing into the enemy tank with lethal precision. The vehicle erupted in a brilliant fireball, its metal carcass joining the countless others littering the battlefield.

"Good shot, Harris!" Ramos commended, his heart pounding in his chest. "Forget about the miss and keep up the good work. We'll see this through."

As the battle raged into the night, the American forces fought with a ferocity and tenacity that belied their exhaustion. By the early hours of the following morning, ninety-six of the one hundred and forty-eight tanks and IFVs that had forded the Yantai River and stormed down the Jingha Expressway were nothing more than burning wrecks. What was left of the 11th Heavy Combined Arms Brigade and the 60th Mechanized Infantry Brigade were forced into withdrawing across the Yantai River to lick their wounds. If Ramos had his way, they would have continued to chase the enemy across the river and push them as far as they could. For now, they'd hold the line and await further orders.

Chapter 16
Celestial Hammers

RAAF Woomera Range Complex
South Australia

Standing in front of the newly arrived military members as they looked on in curiosity, Barbara Young gave a warm, disarming smile as she began to explain why they were here and what was about to happen.

"Good morning, everyone, and welcome to Australia. My name is Barbara Young, but you can call me Barb for short. I'm sure many of you are wondering what this is all about and why you are being asked to sign a nondisclosure agreement before we go any further," Barb explained as folders were handed to the newly arrived military members. "Once everyone has signed the documents, I will explain why you have been chosen to participate in this program, and more importantly, what this program is and how it's going to play a pivotal role in winning this war. I will give you a few minutes to read the NDA if you'd like. But we all know the drill. You were never here, and you saw and heard nothing."

Her comment elicited a few laughs as people reached for their pens. As she was about to speak, she saw a person who looked like he had a question and motioned with a nod of her head for him to speak. "Is this last part serious, Barb?"

"Which part is that?"

"Ah, the last part. The one that says if we're found to have negligently disclosed any level of details about this program, we will be prosecuted and sentenced to life without parole. If we're in the process of actively leaking information about the program, then lethal force has been authorized to stop us from leaking further information," the Space Force pilot read aloud. "I've signed a few NDAs in my career, but this seems a bit extreme."

Barb tilted her head to the side as she replied, "Perhaps it is. But we are at war. A war of survival against a machine that continues to learn from its failures and has the entire industrial capacity of the world's second-largest economy at its disposal. Maybe it's just me, but I suggest signing the document and letting us move on with discussing why you all have been selected to be a part of this program."

A few of the officers grunted at her blunt response before nodding in agreement. Once the documents were signed and collected, the lights in the room dimmed and the meeting began.

Barbara stood at the head of the conference room, her heart pounding with anticipation. She knew the importance of the secret she was about to share with the group of military officers before her. For years, she had poured her intellect and passion into the aerospace and space industries. Now, she was the program director for a project that would change everything.

Clearing her throat, she smiled at her new colleagues. "I'm proud to be the program director for what you're about to become a part of. I hold graduate degrees in aerospace and mechanical engineering and materials science and engineering, and I've had the privilege of working with both SpaceX and Northrop Grumman."

The officers exchanged curious glances, their interest piqued. Barbara could feel the weight of their attention as she continued. "Now that you know a little about me, it's time to reveal the classified orbital strike program you've just joined: Project Celestial Hammer."

Murmurs spread through the room at the mention of "orbital strike," and Barbara noted the surprise and disbelief on some faces. She pressed on, her voice steady and confident. "Celestial Hammer is the latest iteration of the Kinetic Orbital Strike program. Its roots date back to the late 1960s with a project called Smart Rocks."

Barbara dove into the program's storied history, her words painting a picture of ingenuity and ambition. She spoke of the 1980s, when the Strategic Defense Initiative had breathed new life into the project, renaming it Brilliant Pebbles, and later, Project Thor. Though it seemed the program had faded away with the end of the Cold War, it had been revived by the Air Force in the early 2000s as the Hypervelocity Rod Bundles, aimed at developing a nonnuclear bunker-busting weapon.

"The Air Force canceled the program in 2005," Barbara continued, "but it wasn't the end. In 2006, Congress resurrected the project and placed it under the control of DARPA, where it merged with the Falcon Project as part of the Prompt Global Strike program."

Her voice filled with pride, Barbara delivered the final piece of the puzzle. "In 2022, the program was transferred to Space Command and rechristened Celestial Hammer. It's now our responsibility to carry it forward, harnessing cutting-edge technology to create a revolutionary weapon that will change the face of warfare."

As the full impact of her words settled in, Barbara looked into the eyes of the military officers, each now part of the Celestial Hammer legacy. Together, they would defeat Jade Dragon and finally put an end to this bloody war before it killed them all.

****

Colonel Ian "Racer" Ryan stared at the image of the rod his Banshee was supposed to carry. Twenty feet long and a foot in diameter, it weighed in at an improbable two thousand pounds. The numbers didn't add up for a tungsten rod of that size. As Martin Lacey, the engineer from TRW Inc., pulled up the specs, Ian's eyes widened in disbelief. They called them the Celestial Hammers.

Tungsten had always been the go-to material for withstanding the intense heat of reentry. As Ian studied the rod's image, Martin's voice cut through his thoughts. "The Celestial Hammers are possible thanks to breakthroughs in material science. We've come a long way in kinetic bombardment technology since the '80s, primarily due to CarboNanoTech or CNT. They're a composite of graphene and carbon nanotubes, providing unparalleled strength-to-weight ratios. CNT lets us build smaller, lighter, and more agile projectiles that can withstand the extreme heat and stress of reentry."

Ian listened, his concern growing. If Jade Dragon, the Chinese AI responsible for creating a cutting-edge autonomous fighter aircraft, could develop something similar, the allies' supremacy in the skies would be challenged.

As Martin finished his explanation, Ian raised his hand. "Excuse me, Barb or Martin, I have a question."

Barb placed a hand on Martin's arm, signaling that she would handle it, and motioned for Ian to continue.

"I have to say, this program sounds incredible. I wasn't aware this kind of technical challenge had been solved. My question is, how exactly are we going to use these weapons to destroy the bunker housing Jade Dragon?"

"Colonel Ryan, what makes you believe this weapon is targeting the PLA's AI bunker and not some other objective?" Barb shot back.

Ian felt his cheeks redden. "It's an educated guess. Orbital strike programs have historically functioned as nonnuclear bunker busters. To reach bunkers housing Iran's nuclear program, you'd either need nuclear-tipped deep penetrators or an orbital kinetic weapon. But my spacecraft doesn't seem like the right delivery system for this kind of weapon. It should be deployed via satellite from a much higher altitude."

Barb's eyes twinkled with intrigue. "Interesting assessment, Colonel. You're partly right and partly wrong. Have you heard of tectonic warfare?"

Ian's stomach churned, the knot inside tightening.

What kind of weapon are we dealing with here? he wondered.

"Uh, honestly, I can't say that I have. Are you talking about being able to somehow cause earthquakes or something like that?"

The room tensed up as Ian put to words what most of them had just thought. "That's a good assessment, Colonel," Barb replied, smiling. "Once again, you are partly right, and partly wrong. Let me explain something to help everyone understand what it is we're going to do and why it has to be done this way in order for it to work.

"Let's begin with tectonic warfare. It's the strategic use of geological phenomena, such as earthquakes or volcanic eruptions, to cause destruction or disruption. The Celestial Hammers, in this case, are going to be used to hit a specific target Project Cicada has identified that should trigger a seismic event parallel to the Joint Battle Command Center, which we have recently identified as the location where the PLA are housing Jade Dragon.

"The Joint Battle Command Center is a nuclear-hardened facility buried some two thousand feet beneath a mountain in the western district of Beijing. A direct attack against the facility, even an orbital strike from the Hammers or a nuclear-tipped penetrator, will have little chance of success given the depths of the facility and the design and shape of the bunker itself. In order for us to have a chance at imploding the bunker via orbital strikes, we first have to 'crack the egg.'

"This particular bunker was constructed using an oval egg design. The design allows it to absorb tremendous impacts from above as it transfers the kinetic energy down and around the outer shell. However, if the outer hull is somehow cracked, it compromises the entire structural integrity of the facility," Barb explained.

Ian's mind raced as he took in the information, the gravity of the situation settling in as he realized this could actually end the war. But if *they* could come up with this kind of idea, what if *Jade Dragon* got its hands on this same kind of technology? The consequences could be catastrophic.

Barb looked around the room, her gaze resting on each person before she spoke. "Your spacecraft, Colonel Ryan, will deliver a Celestial Hammer to the edge of the atmosphere, where it will release the rods. From there, they'll accelerate toward their targets, guided by an onboard propulsion system. Your Banshee will serve as a stealthy and agile delivery platform, allowing us to strike quickly and without warning. With a little bit of luck, Colonel, we are going to crack the egg. Once that's achieved, we have a satellite that will move into place and finish the job.

"The reason why everyone has been brought to the middle of nowhere in Australia is that we need to test a couple of theories first with these Celestial Hammers before we unveil these weapons against Jade Dragon. Once revealed, the element of surprise will be gone and so will the tactical and strategic advantage these weapons give us. We're going to have one shot at taking Jade Dragon out. It has to count."

Ian sat in stunned silence like the others for a moment as they all considered the implications of this new information. While the potential of the Celestial Hammers was awe-inspiring, the stakes were high. The potential to end the war could literally depend on the actions of those sitting around him. The gravity of it all felt like a weight about to crush Ian.

Then, within the weight of that moment, he smiled as he remembered a cartoon he used to watch as a kid.

Come on, Charlie Brown, don't screw it up now...the whole team's counting on you... Except in this case, the whole world was counting on him.

Chapter 17
You Lost, Marine

5th MarDiv
Toucheng Township, Northern Taiwan

Staff Sergeant Seth Michaels had come ashore in the predawn hours with a unit from the 6th Marine Division. Technically, he was a replacement for the 5th Marine Division. Perhaps it was his misplaced zeal to link up with his newly assigned unit. The first opportunity he'd seen to catch a ride ashore, he'd taken it. Now, as he stood a little further from the beach and the activity of thousands of Marines and thousands of tons of equipment constantly being rolled off and disembarked from the massive naval vessels, he was beginning to question the wisdom of trying to link up with the division reception center on his own.

Since leaving Okinawa, his mind had been spinning with thoughts of *What the hell am I doing here?* and *Why did I volunteer to come back to this?* There was so much going on all around him. Off in the distance he could hear the thunder of artillery fire, the sounds of helicopter blades, and the jet engines high above. Right now, he just felt lost, unsure of where to go next or what to even do.

Prior to being injured, he'd served with 2/8 Marines during the defense of Gitmo. That was where he'd taken a round to the lower back. He'd been lucky: the bullet had deflected off the plate from his vest and bored into his ass. He felt embarrassed a wound like that had kept him out of the fight as long as it had. That was probably why he'd volunteered as soon as he could to return to another unit. When he'd caught a new set of orders to one of the units fighting in Taiwan, he'd thought he'd be happy to get back into the action, but as he'd made the flight from Camp Pendleton to Okinawa, he'd had a long time to think about it, and now he wasn't so sure it had been a good thing to get his wish.

Trying to remember what the embarkation officer had told him about where to head to link up with the 5th Marine Division, he'd somehow gotten turned around. With so much activity and so many vehicles moving all around him, he felt like a lost recruit without a map or a compass and the DI was headed right for him. Sighing, he had been sure of one thing, that the ocean was behind him. But aside from the obvious, that failed to help his current predicament.

157

Shaking his head, Sergeant Michaels fell back on his years of experience as a Marine and did what grunts do when faced with an uncertain situation. He walked towards the largest, busiest main road he could find and then found a reasonably safe spot along the side of it, dropping his seabag and ruck and peeling off his body armor as he sat down.

Screw it. I'm freaking lost, I haven't slept for crap in the last thirty-odd hours. I'll figure things out after I catch a few z's. No sooner had he secured the sling of his rifle around himself and closed his eyes than he'd fallen into a deep sleep. Despite all the noise and the hustle and bustle around him, he was out cold until the moment he felt a stiff kick to his boot.

"You lost, Marine?" His ears registered the gruff-sounding voice. It sounded vaguely familar—then he practically launched himself to his feet as he stood at rigid parade rest. While he couldn't make out the man's face as the sun seemed to form a halo around his head, he knew exactly who was hovering right in front of him and knew he'd better answer his question.

"Yes, Sergeant Major. I am totally and completely lost!" he barked with conviction.

Michaels heard him grunt before his voice boomed, "Is that so? Answer me this, Sergeant. Where are you?"

"Sergeant Major, I'm somewhere in Taiwan!" he shouted back.

"Well, that's a start, then, isn't it, Devil Dog?"

"Yes, Sergeant Major!"

Sergeant Major Savusa bent slightly forward as his eyes bored into him. Then, for the first time in his life, Michaels saw the toughest, scariest man he'd ever known crack a smile.

"Huh. OK, you'll do. Let's grab your kit. We've got someone else to get unlost."

"Aye-aye, Sergeant Major." Michaels tried to grab his seabag, but Savusa hefted it with a single hand as if the thing was a pillow. He grabbed his rifle and heaved his ruck over one shoulder with a grunt and took off after Savusa, who was already widening the distance between them.

For every one step that giant Samoan took, he had to take three just to try to keep up. When they reached the pickup truck, they tossed his kit into the bed. Then, without another word, the truck took off inland.

Michaels had never seen so many Marines moving about in one place. Not even in Cuba—they were just everywhere. There were also what seemed like mountains of supplies, trucks everywhere and the sounds of Marine helos in the air. There was one thing that caused him to do a double take and that was the sight of an MP writing a ticket and handing it to the driver of an MTVR truck.

"Freaking Mud Puppies. You still can't escape garrison even in the middle of World War III," Savusa said with a smile as he turned off the main road and headed towards a small building marked GO/FO Transient.

"What are we doing here, Sergeant Major?" he finally asked, feeling out of place, knowing that GO meant General Officer and he was a lowly sergeant.

"Finding another lost Marine. Hang tight, I'll be right back."

Michaels watched as Savusa walked to the gate, showed his ID card and went inside. A few minutes later, he emerged with a tall blonde woman who was talking on what looked like some sort of sat phone. It kind of reminded him of those large brick-looking phones from movies made during the late 1980s and early 1990s.

While he couldn't hear what she was saying, he could tell she was mad. The moment he saw the star on her collar, he immediately wished he wasn't here. As she approached the truck, he saw Savusa in tow, carrying her bags. She waved Savusa on as she paused just inside the gate. Against his better judgment, he leaned forward to try and listen.

"No, you listen to me! I've got five tons each of 5.56, 7.62, and .45-caliber rounds sitting on your ship ready for offload. So I strongly suggest you have your guys get off their asses and get it done, or I'll be there to climb up *yours* and do it for you!"

She stabbed a button on the phone and made her way to the truck. Michaels didn't know why, but he scrambled out of the vehicle and opened the door for her. She climbed in, and as he got back inside the truck, he looked at Savusa, who gave a wry smile.

"Sergeant Michaels, I'd like to introduce you to Brigadier General Soumoy. She's the new assistant division commander, 5th Marine Division."

Suddenly Michaels felt trapped. Here he was a very junior Marine NCO in a truck with two of the most powerful people in the division. He had an urge to jump from the vehicle but chose to stick around a little longer.

"I'm very pleased to meet you, ma'am."

Somehow his greeting had caused Savusa and Soumoy to burst out laughing. Not sure if it was an inside joke or if he'd said something wrong. He just tried to make himself appear a little smaller if that was possible.

They drove in silence for a few minutes as he thought about who this general reminded him of. Then it dawned on him who she was, and before he could stop himself, he blurted out, "You're the lady who choked out that dude from the 11th MEU, aren't you?!"

Suddenly his face blushed when he realized he'd just referred to a general as a "lady." "Oh, I'm sorry, ma'am," he fumbled.

She laughed at his awkwardness. "Why are you sorry, Marine? That bastard had it coming—and, yes, I'm that lady."

"Holy cow! You're a legend, ma'am."

"Nah, I wouldn't say all that," Soumoy replied dryly.

"Ma'am, at boot camp when we were all going for our tan belts, the drill instructors showed us the video of your fight. They told us it's not the size of the dog in the fight—"

"It's the size of the fight in the dog," Savusa and Soumoy said in unison.

"It really is an honor to meet you, ma'am," Michaels said.

"Sergeant Major Savusa tells me you received a Purple Heart and a Bronze Star for valor at Gitmo. The honor is mine, Sergeant. That was a hell of a fight you guys had on your hands," she said as she turned to pat him on the shoulder.

Michaels glanced over at Savusa, who had a grin on his face.

A few minutes later, the truck came to a halt in front of a sign that read 5th Marine Division HQ. Beneath it, he saw the word Spearhead emblazoned in red and outlined in gold.

As Michaels watched Brigadier General Soumoy and Sergeant Major Savusa head towards the door, he stood there, not sure what to do. Moving to grab his kit, he heard Savusa whistle to him.

"Leave it, Sergeant. The division commander is expecting us."

Oh crap, he thought to himself. "Coming, Sergeant Major," he said, running to catch up to them. *What the hell have I gotten myself into now?*

Chapter 18
Check or Hold, Sergeant?

MSOT 8113
IVO Taigang Hot Springs
Shinchu County

Captain Troy "Chug" St. Onge was in a foul mood. They had chopped the War Pigs to First Platoon, Delta Company, 2nd Battalion, 26th Marine Regiment. Delta Company had been ordered to secure the back door of the upcoming amphibious assault of the 5th Marine Division on the northwest side of Taiwan. They were to go on walkabout, or reconnoiter and mark targets for artillery against the so-called 2nd People's Volunteer Infantry Division. From the reports he'd seen, it was basically a force that the ChiComs had cobbled together and thrown into the fray before the Navy had gained control of the Straits. General Bonwit called the force a delaying action, but Chug knew better. They had been written off as throwaway troops whose sole purpose was to kill as many Americans as possible before the Americans killed them.

The War Pigs were supposed to be assisting First Platoon with their patrol by providing reconnaissance, but the platoon commander, First Lieutenant McCarthy, wasn't having it. His great-grandfather had been a Medal of Honor recipient in World War II, and he was out to prove something. That MSOT 8113 had a Force Recon team with them should have made McCarthy happy. Instead, he'd pushed the special operators to the back of his formation, negating the skill and experience of his one tactical advantage. Chug had rank on McCarthy, but his MSOT was an add-on to Delta Company, so he swallowed this slight and continued the mission.

Staff Sergeant Kushner and his team from 4th Force Recon Company brought the War Pigs back up to one hundred percent team strength. They were down a corpsman and two other critical skills operators, and Master Gunny Walls was still dual-slotted as team chief and operations NCO. Having the Recon Marines made him feel a little better, but being attached to a rifle platoon with a platoon commander with something to prove put him on edge. Not only were they in a thick forest, they were in a valley with a steep climb to get to their next checkpoint. The climb wasn't what was bothering him, though; it was the noise the platoon was making. As Chug looked to his right, he knew that the noise was on Master Gunny Walls's mind as well. Walls signaled to Kushner to slow his Marines down. Not wanting to second-guess his team chief, he slowed his pace as well; besides, he agreed with it. He held up his thumb like the Texas A&M "gig 'em" signal, emphasizing his approval. Then he held up another famous Texas collegiate sign, the longhorn—this was the signal for Walls to switch to their private radio freq so that he could talk to him without having to bunch up the team leadership in case the ChiComs had either of them glassed.

"Master Guns, what are you thinking?" Chug whispered into his throat mic.

"Boss, I don't want to talk out of turn, but Lieutenant McCarthy is moving too fast and is making too much damn noise. We need to hang back."

"I agree, Chief. We hang back so we're close enough to support, but far enough that if the boy wonder walks into an ambush, we don't all get smoked."

He saw they had passed the hand signal to slow down when he did a 360 scan. As they slowed, they also dispersed further apart into an overlapping wedge formation while he moved to the center with his team radio operator.

****

First Lieutenant McCarthy halted his platoon and motioned for his radio operator. He snapped his fingers to emphasize his point. Taking a knee, he slung his rifle. Kit rattled as Lance Corporal Jimenez ran to him. He held out his hand for the radio mic as Jimenez stopped next to him.

"Sir, the signal will not get through. We're deep in this valley and the relay UAV won't be back over us for another ten minutes. We need to move to the top of that ridge if it's urgent."

McCarthy didn't turn around to reply to his platoon sergeant. He slowly exhaled to tamp down his growing frustration with the man.

"Staff Sergeant, I'm aware of that. I'm attempting to contact the Raiders to our rear."

"That's another thing, sir, those dudes are trained for this, and the Force Recon guys really should be out in front of—"

163

"Listen, Staff Sergeant!" McCarthy cut him off with a hiss. "I am the platoon leader, not you. This is my patrol; I'm going to lead it the way I see fit. Check or hold?"

He felt the eyes of his Marines on him and Staff Sergeant Hart. He had attempted to be understanding with Hart, but the man would challenge or reexamine every order he gave. He'd put up with it because he knew Hart had led these men when their last platoon commander prior to him had been killed in the initial invasion of Taiwan. Hart had been a squad leader when the platoon had hit the beach on the first wave to go in. It was just bad luck that both the platoon commander and the platoon sergeant had been together when a Viper AH-64Z had been hit by a missile and crashed, killing them and an entire rifle squad as the wreckage fell to the ground. Hart had taken command of the platoon when the leadership was taken out and rallied them to continue on and secure their initial landing objectives. Two weeks later they'd promoted Hart to staff sergeant, making him the platoon sergeant and awarding him the Silver Star.

That same week, they'd moved McCarthy from the battalion staff to take over the platoon, and the two had butted heads ever since.

Hart glared at him, then grudgingly replied, "Check... sir."

McCarthy could feel the venom in the words but didn't care. He was the platoon commander, not Hart. "Good, that's settled, then," he said as he opened his tactical tablet, bringing up the localized BlueForce tracker app. As the app populated the positions of the platoon members and the MSOT attachment, he frowned when he saw how far the Raiders had fallen back.

He angled the tablet so Hart could see it as he pointed at their position, demanding to know, "What the hell are they doing back there?"

"Sir, it's for tactical dispersion. Far enough away from us so we don't bunch up, close enough to support if we need it."

Snapping the lid of the tablet shut, McCarthy got to his feet in a huff as he grunted, "First Platoon, we're Oscar Mike!"

Stuffing the tablet into his satchel, he unslung his rifle and fell behind the lead fire team as they set out.
****

Chug heard a chirp in his headset—someone was trying to reach him. He turned to see Walls make an open clamshell signal, motioning him to open his wrist tablet, a new piece of tech the Marine SOF units were field-testing. He rested the barrel of his rifle on his forearm as he opened the tablet affixed to it. It was a bendable screen able to display tactical information in real time from the BlueForce tracker app. Seeing the icons for First Platoon, he frowned. They'd almost doubled their speed and were moving away from them at a good clip.

Not happy with what he was seeing, Chug motioned for the Raiders to move to a series of boulders at the base of an incline before making the signal to halt. His flank elements set up security, and he signaled for Walls and Kushner to come to him.

"What's up, boss?" Walls asked.

"Listen, gents, Lieutenant McCarthy is hell-bent on getting into some action. He's moving too fast and making too much noise," Chug explained as he showed them the separation between the two elements on his wrist tablet.

"Young and eager," Kushner said as he spat a glob of Copenhagen on the ground.

"We are not, I repeat, not playing his game. We are going to do what we do, gents, and do it how we do it. Slow is smooth, smooth—"

"Dude, please tell me you aren't about to quote some SEAL crap," Staff Sergeant Kushner said with a smile.

"Well, young Devil Frog, sometimes the squids make sense," Chug said, trying to hold back a laugh.

"What are you thinking, boss? Half a klick or less?" Walls asked, rubbing the gray stubble on his dark face.

"That's affirm, Chief. He's going to tire his Marines in his rush to glory up that ridge. We stay slow and…" He caught himself as he saw Kushner grinning. "We move slow and steady, gents. Let's roll," Chug said as he rose to his feet, ending their little parlay. "Oh, and one more thing. Stay frosty, heads on a swivel. We've all heard about that encounter some Army ODA team had with those ChiCom androids and Colonel Kerns's men."

"They're robots, boss. An android is a machine designed to resemble a human," Kushner interrupted as he adjusted his kit.

Chug looked at Walls, who was looking at Kushner. Then Kushner noticed they were looking at him.

"What? It's true," Kushner explained.

"Staff Sergeant, I never would have guessed you were such a nerd," Chug said. This time he was smiling.

"I'm just saying, boss," Kushner said in a pleading tone as Chug fell in and moved out.

****

Unit 312/Cohort Five
IVO Taigang Hot Springs
Shinchu County

Standing beneath a tree surrounded by dense vegetation, bushes, and hanging vines stood a sleek matte-black-painted humanoid machine. It stood roughly six feet in height with broad shoulders and wide feet with double-jointed elongated toes that looked and functioned more like hands than regular feet. Its arms were an intricate network of steel and servos, each joint double-jointed and precisely engineered to support the use of its metallic fingers. At the tips of the fingers were honed razor-sharp points that promised only destruction for its targets. The Terracotta Killer known as Five Alpha, "TK5A," stood frozen, its face devoid of any expression. As rays of sunshine moved in and out of cloud cover across its emotionless mask of death that lacked any humanizing features save for the V-shaped slits that represented its eyes, it stood firmly anchored to the ground, its programming having placed it in passive sentry mode while it waited to be reactivated or for one of its nearby motion sensors to detect movement, which would turn its systems back on.

Standing in the shadows, TK5A received a burst transmission from Central Command—that reactivated its systems. The V-shaped slits that moments earlier had been devoid of light or life now burned with an orange-yellow intensity as its onboard sensors took in the data and readings of its immediate surroundings from its exterior sensors, which it had deployed prior to powering down into passive sentry mode. As TK5A finished running through a series of internal diagnostic checks, it learned it had been in hibernation for nine hours, twenty-seven minutes and sixteen seconds—since the exact time when it had taken up its current station along the digital fence it had been assigned to guard.

Verifying its power level, TK5A saw that its onboard battery indicated eighty-six point seven percent. It activated its closed-circuit

166

mesh network as it sent an activation code to its nearby partners, Terracotta Killer Five Bravo, "TK5B," and Five Charlie, "TK5C," both standing beneath a similar tree some twenty-five meters to its right and left. As the three TKs shared data between themselves, TK5A sent a one-word response to Central Command, "Orders?" and awaited a reply.

The response was swift, clinical, and clear. "The geofence along sector Lima-Two 'L2' was penetrated twenty-three minutes and forty-two seconds ago. Dragon Bird was deployed to investigate. Identification of enemy forces entering restricted area has been confirmed." Video footage taken by the Dragon Bird scout drones was downloaded to TK5A to aid in its identification of the hostiles. "Cohort Five has been authorized to use deadly force—no friendly forces nearby—weapons-free. Execute immediate removal of unauthorized personnel from the restricted space. Coordinates and tracking data to follow."

As the data from Central Command was transferred to TK5A, it shared the data with 5B and 5C and the robotic killers developed a plan for how they were going to dispatch the intruders.

Moments after receiving the alert and instructions from Central Command, the three TKs began to advance towards the hostile targets. 5A and 5B released the safeties from the QBZ-191 battle rifle as they moved them to the low ready position while 5C made the QJY-201 medium machine gun ready for action as the trio set out towards the intruders.

As TK5A moved with an eerie grace that defied its inhumanity, it switched from thermal sighting to electro-optical sighting and reached out across the Cohort mesh network, instructing TK5B to switch its visual sensors to thermal while TK5C switched to multispectral band imaging. This specialized sensor would send a radar pulse outward in the direction of the geofence as it mapped the terrain in front of them, comparing it against its known mapping of the area to verify they were heading in the right direction.

With their direction and bearings assured, the trio ran with fluid and smooth motions, their movements purposeful and without hesitation. As they picked up speed, the trio was now converging on the intruders at four times the speed of the enemy. It calculated the time to encounter at just under ten minutes given their current pace.

"Query," TK5A announced. "Do you concur that location 2274 is a more optimal site to interdict the intruders?"

"Answer, affirmative," came the near-instant reply from the other TKs. The trio adjusted their speed to allow themselves to arrive just ahead of the intruders' own arrival at the cross point.
****

The incline of the ridge had set First Lieutenant McCarthy's lungs on fire. It wasn't so much the elevation that was getting to him. It was fighting through the thick vegetation and the vines and roots that seemed to reach out and try to hold him back. With each step, his muscles screamed for him to stop punishing them. He tried to regain his strength through some deep breathing exercises, but all it seemed to achieve was to make him more tired and make it that much harder to go on.

Pausing for a moment, he looked up and briefly smiled. Not too far ahead looked to be a clearing. Not wanting to look weak in front of his Marines, he devised a plan to build a break for himself using the cover of doing a head count as they passed him. Then when the last Marine passed him, he'd call a ten-minute bio break so it would come off like he was doing them a solid when in reality he was hoping to give his muscles a break.

When he reached the edge of the clearing a few minutes later, he found himself bent over at the waist, breathing heavily. The sweat stung his eyes as he tried to catch his breath. A few seconds later, he was about to step into the clearing when Staff Sergeant Hart grabbed him by the drag handle on the back of his body armor. He turned violently, knocking Hart's hand away.

"Get your hand off me! Just what in the hell do you think you're doing?" McCarthy demanded.

"Sir, you know better. We don't go into a clearing without establishing far security first!"

McCarthy knew Hart was correct, but he glared at him for a long beat before he pointed to the two closest Marines.

"You two, establish far-side security now!"

Both Marines grunted out what passed for an "Aye-aye, sir."

As they moved past him and the platoon sergeant, McCarthy and Hart took a knee. Then Hart motioned for the rest of the platoon to take cover and for the squad leader to take charge.

McCarthy was pleased to hear the junior NCOs issue commands to establish flank security as the squads fanned out into a loose one-eighty perimeter. Then he focused his attention back to the front as the two Marines cautiously entered the clearing. He looked over to Hart, who was looking up into the trees. At what, he wasn't sure, but something had his attention. Hart rested the barrel of his rifle in a tree notch and used his nonfiring hand to adjust his combat optic.

McCarthy looked forward again and saw that they had established the far-side security, signaling the all clear. He nodded to Hart, who gave the signal to move the platoon towards the far side. As Second Squad passed him, McCarthy fell in behind them. As he watched First Squad reach the far side of the clearing, his world suddenly exploded as eruptions enveloped the Marines he was looking at.

BOOM! BOOM! BOOM!

McCarthy blinked in shock as he saw the limp, torn, and mangled bodies of First Squad falling to the ground around him. Then the pressure wave of the explosions hit him like a sledgehammer, throwing him backwards to the deck.

When he opened his eyes, he wasn't sure at first what he saw. Then it dawned on him—the green flashes of light zipping around him were tracer fire crisscrossing above him. Despite seeing the flashes and knowing what they were, he couldn't hear anything over the ringing in his ears. He rolled onto his stomach and began crawling back towards Staff Sergeant Hart.

As he tried to blink his blurred vision into clarity, he saw the rest of the platoon getting online and firing in a 180-degree arc to their front. Even though he couldn't make out what Staff Sergeant Hart was saying, he watched as he issued orders to the Marines. He made eye contact with him, and Hart shook his head and rushed forward, reaching out his hand to him. McCarthy extended his arm and grabbed it, feeling himself yanked to his feet so hard he felt as if his shoulder had been pulled from its socket.

"Ambush front, enemy numbers unknown, sir! What are your orders?"

The words made sense to him, but his mind was in a fog and he couldn't find the right words to reply. He felt his head snap to the right as Hart slapped his helmet.

"Sir, pull yourself together and get into this fight!" Hart yelled over the thunder of gunfire.

****

TK5A watched as the intruders reached the clearing. One stopped and bent over. TK5B zoomed its focus and directed its internal microphone towards the intruder. TK5A observed that the intruder's breathing was labored and their heart rate was elevated. TK5A reached out to 5B and 5C, and in a microsecond, they reached concurrence to alter the cohort's attack plan. Based on amplified sounds, all the intruders had elevated heart rates, which would hinder their reaction times, reducing threat reduction time estimations by half.

TK5A saw the first human stand, then stop as a second spoke. *Curious*, TK5A thought, as there seemed to be a moment of violence between the human soldiers. It tilted its head and received a thermal feed from 5C, then switched to 5B's electro-optical feed. They counted forty human soldiers with elevated aspiration. Two of the soldiers moved forward, and TK5A signaled for all cohort units to remain still. As the soldiers moved into the open, it sent targeting priorities based on greatest threat, proximity, and probability of the soldiers' reaction to the closest TK.

When the tenth soldier entered the clearing, TK5A signaled the others, and in unison, each fired a 40mm grenade at the closest combatant. Simultaneously, the first grenade detonated at the feet of the two who had crossed first, the second at the average head level of the soldiers, and the third three meters above the ground.

TK5A noted that all organic life signs within the blast radius were zero or lowering towards zero. It removed them from the threat matrix, determining they no longer posed a danger. Tilting its head again, it detected organic short-range radio frequencies.

TK5A linked with the geofence and the rest of the TKs assigned to this sector. The narrow bands were now jammed at location 2774. It then targeted an organic that was attempting to retrieve an injured organic and shot them both in the head.

****

Staff Sergeant Kushner raised a balled fist to halt the element as soon as the sound of the explosions reached them. Master Gunny Walls turned to Chug, all pretense of stealth now gone.

"Looks like McCarthy got his wish!"

"OK, gents, it's time to do what we do! We've got Marines in contact with an unknown enemy. Prepare for close combat."

"What's the plan, boss?" Walls asked as he and Staff Sergeant Kunze both began changing the upper receivers on their M27 IARs.

"We split in two and approach from the obliques. Let's get some eyes. I think it's time you guys got to play with that toy of yours."

"Oorah! I'll tell the kids to get the Black Hornet airborne!" Kushner exclaimed, excited at the chance for his squad to finally use the microdrone they'd carried for weeks.

"Just make sure it's synched to me for C2. I'll direct them to targets. Weapons-free once we link up with First Platoon. Questions?"

Kushner looked disappointed that his guys wouldn't get to direct the drone themselves. He knew Chug was right, though; they would need every rifleman online for whatever this lieutenant walked into.

"OK, Devil Dogs! Let's roll!" Chug declared as he took off towards the sounds of the gunfire.
****

McCarthy's ears were still ringing, and he couldn't focus. Hot brass from Staff Sergeant Hart's rifle was raining down on him. He fumbled for his rifle, which was still attached to his body armor. He checked to make sure a round was chambered, then rolled over as he fired his weapon. After the third burst, he got a misfire—the brass was hung up in the chamber. As McCarthy rolled to his back to clear it, a searing pain hit his shoulder when a burst of fire stitched the ground where he'd been a second before.

"I'm hit!" McCarthy yelled in pain. The feeling in his left arm faltered.

Hart looked down at him and knelt to render aid, but suddenly, his head snapped violently to the left, causing him to fall. McCarthy immediately thought his platoon sergeant must be dead, but he pushed through the pain to crawl around Hart and check on him.

"Sir, I think we're fighting those robot things the intel guys told us about," Hart said.

McCarthy wasn't sure that he'd heard him correctly, but he could read his lips.

"Robots?" McCarthy yelled over the automatic weapons fire. "Like the ones Colonel Kerns reported?"

"Yes, unless you've heard of different ones!" Hart yelled back.

McCarthy felt a rush of adrenaline overtaking him at the thought of running into those killer robots he'd heard those Green Berets talking about with Colonel Kerns. He needed to get his Marines the hell out of here. If they were up against these "Terminators," they didn't have a chance. They had to break contact—immediately.

"We need artillery now!" McCarthy yelled.

"We can't, the comms are down," Hart responded. "We seem to be in a dead zone, or we're being jammed. We're on our own."

"OK, then. We can't stay here! It's time to bug out."

"Yes, sir!" Hart said as he fired several bursts toward the direction where the red tracer fire was coming from.

All of a sudden, two Marines to his right disappeared in a cloud of smoke and fire as another grenade exploded over them. This time McCarthy and Hart were splashed with blood and peppered with shrapnel from the explosion.

"Marines, we're leaving! Fall back!" Hart yelled.

Then McCarthy saw a shadow pass over them and felt the impact of something big thud against the ground behind him. In a split second, Hart raised his rifle and was pointing it at him before he had a chance to scream. The rifle spat fire in his direction as he threw himself to the ground.

McCarthy scurried forward as Hart walked towards him, firing the entire time. As he rolled over, he saw one of those Chinese robots. Had he not seen it with his own eyes, he wouldn't have believed it.

It stood about six feet tall and was outfitted with a chest rig loaded with magazines. The bullets that Hart was pouring into it were bouncing off. Hart had targeted the machine's firing arm, hitting it with round after round. Each time the machine tried to raise the rifle, another 5.56mm round would slam into the arm or the QBZ rifle, lowering it a fraction, preventing it from leveling the weapon and killing them. Then McCarthy heard a click as Hart's weapon went dry above him.

"Damn it!" Hart yelled.

The color of the machine's visor glowed for a second and it tilted its head, raising its rifle at an unimaginable speed. McCarthy closed his eyes, expecting to die.

Wham!

His eyes shot open as the machine stumbled to its left. Sergeant Booth from Third Squad had used his rifle like a baseball bat, hitting the Terminator for all his worth in the side of the head. The robot stumbled briefly from the hit it hadn't anticipated before it righted itself. As the robot tried to bring its own weapon to bear against this new threat, Sergeant Booth again swung the rifle like a baseball slugger, only this time, the machine caught it midswing with one of its hands while its other hand continued to grip its own rifle.

In the blink of an eye, it ripped the weapon from Booth's grasp with such force it snapped one of his wrists with a sickening crunch. The Marine howled in pain right before a blur of action slammed in the side of his head—now the robot used Booth's own rifle as a club against him. The hit was so fierce and sharp, he just collapsed to the ground in a lifeless heap.

The robot swung around to face McCarthy, and the fear of the moment almost completely overwhelmed him. In a sort of dissociated haze, he heard the bolt of his M4 slam forward. He tried to raise his wounded arm, but it seemed to be growing weaker by the second. Pain like nothing he had ever felt before shot through his shoulder and into his chest. He could see he wasn't going to outmaneuver the robot no matter how hard he tried with his wounded arm. Then, just as he was certain he was about to be riddled with bullets, Staff Sergeant Hart had again started putting rounds on target, repeatedly hitting the robot's arm with the rifle, sending sparks flying off the metal of the machine.

At that point, McCarthy was somehow able to get his own rifle into the fight. He tried to shoot at the machine's center mass or just below the neck, where it looked like it might have a vulnerability. Then he heard the sound of at least two Marines shooting at the robot. McCarthy couldn't tell if the bullets were doing any actual damage, but the Terminator was steadily moving backwards.

The hailstorm of steel-core 5.56mm bullets hammered their way into its exoskeleton. The QBZ rifle the robot had momentarily tried to use as a shield was shot to pieces in seconds. Then the machine flung the remains of the rifle at the closest Marine. The damaged weapon slammed into the Marine's face with a wet thud, and the Devil Dog fell backwards and rolled a few feet down the hill and out of sight.

Corporal Garza, the machine gunner from Fourth Squad, had run up next to Staff Sergeant Hart and he screamed at the top of his lungs, "Die mother—" as he held the squad's M240L machine gun tight into his shoulder and squeezed the trigger tight.

The machine gun spat fire out its barrel. The 7.62mm slugs came rushing out at such a high rate of sustained fire that the barrel glowed from overheating. As round after round of the heavier slugs crashed into the robot's armored chest, it stumbled backwards until one of its feet caught on something, causing it to momentarily lose balance and fall awkwardly to the ground. By now, the remaining members of Fourth Squad converged on the machine, hitting it with a continuous volley of fire, keeping it pinned to the ground despite its many attempts to get up.

McCarthy dropped his spent magazine to the ground below. The air around him smelled of battle, and despite the searing pain in his arm, he felt like they just might survive the next few minutes. He slapped a fresh magazine in place and hit the bolt release, chambering the first round.

As he aimed for the remnants of the machine, he saw Lance Corporal Garza, the only female in the platoon, swing her M27 automatic rifle to one side, unslinging a Benelli semiautomatic twelve-gauge shotgun. Then, without a moment to spare, she leaped towards the machine faster than McCarthy would have thought her five-foot-five-inch frame could move with seventy pounds of body armor and gear. Somehow, she landed near the machine's robotic head, just in time to place the muzzle against it and pull the trigger. The Benelli barked fiercely as the twelve-gauge slug blew a hole out the other end; the machine's circuitry, optical sensors, and cameras ejected from what constituted its head.

For a brief moment, the Marines stared on in shock at what had just happened. Garza took a couple of steps back, the barrel of the Benelli still smoking. Then the unthinkable happened. The robot's left foot, now functioning more like a hand, grabbed McCarthy by the ankle, yanking him hard off his feet. He crashed on his tailbone and yelped in pain, stars briefly blotting his vision. The next thing he knew, he was kicking violently against the tightening grip against his ankle.

This robotic killing machine was like the Energizer Bunny—it just kept going, returning from the dead as Lazarus did when Christ called out his name. As this freakish mechanical killer robot sat up, McCarthy saw pieces of plastic and filament fall from the ruined carapace of what had once been its head, where sparks flew as exposed wires began to arc. The Marines staring on in horror at the partially headless machine raised their weapons to unleash a torrent of armor-piercing rounds once again. Garza beat them to the punch as she pulled the trigger again and again. The Benelli's steel-core slugs punched fist-sized holes through the metal frame and the machine convulsed one final time before slumping over at the waist, motionless at last.

McCarthy let out an audible sigh of relief that it was finally dead, this nightmare over. Then his ears heard something he could only describe as a series of bloodcurdling screams, wails, and taunts being hurled at them from the depths of the jungle. It sounded to him like the very pits of hell itself had been opened and some terrifying creature was crawling out for him and his Marines. As the noise grew closer, their eyes turned in its direction until they spotted movement within the jungle, confirming this bad dream was far from over.

Instead of just one of these robotic killing machines steadily advancing towards them, they now saw *two*, jumping and leaping between trees and branches. It was as if they had emerged from the pages of a Stephen King novel—a pair of evil monkeys steadily closing in on them. McCarthy joined with his Marines, shooting desperately at the bobbing and weaving mechanical creatures, until suddenly they were upon them like a pair of jackals.

As McCarthy dropped yet another spent magazine, he saw one of the machines had landed just behind Lance Corporal Garza. It attempted to slam her face with a backhanded slap but missed—Garza had somehow managed to arch her body just outside its reach. She leapt backwards, creating the space she needed to bring her Benelli to bear.

When she fired the first shot at nearly point-blank range, a four-inch chunk of metal, wiring, and circuitry blew out the upper chest of the ghoulish machine that continued to blast their ears with its ghastly noise. Then, before she could get a second shot off, it recovered from the hit to its chest, lunging forward with an outstretched arm as it sought to grab her.

Before any of the Marines could intercede or attempt to come to her aid, the crazed warbot had grabbed her by the throat, lifting her into the air. She struggled against its ever-tightening grip. When her life was literally squeezed from her, this soulless creature tossed her aside like a rag doll, disappearing into the knee-high underbrush of the clearing they had been fighting in.

Seeing everything unfold the way it had reminded McCarthy of a film his older brother had let him watch when their parents were out one evening—*The Matrix*. The way the main character in the film had been able to shift and contort his body as he anticipated, then deftly evaded the barrage of bullets fired at him was something his childlike mind could never forget. But what was happening to him and his Marines wasn't *The Matrix*—this was real life, and it was happening in front of him.

McCarthy found himself screaming like a savage animal gone feral as he joined with his Marines, firing relentlessly at the machine that had just murdered Garza. He suddenly felt an overwhelming sense of unbridled hate at this...*thing* that was ripping through his men, one after another, like they were GI Joe figurines and not flesh and blood. It was as if everything around him began to slow down—almost as if McCarthy was viewing the events frame by frame as they were happening.

The remaining Marines around McCarthy fired as rapidly as they could, landing round after round into the warbots, hoping beyond hope that just one of their bullets might hit something of importance— something that might disable or outright kill it. Then one of his Marines was thrown violently, crashing into him with enough force to topple both of them to the ground. Momentarily dazed from the body check, McCarthy looked past the limp Marine lying across him. Both of these diabolical machines were now wielding two weapons, one in each hand, firing at different targets with relentless accuracy.

McCarthy tried desperately to free himself from the giant Marine he knew to be his sparring partner, Sergeant John Bobo, who had crashed into him moments earlier. With one of his arms still not fully functional, all McCarthy could do was scream in frustration as he desperately tried to push and squirm his way out from underneath the six-foot-three-inch-tall, two-hundred-and-thirty-pound Marine and the seventy pounds of body armor and gear now pinning him to the ground.

"Frag out!" shouted someone nearby.

McCarthy caught movement in his peripheral vision. Craning his neck to see where it was headed, he caught sight of the grenade sailing towards the Terminator closest to him. Then it put down one of the two rifles it had been holding to free up a hand, catching the grenade like a veteran outfielder for a Major League Baseball team, all the while not even looking in the direction it came from. In the same fluid motion it had caught the boom-ball, it tossed it right toward McCarthy. The grenade thudded off the chest of Sergeant Bobo before rolling off to land next to McCarthy's injured arm.

In that instant, McCarthy knew he was done. He was pinned beneath Bobo and this thing was about to go off. He couldn't do a damned thing about it. As memories flashed through his mind, he felt something grab the handle at the top of the back of his body armor. McCarthy was yanked backwards while Bobo's limp body was rolled on top of the grenade. He vaguely heard the voice of Staff Sergeant Hart yelling, "Hit the deck!" as two wildly different explosions occurred almost simultaneously.

BOOM!

Crump!

The closer-sounding dull thud that momentarily lifted Bobo's body off the ground paled in comparison to the grenade that went off near the other side of the clearing, where the ambush had originated from. As McCarthy's brain began to register more than just the muffled boom reverberating through the soil, he felt a searing pain tear into his boots as hot fragments tore into his feet, perhaps severing a toe or two. His vision blurred again, but this time it was from debris raining down from the other grenade.

McCarthy pushed aside the pain he felt in his feet, toes, and arm. One of the robotic killing machines appeared to have taken the brunt of the blast from one of the grenades; it stumbled momentarily from the concussive force.

The machine's partner in this horrific nightmare McCarthy found himself unable to awake from had lost its left hand and the rifle it had been carrying. It leveled its gaze in their direction and began to walk toward them. It moved with a slight limp due to its mangled foot, but it relentlessly advanced nonetheless.

McCarthy's hands searched for his rifle. He pulled against the sling, only to realize it had been cut, and his weapon was no longer attached to his body. Pushing the question of what had happened to his rifle aside, he grabbed for his service-issued Sig Sauer M17 and leveled it, firing the handgun he knew was worthless against this armored beast as it continued the methodical process of reloading its rifle.

The machine hit the bolt release to load the next round into the chamber. When the rifle moved to aim directly at him, McCarthy realized for the second time that day that his time was up. There was no way of dodging the bullet being aimed at him. In that moment, whether it was nerves, fear, or just an overwhelming sense of having to urinate, he felt warm liquid running down his leg. It was almost as if his soul was being released from his body. Never before had he been so scared, yet so sure of what was about to happen. He was about to die by the hand of a damn machine, a robot built for the sole purpose of waging war and killing humans.

The machine took a half step towards him before stopping dead in its tracks. It was still aiming the QBZ at his face, but for some reason it had held its fire. As it turned, McCarthy saw half of its head explode, its body momentarily rocking to the side as it pulled the trigger. The bullet zipped right past his head, thudding harmlessly into the dirt.

Then came the unmistakable *bam, bam, bam* sounds as large-caliber slugs pounded the metal frame of this terror weapon, sparks erupting from the repeated impacts hammering the machine. McCarthy's ears registered the loud reports of what had to be a fifty-caliber weapon being fired at these beasts of war.

Oorah, Devil Dogs, he thought. He realized this sudden unexpected salvation had to be coming from the Raider element that he had chided for lagging behind.

Chapter 19
The One That Got Away

March 8, 2023
Point Loma, California

A year before hostilities broke out with China, Commander Kurt Helgeson was attending a conference at Point Loma Naval Base and wanting desperately to escape the boredom and monotony of the endless PowerPoint briefings. As the last briefer opened the discussion to questions, he rose from his seat in the room's portion reserved for up-and-coming officers who hadn't been selected for command but were still expected to sit through the commander training. The sting of being passed over for his first shot at a command of his own was still fresh in his mind. The squadron commander had told him he'd command a boat soon, but he wasn't sure he believed it. He'd graduated at the top of his class at the United Kingdom's "Perisher" submarine commanders' course last year; maybe it was ego that had led him to believe they would hand him a boat, but he'd paid his dues and had damn sure earned it. His rise to commander was fast by US Navy standards, but now he leaned more towards hanging up his uniform for good. It wasn't like they were at war, so why hang around?

Exiting quickly, he walked to his rental car and drove to Tom Ham's Lighthouse, a favorite seafood restaurant of his, which overlooked North Island Naval Air Station. He hated to wear a uniform in public when off duty and trying to wind down, but the need to be away from base and the Navy had propelled him to make this rare exception.

After he parked his car, he walked toward the entrance. As he opened the door, he heard a group behind him. Hearing female voices, he held the door and stepped aside so they could enter.

"Lieutenant Helgeson?"

His heart felt as if it were going to explode in his chest. As he turned, he saw Juliet Nolan. If anyone could be "the one," it was Juliet. She'd definitely been the one that got away. He stood dumbfounded for a moment before he muttered, "It's Commander now…"

In the space of a long five seconds, he thought of a thousand things to say, but nothing came out. He just stood there holding the door, staring at the most intelligent and beautiful woman he'd ever known.

"Oh, my! Excuse me, Commander," she said, enunciating each syllable. "I see you're still a man of few words."

She laughed and embraced him in a hug, kissing his cheek.

"Sorry, Juliet, I just wasn't expecting to... what are you... it's fantastic to see you," he stuttered as he tripped over his tongue.

"I'm here for a wedding," she said as she looped her arm through his.

"Oh?" Helgeson said, hoping with a pang of jealousy that she wasn't somehow referring to her own wedding.

"Yes, my cousin Corrine gave her fiancé the ultimatum, and he finally caved."

She began laughing at her own joke and snorted, which caused him to laugh. Her laugh had always been infectious. She must have sensed the sudden shift in his mood, because she leaned in and whispered, "There's only one man for me. He's out there somewhere. He just has to realize it."

He turned and looked at her. She winked at him, and his heart stopped again. Smiling at her, he said, "Can I buy you a drink? Old Fitzgerald neat, was it?"

"Why, Commander Helgeson, a girl could get the impression she's fancied by you!" She winked at him, flashing a devilish grin. "Any other time, I'd graciously accept, but I'm a bridesmaid... never a bride. So, duty calls."

"Of course, silly of me, I understand."

She kissed his cheek again and held his gaze for a long moment. "It was good to see you, Kurt."

"Likewise, Juliet" was all he could say as he felt the lump in his throat threaten to choke him. She turned to walk away, then paused and turned to face him again. She reached into her purse and held a card out to him.

"Here's my number, Kurt. Why don't you call me when you're done with the Navy?"

"Funny story," he said as he took the card.

"Oh, do tell."

"I'm actually thinking about retiring. This peacetime Navy is for the birds."

She looked deeply into his eyes and smiled. Before he knew what had happened, she walked to him and kissed him. His mind flashed

180

to the film *The Sandlot* when Squints kissed Wendy Peffercorn. After what seemed like forever, she pulled back and smiled.

"You can only have one true love, Kurt. If you're leaving the Navy, call me."

He watched her walk away, and he felt numb all over. "What the hell just happened?"

He made his way to the bar on the far side of the restaurant, but he could still hear the bridesmaids laughing and having a good time. He couldn't stop thinking of Juliet, so much so that the bartender asked him if anything was wrong with his food. He looked down at his forgotten halibut. As he paid for the meal he'd barely touched, he heard his name called again.

"Helgeson! Holy crap, old boy! I've been looking for you!" exclaimed a stocky officer named Grimes as he charged over to where he sat.

"You found me. How did you find me?"

"I had the N2 geolocate you."

"Why? We're off duty."

"You left so fast after today's session, you missed it, man!"

"Missed what?"

"Admiral Patel showed up looking for you."

"Come on, man, you're pulling my leg. Why would he be looking for me?"

"Man, you are dim. You didn't hear this from me; I was going to call you after what I overheard, but I just got in my car and raced over."

"Well?" Helgeson said, growing agitated.

"Dude, he's giving you a boat! You're getting SSN-775, the *Texas*!"

Helgeson stood there dumbfounded. Grimes grabbed him by the shoulders and pushed him back to the bar.

"Barkeep, two Anchor Steams! My pal here just got named skipper of a fast-attack sub!"

There were a few polite claps in the bar and a few older patrons raised glasses to him. As Grimes handed him his beer, he turned to the entrance to the bar and saw Juliet. The smile was gone from her face, and he saw in her eyes a sadness that made him realize that for her, he was the one that got away.

****

October 2026
USS *Texas*

Captain Helgeson sat in his stateroom, staring at his computer screen and the email he'd written at least a dozen times since the war had begun. Glancing at the clock on his wall, he saw he had five minutes left before the photonics masts of the *Texas* slipped beneath the waves. If he didn't send it now, he didn't know how long it would be until he had another chance, if he ever did. He hated this feeling. Like a teenager again, trying to work up the courage to ask the girl of your dreams out. It was silly in the grand scheme of things. This wasn't a life-or-death tactical decision. It was an email to a woman his heart had pined over for more than a decade. He hadn't spoken to her in three years, and yet here he sat like a lovesick puppy, agonizing over sending a damn email. The last time they had spoken was during a chance meeting in Point Loma. So much had changed since then, yet thoughts of her were never far from his head. A pounding on the hatch of his quarters pulled him from his thoughts.

"Enter," he said with an authority in his voice he wasn't feeling at the moment.

Newly commissioned Ensign Allen, formerly OC2 Allen, stuck his head in the door.

"Sir, the XO sent me to fetch you," Allen said, pointing at his watch.

Helgeson continued agonizing over whether or not to send the email.

Now or never, Kurt, he thought to himself.

Taking a deep breath in, he hit send. The icon spun for a second and then disappeared. The email was encrypted, and once it reached Fleet HQ, it would be decrypted and sent to its intended recipient as if it was a normal email. No turning back. Now it was time to put on his game face. He had a war to fight. Making the mental switch from lovestruck puppy to apex underwater predator, he went to work.

"Those bars look good on you, Ensign," Helgeson said as he unplugged his commander's tablet from the charging cable.

"Honestly, sir, I'm still not used to it. Thank you again for recommending me for a direct commission, and thank you for fighting to keep me on the *Texas*."

Helgeson smiled. "As much as I hate to admit it, we're a family on this boat. I used to say that no matter how mad my mother got at me, she'd never send me to war."

Ensign Allen laughed as he stepped aside, allowing him to pass.

"Allen, why do they call you Woody? Is it because of the actor?"

Allen visibly blushed at his question as they walked down the passageway towards the Conn.

"No, sir, they call me Woody because I grew up pretty poor in Alabama. The kids from the good side of the tracks called us peckerwood. It's another term for poor white trash, sir. One day I just got sick of it and beat the snot out of one of the rich kids. After that all my friends started calling me Woody. Kind of like a badge of honor. It just kind of stuck."

Helgeson belly laughed as they walked into the Conn, causing all eyes to turn towards him. He knew the crew hadn't seen him laugh in quite some time, but he couldn't help himself.

"XO, I have the Conn," he said while still laughing.

"Aye, sir, you have the Conn," Commander Evans responded with a look of surprise on her face.

"XO, status report on our rendezvous with the *Owasso*?"

"Sir, *Oklahoma* confirmed rendezvous in our last message download while we were at periscope depth."

"Very well, XO. COB, time to rendezvous?"

"Sir, time to rendezvous is ninety minutes present speed."

Helgeson opened the timer icon on his tablet and set it for eighty-five minutes. Then, with a swipe of his finger, he flicked the timer to his primary commander's display near his chair. He placed his tablet in the cradle on the side of his chair before turning to walk toward the master plot.

"XO, COB, come on over."

Commander Evans and Chief Schmall stood across from him at the plot.

"What do you got, Skipper?" COB said in his characteristic southern drawl.

Helgeson pulled up an overlay of their rendezvous with the Orca *Owasso*. He slid it to one side of the digital plot and opened their latest mission order on the other side. Tapping the glass, he motioned for his XO and the COB to read it. Crossing his arms, he exhaled and gave them a few moments to digest the contents before asking them for their thoughts.

"Well, that's odd, sir," Commander Evans said as she drummed her fingers on the edge of the plot.

"Yeah, that's kind of what I thought. I was hoping our latest download would include an update or maybe some additional details. This seems to be about as much as we're going to get."

"Well, sir," COB began, "there isn't too much left of the PLAN for us to kill. Especially after the recent action by Task Force Dupre. They went on a bloody rampage in the Yellow Sea, sending more than forty-five vessels and subs to Davy Jones' Locker."

Helgeson grunted in agreement. "True enough, COB. I read the after-action report of their campaign. It was impressive, even if they did sustain some losses. They arguably finished off the PLA Northern Fleet. But something about this set of orders screams OGA to me."

Evans and Schmall groaned quietly at the mention of the CIA's alternative name—Other Government Agency—often used by military members.

Hearing their displeasure, Helgeson held up his hands in a placating gesture as he tried to explain, "I know what you both are thinking, and I don't disagree. The mission tasking we received is vague, and while it's not always a good idea to assume as it gives you an opportunity to make an ass out of you and me, in this case, it's really the only thing that comes to mind. Someone high up in the food chain wants us to link up with the *Owasso* for reasons unknown, so that's what we're going to do."

"If the *Owasso* is close enough to rendezvous with us, then isn't the *Oklahoma* close enough for the mission tasking?" the COB asked.

Helgeson was about to respond when he saw Commander Evans working on something on the plot screen. She shifted the screen to display the sea floor topographic map. As he silently observed what she was up to, the COB leaned over the plot, breaking the cardinal rule of not placing anything atop the multimillion-dollar piece of equipment.

Helgeson let it go for the moment as he was more interested in what the XO was on to.

"Skipper?"

Helgeson suddenly realized he hadn't responded to the previous question as he pulled himself away from staring at the screen. "Sorry about that, COB. That's technically true, but the *Oklahoma* isn't the *Texas*. Commander Jacoby is a great sub driver, but his boat is nowhere near as capable as we are. Besides, ours is not to reason why."

He was about to say something else when Commander Evans expanded the image on the plot.

"Sir, I think I know why it's the *Texas*."

"Oh? OK, XO, let's have it."

"Sir, whatever we're going to be asked to do, I think we can safely assume it will be because of our prior navigation and hydrographic studies in the home waters of China. We were able to sail in and maneuver undetected along much of the East China Sea coastline."

"That's true, XO, but we don't have the same UUVs that we did then. These new Orcas are untested and I'm not ready to take them into a fight."

"I can understand that, Skipper. Losing the *Dallas*, *Killeen*, and *Lubbock* was almost like losing the family pets, if that makes sense."

"It does, XO, and replacing our pets with new ones makes me feel guilty in an odd way, but we are a ship of war. Taking new untested weapons into enemy waters makes my Spidey senses tingle," Helgeson said with a laugh. He noticed Ensign Allen casually trying to eavesdrop while doing his best to appear not to be.

"Ensign Allen, join us at the plot," Helgeson called over.

"Aye, sir," Allen said as his head slightly bowed. His subtle gesture reminded Helgeson of a schoolboy who'd just been called to the principal's office.

As Allen joined them at the plot, Helgeson slapped him on the shoulder and smiled. "It's OK, Ensign. When you're in the Conn, you're supposed to pay attention to what's going on."

"Sorry, sir, I heard you mention the Orcas, so I started to pay attention."

"Tell me about them," Helgeson said, all business once again.

"Well, sir, the *Pecos*, *Temple*, and *Bexar* have been with us since we received our last resupply and refit at Isla Socorro. Per your instructions, all data from the *Dallas*, *Lubbock*, and *Killeen*, as well as all war data to date, have been uploaded into their systems via big brain uplink. Each individual Orca has the data of every single Orca the Navy has fielded to date."

"That's all well and good, Woody. My primary question is can they fight?"

"Sir, those machines are better than the ones they replaced. We run systems diagnostics here at our station and we programmed them to initiate self-diagnostics each midwatch. To date, we've seen zero issues, glitches, or ghosts in the machine."

Helgeson pondered this for a moment. He'd had a gnawing suspicion that this ChiCom super AI would somehow figure out a way to infiltrate their Orcas and turn them against the *Texas* one of these days. *I have to put this concern to bed or it's going to eat me up...*

"Allen, hypothetically, is it possible for the ChiComs to penetrate them electronically or wirelessly?" As Helgeson stared at Allen, he pictured actual gears turning in the ensign's head as he thought about the question.

"Sir, no way. When the Orcas receive their program packets, their brains, for lack of a better term—they're encased in such a way that no signals can get in or out until it's connected to the Orca itself. Then it must go through its initialization runs. I'm not sure of all the ones, zeros, and trons. But the programmers have something like thirty thousand encryption and decryption algorithm protocols that must be answered before the Orca itself will pair with its digital brain. If there's any deviation from tolerable parameters it's allowed to accept, then its pairing will be unsuccessful. The brain has to be tested for defects, programming errors, data corruption and outside intrusion before it's allowed to pair with the Orca—essentially its body if you will."

Helgeson rubbed his chin unconsciously as Allen explained the technical aspects of how the Orca actually worked. He stopped doing it the moment he realized he'd slipped back into the habit. It was an unconscious tic he'd developed, and it had grown to annoy him greatly.

When Allen finished explaining more of the security features, Helgeson then asked the next burning question he needed an answer to. "OK, Allen. You've assured me of their security protocols. One final question, and I want an honest opinion. Can they fight?"

Allen stood a little taller as he answered confidently. "Sir, these weapons are, and I hate to say it, better in every way than the Orcas they replaced. If we have to fight, just say the word, sir, and I'll turn 'em loose."

Chapter 20
It's Chucky

MSOT 8113
IVO Taigang Hot Springs
Shinchu County

Chug looked to his right, straining to see the Raider closest to him beneath the dense vegetation of this quasi-jungle-slash-forest they'd been moving through. *I've never seen bamboo trees intermixed within a regular forest*, he thought privately as the Raider gave him a nod. It was killing them right now not to rush forward to the aid of their brother Marines, but he knew if they didn't do this right, they'd get chopped apart just like McCarthy's platoon had been. Having gotten the nod from the Raider he was waiting on, he gave the go-ahead.

"In position," he said into his throat mic, barely above a whisper.

Click, click, click.

When he heard the three-click reply, he responded with three of his own, sending the War Pigs into motion as they collectively advanced towards the sounds of gunfire.

When Chuck had received the intel brief prior to heading out of this patrol, he'd insisted on his Raiders bringing the Beowulf .50-caliber upper receiver on the patrol with them on the off chance they stumbled upon some of these Terracotta Killers. When the intel guys assessed there might be some of them operating in the vicinity, he wanted to make damn sure they had a viable means of taking them down. Once the shooting had started and they'd gotten a glimpse of what was happening via their drones, he was glad he'd listened to his gut instinct on this one. At worst, carrying the upper receiver and a pair of mags for it would mean some extra weight. If there was one thing he'd learned during this war, it was that it was far better to bring something along and not need it than need it and not have it.

With the War Pigs now as the hunters, they began to stalk their prey, who were now distracted by the chaos of battle—something they planned to use as they crept closer to the enemy. As the Raiders stealthily moved forward, Chug postulated how he thought these machines might fight if they fought remotely like humans.

In a gunfight, when wearing body armor, you want to position yourself so your frontal armor, the section where your armored plate is located, is always facing the enemy. If you're going to take a hit, try to make sure it's in a section of armor with the most protection.

If this theory of his held true, then the best angle of attack should be the side profiles of the machines. If his Raiders could get lucky and glass a TKs from a position of advantage before having to engage them head-on, then that was what they'd try to do.

As Chug's team moved closer to the sounds of battle, they started to hear commands and warnings being shouted between the squads.

"Reloading!"

Ratatat! Bam! Ratatat!

"Watch out!"

"Aaahhh, I'm hit! Corpsman, corpsman!"

Approaching the edge of the clearing, they caught a glimpse of the desperate fight unfolding on the other end of the clearing. *My God! Look at those bastards…. this ends now!* Chug ordered his marksman with the Beowulf to open fire and cover their advance—they were going in.

"War Pigs! Follow me!" Chug shouted as he leapt to his feet and charged forward.

Crack! Crack! Crack!

His marksmen fired, announcing their entry into the fray as the first of three of the fifty-caliber slugs smashed into the nearest machine. The bastard had been towering over a fallen Marine and was about to shoot him. The 9mm bullets from the poor guy's pistol just bounced harmlessly off its frontal armor until the three jackhammers had nearly knocked it to the ground. With the element of surprise now gone, Chug and his War Pigs charged headlong into the fray—weapons ablaze.

Chug fired his SCAR-L while on the move as he focused his fire on the same TK his marksmen were hammering the hell out of. This was where years of training and hundreds of hours on the range meant the difference between staying calm under fire and being a statistic.

Hurdling over a fallen tree, Chug spotted the point on the machine he thought might be a weak spot—the right side of the machine's upper chest. Aiming for it, he started hitting it over and over as he shared his idea with the others. Meanwhile his marksmen continued to pound into it like a sledgehammer over and over again, the kinetic energy reverberating across the electrodes, servos, circuitry, and wiring that controlled it.

When Chug paused along the side of a tree, he dropped the spent magazine into his drop bag and grabbed for another mag. Then he saw something in the machines he hadn't expected to see. Confusion, or at least momentary disorientation, as the TKs looked to have been taken by surprise by the sudden arrival of his force.

He spotted at least one of them that had been destroyed, but two others were now reacting to the new attack. They started falling back into the trees, using them for cover as they withdrew, extracting themselves from the fight until they could reorganize themselves for a better attack.

Chug saw what was happening and thought, *I'll be damned if I'm going to let those TKs get away.*

He shouted into his mic, "Team Two, go, go, go! Close the trap now!"

As he called an audible to the plan he'd originally envisioned, the Force Recon Marines he'd directed to flank the TKs now moved to close the distance themselves and get in the fight. The TKs were now being bracketed from three angles of attack. That was when they launched themselves into the nearby trees. The buggers had just gone vertical, changing the dimensions of the fight as they moved rapidly from branch to branch in a way he couldn't understand.

So you want to go Predator on me, eh? Let's see how you like my little friends…

Sliding next to First Lieutenant McCarthy, who'd managed to find a rifle to get back in the fight, Chug flipped open the wrist tablet, finding the drone icon as he traced his finger from their present location to the TKs monkeying around in the trees as they continued to fire at his men.

"They're too damn fast! I can't seem to get a solid shot or two on 'em," McCarthy yelled to him, some blood dripping near his ears.

Chug laughed an evil laugh and countered, "Watch and learn how it's done, Padawan!"

Zipping over their heads and racing right for the TKs were the six D40s they'd launched just prior to heading out. The Drone 40 was an unmanned aerial system with a twenty-kilometer range and sixty minutes of loiter time, and it packed enough explosive charge to disable a light armored vehicle or a handful of soldiers nearby when it detonated. Having fired the D40s from their grenadiers' M320s, they'd been waiting patiently for a target, and now they had one.

One of the TKs must have spotted the D40s coming at them as it stopped swinging. It twisted the trunk of its body 180 degrees on some sort of double joint, because its legs and head looked to still be facing the other direction while its chest was now pointing in the direction of the drones. Then as it hung there from one of its arms, the joint in the other arm turned it to face the drones and it reached for the QBZ rifle hanging by its sling. It then fired rapidly at the drones closing in on the two of them, and to Chug's astonishment and disbelief, it blew three of them up before they could land a hit. Then two of three D40s scored a hit as they rammed into the TK, blowing it to pieces, leaving just the single arm still gripping a tree branch.

The other TK leaped from the trees like a jaguar as it looked to jump behind the trunks of several trees in an apparent move to try and shield itself. Chug was midway through cursing up a storm when he saw the D40 pull back on its throttle, its time to impact now altered, successfully plowing into the TK as its charge detonated. The force of the explosion spun the robotic killing machine off course to crash headlong into a nearby trunk before falling to the ground in a heap.

If Chug hadn't seen this with his own eyes, he would have sworn whoever told this story was lying. But as he looked down at the wrist tablet still controlling the ISR D40 variant, he smiled and gloated to himself, *I win! We recorded it!*

In that singular moment in time, he felt like a kid at Christmas. He'd deployed a seventh D40 to provide ISR support just in case the TKs managed to slip away into the trees. Now he had a recording of the TKs in action and an epic video of them being blown apart.

"Make sure it's destroyed!" Chug shouted as he saw Walls, Kushner, and Kunze approaching the wreckage.

With guns up, the Raiders fanned out in a wedge as they approached where they thought it had landed with cautious optimism.

Then Kunze asked, "Uh, boss, where the hell is it?"

"Quiet!" Chug hissed as he scanned to their left, then to their right. *Something doesn't feel right...is that a hissing noise?*

Then Chug saw it, shouting, "Down!"

Zip—Zip!

Two basketball-sized rocks rocketed through the space where his head had just been moments before he ducked.

"Ooofff," Staff Sergeant Kushner yelped as one of the rocks slammed into his chest.

Chug was in the process of bringing his rifle up when he heard the rustling of leaves and a blast of movement flashed in front of him. The next thing he knew, he was being thrown backwards, off his feet, and he heard a loud cracking sound from the level 4A chest plate, which had been shattered by the punch to the chest he'd just taken.

As he crashed to the ground near Kunze, who was in the process of trying to draw his M17 pistol after the sling of his rifle had gotten tangled on something attached to his equipment, the TK that had punched Chug was on them like white on rice. Before either of them could react, the bastard stomped on Kunze's knee, the sound of it snapping almost causing Chug to vomit as his friend howled in agony.

As Kunze tried to sit up, reaching for his knee, he was flung through the air like a rag doll and bounced off a tree. In that moment, Chug's eyes met with Gunny Walls's, and in an instant, they both reacted without hesitation or regard for their own lives. They pounced at the TK, knowing their lives depended on what happened in the next thirty seconds.

Master Gunny Walls went low as he braced himself just behind the back legs of the machine. Then Chug lowered his shoulder as he dove into its chest. As he crashed into the robotic killer, it stumbled backwards, tripping over Walls as it flailed about and fell.

Chug grunted hard as he and Walls tried to keep the TK's arms pinned below it and leverage their weight against the machine.

"What the hell do we do now?"

"Hell if I know! This was your dumbass idea!" Walls retorted through gritted teeth.

They held on as long as they could, but the TK thrashed about and bucked its hips, steadily squirming itself free of them.

Chug knew if it got one of its arms free, they would be dead. They were fighting for their lives and time was running out. There was no way he could reach any of his weapons, and Chug knew Walls was in the same boat.

Then, despite their best efforts, it righted itself using its double-jointed hips, knees, and ankles, bringing Chug along with it as he held on for dear life. There he felt an explosion of pain across his nose as it crumpled beneath the impact of a vicious head butt.

With blood gushing down his face, his grip slipped away. The machine grabbed him by his body armor with one arm and lifted him off the ground. Through tearing eyes, Chug could see its arm drawing back as it balled its fist to deliver the killing blow.

Master Gunny Walls grabbed its fist before it rearranged Chug's face. Then, like the doll Chucky from the 1988 film *Child's Play*, the TK's head turned a full 180 degrees to face Gunny Walls, and the machine's hand transformed and reversed itself, seeming to morph around Walls's hand before crushing the bones in it.

While Chug dangled helplessly in the air, flailing about to try and help his friend, he heard a familiar voice. "Hey, asshole!" yelled Staff Sergeant Kunze.

The TK turned to face the new threat as an object crashed into its face.

Thump!

The 40mm smoke grenade cracked part of the TK's face. It instantly dropped Chug and Walls as it spun around to face Kunze. Chug and Walls rolled away as Kunze finished loading another grenade.

When Kunze looked at Chug and Walls, they waved frantically, shouting, "Too close. Back up!"

"Oh, crap!" Kunze shouted as the TK emerged from the blue smoke. Having backed up further, he fired again.

Thump!

Once again, the grenade was too close to arm and it fell harmlessly to the TK's feet.

Kunze cursed loudly as he desperately tried to reload. But now the TK was stalking towards Kunze—closing in on him.

Boom!

Chug flinched this time as he saw the TK stagger from the impact. That was when he saw Walls holding his Beowulf with his left hand, trying to steady his aim. The TK diverted its course away from Kunze, now unsteadily heading towards Walls.

Boom! Clang!

Walls's second shot slammed into the stomach section of the TK, causing it to stumble backwards.

Boom! Clang!

Walls's third round hit the TK dead center in its chest. It staggered back a step from the hit before trying to walk forward again.

Boom! Clang!

This time Chug saw Walls's next hit had nailed something vital, as the machine seemed to lose its ability to walk straight.

Gunny Walls approached the machine, confidently aiming towards its head as he fired. This time he blew most of it apart, and the TK finally collapsed to the ground. Sparks and smoke started to emanate from it. He finished the magazine off, plugging three more rounds into the beast just to make sure it was taken off-line this time.

"Is it dead?" Kunze asked.

"Yeah, I think so…or at least it stopped moving," Walls replied as he reloaded the Beowulf just in case.

As the three of them stared at the wrecking machine, a sudden calm washed over them as the realization set in. It was over. They had survived when so many others hadn't.

As the cries of the wounded echoed about, Doc Swanson, the War Pigs' medical corpsman, moved with a renewed sense of purpose. His job now was to save those who could be saved and make comfortable those who could not.

Swanson and Doc Simpson from First Platoon set up an aid station in the fight's aftermath. The results of their victory had come at a grisly cost, as they often had in this war. Thirty-one of the forty Marines had been killed in action, while the remaining nine had all been injured.

Chug stood near the aid station, looking at the rows of bodies lying next to each other while they waited for the Dustoff. Somehow his Raiders had gotten off easy, if that was what you called losing two of your men. The Force Recon Marines had fared a little better, Staff Sergeant Kushner being their only loss. When Chug looked over to First Lieutenant McCarthy, he actually felt bad for the guy. His first official outing as the platoon commander had resulted in the loss of thirty-one of his Marines—damn near his entire platoon, wiped out.

Had this happened against a regular ChiCom line unit, Chug would have half a mind to have him brought up on charges for the negligent way he'd led his Marines trekking around like a stampede of elephants. But they hadn't encountered a line unit. They'd run smack-dab into the wood chipper of some kind of new robotic killing machine. It had been unlike anything he had seen, so Chug cut him some slack,

"Oh crap!" blurted Corporal Butler just as Sawtell saw a missile leap out from underneath the overpass. The object closed the distance in fractions of a second.

As the missile raced towards the Australian tank, the vehicle's active protection system or APS reacted to the incoming threat and the Trophy system fired its countermeasures. The blast of tiny projectiles into the path of the missile caused it to prematurely explode before it slammed into the tank. Within seconds of the first missile firing, several more emerged from beneath the overpass and the nearby tree line to the left of the four-lane road. The missile streaks were rapidly followed by multiple strings of tracer fire likely coming from the same infantry fighting vehicles that had fired the ATGMs.

The lead Abrams fired its smoke grenade launcher as an airburst around the vehicle, creating a thick blanket of smoke to obscure the missiles from scoring further hits. As the Abrams's Trophy system reacted once more to the incoming threats, some missiles began exploding while others were thrown off course by the countermeasures aboard the four tanks of the platoon. Then the lead tank fired its main gun, belching flame and smoke as the gunner reacted to the ambush.

Sawtell watched with rapt attention as the tank's first shot nailed one of the armored vehicles, the one that had fired the first missile at them. No sooner had they destroyed the IFV than a string of tracer fire ricocheted off the turret of the Abrams—another IFV had unloaded on the tank with its 30mm autocannon. The tank fired again, scoring another hit as the explosion ejected the turret of the Type 08 infantry fighting vehicle, sending it high into the air.

"Oh damn!" exclaimed Corporal Butler just in time for Sawtell to see one of the ATGMs slam into the side armor skirt of the second tank in the tank column.

The tank was moving forward when it was hit. While Sawtell wasn't sure what kind of damage the Abrams had just taken, the most obvious damage to the tank was that the track had split and it looked like one or more road wheels had been destroyed. Someone in the vehicle had smartly deployed the tank's smoke grenades as it bathed the armored beast in a blanket of white clouds. Then came a flash against the side of the turret, followed moments later by the ammunition exploding. Jets of flame instantly shot into the sky as the blast doors performed as designed and kept the crew safe.

197

As Lance Corporal Lydia Kellner continued to provide them with an aerial overview of the evolving battle, Sawtell saw the third and fourth tanks move forward past where the second tank had just been destroyed as they moved to get in the fight. When the third tank had barely advanced past the burning wreck of its comrade, its Trophy system activated and it knocked another ATGM down before it could hit the tank. Then the gunner or tank commander spotted the threat that had fired on them and returned the favor.

One of the ZTZ96s fired its main gun from beneath the overpass towards the fourth Aussie tank as it came abreast of the first one. The ZTZ missed, its sabot round sailing between the two Abrams tanks like a giant lawn dart. Then the fourth tank fired its own sabot at the ZTZ, only this time they hit. Sawtell wasn't sure if the round had glanced off the tank or potentially missed when suddenly it blew apart. As Sawtell continued to observe the drone footage, he saw the remaining three tanks of the platoon continuing to engage the remaining armored vehicles and wondered when his platoon and unit were going to get the order to advance and support the tanks. Just then, he spotted a pair of ASLAVs he knew had to have come from Bravo Squadron. *Why are they sending the ASLAVs when they could send us?* he thought angrily at whoever had ordered the less-capable vehicles into the fight rather than send his unit in the Boxer CRVs.

No sooner had he questioned the wisdom of the decision when one of the ASLAVs was hit by what appeared to be a tank round while the other took an ATGM hit, disabling the vehicle. The soldiers aboard the disabled vehicle bailed out the back as best they could. Some of the enemy vehicles still in the fight began to crisscross the highway with withering barrages of 25mm and 30mm rounds, catching some infantrymen in the open while causing the others to scurry for cover.

"Bravo One-Six, Bravo Actual. Advance to T1. I say again, advance to Tango One. How copy?" came the voice of Major Keogh, their company commander, giving the long-awaited order to advance.

A grim look of determination spread across Sawtell's face as he lifted the hand receiver to his lips. "Bravo Actual, Bravo One-Six. Good copy. Advancing to Tango One. Out."

The Boxer CRV lurched forward the moment he was off the radio and their mission was officially a go. While the Abrams and ASLAVs continued to assault the enemy positions head-on, Bravo

Company, led by Sawtell's First Platoon, was going to approach through a nearby tree line in hopes of catching the defenders by surprise. While the CRVs moved through the trees and underbrush, the sounds of the battle further to their right continued to grow in intensity. In addition to the sounds of tanks and heavy-caliber machine guns, the sounds of artillery joining the mix only added to the urgency of finishing the enemy off before they could bring more resources or reinforcements to the fight.

"Ah, damn it! They got our drone," cursed the platoon's drone operator, Lance Corporal Kellner.

"How quick can you get another one up for us?" Sawtell quizzed, suddenly realizing his eyes on the greater picture around them were gone.

"Not long, sir, but we would have to stop so I could launch it," she explained.

While he wanted nothing more than to stop and get another drone in the air, he knew timing was going to be everything with this attack, and right now, they didn't have minutes to spare. They had to get across the expressway and establish another blocking position on the other side before the PLA reinforced this position.

Finally he shook his head in response to her question. "We can't stop. Not right now. Once we do, Kellner, I need you to get your eyes in the sky and start seeing what you can to help me direct my squads where to go and where to focus our LMGs once the shooting starts."

The lance corporal listened intently to his instructions, nodding along in agreement. Shortly after the landings a few months back, the Army had started integrating drone operators and targeteers into company- and platoon-level formations. As commanders had a greater sense of awareness of their surroundings, they could more effectively direct where to have their forces concentrate their efforts, like where to position or direct the machine-gun fire from the squad's machine gunners or the mortar platoon's indirect fire support.

"Heads up, Lieutenant! We're about to exit the tree line. This places us near that farm just south of the main intersection at Tango Three. Do you want us to dismount you guys while we're still in the tree line or try and get you closer?" asked the vehicle commander. The CRV bounced and jostled around a bit as it pushed its way through the trees and underbrush.

Sawtell thought about that for a moment, then made the decision. "Sergeant Riley, stop the vehicles here. We'll dismount and look to engage on foot. I want you to stand by with your vehicles and be prepared to engage targets of opportunity and provide fire support should we call for it."

"Copy that, Lieutenant. I'll pass the word," replied Sergeant Riley, the troop commander for the platoon's four CRVs.

As the vehicle came to a halt, it was still in the tree line, giving them momentary cover. When the hatch to the troop bay finally opened, Corporal Butler shouted some orders as he took charge of the soldiers exiting the CRVs, who raced towards the tree line.
****

Corporal Roderick did not agree with this part of the plan Lieutenant Sawtell had come up with. He felt they should use the speed and firepower of the CRV to push through the enemy lines before dismounting the vehicles. Seeing the scared look on the face of Private John Federspiel, Roderick kicked his foot with his own. "Hey, mate, it'll be all right. You just stick with me, OK?"

The young kid looked barely old enough to shave let alone serve in the Army as he nodded his head in agreement. Federspiel had joined their platoon six days earlier. Just two days prior to the start of ANZAC's latest offensive, they'd gotten bogged down in the central highlands after pushing inland from the beach. If the attack worked, they'd finally be back on the move after being stuck in place for a while.

"Stand by to dismount!" shouted the vehicle commander as they felt the CRV veer off to one side before coming to a halt. As soon as the vehicle stopped, the rear hatch came alive and allowed them to rush out of the vehicle.

"On me, Second Squad!" Roderick shouted as he ran to the right before turning to begin rushing towards the tree line.

"Get those Javelins up and take those vehicles out!" shouted one of the sergeants.

Roderick pointed to the pair of soldiers carrying a set of Javelins on their shoulders. "Get the Javs set up and ready to use. If you spot a tank, go for it. Otherwise, start hitting IFVs and APCs in that order."

The woods came alive around Roderick with soldiers shouting and preparing to fight while the sounds of battle raged in the distance.

He had a surreal feeling like he had been here before, like déjà vu or something he couldn't explain. Then, just as he saw his Javelin teams were about to engage some enemy vehicles, he caught sight of something moving on the far left flank of their position. As he turned his head to see what it was, he felt something spray the side of his face as the soldier standing next to him fell to the ground. Then he heard the crack of a rifle and felt something zip through the air right in front of his face as his instinct took over and he dove for the ground.

"I'm hit! Medic!"

"We're being attacked from the left flank!" someone shouted urgently.

Crack! Crack!

Roderick heard the two single shots and felt pretty certain two more of his platoonmates had just been hit. *What the hell is sniping at us and why can't we see it?* He cursed angrily as people shouted warnings to each other and tried to call out locations where the sniper or shooter might be. With each crack of the rifle, another one of their mates was hit. Using the radio, Roderick asked the lieutenant to see if the sensors aboard the CRV might be able to help them figure out *who* was shooting at them.

****

"Come on, come on, Kellner. We got to figure out where that sniper is or what's taking our guys out," Lieutenant Sawtell urged. She'd just moved the drone over to this side of their flank as they looked frantically to find whoever was taking their people out.

"I don't know, Lieutenant. I can't spot them. They've got to be coming from this direction," Kellner explained as she tried to contain her growing panic at not finding whoever was picking off their platoonmates.

Sawtell looked over to Sergeant Riley as he used the more advanced optical targeting computer aboard the CRV. He just shook his head. "I can't find—"

"Wait, Riley, go back one second," Sawtell interrupted as something caught his eye. As Riley moved the optical scanner gradually to the left, he spotted it, or rather, he spotted something he hadn't expected.

"Whoa, what the hell is that?" Sergeant Riley blurted out as Kellner gasped when whatever this machine was seemed to stare right at them. Almost like it knew they were looking at it before it darted off and out of sight.

Pushing the million thoughts flooding through his brain to the side, Sawtell pulled Riley and Kellner back to reality. "Listen, we can figure out what that thing is later on. Right now, it's killing our platoonmates and that's something we have to stop. Kellner, see if you can help us spot it again with your drones. Riley, the moment you see that thing, you need to hit it with the gun. We got to take that thing out."

As the minutes continued to tick by, more cracks from the rifle were heard, followed by more cries for a medic or just shouts of panic as this mechanical sniper continued to one-shot anything that showed itself. Sawtell got on the radio, hoping to call for help while reporting what they were encountering. Instead of being offered some help, he learned others were encountering the same thing. Just when he was about to scream in frustration as yet another one of his soldiers cried out in pain at being shot, the autocannon fired a double-tap of its 30mm air-bursting munition.

"I got it! I nailed the bastard!" shouted Sergeant Riley as he pointed excitedly to the monitor.

Sawtell looked at the monitor, still somewhat unsure of what exactly he was looking at. Riley pointed to what looked to be the lower torso of the machine they'd seen moments earlier shooting at their people. *If that's the legs, then where's the rest of it…?* No sooner had he had this thought than Riley moved the camera slightly and zoomed in. "There, that's it. That's the rest of it after I hit it with the thirty mike-mike," Riley boasted proudly as Sawtell and Kellner looked at the remnants of what looked to have been some kind of robotic killing machine.

Turning to look at his two soldiers, Sawtell said, "Tell me someone recorded what just happened."

Lance Corporal Kellner smiled. "Oh, I recorded it," she said as she typed something on her tablet before looking up at them. "And I just sent a copy of the video file to myself and the two of you, just in case no one wants to believe us. But, sir, what the hell did we just see? Because that thing sure looked like a killer robot from some kind of dystopian sci-fi novel if you ask me."

"Yeah, really, what the hell was that?" Riley asked as well.

Lieutenant Sawtell looked at the two of them for a moment before commenting. "I'll tell you what we just saw—we saw the future of warfare, and it scares the hell out of me."

Chapter 22
The AquaXpress

USS *Oklahoma*
Yellow Sea

Petty Officer First Class Hugo "Boss" Moretti finished stowing the gear he'd been told to pack aboard the *Owasso* as the *Oklahoma* got underway for another mission. The *Owasso* was one of the two midget submarines the SEALs used for clandestine operations. While it was public knowledge that the advanced SEAL delivery system or ASDS had been canceled back in 2009, what few were aware of was that the cancellation and the very public failures of the program had been intentional misdirects, designed to make the nation's adversaries believe the system wasn't an operational reality when it was. Thus far, it had managed to avoid being outed by the Chinese AI and was among one of the few hidden platforms they had been actively using against it.

While Moretti enjoyed being one of the few guys to be able to operate it, he really wanted to get to working more with his SEAL brothers or maybe another opportunity with Chug and the War Pigs. There was an old SOF adage, "Two is one, one is none," and right now he was feeling every bit the "one is none," and it wasn't a good feeling, growing worse the longer he stayed away from the SEAL teams.

While he would do anything to get himself back in the thick of the action as the war looked to grind on into another year, he had finally come to peace with the newfound purpose Captain Troy "Chug" St. Onge had so lovingly assigned him—the AquaXpress—delivering the nation's warriors from the depths of the sea. Thinking back to his time working with the Raiders, he felt bad when they'd been reassigned to another mission set only days later to discover his rotation aboard the *Oklahoma* had not only been extended but was likely to last for the duration of the war this time. He'd established a reputation as the driver for these kinds of underwater delivery vehicles.

Generally, he didn't mind serving aboard a sub and usually got along with most people he came into contact with. But this rotation aboard the *Oklahoma* had him feeling increasingly alone and isolated from the tight-knit community of SEALs. When the *Oklahoma* had set sail from Guam a few weeks early, he'd suspected something was up.

What he hadn't expected was that the reason for their expedited departure had already come aboard while he had been finalizing his taxi for departure aboard the mothership.

When his shift ended the first day they were underway, he was on his way to the separated compartment aboard the sub where they stored their gear and the operators hung out. The space had been created to keep the operators and their gear away from the crew until it was time to deliver them to where they were going. As he neared the hatch, a figure emerged, catching him off guard as he hadn't realized the "special" passengers had already come aboard.

"Oh, I'm sorry. I didn't realize we had guests aboard," Boss said as he greeted the equally surprised man who stood in front of the hatch.

"Ah yes, we came aboard just before the captain shoved off. You must be Petty Officer First Class Hugo Moretti," the man said as he extended his hand. "I'm Carson Ngo, it's good to meet you."

Moretti shook his hand. "Hi, Carson. You can call me Boss. Everyone else does. Am I allowed to enter, or have I been given the boot out of my space?"

The man seemed to realize he was blocking the hatch and stepped aside. "No, nothing like that, Boss. You're welcome to come in. I'll introduce you to my compatriot. I hear you're quite the driver for these new underwater delivery vehicles. I actually just came from Taiwan; I had infiltrated the island sometime prior to the invasion with an SF team using a similar method," Carson explained as the two of them made their way into the compartment.

As Moretti followed the mystery men into his space, he almost did a double take.

Women... Agency types, he thought to himself.

The women stood as he approached.

"Nat, this is Boss, the Navy SEAL who's going to assist us for a little," Carson announced as the two shook hands. Then he explained, "Now that the introductions have been made, if it's OK with you, Moret—sorry, Boss—Nat and I are going to continue our mission prep until we reach our next destination. If you'd like"—Carson handed Boss a folder marked Top Secret—"you can read up on your new orders and how you fit into what's going to happen next."

Moretti took the folder, surprised by the sudden turn of events as he thought he was going to stay aboard the *Oklahoma*. *OK, this just got interesting. Let's see what I just got signed up for…*
****

A Few Days Later
Owasso

Moretti looked at the depth display for the third time in as many seconds. The currents were stronger than initially anticipated and he was having a hell of a time keeping the bow of the *Owasso* pointed in the direction of the USS *Texas*.

Beep, beep, beep.

The sudden noise alerted Boss that they'd drifted off course again as he glanced at the depth gauge to verify why the beeping had started. As he moved them back to the heading he'd been given, the beeping turned off and he was back on course once again.

The constant fighting of the underwater current was making it challenging to stay on course and on time for their rendezvous with the *Texas*. As he glanced at the clock near his control, he was surprised they'd managed to stay this close to the original time hack for the linkup with the *Texas*, but somehow, they'd managed to stay on track.

"How are we looking, Boss?"

"We're on schedule if that's what you want to know," he replied casually.

"I suppose this is where things get tricky, isn't it?" Carson asked as he stood behind him.

"Yeah, you could say that. I know you can't see it right now, but the *Texas* is about two hundred meters straight ahead," he said, pointing before adding, "and probably about another hundred and fifty meters below us."

"Below us? Can we go that much deeper?"

"Not a chance. We're about to reach our designated linkup point. Once we do, the *Texas* will come up so we can begin the docking process and come aboard," Moretti explained.

"What happens to the *Owasso*?"

"Do you really need to know?" Moretti asked as he turned to look at the spook.

Carson shook his head, acknowledging he didn't.

Moretti turned back to the controls as he finished guiding the *Owasso* towards the *Texas* and completed the first part of their new mission.

****

Wardroom, USS *Texas*

Sitting in the wardroom with his newly arrived guest, Captain Helgeson finished reviewing the set of sealed orders they'd brought for him to read. He'd suspected their mission had something to do with one of the intelligence agencies, and he'd been right. The man and woman sitting across the table from him hailed from both the CIA and Army intelligence. While he wasn't privy to the nature of their mission once ashore, it had to have been deemed important enough to justify the Navy risking its most advanced submarine to approach one of China's largest and busiest port facilities. While much of the Chinese Navy might be resting at the bottom of the ocean, some threats to the *Texas* still existed, like the autonomous catamarans outfitted with antisubmarine warfare equipment, or the aerial drones Jade Dragon had used extensively to hunt and destroy numerous American submarines off the east coast of China.

Helgeson handed the orders to Commander Evans to read while he questioned their guest. "Carson, is it?" he asked of the man who looked to be in his early forties.

"Yes, Carson Ngo, but you can just call me Carson," the man Helgeson knew to be CIA replied.

"Carson, I reviewed the orders, and something seems to be missing from them. There aren't any details about when we're supposed to retrieve the two of you. Is that not part of the deal?"

The CIA operative placed his hands on the table as he calmly replied, "No, you're correct. This is a one-way mission. No sticking around longer than necessary to drop us off."

Evans leaned over as she commented softly, "These are extremely shallow waters. It's going to be very tricky getting them close enough to even get them ashore."

Carson must have heard the comment as he interjected before Helgeson could say something. "Sorry to intrude, Captain. We understand the risk to your boat in the shallows. That's why the *Owasso* was brought along. You get us as close as you safely can. Then we'll rely on Petty Officer Moretti to get us the rest of the way with the *Owasso*, after which we'll swim ashore and continue on with our mission."

Helgeson stared at Carson for a moment. He didn't like this set of orders one bit. It was placing the *Texas* at far more risk than he thought was acceptable. Without knowing the nature of Carson's mission, he was having a hard time accepting the danger he was being asked to place the *Texas* in. If they were detected…there would be little room for maneuver at these depths.

"OK, Carson, I guess we'll have to get you as close as we safely can. Then it will be up to Moretti and the *Owasso* to take you the rest of the way to your destination. For now, I'd like the three of you to stay out of the way of my crew and let us do our jobs. If something changes between now and our estimated time of arrival, I'll let you know. Dismissed," Helgeson said as he stood and made for the exit.
****

Captain's Quarters, USS *Texas*

Carson Ngo met Captain Helgeson at his quarters. Carson knocked twice on the door and waited. When it opened, the captain stared at him for a moment. "Come in. I've been expecting you. I don't have long. I'm on watch soon. I suspect you want me to retrieve the box that was placed in my personal safe with a special note that it was for 'your eyes only'?"

Carson smiled as he gave a curt nod but didn't say anything.

Helgeson stepped back as Carson entered. The captain walked over to his safe and used his body to shield his unlock procedure. When the door popped open, Carson caught a glimpse of the biometric and numerical lock on its front. Helgeson did a good job of shielding the contents of the safe, but as he pulled a thin metal box from within, Carson knew exactly what Langley had left for him.

"OK, Mr. Ngo. I've done my part," said Helgeson. "I've safeguarded your box, ensuring that no one—to include my own XO, COB, or anyone else—knows the Agency placed it aboard prior to our leaving." Helgeson handed the black box over to him. "Is there anything else you need other than some time alone to review its contents?" he asked.

Taking the locked container from the captain, Carson scanned the sealed edges to make sure it hadn't been tampered with. "I'll need between one and two hours alone," he replied. "I'll also need an armed guard posted outside the room. The only person allowed to enter—and only once I say it's OK—is you."

When Carson didn't hear an immediate reply, he looked up. Helgeson was glaring at him. "I'm sorry for the inconvenience, Captain. This contains highly classified and sensitive material. Beyond top secret. That's all I can tell you."

Helgeson stared at him for a moment. Then he slowly nodded. "OK, Mr. Ngo. I'll play your game. I'm going to post Petty Officer First Class Hugo Moretti to stand guard." When Carson didn't immediately respond, he added, "He goes by the call sign Boss. The SEAL that drove you here in the *Owasso*—ring a bell?"

Carson felt his cheeks redden. "Ah, yes, of course, Moretti," he responded. "He told me his call sign came from his Italian surname. He'll be fine, Captain."

"Good, 'cause he'll be on his way here in ten minutes. I'll go ahead and stand outside the door so you can begin. I'll knock twice, then twice more to let you know he's arrived and I'm on my way to the bridge. If you need anything further"—Helgeson pointed to the phone built into the wall next to his table and his bed—"you pick up one of those and you ask for me. That'll connect you to the bridge. If I'm not there for some reason, they'll be able to find me if it's something urgent. Boss will be standing outside."

"Thank you, Captain. Sorry again for the inconvenience and the cloak-and-dagger nature of all this," Carson said as Helgeson left the room to stand outside until his armed guard showed up.

Carson blew some air past his lips. He finally found himself with some solitude. He took a seat at the compact table, placing the sealed black metal box on it. With the urgency and the high stakes of the mission he'd been sent on, the Agency had been forced into merging efforts with MI6.

Withdrawing a knife from his utility belt, Carson cut the seals along the edges of the box. Then he placed his hand atop the glossy material at the center of the box, holding it in place for three seconds. A soft blue light moved from the tips of his fingers down to the base of his palm. When he withdrew his hand, he saw an outline of it in the semitransparent bluish-lit material. A series of biometric signatures across his palm, thumb, and fingers highlighted momentarily before turning green. Then the top of the box hissed slightly as the air inside escaped to reveal its contents.

Inside the box were a pair of files. He reached in and pulled the first one out, leaving the other one inside for later.

The first file had special markings, denoting it was from British intelligence. This wasn't just a sensitive file—it was a special access program, classified beyond top secret and the reason he had requested the armed guard to stand watch outside the door while he read it.

Opening the file from MI6, Carson saw a photograph of a woman named Alexandria "Alex" Mak. She was a deep-cover operative with a background similar to his own.

Alex had been born in Hong Kong to parents who had also been part of British intelligence. They had died tragically in service during her senior year of high school. Later on, as she'd prepared to graduate from Oxford, a former colleague of her parents had recruited her into MI6. Carson found her background, skills, and abilities intriguing. Her dedication to infiltrating a Chinese management consultancy firm linked to Jade Dragon was unmatched. MI6's strategic vision in pursuing the Chinese AI was commendable.

I'm not sure our own Agency would have had this kind of strategic patience, he thought.

During her long-game play to gain access to the right information from the Chinese, many other MI6 operatives had been uncovered by Jade Dragon. When they'd been found, not only had they been executed, but any of their family in the United Kingdom had been assassinated as well. Somehow, Alex's superior intellect and wit had allowed her to remain under the radar for over seven years.

As Carson continued to read through the information she'd uncovered, his jaw dropped. *Wow, it sounds like they might know where those robotic soldiers are being produced. If that's true, this will be a game changer…*

Carson closed Alex's file and placed it back in the box, reaching for the dossier on Major Natalie "Nat" Chen, the lone military member accompanying him. Opening the dossier, he stared at the service photo of Major Chen. Nat, as she preferred to be called, was part of the Army's Intelligence Support Activity. His own Agency knew it by the term "The

Activity." Inside the SOF community, it went by another name—Task Force Orange.

Born in San Francisco to Chinese immigrants, Nat had excelled academically and athletically. After attending West Point Military Academy, she had become an intelligence officer and had eventually been recruited into the Army's Intelligence Support Activity group. Her extensive military training and experience made her a formidable addition to the team. If things went awry, her lethal skills would prove invaluable.

After he finished reading about her education, language skills, military schools, and awards, Carson dug into the descriptions of her military actions and classified operations. Nat, being fluent in Spanish, had apparently spent a lot of time in Cuba, Venezuela, and El Salvador.

However, the most interesting story was about her time during the Russo-Ukrainian War. Natalie had worked with a deep-cover CIA operative who was living as a general in the Russian Army. In that role, she had donned a uniform and patches consistent with the Russian Far East and posed as the general's aide. They had gone to a meeting in the Donbass region with the man who was going to be the governor of that region and several of his closest advisors, and somehow Nat had managed to slip poison into the vodka bottles that were being served to the group.

Holy crap, he realized. *I always knew that Russian leader and his aides had been assassinated, but I had no idea this was how it went down.*

Closing Nat's file, Carson placed it back in the metal box. Sitting back in the chair, he pondered their chances of success. With the Chinese AI Jade Dragon continuing to reveal superweapons like the Terracotta Killers and the Shadow Dragon UCAVs, the balance of the war was threatening to tip in China's favor. With the fate of the war at stake, time was not on the allies' side.

As Carson looked at the files of his two teammates, he felt a glimmer of hope. They just might actually pull this off.

No longer needing the files, he closed the box and pressed down until he heard it click. Satisfied it was sealed, he placed his hand over the semitranslucent material that verified his biometrics. When it scanned his hand this time, it illuminated a soft red color. When Carson continued to hold his hand in place for a moment, he heard a couple of soft pops before the light dimmed to nothing. He removed his hand, and a single word appeared for a few seconds before disappearing—*cleared*. A capsule inside had broken open, its contents disposing of the two dossiers, leaving nothing more than a liquid mess should someone break open the box.

Good, one less thing to worry about. Now to see if Captain Helgeson might be so kind as to eject this out the tube to the depths below, thought Carson. *My work here is done.*

He smiled to himself, thinking that together, they just might be able to pull this off. Their combined skills and expertise, coupled with the urgency of their mission, would drive them to perform beyond expectations, united as one force against the imminent threat of Jade Dragon.

Chapter 23
White Dolphins & Star Wars

Three Days Later
Owasso

Boss watched patiently as Carson and Nat stuffed their kit in the stowage compartment beneath the deck plating. To his eye, their dry bags looked small compared to what he was used to working with. Then again, they weren't packing weapons, and he knew their mission wasn't to mix it up with the CCP.

His orders were specific—drive them to the nearby shore and cut 'em loose. It was ops like this that reminded him why he was a SEAL and not a spook. The idea of infiltrating China without a full combat load and a platoon of SEALs at his side made him shudder.

This spy stuff's for the birds, thought Boss. *I'll stick with the AquaXpress...I'll bet the pay for their line of work is pretty crappy too. It's still a government job, after all.*

As he worked his way through the *Owasso* system checks before getting underway, Boss realized he didn't know the first thing about his passengers. If he had been transporting SEALs or even some jarheads from MARSOC, there was a decent chance he would have known them or known *of* them. But these two...he didn't have a clue.

Bliss is its own reward. He smiled at the thought of that simple truism.

When Boss looked into the mirror that let him see into the passenger compartment behind him, he caught sight of the spook they called Nat, who was in the process of putting her wetsuit on. He admired how it hugged her athletic curves like a second skin, accentuating her figure. He didn't realize he was staring until she looked up and met his eyes. His cheeks flushed as she smiled before blowing him a kiss. He snapped his head to the side in embarrassment as he heard her say something in Chinese—he couldn't tell the difference between Mandarin or Cantonese with his poor language skills.

Then he heard Carson reply to her and they both laughed. No doubt at his expense.

"Boss, she said you've been under the water too long, and that maybe you'd like to come ashore with us and get some fresh air," Carson called out to him. Although he'd heard the man speak flawless English in the past, he suddenly spoke as if he'd been studying English at a second-rate community college to prepare for his citizenship exam.

Boss was puzzled by the sudden change. "I can see you are confused, so let me help," said Nat. "Carson and I are now thinking in Mandarin. We are practicing how to translate in our minds before we speak. The two of us are about to enter the literal belly of the beast. Once we leave the *Owasso*, we won't speak to each other in English until our mission is over. Our lives and our mission depend on us becoming completely Chinese."

Boss nodded his head at the explanation.

Yep, there's no way in hell I could be a spook like that, he told himself. In his mind, being a SEAL was simple: shoot, move, communicate, and repeat.

Having completed his systems check, Boss stood before stepping past them to head toward the opened hatch. Looking down into the *Texas*, he saw a sailor standing at the bottom, waiting for him to give the signal. Once he gave the guy a thumbs-up, they both moved to close their hatches and prepare to separate. Boss had been operating the *Owasso* for so long, he'd started to feel like he'd formed a bond with the *Owasso*, like Han Solo and the Millennium Falcon. As he closed and dogged the hatch separating them, Boss felt more than heard as the *Texas*'s hatch close beneath them.

Boss turned back to his passenger. A pair of Draeger rebreathers hung on the wall near some additional scuba gear. Turning to look at Carson and Nat, he offered, "Are you sure you don't want to use the Draegers? I'll be happy to give 'em to you," he offered.

Carson and Nat both shook their heads before Carson explained, "We appreciate the offer, Boss, but we have to decline. We can't take any chances of them being discovered. If they were and the information concerning how they were discovered was shared with Jade Dragon, who knows? Maybe it might connect some dots or make some rather accurate assumptions. We can't afford the risk. Besides, once we leave the *Owasso* it'll be a short swim. We've got Chinese knock-off SMACO mini-dive tanks we're going to use. If they're found, it will raise less suspicion than a Western setup would. Fishermen use these to clean the hulls of their boats and for shallow dives. They may look old, but they're quite new. They've just been made to look old."

214

Boss understood their concern. The teams were the same way when it came to equipment loadouts for particular missions. Taking a breath in, he said, "That makes sense to me, Carson. So you both know, I can only get so close to the mouth of the Duliujian River. Maybe one hundred meters from where the river empties into the bay. We just don't have any reliable hydro studies upriver—especially ones with enough details for me to navigate it. But it looks like there are plenty of places to come ashore from the river once you reach it."

"Ah, that's OK, Boss, no need to move closer to the river," Nat replied. "Just getting us as close as you have is a risk. No need to increase your odds of getting caught for us. Just get us as close as possible and we'll take it from there. And you're right, there are good places to come ashore once we swim further up the river. I forget sometimes that you're a Navy SEAL and probably understand where to come ashore better than us. It would be nice to get your opinion on the location we chose, but I hope you won't take offense if we keep that to ourselves. It's nothing personal…you know, just in case."

Boss nodded slowly as her meaning sank in. If he somehow got captured, he *couldn't* give up their location, even under torture.

"I agree, good call. OK, then, let's get started," Boss said as he sat in the driver's seat. Turning the power on, he started running through his final systems check before getting them on the move.

He, Carson and Nat took their seats and buckled in. Then he reached for his headset, affixing it to his head and turning the ship-to-ship channel on.

"*Texas, Owasso.* Requesting permission to detach."

"*Owasso, Texas.* Permission granted. Rendezvous coordinates were just fed to your system. We'll see you in a few hours. Good luck."

"*Texas, Owasso.* Copy all. *Owasso* out."

He severed the connection, then started the decoupling sequence to get them going. A few seconds went by as the *Owasso* and *Texas* drifted apart.

When the system status came to life, it showed the *Owasso* was hovering two meters above *Texas* as all systems showed green—operating normal. Checking the oxygen levels first, he then looked over the ballast tanks before manually checking his steering planes.

"All systems check green. *Owasso* is good to go," Boss announced over his shoulder before he saw Carson and Nat staring

215

intently at him. Smiling to ease the tension, he said, "At AquaXpress we know you don't have a choice when clandestinely entering the People's Republic of China. If you're not a frequent diver with AquaXpress, you can join today once you fill out a customer survey telling us about today's experience. Now I'd like to invite you to sit back, relax, and enjoy this three-hour trip as we take you to the terminal."

We were never here.

By the time Boss had finished his little spiel, he heard Nat trying to stifle a laugh before Carson lost it and belly laughed hard, causing Nat to join in.

"OK, folks. Time to drive it like I stole it," Boss announced as he turned his holo-screen on.

The world around him illuminated. Boss activated the pre-plotted position and increased their speed to twelve knots. They were off like it was the Daytona 500.

****

Conn, USS *Texas*

Helgeson watched the 3-D render of the *Owasso* as she angled up and away towards Binhai Bay. His arms were folded, and he felt tense. There wasn't a ChiCom vessel within two hundred miles of the *Texas*. Not that the People's Liberation Army Navy had anything left that posed even a remote threat. Not one to take more risk than was necessary, he deployed the Orcas on his flanks and one to his rear.

The tension he felt in the air wasn't for the *Texas*. It was for the *Owasso*. Boss was on his own out there and nothing could help him should he get into trouble. The waters were just too damn shallow for *Texas* to go in if *Owasso* got into a jam. He wondered if his parents had felt like this as they'd waited for him to come home when he'd borrowed the car.

"Officer of the Deck, set time to rendezvous on the master plot and all stations," Helgeson said tersely. He felt the throbbing in his head come back and for a fraction of a second the edges of his vision began to close in. He shook it off and focused. He didn't have time to deal with another damn headache.

You probably have a TBI, he recalled the doc telling him after he'd been knocked about during one of their underwater duels.

"Set time to rendezvous on master plot and all stations."

"Nav, as we discussed, let's do some lazy eights at fifteen knots to the rendezvous." Before the Nav could echo his order, he continued. "Weps, prep tubes one through four with our Mk 50 specials. Open the outer doors and stand by."

Both officers echoed his commands as his XO, Commander Evans, faced him from across the plot.

"Sir?" she said, looking puzzled.

"We've come too far to be surprised by anything," Helgeson said as he rubbed the back of his neck. "OOD, battle stations quiet."

"Battle stations quiet. Aye, sir."

Plucking the mic from its cradle, he turned the knob to the channel he wanted and pressed the talk button.

"Maneuvering, Conn."

"Conn, Maneuvering," came the robotic reply.

"Prep for ultra quiet, and ready the microreactor."

"Prep for ultra quiet, and ready microreactor, aye."

A few minutes later, the mic squawked for the XO, and she answered the call.

"XO."

Helgeson watched as she listened to the call and checked the information she was receiving against her XO's tablet.

"XO out," she said and placed the mic back in the cradle on the bulkhead next to her head.

"Sir, ship ready in all respects. All stations answer rigged for battle stations quiet," she relayed confidently.

"Thank you, XO."

Walking towards him, she leaned in, whispering, "Now what?"

Whispering back, he replied, "We wait."

****

90 Minutes Later
Owasso

As they continued toward the river, the sonar aboard the *Owasso* detected activity above them. Unsure what it was, Boss queried the big brain to see if it was among its library of known contacts. A moment later, the screen displayed several of the ChiCom autonomous catamarans. His blood pressure began to rise and he was forced to take several slow deep breaths to regain control. Then he heard a sound that made all submariners' blood run cold.

Ping... Ping... Ping...

****

Conn, USS *Texas*

"Conn, Sonar!" came an excited voice over the speakers.

"Sonar, Conn," Helgeson replied, his voice sounding far calmer than he felt.

"Sir, active sonar in the vicinity of the *Owasso*."

"Classify and distance to contact, relative bearing to *Owasso*?"

"Sir, three...belay that. Contacts are classified as four Type-A55 USVs. I can't get an exact distance, but they're closing with the *Owasso* from multiple directions."

"Damn," Helgeson hissed.

"Sir, what can we do?"

"Nothing. There isn't a damn thing we can do, XO. Boss is going to have to figure it out."

****

Owasso

Work the problem! Boss thought to himself. He'd switched on the 2-D holographic display at the front bulkhead of the Conn. He was seeing an approximation of what was outside and above them in real time. It was a computer-generated rendering, which made the data he was being bombarded with easier for his mind to comprehend. He knew that they were at a depth of twenty-two meters, and he had roughly five more meters beneath him before he'd scrape the bottom.

Come on, think. That's it...

He flipped three switches to his right, activating the tactical display. With his left hand, he flicked the tactical display to the main display in front of him. It overlaid itself and offered him a 3-D rendering of the world around him in a 360-degree arc.

Ping... Ping... Ping...

"Boss, what can we do?" Carson asked.

218

Boss looked into the mirror that allowed him to see his passengers. He could see the tension on their faces. That feeling of being helpless washed over him—their lives depended on what he did next.

He returned his gaze to the instruments and readouts. "I'm working the problem, Carson. Just give me some room." He could hear the heavy breathing of his passengers and knew they were scared. He couldn't do anything about that, so his mind blocked them out and focused on getting them through this.

Then for some reason, a report he'd read about these ChiCom USVs popped into his mind. Their design was a total rip-off of the US Sea Hunter, virtually down to their guts.

It's a long shot...but I'll bet it'll work, he thought as an idea began to form, a plan that might save their asses. The pings were loud, but they weren't targeted at the *Owasso*—they were actively pinging on broadband. They were looking, but that was all. They weren't hunting. He was about to give them something to chase.

Boss's fingers danced across his keyboard and controls as he opened the outer doors to the *Owasso*'s pair of torpedo tubes. These weren't the larger traditional tubes but the ones that fired the smaller light torpedoes. Entering the master arm code, he took a second to find what he was looking for. As he scrolled through the acoustic packages, he found the one he was after. With sweat rolling down his face, he entered the four-digit code, loading the software into the torpedo, and then fired.

With a whooshing sound heard throughout the *Owasso*, he'd fired the pair of Mk 54 MOD 3 torpedoes, sending the smaller lightweight hybrid torpedoes in two different directions away from the *Owasso*. Within seconds of being sent on their journeys, they started emitting a high-pitched noise as the torpedoes moved erratically away from the *Owasso* and flooded the area with its computer-generated noise.

For a few moments after he'd sent the decoys on their one-way missions, the pings of the catamarans grew louder as they closed in on the *Owasso*. Then, as the Mk 54s swerved across the paths of the USVs, they increased their noise and accelerated further away.

Boss held his breath as he waited to see if they'd take the bait. Then to his relief, he saw the first reaction. The closest ChiCom USV turned away from the *Owasso*, the sounds of its propeller blades kicking into high gear as it looked to give pursuit to the newly acquired target. Moments after the first USV altered its course, the others joined in and they split into teams, chasing down the two decoys leading them further away from the *Owasso*.

Feeling relieved, he checked their position and distance to the drop-off point. Listening for the USVs a final time to make sure they'd fully taken the bait, he nodded to himself before taking the headphones off and laughing quietly that his plan had actually worked.
****

Conn, USS *Texas*

"Sonar, Conn. Status report," Helgeson called out. When he didn't get an immediate response, he stood from his seat and went to the sonar station behind the Conn to see what was going on.

As he stuck his head into their fiefdom, he snapped, "Status report, now, mister!"

"Sir, sorry, I…it's strange, sir. Here, you just have to listen," the young sonarman stammered at Helgeson's surprise visit. He held a set of headphones for Helgeson as he approached. "Sir, I'll play it back from the time the *Owasso* got pinged the first time to what's happening now."

Helgeson placed the headphones on and made a spinning motion with his finger to hurry this along. He felt his annoyance growing the longer this took. *I just wanted a status report…not to waste time doing what should be your job*, he thought angrily to himself as the seconds ticked by.

As he continued to listen to the *Owasso* making turns at ten knots or less, he started to hear the USVs initiate their sonar pinging as they sailed towards the vicinity of the *Owasso*. Just as he was about to snap at the sonarman for wasting his time, he heard something he hadn't expected. The *Owasso*'s outer torpedo doors began to open. *What the hell is he doing?* As questions flooded his mind, the sounds of torpedoes being fired were unmistakable.

Helgeson was about to order the *Texas* to begin maneuvering and accelerate to flank speed when he heard something else—a loud noise that suddenly brought a smile to his face. *Nice freaking move, Boss…you just saved the mission…hell, you may have just won us the war if their mission succeeds…*
****

With the situation of the moment now under control, Boss turned around to face his passengers and explain what had happened. As he did, it was evident even in the dim lighting of the Conn that the color had drained from their faces. Carson and Nat looked petrified.

Boss held his hands up in mock surrender. "OK, that was tense, so let me explain what's going on. We aren't out of the woods just yet, but the immediate danger is over. It's safe to breathe again, we're safe for—"

"What…wait, what just happened?" stammered Nat as she interrupted.

"More importantly, Boss, has whatever that was compromised the mission?" asked Carson as he tried to stay focused.

"In a nutshell, I spotted four PLA Navy USVs, which are carbon copies of our own Sea Hunter autonomous surface vessels, which we use in antisubmarine warfare operations. They're catamarans designed to prowl the seas looking for subs like us and the *Texas*," Boss explained to looks of shock and surprise from his guests.

"Whoa, that sounds crazy," Nat managed to say.

Carson then asked, "What did you do? I heard some whooshing noise around us. What happened?"

"Oh, that. Yeah, I don't take well to being hunted, so I fired a pair of torpedoes—"

"Wait, what the hell did you just do?" Nat hissed at him with something resembling anger as her eyes bored into him.

"Whoa, hold up. Before you guys lose it, let me tell you something. Those torps I fired won't attack 'em. They're decoys. Those USVs are hunters—like ours. I needed to give them something to hunt. Something to chase, so that's what I did," he rapidly explained before they yelled at him further.

Carson placed his hand on Nat's arm, then in a calmer voice, he asked, "You launched decoys? You realize this compromises our entire mission once they recover those decoys, don't you?"

Boss bristled at the accusation, calming himself before he replied. He explained, "No, Carson, that's not how this works. What I fired was one of our advanced hybrid torpedoes for situations like this. In the forward cone of the torpedo and along the sides are specially designed acoustic inducers." Seeing the confused looks as they stared blankly at him, he further explained, "I don't know if either of you have gone duck hunting or not. But your dog hears the sound of ducks. They tend to give chase unless you hold them back. Think of those USVs as our dog and those acoustic decoys I fired as ducks. The noise they emitted caused the USV to chase 'em and lead them away from us. To further aid in my ruse, I specifically programmed the makers to mimic the sounds of a pod of endangered Chinese white dolphins."

"Wait, what, how, how did you…?" Nat's words faltered as she tried to keep up.

Boss smiled. "Ma'am, I know it's hard to accept, but the People's Republic of China has tree huggers. In the heat of the moment, I took a chance on this. The odds were long, but the payoff was worth it. Those white dolphins they're mimicking are so endangered that Chinese fishermen are required by law to report them in the wild if encountered." He paused to run his hands through his hair as he wiped the sweat along the edges. "Early in the war, we got a strange report through Greenpeace of all people about an encounter they observed with some Chinese warships. Apparently a PLA Navy flotilla was in the process of putting to sea when their transit through the opening of the port was delayed after a pod of these white dolphins was spotted in the area."

"You got to be kidding me," said Carson, who visibly relaxed.

Boss held his hands up. "To be honest, maybe it's all BS misinformation from this AI. But in the moment when those USVs were closing in on us, I figured it was worth a shot. If those USVs were being manned by sailors, I don't think it would have worked. If I had waited and hoped for the best, chances are they would have found us soon enough and we'd be dead." He let that hang in the air for a moment before continuing. "All I know is that there is some low-level bureaucrat or environmental activist in China who got some law put into place to track these kinds of biologics on the endangered list and, should I ever find out who that person is, I'm going to buy 'em a case of Maotai for saving our asses."

His last comment caused everyone to laugh as they calmed their nerves, and he got the *Owasso* back on the move.

As Boss approached the insertion point, he kept an eye on how close he was to bottoming out as the water continued to get shallower the closer they got. It had been ninety minutes since their scare with the

USVs. So far they hadn't spotted anything else to ruin their day, unless his sensors had failed to detect a sunken vessel along their path.

Craning his neck to shout back into the compartment, he said, "We're five mikes out. Almost there."

With the distance to the drop point measuring in tens of meters, he slowed the *Owasso*, allowing its forward moment to glide them into position. Turning the autopilot on, he let the computer run through its paces as its sensors made a final check of the area before rising to ten meters below the surface. Once they were in hover mode, he got up and prepared the vessel to leave his passengers behind.

Boss moved to the hatch they'd use to exit the *Owasso*. He undogged the latch on the deck locker and pulled the bags out from below.

While he was grabbing their gear, they exchanged the wetsuits they'd worn for the ride with the dry suits they'd need for this part of the mission. As they donned their fins and hoods, he watched as they expertly checked each other's equipment a final time before resealing their waterproof bags.

Boss wasn't sure why he felt better about their chances when he saw their suppressed Sig Sauer P229s pistols, but he did. He knew where they were going and what they were up against. Maybe having the ability to defend themselves made him feel like it wasn't a suicide mission. Unsure what more he could do while they prepared to leave, he stuffed his hands in his pockets and waited for the dive light to let him know they'd reached ten meters and it was safe to exit.

"It's time, folks," he finally said as the dive light turned green. He opened the hatch below and the smell of saltwater filled the compartment. Looking into the hatch and seeing the blackness of the water, he knew it was cold and was glad they were wearing dry suits.

He looked at his watch and saw it was 2150. They'd have around seven hours of darkness to do what they had to do before morning twilight arrived.

Carson gave a nod, inserting his regulator into his mouth and lowering the bag attached to his belt into the water before lowering his legs and disappearing into its depths.

Nat hesitated for a moment before she walked to Boss and kissed him. At first he put his hands behind his back, unsure of how to react. Then, somewhere inside his lizard brain, he said "screw it" and leaned forward and kissed her back. He was single, so why not?

They kissed for a few seconds before she broke away, saying, "For good luck."

Boss laughed and she tilted her head to the side with a questioning look. "Like in *Star Wars*?" he said, smiling.

She just looked at him with the same puzzled look on her face before replying, "More like I'm about to go on the most dangerous mission of my life and just wanted to kiss a man once more before I possibly die."

"Oh, damn, I'm sorry I—"

She winked at him playfully. "And, yes, Your Highness, like *Star Wars*."

Then she turned and inserted her regulator before disappearing through the hatch, leaving barely a ripple in the water as she vanished.

Standing in the now-empty *Owasso*, he thought about the kiss for a moment before closing and securing the hatch. *How weird is war where you can run into a smoking hot 007 and share a kiss before she slips beneath the water to go kill bad guys...I sure hope I can find her after this war's over...*

Chapter 24
Spy Games

Three Days Later
Haihe Bund Park
Binhai, China

Alexandria "Alex" Mak had meticulously crafted her morning routine, rising daily at 4 a.m. to go running along the waterfront with her backpack. Over the months, her presence had become a familiar sight to the few early risers and shopkeepers she encountered. To create some opportunities to speak with the occasional person along her runs, she'd periodically stop for various calisthenics, such as sit-ups, push-ups, and jumping jacks. As summer transitioned into fall, she made a few friends and engaged in casual interactions with those she met on her morning runs or after work as she built her predictable routine. This was all part of her plan to blend in with the background noise of daily life as she disappeared in plain sight.

After completing her last assignment with McKinsey & Company in Shanghai several years prior to the war, Alex had been ready to move on to the next step in establishing the bona fides that would eventually lead her to the assigned target she'd been dispatched to infiltrate in China. She'd applied to a similar management consulting firm by the name of China International Capital Corporation. CICC kept her working in the management consulting field until she was eventually able to secure a consulting position with Tianjin Yoshida International Logistics, her primary target. It had taken her over seven years, but Alex had achieved what no MI6 operative had before—the infiltration of TYIL, a front corporation British intelligence believed Jade Dragon was using to build autonomous weapons.

Wearing her running gear, Alex exited her apartment, starting her morning routine with stretches before setting out on her run. Five minutes in, she passed the large white metal wavelike structures, beautifully lit at night like a celestial bridge. Binhai was a stunning area, with its large flower displays and enormous sculptures. During these quiet moments, she could almost forget the ongoing war. However, Alex was always aware of the personal risks involved; if discovered as an MI6 operative, she would face insidious and terrifying forms of torture until she had confessed everything—then they might allow her to die, or hold her hostage for a prisoner swap, if she was lucky.

As Alex rounded a curve near the end of her run, she approached the meeting point—a globelike structure still illuminated in the predawn light. Monitoring her surroundings, she saw no one, as usual for this time of day. As she transitioned from running to walking for her cooldown, she passed a statue of a woman in a heroic running pose. But it wasn't the statue that caught her eye; it was the image of an older gentleman with a cane being helped along by a younger female companion, walking towards her and the bench they were both closing in on.

This particular bench was where Alex routinely stopped to perform basic stretches during her cooldown. Upon reaching it, she grabbed a bottle of water from her running pack and took a drink before placing the bag down on the bench. She fiddled with her shoelaces and stood to stretch her calves.

The older man and the younger woman continued to approach. "You might want to hurry up and get back inside," Alex called out to them in perfect Mandarin, one of the seven languages she spoke fluently. "It's supposed to rain soon."

"Oh, I thought they had forecast an Old Man's Summer for the next few weeks," the woman replied.

Alex smiled at the response, recognizing the coded challenge phrase. "Old Man's Summer" didn't just mean that the warm weather would continue—it meant they hadn't been discovered coming ashore or en route to meet her. Reaching for her bottle of water, she took another drink and casually moved her running pack from the bench to the ground, nudging it against the trash receptacle with her foot.

Holding her water bottle, Alex turned to the woman. "I'd always thought of it as an 'Old Tiger Autumn,'" she replied, giving her the return challenge phrase. "Well, either way, then I suppose we should take advantage of the warmer weather before winter sets in. I still have some of my morning routine to finish before work. Have a good day."

"You as well," the woman replied as Alex resumed her cooldown routine.

****

Later That Evening

Alex Mak's Apartment
Binhai, China

"All right, Carson," Alex said as she placed a bag of makeup on the table next to him. "Let's work on your appearance a little, shall we?"

"What, you didn't like my 'old man' look?" he replied with a smirk.

Alex smiled coyly as she rifled through some supplies she'd retrieved from her bathroom. "Some men try to appear younger, more virile, as they dye their gray away," she said with a seductive smile before continuing her playful banter. Nat looked on with amusement as she sat opposite him. "Today, honey, we are going to have you embrace your age to the fullest."

They all laughed, which was good. The start of the day had been intense, trying to avoid the surveillance state that abounded all around them, but they had made it through the first crucible. Now they had to make it through a few more.

While Alex worked on Carson's hair, they shared some details about their backgrounds as they tried to get to know each other a bit more and build some trust between themselves. Carson knew about her affiliation with MI6, but Natalie didn't, so she was very interested to hear her story. Alex actually enjoyed talking about her past; it was one of the few times she was able to speak about her parents, who had also been MI6. They had died tragically in a car accident when she had turned eighteen, but not before they had passed on their vast knowledge of languages and spy craft. Espionage was in Alex's blood, and apparently, it was now part of the family legacy too.

"Your turn now," said Alex, turning to the young female Special Forces companion.

"Right. Well, that's going to be hard to follow up, Alex. You have such an amazing story and, wow, your family too. So about me. As you know, I'm Natalie Chen. Everyone calls me Nat for short," she began. "I'm the youngest of four kids. I was raised in San Francisco by my parents, who fled China shortly after the Tiananmen Square protest. I don't know too much about it other than my parents seemed to have gotten caught up in some sort of youth movement that ultimately led to them having to flee the country."

Nat shrugged at her story as she continued. "Ultimately, it seems to me like it worked out for them. They got to live the American dream and have a large family, something they never would have been allowed to do in China. During my senior year of high school, I started to get interested in the Army after a recruiter came to our school during a career fair. One thing led to another, and before I knew it, I had applied to and was accepted to West Point."

"Wow, impressive, Nat. That's like getting into Sandhurst back where I come from," said Alex as she finished up a few cosmetic touches to Carson's face, having finished dyeing his hair. "What intriguing field did you study?" she asked.

Nat tried not to laugh at her question. "Oh, nothing very exciting. Trust me. I may have been a track all-star, but I was a total geek in school. A nerd's nerd. I was big in tech and computers, things like that. At the Hudson School for Boys—that's what us 'girls' call the Point when the guys aren't around—I studied computer science and cybersecurity—"

"Whoa there, Q. You really are a 'nerd's nerd,'" Alex interrupted. "How'd you end up in this line of work?"

Nat smiled at the reference to the James Bond quartermaster known as Q in the fictional film and book series. "My first couple of years in the Army, I worked as an intelligence officer supporting the 3rd Special Forces Group out of Fort Bragg—um, I mean Fort Liberty." Nat smirked devilishly at the new name they wanted everyone to start calling Bragg. "I was part of the brigade headquarters element. One day, following a jump on a joint exercise in Jordan, someone mentioned a need for more women inside JSOC. Apparently, women have this unique ability to either turn heads and capture a room or stealthily walk in without being noticed by men."

"Ah, yes. We do have that ability—don't we, Carson?" Alex shot him a wink and his cheeks blushed.

"In any case, that's kind of how I got into this world. I probably spent twenty-four months in training before I went on my first operation in Syria. After spending some time in that AO, I was in Afghanistan until the fall of Kabul, and then I put in time at the 'embassy' in Kyiv. It's been nonstop since the war started. Being fluent in Mandarin, Cantonese, Arabic, Hebrew, Farsi, and Spanish, I've been kept fairly busy. I'll admit, I was pretty stoked when I met Carson here and he told me about our mission," Nat explained as she summed up her experience.

Alex smiled approvingly at Nat. Then, handing Carson a mirror to look at her handiwork, she said, "I daresay, old man, we have added a few years to your look. I think you should do fine now."

Carson looked at himself in the mirror, then looked up at her, a glint in his eyes. "Am I a Silver Fox or a Gray Wolf?" he asked.

The two girls laughed before Nat replied, "A Silver Fox for sure."

"If I was back home and on the prowl, I'd bag and tag you for sure," Alex added for good measure.

Now the three of them laughed. They'd started the day as strangers—two teams forced into working together for a common good. Now they were a team, ready for the next challenge to begin.

****

Alex Mak's Alternate Apartment
Langfang, China

Alex had meticulously crafted a cover story with Tianjin Yoshida International Logistics to justify her stay in Langfang for a couple of weeks. With her travel documents and her innate talent for deception, she'd created a pair of convincing papers for Nat and Carson as well. In the event they faced an encounter with the authorities, the trio would be well prepared.

Prior to Carson and Nat's arrival, Alex had secured a nondescript apartment in close proximity to Peng's family. Since Alex had lived in China for years, the three agreed that she would be the one primarily venturing outside the apartment when the need arose. One of her first tasks was to locate Peng's parents, which she accomplished with relative ease.

As they monitored the grandparents, they looked for signs of surveillance or countersurveillance, anything that could hint at the family being watched. After more than a week of careful observation, Alex turned to Carson for his opinion.

Carson leaned forward on the couch, the dim light casting shadows across his face. "There's still a lot we don't know about this

229

Jade Dragon. It's possible it believes Peng was killed or captured in Taiwan and thus calculated no further need to surveil the grandparents."

Alex brought her hands to her chin, her eyes narrowed as she considered his words. "It's also possible it has other electronic means of tracking them without needing boots on the ground."

Carson nodded, a hint of a smile playing on his lips. "That's true as well. If I may, Alex," he said, and she gestured for him to continue, "sometimes when a bear wants some honey, it has to stick its paw in the honeycomb. It might get stung, or it might not. But one thing's for sure—it'll get some honey."

Alex laughed. "What the hell does that mean?" she asked, her British accent coming out strongly. She turned to Nat for support. "What's this talk about honey and bears?"

Nat couldn't suppress a grin as she held her hands up in mock surrender, feigning confusion at Carson's analogy.

"It means," Carson interjected, his voice betraying his amusement, "sometimes you have to risk getting stung to get what you want. We may have to take a chance and contact the grandparents so we can get this ball rolling. Time isn't on our side here. Once the signal comes—we'll have hours, not days to act."

The jovial mood in the room subsided. Alex's eyes locked on to Carson's, and she nodded in agreement. The tension in the room grew palpable, a potent mixture of adrenaline and anticipation. Their mission hinged on their ability to navigate the complex web of espionage. They knew the stakes were higher than ever.

****

The Following Week
Langfang Nature Park

The air was crisp and tinged with the unmistakable scent of autumn leaves as the team surveilled the grandparents. The team had been on their case for over a week, learning their daily routines. During one particularly close encounter at the bustling market, Nat had demonstrated her prowess with electronic gadgetry by piggybacking off the grandparents' Bluetooth connection. With deft precision, she'd paired their phones to a software app that allowed them to eavesdrop on all incoming and outgoing calls, even covertly activating the phones' microphones and cameras without detection.

The revelation that Jade Dragon wasn't the only one capable of electronic espionage was a game changer, and Alex couldn't help but admire the resourcefulness of her American counterpart.

Mr. and Mrs. Liyuan, like many of their generation, thrived on routine. The team observed them meticulously as they went about their day-to-day activities, dropping their granddaughter Mei off at the state-funded preschool program on Mondays, Wednesdays, and Fridays. On those days, the grandparents tended to errands such as shopping, except for Fridays, when they volunteered at the civics hall, contributing to the war effort in their own way.

Tuesdays and Thursdays were different, though, as the couple always spent time at Langfang Nature Park with Mei, weather permitting. Alex marveled at how Chinese society appeared to be almost oblivious to the ongoing war, sheltered by carefully crafted news articles, talk shows, and other TV programs. Jade Dragon had indeed manufactured a surreal bubble for people to exist in.

As the team observed the grandparents entering the park with Mei, Alex couldn't help but smile at the joy radiating from the child in her stroller. Families filled the park, despite the absence of many younger men, who had been pulled into the war. The laughter of children playing among the trees or watching ducks swim in the lake served as a poignant reminder of what they were fighting for.

Carson and Nat took their positions while Alex kept a vigilant eye on the unfolding scene. The tension in the air was thick, their nerves wound tight as a clock spring. It was time for some honey. Carson was about to make his move.

Alex sat inconspicuously on a bench, her eyes hidden behind dark sunglasses as she pretended to read a popular book for women her age. Through the earpiece, she whispered, "Don't let us down, old man. It's on you."

From her concealed overwatch position, Nat watched intently, her finger on the trigger of her silenced sniper rifle, ready to provide cover if needed. She communicated discreetly through her earpiece. "Carson, they're near the lake now. You're clear to approach."

Carson, in his masterful disguise as an elderly man, slowly hobbled toward the Liyuans, his cane tapping rhythmically on the paved path. His every movement was carefully calculated to avoid arousing suspicion.

With her heart pounding in her chest, Alex continued to monitor the situation, her gaze flicking between the scene unfolding before her and the other park-goers, ready to react at a moment's notice. "Carson, remember to maintain your cover. We can't afford any slipups."

The tension mounted as Carson drew closer to the Liyuans, the other operatives holding their breath, waiting for the precise moment to act. In the world of espionage, the line between success and failure was razor-thin.

****

Carson briefly studied his reflection in the puddle of water near him as he waited for the light to change before continuing his stroll to the park. He marveled at how Alex had subtly aged his face with makeup and a little dusting of gray in his hair. Alex's skill in applying the disguise far exceeded his own, and he couldn't help but feel a grudging admiration for her expertise. The park's entrance loomed ahead, the crisp autumn air filled with the laughter of children and the chatter of families.

Showtime, he thought.

Mr. and Mrs. Liyuan pushed Mei in a stroller, the little girl's eyes sparkling with wonder as she looked about while her grandparents pushed her through the park. Carson sensed an opportunity, and as they approached, he reached out to the child, contorting his features into a comical expression. Mei's laughter bubbled up, and the Liyuans glanced at him, smiling.

"What a beautiful child," Carson remarked, his voice warm and engaging. "I'll bet she must enjoy the blooms of the flowers here. If you look over there, you can see the asters bloom in the meadow's embrace."

The couple's eyes flickered with recognition at the mention of the family code phrase. Mrs. Liyuan, however, maintained her composure, responding, "She does. Our Mei enjoys the tapestry of colors as they unfurl across the meadows here."

Carson's pulse quickened as the exchange of code words proceeded smoothly. The tension in his chest eased slightly, but he remained vigilant, knowing the stakes were high. He gestured toward a nearby garden bed, saying, "You know, I believe those are marigolds in the garden over there."

Mr. Liyuan followed Carson's gaze, nodding in agreement. "They are. They say their golden eyes guard the gates to the park. Do you come here often?"

Relief washed over Carson as the final code phrase confirmed that it was safe to speak. "No, a friend told me about this park. She said it was beautiful this time of year," he replied, giving the couple a slight nod before surreptitiously slipping his phone into the stroller near Mei's diapers.

"Do you think your granddaughter might enjoy looking at the flowers over there?" he asked, subtly motioning with his head.

"I think she would," Mrs. Liyuan agreed, placing her own phone discreetly next to his as she lifted Mei from the stroller. Her husband retrieved a bottle of milk, placing his phone next to Carson's with equal stealth.

With Mei cradled in Mrs. Liyuan's arms, the four of them meandered toward the flower bed, where the vibrant hues of sedum, asters, and marigolds still bloomed. Carson kept up the facade of a casual park-goer, delighting Mei with peekaboo faces while he spoke in hushed tones.

"Your daughter, Dr. Peng Liyuan, is alive and doing well. She's the one who gave me your family code word and asked me to speak to you," he said, pausing for a moment to focus on Mei's laughter. "I need the two of you to trust me, as your daughter has, and you will see her again soon."

Mr. and Mrs. Liyuan exchanged solemn glances before nodding, their determination evident as they joined Carson in entertaining their granddaughter. The weight of their decision to trust a stranger with their family's fate hung in the air, but their love for their daughter and granddaughter clearly spurred them on.

Carson continued, his voice barely audible over the rustling leaves and distant laughter. "You are about to receive a letter. In it, you will be informed that you have won a vacation to the Tianjin Eco-City Hotel, with accommodations and a spa package. It's that former Hilton hotel the government confiscated at the start of the war."

The Liyuans' brows furrowed momentarily. Carson pressed on. "The trip is real. But I'm afraid you won't have much time to enjoy the pampering. Don't look, but that woman sitting on the bench reading a book directly behind me—she's safe, she's with me. She has some regular business at the hotel and comes there often. When the time is right, she will find a way to connect with you there. When she does, have everything you want to bring with you on your person. You will not be able to bring anything else. It could attract the wrong kind of attention. She will lead you to a safe house where you will begin the next step in your journey."

Mr. Liyuan's eyes darted to his wife, apprehension clear on their faces. Still, he puffed out his chest and straightened his spine, ready to face whatever challenges lay ahead.

"For now, pack light," Carson advised. "Bring only what you absolutely need to the hotel, and remember, you can only bring what you can carry with you when it's time to leave. If you must, you could slip something inside the baby bag, but I'd save that for the baby."

He leaned in. "This should go without saying, but only communicate the contents of the letter to those who might specifically miss your presence, such as Mei's preschool or your volunteer coordinator for the first aid kits. And do not share more than you need to. If anyone calls the hotel, they will be able to verify the legitimacy of your travel, but we don't need people poking around because you told some friends about your fortune."

"What about our cell phones? Electronic devices, things like that?" Mr. Liyuan inquired, his voice laced with concern.

"Leave them at home. They can be used to track," Carson replied. "I'm sure this is quite overwhelming. But stay calm, and it will all be over soon. Your daughter trusted me enough to send me to you. Trust me now to bring you to her."

As they returned to the stroller, Carson tickled Mei's cheeks, making her giggle. His hand moved deftly, retrieving his phone from the stroller. After a brief farewell, he ambled toward Alex, who had closed her book and risen from the bench.

The Liyuans disappeared from view, their figures retreating past the eight statues of white elephants that lined the path leading in and out of the park.

Alex sidled up to Carson, her voice barely audible. "Do we have some honey, or did the bear get stung?"

Carson and Alex walked toward the white elephants leading to the exit, their conversation a silent exchange of subtle gestures and facial expressions. "The bear has some honey—minus the bees," he confirmed.

Nat trailed behind them, her sharp gaze scanning the park for any signs of surveillance that might have detected their clandestine meeting. As the trio neared the safe house, she tapped her mic twice, signaling the all clear. The tension that had hung over the scene like a heavy cloud dissipated, replaced by the promise of hope and reunion. The Liyuans had taken the first step on a dangerous journey; now they needed them to follow the plan and stick to it.

Chapter 25
Did You Feel That?

RAAF Woomera Range Complex
South Australia

Racer's hands trembled slightly on the controls as he leveled the Banshee out at angels one hundred. This test was critical—failure could mean the end for the allies. The secrecy surrounding the kinetic weapon and the mission they were preparing for allowed just one shot at success, with a second chance only if they botched it.

As the targeting computer came online, Racer's heart raced. He brought up the coordinates for the hammer one final time. Dr. James Wharton from DARPA had been adamant about each hammer hitting its precise target. They were going to drop three of the Celestial Hammers along the Nuyts Arch fault line, testing the potential to generate a seismic event. If this test succeeded, they might have found the key to turning the tide of the war and destroying the bunker housing Jade Dragon.

"ARTUμ, take control of the aircraft and continue on course to the drop zone," Racer said, his voice tense.

"That's affirmative, Colonel Ryan. I have the aircraft," the smooth voice of Morgan Freeman replied, offering a brief moment of levity in the high-stakes mission.

As the targeting computer highlighted the three Celestial Hammers, Racer marveled at the TRW engineers' solution to the strength-to-weight ratio problem. The fate of the war could depend on these Hammers. He was going to drop three of them, each with a different experimental feature, at five-minute intervals.

"Colonel Ryan, this is Dr. Barbara Young from the ground control team," a voice crackled over the radio, sounding as tense as he felt. "Are you ready for weapons release?"

"Ready, Dr. Young," Racer replied, his voice firm.

"Good. Our future could depend on this test. Proceed with the first hammer, CH1."

Racer selected CH1, entered the authentication code, and released the weapon. His heart pounded as it plummeted toward its target. He switched to the next hammer and repeated the process. Racer didn't know the differences between the three Hammers other than the fact that he'd been assured none of them were nuclear.

With the last hammer released, his part in the test was complete. Sweat beaded on his forehead. "All Celestial Hammers deployed, Dr. Young. What's the next step?"

"Thank you, Colonel. We'll analyze the results and hope for the best," she replied, her voice strained. "Now, please return to base."

Racer directed ARTUµ to set course for RAAF Woomera. The remote facility was desolate and uninteresting, but it was the only place they could maintain secrecy. He prayed the results would be conclusive and the release of this weapon would prove to be the turning point in the war. If not, he dreaded to think what might come next.

****

RAAF Woomera

Dr. James Wharton studied the data from the three separate tests, a satisfied smile playing on his lips. He knew the importance of the nose cones equipped on the Celestial Hammers. It was his work in deep-penetrator munitions that had led to the funding of Project EGIC. The Energy Guided Impactor Cone was a game changer, and the Ultradense Nanometal-5, or UN5, was the revolutionary material that made it possible.

Lost in thought, James barely noticed the door creak open. Looking up, he saw Barbara, the liaison officer. Suppressing a groan, he forced a smile. "Barb, I thought you were giving me until noon to analyze the results."

Barbara grinned. "Sorry, James, but I couldn't contain my excitement. Those seismic results are incredible!" she gushed. "You *have* to tell me how you came up with the idea for the UN5 material."

James leaned back in his chair, recalling the long nights in the lab. "It was a team effort," he replied modestly. "The Air Force Research Laboratory and the Lawrence Livermore National Laboratory both contributed. We were looking for a material with a high strength-to-weight ratio and superior thermal absorption properties. The combination of depleted uranium, tungsten, and the NanoLattice material from Livermore was just the ticket."

As they discussed the results, Barbara listened intently, realizing that she had underestimated James's theories in the past. "You've really outdone yourself this time, James. So, what are your thoughts on the warhead types?"

James considered the options. "We need to bore hundreds of feet. I propose using a combination of high-explosive penetrators and thermobaric warheads. The first three Hammers will dig out a deeper tunnel, and the last one will create overpressure to collapse the bunker."

Barbara furrowed her brow, considering the implications. "Interesting. And you think the SB-1 Banshee can handle such a payload?"

James nodded confidently. "The Banshee was designed for this exact purpose. It can carry four Celestial Hammers, making it the perfect delivery system."

Barbara's eyes narrowed. "Dr. Wharton, how confident are you in this approach?"

James paused for a moment. "There's always a risk, Barb, but the tests speak for themselves. With the right execution, I believe we have a real chance at defeating Jade Dragon."

Barbara placed a hand on his shoulder, her expression earnest. "Thank you, James. Your dedication and expertise have given us hope when we needed it most. Now, let's make sure we're prepared for the fight ahead."

As the two continued their discussion, the future of the war hung in the balance. But with the Celestial Hammers and the genius of Dr. Wharton, the allies finally had a fighting chance.

Chapter 26
Bonwit's Berserkers

5th MarDiv "Bonwit's Berserkers"
Division HQ
USS *Bougainville*

Major General Bonwit looked at his senior staff and RCT commanders. He felt they were ready. His new XO, Brigadier General Soumoy, had worked some logistical miracles, acquiring the resources and operational support elements from the Navy and Air Force beyond anything he'd thought possible. She knew what he needed to accomplish the task and made sure he had it. Now it was incumbent upon him to make sure his field commanders employed the tools and resources of the division and defeated the enemy. The time for planning was over; now it was time for action.

"Twenty minutes ago, we rounded the northern tip of Taiwan and officially entered the Strait," Bonwit explained. "Admiral Blandina said we should arrive off the coast of the Xinwu District in roughly three hours. Colonel Kerns, I want your RCT in the water and hitting your beaches within an hour of the fleet's arrival. I want RCT 27 ready to heliborne you to your objectives inland within ninety minutes of RCT 26 hitting the beach."

Bonwit turned to Colonel Givens, his newly promoted colonel he'd selected to lead RCT 28 after the previous commander had been killed a few weeks back. "Shannon, you've done a good job getting your Marines ready for this. I'm counting on RCT 28 as the division reserve force to be the spear we thrust into the enemy's side once we've opened a breakout or found a seam in their lines to exploit."

"You can count on us, General," Colonel Givens replied confidently. "We're ready to go and chompin' at the bit."

"General, are we still running with these call signs for this op?" asked Colonel Ray, whose RCT would go by the call sign Thor. He had given his commanders and senior staff Nordic call signs for this operation. After more than two years of war, he felt it was time to mix it up with the call signs and let his Marines vote on a slate of potential names that could be used. Had he known how excited they would have gotten over choosing the call signs for the RCTs and division staff, he would have started this from the beginning.

"Ah, what's the matter—Thor?" Colonel Kerns teased. "You don't like our Nordic call signs in honor of temporarily renaming the division to Bonwit's Berserkers?"

"I think he's jealous you got Odin and I'm Loki. We got the cool guy names," ribbed Colonel Givens as the jokes started to flow.

Bonwit let it slide for a moment, then raised a hand to silence them. "OK, kids, time to calm down. Don't make me get your mother. Savusa has been extra grumpy since someone swiped his bag of Invader coffee. He's still got a reward out for information on what jarhead was stupid enough to mess with the sergeant major's brain juice on the eve of an invasion."

An awkward laugh filled the room as everyone eyed each other suspiciously.

"Kerns, RCT 26 is now RCT Odin," said Bonwit, getting back to business. "You guys are first in the rotation. Expect stiff resistance and get off the beach ASAP. Push inland to get out of their kill boxes. Ray, RCT 27 is now RCT Thor. Once Odin's ashore, then Thor will take to the air and heliborne assault your key objectives. That leaves you, Givens. RCT 28 is now RCT Loki. While I'm keeping you in the kennel, once an opportunity presents itself or Odin or Thor run into trouble, I'll cut you loose so your Marines can get in the fight. Let's show these ChiComs what the Berserker Division is all about—slaying America's enemies and stackin' bodies for God to sort out later. Oorah!"

"Oorah!" everyone shouted back.
****

3rd People's Militia Regiment
China University of Technology
Hsinchu County, Taiwan

BOOM! BOOM! BOOM!
The thunderous roar of explosions erupting nearby bounced Major Zhong Jin off his bed. His body crashed into the floor.

What the hell am I doing down here? he thought to himself as he groggily struggled to open his eyes. Slowly, his brain pushed through the pharmaceutical lullaby he'd come to rely on at night.

BOOM! BOOM! BAM!

Holy crap! We're under attack! he realized, now understanding how he'd ended up on the floor. He hadn't rolled off the bed. He'd been tossed from it and somehow managed to sleep through the explosion. Grabbing for something to help him up, Zhong flicked the light switch. To his surprise, it still worked. Searching the room, he found what he was looking for. He sat on the bed and reached for his prosthetic leg.

He cursed himself for having slept through some of the attack as he rapidly threw on his uniform. Standing next to his bed, he grabbed his kit and hoisted it over his head before it settled on his shoulders. He cinched the straps, the body armor and pouches now tightly held against his body. Down the hall, he heard shouting as more explosions erupted outside.

They must be hitting the beach. They're hammering it hard right now!

Checking the time, Zhong saw it was 0515 hours. Not bothering with checking himself in the mirror, he grabbed his rifle and bolted down the hall toward the duty officer. As he neared the end of the hall leading towards the building's entrance, he saw a reflection of the lieutenant against the plexiglass message board sitting at the duty station near the entrance. Then a flash illuminated the room and the lieutenant disappeared into a red mist as the pressure wave of the explosion blew thousands of shards of glass and debris into the foyer.

Zhong twisted his body to the left as the blast tossed him to the floor. He lay still for a moment; more explosions erupted outside. He shook off the fog clouding his head as new sounds filled the air. Cries from the wounded, screams of pain and calls for help soon filled the building as its occupants reacted to the bombs exploding around them. Pushing himself to his feet, Zhong felt a stinging pain in his hand. When he looked at the injured appendage, he saw blood oozing around a shard of glass protruding from between two tendons.

"Major! There you are. Are you OK, sir?" a familiar voice called to him as he approached.

Zhong smiled when he saw the face of Master Sergeant Second Class Han as he handed him a bandage. Zhong willingly accepted the dressing, then winced as he pulled the shard from his hand before wrapping the wound and grabbing his rifle.

"Thank you, Master Sergeant. I'll be fine, but right now we need to get to the general and assess the situation. It sounds the like the Americans have decided to pay us a visit," Zhong shouted cockily, like he didn't have a care in the world as explosions continued to bombard the area around them.

"Ah yes, sir, I agree. But I can't seem to find the general," Han replied, his voice cracking with fear. "When the bombs started to go off, I ran to his quarters to alert him of the attack. But he wasn't there, and it looks like his car and driver are gone as well."

As Zhong listened to Han speak, his blood boiled. He knew exactly where the general had snuck off to and who he was likely with.

"Get my vehicle, Master Sergeant, and mount up the guard force! We need to get to the general now! The Americans are coming, and he needs to lead us before they arrive."

As Master Sergeant Han rushed out of the building shouting orders and commands, Zhong felt a buzzing in his pocket and knew someone was trying to reach him. He grabbed the encrypted phone from his pocket, his jaw clenching the moment he saw the name on the caller ID—Brigadier General Qi Guo. He took a breath as he accepted the call, knowing what would come next.

An excited voice shouted, forcing Zhong to hold the phone away from his ear. "It's really happening, Major Zhong! The Americans are attacking! You must activate the reserve battalion and have them sent them to me now!"

Zhong tried to maintain his composure. "I understand, General Qi. I need to know where you are, comrade General. We checked your quarters, but you weren't there. Where are you?" he asked, knowing his question sounded accusatory.

"What? Where am I? There isn't time to explain, Major! We are under attack. Track my signal and dispatch the reserve battalion to my location now!" the general snapped before ending the call without bothering to wait for a reply.

Unbelievable. The Americans are attacking, and this fool is hiding at a whorehouse…what did I do to deserve this punishment?
****

Four Hours Later
Aerial Command Post

Bonwit looked on in awe of the fleet below as he peered through a window in the Osprey. Colonel Kerns's RCT Odin had just reached the beach after encountering minimal enemy fire. His lead elements appeared to be making short work of the poorly defended beach as they cut a path inland for others to follow.

"It looks like the intel was right about the Xinwu District," said Colonel Philip Daniels as Bonwit peered through the window. "One of our recon elements further inland just sent a report in after securing their objective. One of the soldiers they captured confirmed he was part of the People's Militia. He said the district is being defended by the 3rd People's Militia—Kunming Regiment."

Bonwit pulled away from the window. "Huh, is that so?" he asked rhetorically. "Well, I guess the intel weenies finally got it right. No offense, Phil—it's just nice to see our ability to acquire information seems to have finally gotten better as the war progresses."

"None taken, sir, and you're right. Intelligence is an imprecise trade that's only as good as the inputs it receives. It does confirm for us that if we're facing a PM regiment here, it's likely these neighboring districts are also being garrisoned and manned by similar PM regiments," Colonel Daniels elaborated as Bonwit moved towards the table and chairs he typically used when aboard the division's aerial command post.

Shortly after the Cuban invasion, the Marines had converted a pair of division MV-22s into an aerial command post. The newly converted Ospreys had finally rejoined the fleet after the initial landings at the start of the Taiwan operation. The interior space of the Osprey, which could once ferry up to thirty-two Marines into battle, had now been converted into an airborne operations center. The center of the cargo hold featured a bench for the computers, radios, and the comms equipment necessary to manage the division. Seated along opposite sides of the bench were Bonwit's officers and NCOs responsible for receiving the data flowing in from the division's drones and units below. Affixed to the walls of the Osprey were a trio of monitors, able to display whatever they deemed necessary.

"This is good news about the militias. Do we know if the 71st Group Army has started moving units in our direction yet or if the 72nd

243

Group Army has started to react to our presence?" Bonwit quizzed. The last thing he wanted to see happen was for his division to get squeezed on both sides by a desperate PLA commander.

"Nothing major just yet, but that will likely change in the coming hours as they try to figure out what they want to do next," Daniels responded before grabbing his tablet to pull up some digital maps of the area to share with him.

As Bonwit examined the current disposition of the enemy units in relationship to his own, he felt confident he'd found the squishy spot in the enemy lines. *If it's mush...push...* was the adage that came to mind.

"This is good work, Phil. Now how about those drone feeds everyone swore we'd have available once the landings started? If we're going to help the RCTs find some openings in the enemy lines to exploit, then it might be nice if we could keep 'em from getting zapped," Bonwit chided. Both sides had gotten adept at taking each other's drones down the moment they saw them.

"Here you go, sir," Sergeant Michaels offered. He handed him a tablet showing a four-way video split.

"Ah, excellent. This is good. Now let's try and keep 'em from getting destroyed long enough for us to get some use out of them," Bonwit replied as he took the tablet.

"I'll get out of your hair, sir," offered Daniels as he returned to his seat.

Looking at the drone feeds, Bonwit found the one he was after. It was a feed set up in an overwatch position a few kilometers behind RCT Odin. He tapped the image, bringing forward a larger view of the situation. Using the controls to the drone's camera, Bonwit zoomed in to get a better view.

Once he could see the beach and shoreline more clearly, Bonwit could tell it had taken a beating from the earlier shore bombardment. The Ticos and their 155mm cannons had worked the area over, hitting machine-gun emplacements and assorted trench networks that looked to have been haphazardly constructed.

When Bonwit zoomed in to get a better look at the defensive works, he was confused by what he saw. They were a mess. They were poorly laid out, with few if any connecting trench lines and not enough fortified gun emplacements to provide effective interlocking fields of fire. In short, they were nothing like the defensive works he'd

244

encountered in Venezuela or on the eastern side of the island. Bonwit realized in that moment how big of a break they'd caught, facing a militia unit instead of battling hardened ChiCom regulars.

As Bonwit continued to watch the drone feed, he saw that the first echelon of amphibious combat vehicles had reached the shore. Not far behind the ACVs was a line of the smaller landing craft bringing ashore some armored trucks, followed by the larger landing craft utilities bringing ashore the LAVs and other armored vehicles they'd need to expand inland.

As the units of RCT Odin moved inland past the beach areas, the enemy resistance seemed to melt with little more effort than driving towards them and firing a few rounds in their direction. Then Bonwit observed pockets of militia throwing their weapons down and surrendering at the first sight of a Marine. At first, it looked like a squad trying to surrender. Then it grew into a cluster of twenty or thirty trying to surrender at once. For a moment, Bonwit wondered if the entire enemy regiment might surrender. Then Kerns's units hit a few pockets of determined fighters, dashing his hopes of a quick collapse.

Bonwit had discounted the possibility of encountering formations of militia on this side of the island until the landings had started. The more he saw his Marines encountering them, the more he was starting to believe the rumors he had heard about these so-called People's Militia units. Up until now, the Marines had not encountered many of them in Taiwan. Most of these PM units were fighting in northern China, against the Russian-NATO force and now the US-led Eighth Army. With casualties among the regular ChiCom units off the charts, the Chinese President, Yao, seemed to be grabbing civilians off the streets and throwing them into these militia units to be hastily outfitted and driven to the front.

Bonwit shook his head in disgust at the idea of sending these ill-equipped, poorly trained civilians directly into combat with little regard as to whether they lived or died. He recalled how that had happened during the initial months of the Russo-Ukraine War. It had led to enormous casualties on both sides until they'd exhausted themselves during the second year of the war. In many cases, these valiant Ukrainian soldiers were dying not because they couldn't be saved but because they didn't have access to basic first aid or the knowledge to use a tourniquet to stop the bleeding.

"Sir, you got a call," interrupted Staff Sergeant Michaels.

Bonwit grabbed the hand receiver. "Go for Berserker Actual."

He smiled after saying Berserker. Rather than force his Marines into using the older division motto, he'd leaned into the new one they had created.

"Berserker Actual, Odin Actual. Report ready to transmit. How copy?" came the voice of Colonel Kerns. His RCT had encountered light and highly disorganized resistance on their approach to the beaches. Once they had reached the defensive works, they'd run right through them and proceeded to move inland.

"Odin, Berserker. Good copy. Go for report."

A moment later, the SINCGAR frequency-hopping radio chirped as the connection synched. "Berserker Actual, Odin One has reached Jorvik-Two-Alpha. Odin Two has reached Jorvik-Two-Bravo. Break. Odin One is now advancing northeast towards Jorvik-Three-Alpha and Three-Bravo. Break. Odin Two is now advancing east towards Jorvik-Four-Bravo, Four-Charlie, and Four-Delta. How copy?"

Bonwit hastily scribbled some notes as Kerns continued his update. He then breathed a sigh of relief when Staff Sergeant Michaels placed a map on the table between them. He started following along using colored dry-erase markers to highlight the current and future locations of Odin One and Two.

"Odin, Berserker. Good copy on all. Break. What is the status on Odin Three? Jorvik-Eight-Alpha through Eight-Bravo look to have minimal protection. How copy?"

Jorvik-Eight was the location of the former Republic of China Hukou Army Base on Shengli Road. It had been bombed many times over since the PLA had invaded.

Bonwit hesitated a moment before responding. He wanted to grab the Hukou Army Base as much as his Marines did. His only concern was getting a force too far out in front of him and suddenly finding them cut off from resupply or help should they run into stiffer enemy resistance. Sighing, he reluctantly replied, "That's a good copy. Raven Five confirms Jorvik-Eight is minimally protected. Break. Based on your report and the ISR we have of the area, I'll release Odin Three to seize Jorvik-Eight. Break. Raven Four has detected minimal force near objective Mercia-One. How copy?"

"Huh, could they really have left Mercia-One wide open like that?" Bonwit thought out loud. Mercia was what they had labeled a nearby defunct Taiwanese air base. If they could grab it and turn it into a functional air base again, then it could go a long way towards rebasing the division's attack helos and maybe some aircraft for faster turnaround times to better support his infantry.

"Odin, Berserker. What's the status of those POWs? Do you have a count yet?"

Bonwit was starting to get concerned that his lead elements were getting overwhelmed by the number of prisoners that were surrendering to them. He needed those units pushing inland away from the landing zones—not tied down babysitting prisoners until another unit could take them off their hands.

"We're encountering more units surrendering as we push further inland. Break. I've tasked Odin One-One with creating a POW collection point near Jorvik-One-Delta. Break. We need to push a unit forward to take 'em off our hands. How copy?"

I guess we better get the MPs on the next rotation to the shore, Bonwit realized.

"Odin, copy all. I'll move up the MP rotation. Continue with your objectives. I'm going to release Loki with orders to seize objective Mercia-One. Out," Bonwit said, ending the call.

Then he turned to his operations officer. "Send a message to Colonel Givens. Tell him I'm releasing his Loki elements. Tell Colonel Givens his orders are to seize objective Mercia-One and expand and hold the perimeter."

The next hour was tense as Bonwit continued to observe his units moving further inland towards their second- and even third-day objectives. Given the brutal savagery of the fighting his Marines had been encountering with units from the 71st Group Army, he had expected to meet more resistance than what they had so far. Not that he was complaining about a lack of fighting. It just felt too easy, and if something was too easy in war—it was usually a trap.

Are we being drawn into something we haven't spotted yet? he wondered. *Something feels strange about this...*
****

IVO Fugang Old Street

247

Hsinchu County, Taiwan

Major Zhong Jin was glad to have Master Sergeant Han do the driving at that moment. They were heading towards the location where General Qi Guo had spent the night before the Americans had attacked, and the university that they had converted to a command center was toast. A pair of cruise missiles hit the building as they were leaving the compound to pick up the general. He was glad they'd agreed to move the headquarters operation center into the university's basement. While Zhong wasn't sure if anyone had survived the attack or not, it did give them a better chance than leaving the HQ on the third floor of the main building.

While Master Sergeant Han drove their convoy through the various winding roads connecting the tiny villages and towns together, Zhong was on the radio trying to reach one battalion commander after another to get an update on what was happening. His level of frustration grew with each attempt to speak to one of the colonels. Two of them were nowhere to be found while another had been killed—an artillery round had scored a hit against the building he was sleeping in.

Another pair of colonels were also unavailable, much to Zhong's chagrin. Their seconds-in-command swore they hadn't abandoned them. They were last seen together in one of the command posts in the Xinwu District, not far from the beach. Apparently, the place had been hit by a missile or guided bomb from an American warplane. He'd been told it was a smoldering ruin.

"We're not far, Major. Maybe five minutes," Han shouted to be heard over the sounds of explosions, helicopters, and gunfire happening all around them.

"Just try and get us there alive."

Zhong tried not to flinch at the sounds of explosions that ebbed and flowed as they sped along the county roads toward the location where the general had snuck off to. When Zhong looked in the direction of the coast, he could make out some faint images of vessels far off. Closer to the shore, he could see smaller vessels bobbing in the waves as they crept towards the beach. Periodically, he'd spot an explosion or two from one of the howitzer batteries he'd convinced General Qi to dedicate for shore bombardments. He knew if the Marines landed along the Xinwu District, he'd be hard-pressed to throw them back into the sea, but if they could get lucky and score a hit or two against some of the landing craft or amphibious assault vehicles, it might do some damage and buy them more time for help to arrive.

"Hold on, Major. The bridge is destroyed," Han announced. "I'm going turn on that road that runs next to the river that bridge crossed. I think we can ford the river. If we can't, there's another bridge a mile or two further down the road," Han explained as he braked sharply before turning abruptly onto a new road.

No sooner had he turned off the main road than they saw short flashes of red light zipping through the air. Chunks of asphalt and cement were ripped from the road and thrown into the air. Zhong clawed at the bar above his head as Han swerved to one side before swerving to another as tracer rounds zipped around the vehicle. The thumping of helicopter blades grew louder until Zhong spotted a Marine Viper attack helicopter not far away.

"It sure would've been nice if we had some air cover or SAMs, wouldn't it?" Master Sergeant Han joked as he placed another cigarette in the corner of his mouth.

"I agree, Sergeant. For now, let's try and make it to the general before we get blown up or shot to pieces to one of those helicopters," Zhong replied as he tried to remain stoic and in control of his fear. When they'd left the university, they had started with ten vehicles; now they were down to three.

"Major, that building next to the corner should be it. That's where the general should be waiting for us."

Zhong spotted the building at the end of the street. The vehicle slowed as they approached until he stopped in front of it. Before he got out of the vehicle, Zhong explained, "Listen to me, Han—once we get the general into the vehicle, I need you to listen to me and ignore whatever orders he gives you.

"General Qi Guo is the regiment commander in charge of the defense of this area. Right now we are under attack, likely by the American Marines, and this sorry excuse for a general is not going to be allowed to slither away into the shadows to hide while his soldiers die in the very defensive works he failed to ensure were being properly built. Once I get him in the vehicle, I need you to drive us to the alternate command post. We can resume command of the regiment from there and get the battalions deployed to their sectors if they haven't already."

******

Midafternoon
5th MarDiv "Bonwit's Berserkers"
Aerial Command Post

It was nearly 1400 hours when Major General Bonwit ordered his aerial command post back into the sky. They had returned to the *Bougainville* for fuel a couple of times throughout the day, but nothing beat the sight of his division unfolding itself from the ships to the shore—then from the shore inland. While it was certainly easier and less cramped to manage and oversee the division's mission objectives from the LHA's tactical operations center, seeing his units moving about the battlespace gave Bonwit the ability to determine firsthand what his forces were encountering so he could better devise a means to overcome it, which just couldn't be done aboard a ship.

As the pilot took them closer to the shore, Bonwit could see it was abuzz with activity. The large landing craft utilities and other landing craft were hurriedly bringing his armored vehicles ashore along with more of his trucks and JLTVs. It was a race now to get his forces ashore with as many of their supplies as possible before the larger PLA formations to the north and south advanced toward them. His units needed to grab a series of choke points and strategic positions, which his engineers would rapidly transform into defensive redoubts. He was under no illusions about what would happen to his division if either of those larger PLA group armies decided to refocus their efforts against his beachhead and throw the division back into the sea.

"Excuse me, sir," interrupted Staff Sergeant Michaels as he gave the radio hand receiver to him. "It's Brigadier General Soumoy on the line. She said it's important."

Bonwit raised an eyebrow as he took the hand receiver. "Huh, I guess we'll see in a moment, won't we?" he remarked, mostly to himself.

Sergeant Michaels grinned as he tried to listen to the one-sided conversation.

"Freya Actual, Berserker Actual. Send it," Bonwit said as he used Soumoy's call sign for the first time of the day.

"Berserker Actual, don't ask how, but I just came into possession of a mix of Jackal XD500s. Break. I believe RCT Odin had requested additional Jackal support. Break. How would you like them distributed to the RCTs? Over," Soumoy explained, having once again managed to find a stash of supplies that wasn't supposed to exist.

"Freya, how many Jackals did you say you found? Over."

"Berserker, sixty-four. An even split of sixteen to each RCT with four of each model available. Should I arrange for delivery to the RCTs? Over."

"Did I hear that right, General?" Colonel Daniels asked, his left eyebrow raised in doubt. "The XO managed to find sixty-four Jackals for us?"

"Yeah, it looks that way," Bonwit confirmed. "Is there an RCT that needs 'em more than another? She's asking where to send them right now."

The G2 held his hand up as he grabbed his tablet and scooched over to his table. "Sir, we just got a Raven report from Hukou Township. Just beyond the village, you can see an enemy force starting to marshal some armored vehicles and a few tanks to support them. I can't say when they'll attack or if they'll attack, but this is RCT Loki's AO, and if they do attack, then his units are going to be in a world of trouble. Most of our armored vehicles and trucks are with RCT Odin and Thor. I'd send eight Jackals to their RCTs and send the forty-eight others to Loki's units. They'll need 'em more should that force make a move on them."

Bonwit was concerned about sending more helicopters into Hukou. They'd already lost two MV-22s to MANPADs. He wasn't keen on adding some of his Super Stallions to the list. Then again, if the ChiComs were organizing some sort of armored force to attack his landing zones, then Colonel Givens was going to need the firepower they could bring to a fight.

Bonwit shook his head. He didn't like his options. "Freya, the G2 just made me aware of something. Here's what I want you to do. Send eight Jackals to RCTs Odin and Thor. Then send the remaining forty-eight to RCT Loki. Out."

When Bonwit saw the concerned look on the face of his G2, he felt like they weren't out of the woods just yet. The militia regiment they had pounded on throughout the day just might have a little fight still in them.

251

****

3rd People's Militia Regiment
Hukou ROC Army Reserve Camp
Hukou Township, Taiwan

General Qi stammered for words that wouldn't come. His eyes widened at the sight of Major Zhong's pistol, now inches from his face. "You can't do this!" he blubbered as he became emotional. "I am a general…my father is a senior Party official, and my brother is a political officer in the Air—"

Pop, the pistol barked.

The bullet hit Song squarely between the eyes, and his body collapsed in a heap. Zhong heard audible gasps and murmurs of concern from Song's acolytes, who couldn't believe he'd just been shot like that. Zhong turned to face them, the pistol in hand. He pointed his free hand at Captain Yang Yong, Song's political officer.

"Captain Yang was present during the call with Major General Huang, the commander of the 71st Group Army and his political officer. General Qi Guo was an embarrassment to the People's Militia, the Group Army commander, his family, and the nation." Zhong spoke forcefully, wanting to make sure everyone understood what happened to those who failed China.

"The 3rd People's Militia Regiment was responsible for the coastal defense of Hsinchu County. The 71st Group Army was counting on our regiment to do what we said we could do and defend the coastal areas long enough for reinforcements to arrive.

"Do you want to know how long we lasted? How long Lieutenant Colonel Lei's Dianchi Battalion lasted before he surrendered his force?" snarled Zhong, his words laced with the venom, scorn, and disgust he felt towards the unqualified commander.

"Twenty-seven minutes! That's how long Lieutenant Colonel Lei's battalion fought the Americans before giving up! As of this moment, General Huang has placed me in command of what's left of the regiment. We are going to fight. We are going to defend our homeland from these foreign invaders. We shall water the land with their blood, or we shall throw them back into the sea," Zhong exclaimed loudly, pounding his fist on the table nearby.

252

"Our regiment has been given new orders," Zhong continued. "I want Major Li, Captain Chen, and First Lieutenant Sun to stay here. Everyone else…get out!"

As the room cleared, the reality of the situation sank in, and Zhong knew they were not long for this world given the way things had gone so far. From the moment he'd retrieved that odious piece of garbage from the whorehouse where he'd stayed the night, battalion after battalion had been cut to shreds by American Marines or had simply given up. On several occasions, he had blocked General Qi from ordering his commanders to fall back to the Army Reserve camp, until eventually, General Huang had been made aware of what was happening and ordered Zhong to take charge of the regiment and fix the problem.

Staring at the recently updated map taped to the wall, Zhong wasn't sure there was much he could do at this point to turn things around.

We started the day with eight battalions…we have two left.

Zhong turned away from the map, fixing his gaze on the three officers he deemed moderately qualified to hold their positions. He'd asked them to stay behind because they were the only ones he felt reasonably confident about placing in charge of the remaining force he had left.

Looking first to Major Li Qiang, he said, "Major, you're now in charge of the Lugu Battalion. I don't trust anyone else. As much as it pains me to admit this, since the Marines have established a beachhead and even now are assaulting the Hukou Army Base, we are now being asked to form small hit-and-run ambush teams to sow chaos and cause problems for the Marines. This is a task that is beyond what I think our militia force can effectively do, but we will try and continue to stall their advance while we wait for additional units to arrive."

For the next hour, Zhong passed along as much as he could before sending them out. He knew he was likely sending them to their deaths, but what choice did he have? Surrender wasn't an option, and the word *quit* wasn't a part of his vocabulary.

When it was down to just him and First Lieutenant Sun, Zhong explained the importance of the mission General Huang had tasked them with, clipping the wings of the Marines and forcing them into a street fight. This strategy would sap the energy of the allies and drain material support in Taiwan so it couldn't be used on the mainland. Zhong pointed to the two OD Green cases stacked against the back of the room, and once his eager lieutenant realized what was in them, a devilish grin spread across his face.

"Are those what I think they are? Flaming Arrows—Norinco's newest QW-3 man-portable air-defense system?" Lieutenant Sun asked. There was no question these fourth-generation MANPADs were vastly superior to the HN series, which were little more than copies of the Soviet Strela MANPADs.

"Lieutenant Sun, I must admit I didn't think you would know much if anything about MANPADs. But, yes, those are the QW-3s," Major Zhong confirmed. "These are the ones that use those dual-mode seekers—infrared and ultraviolet. They are also the ones that include a passive countermeasures system. That's the whizbang stuff they tell me reduces the likelihood of it getting spoofed and chasing after a flare or some sort of chaff canister decoy. Basically, that means it'll be damn hard for those Marines to try and evade one."

"This is incredible, Major. Does this mean the mission you want to use me and my platoon for involves going after helicopters?" the lieutenant inquired, doing his best to contain his excitement.

"Um, sort of, I suppose," Zhong responded. "Let's just say I think it's time we invited your platoon to come join us here. I want to make sure you guys also know how to use those." Zhong motioned with his hand to a series of stacked OD Green cases similar to the ones containing the MANPADs.

Lieutenant Sun furrowed his brow as he hesitantly read the words. "Hongjian-12—I don't seem to recall what this stands for. I only know about the Norinco QW system because my older brother is a supervisor at the plant that makes them. What does it do?"

Zhong smiled. "Lieutenant, have you heard of the term 'antitank guided-missile system' before?"

"Ah, you mean the fire-and-forget ATGM or something like that?" he quizzed, still unsure.

Zhong laughed at his hesitation. "Yeah, it's something like that. Go get your platoon. Now that Qi Guo can't inadvertently get us all killed, I think it's time I show you what I used to do before I lost my leg back in Venezuela…"
****

254

0328 Hours, Following Morning
IVO Hukou Army Base
Hukou Township, Taiwan

Major Zhong Jin stood at a vantage point overlooking the Hukou Army Base, binoculars pressed to his eyes. His pulse raced as he watched the American Marines working on the flight line, adrenaline pumping through his veins. The invasion had been swift and merciless, and Zhong couldn't help but feel a sense of frustration at the rapid progress of the Marines. It was a question he could only ponder after the war.

"One minute," Lieutenant Sun's voice crackled over the radio.

Zhong glanced down at the DJI drone controller in his hand, the live video feed revealing the preparations of the militia platoon. In less than sixty seconds, they'd find out if the hurried training on the Red Arrow–12 ATGMs had paid off. The Marines had wasted no time in capturing the base and getting the helipads operational. Now, choppers streamed in, bringing reinforcements and supplies.

Despite his determination, Zhong was a realist. With just three Red Arrow–12 fire-and-forget ATGMs and a pair of QW-3 MANPADs, there was only so much Lieutenant Sun's platoon of militiamen could do. To make matters worse, the betrayal of Major Li weighed heavily on his mind; the memory of Li's surrender of the entire Lugu Battalion was still fresh and painful.

Shaking his head dismissively, Zhong tightened his jaw. He hoped the militiamen wouldn't falter at the last second, a dangerous trend he'd noticed among the militia units. The stakes were high, but he had to believe they could make a difference.

"Thirty seconds," Sun's voice came through the radio again, the anticipation palpable.

Zhong's fingers tightened around the drone controller, his eyes never leaving the live feed on the small screen. The militiamen were in position, their camouflage blending seamlessly with the vegetation and natural terrain. Sergeant Yang's squad, armed with the Red Arrow–12 ATGMs, tensed as the countdown continued.

"Ten seconds," Sun whispered, his voice laden with the gravity of the situation.

Zhong's heart pounded in his chest, his nerves fraying as the seconds ticked by. The militia platoon was inexperienced, but their determination was undeniable. He knew their bravery and their lives were in his hands, and he was determined to make their efforts count.

"Fire!" Lieutenant Sun commanded, his voice resolute.

Sergeant Yang's squad sprang into action, launching their ATGMs at the unsuspecting Marine vehicles and fuel bladders. The missiles cut through the air with deadly accuracy, their fiery tails streaking toward the enemy. The Marines scrambled in response, some diving for cover while others attempted to return fire.

"Sergeant Yang, report!" Lieutenant Sun demanded, the urgency in his voice betraying his own nerves.

"Two vehicles destroyed. One fuel bladder hit!" Yang replied, his voice strained from the chaos of battle.

A surge of pride coursed through Zhong at the small but significant victory. It wasn't enough to turn the tide of the battle, but it would buy them time and disrupt the Marines' operations. Zhong quickly refocused on the drone's feed, scanning for the AH-1Z Viper attack helicopters that were sure to respond to the attack.

"Corporal Liu, stand by with your QW-3 MANPADs," Lieutenant Sun ordered, his voice tense with anticipation.

The chaos on the ground intensified as Zhong saw the pair of Viper helicopters in the distance head towards the fight they'd started. As they closed the distance to the base they were attacking, he could hear their rotor blades slicing through the air, a menacing reminder of their deadly firepower. The noise was deafening, but Zhong remained focused, his eyes glued to the drone's screen.

"Vipers incoming!" Zhong warned over the radio, his voice steady despite the pounding of his heart.

Corporal Liu's squad sprang to action, their QW-3 MANPADs at the ready. The militiamen crouched in their concealed positions, their eyes trained on the approaching helicopters. Time seemed to slow as the Vipers bored down on them, their sleek frames bristling with weaponry.

"Now!" Lieutenant Sun barked the order.

Corporal Liu's squad fired their MANPADs, the missiles arching skyward to meet the advancing Vipers. As the missiles closed in on their targets, the fate of the militia platoon hung in the balance.

Two direct hits sent plumes of smoke and fire into the sky. The AH-1Z Vipers erupted into flames, spiraling to the ground in a pile of mangled, burning wreckage. The Chinese soldiers cheered, their spirits momentarily lifted by the small victory.

But the battle was far from over. The Marines regrouped, their discipline and experience shining through as they launched a devastating counterattack. Mortar rounds and machine-gun fire rained down on the militia platoon, pinning them down and cutting off their avenues of retreat. One by one, the Chinese soldiers fell, their desperate cries echoing through the air as they succumbed to their injuries.

Zhong watched helplessly as Lieutenant Sun tried to rally his men, shouting orders over the cacophony of gunfire and explosions. Sergeant Yang was hit, slumped against a tree; his lifeblood stained the ground beneath him. Corporal Liu, too, was struck down, his lifeless body cradling the remains of the QW-3 MANPAD that had brought down the Vipers.

"Major Zhong, we need to withdraw!" Sun shouted into the radio, his voice strained and choked with emotion.

But Zhong knew it was too late. The Marines had them surrounded, their superior firepower and training quickly overpowering the beleaguered militiamen. The drone's feed painted a grim picture, with the bodies of the Chinese soldiers scattered across the battlefield like rag dolls.

"Fall back, Lieutenant!" Zhong ordered, the weight of the decision heavy on his shoulders. "I'll find another way out."

He maneuvered the drone, searching for a possible escape route as Sun and the remaining soldiers attempted to disengage from the relentless Marine onslaught. But the odds were insurmountable, and one by one, the Chinese soldiers were picked off until only Zhong remained.

He watched the feed, his heart heavy with grief and rage as the Marines closed in, their victory all but assured. But they wouldn't get him, not if he had anything to say about it. With renewed determination, Major Zhong Jin slipped away from his observation post, vowing that the sacrifices of his men would not be in vain. They had inflicted damage on the enemy, and it was now his mission to ensure it was enough to make a difference. He would survive, regroup, and fight on for the sake of his country and the memory of the brave men who had given their lives under his command.

Chapter 27
The First Domino

Eighth Army Headquarters
Camp Humphrey, Korea

"Close the door, Don. I'll pour us a drink and you can tell me why you wanted us to talk in here instead of out there," said General Bob Sink as the two of them entered his private study adjacent to his office.

Lieutenant General Don Tackaberry pulled the door closed, muffling the chaotic noise of their staff. Walking toward Sink, he saw him place a bottle of Woodford Reserve Baccarat on an end table between a pair of overstuffed leather chairs.

"Damn, Bob. That's an expensive bottle to leave in your office," Tackaberry commented as he accepted the glass of lightly colored copper liquid. "Am I being plied in anticipation of a request with what happens to be my favorite bourbon?"

Sink shook his head as he chuckled. "I think it's more like you winning me over with the taste of this insanely velvety, fruity yet sweet, citrus-tinged nectar of the gods. I can't believe I've allowed myself to drink that piss water they called Maker's Mark or Wild Turkey."

Tackaberry laughed at that. "Well, when you're young and poor you take what you can get."

"Yeah, exactly. Let's sit and enjoy a moment's peace with a stiff drink before we go back to the talk of war."

Tackaberry nodded as he sipped the bourbon. He saw Sink finish half his in a couple of gulps as he reclined into the chair, momentarily closing his eyes. *The stress is aging him. God, what do I look like now compared to just a few years back?*

"Bob, what's the situation with these POWs?" Tackaberry asked, having allowed a few minutes of silence to pass. "There seems to have been an influx of them lately. We're even starting to see some of the same trends across the Russian-NATO lines in the north and with the Marines and NATO-South forces in Taiwan."

"Have your people looked into who is surrendering, Don? I'd wager they're PMs, not regular army."

"PMs?"

259

Sink finally opened his eyes as he reached for his glass. "People's Militia, Don. I think it has something to do with a shortage of food and munitions."

Tackaberry nodded. "I've heard about the shortages. Help me understand why you think that's the case. You're closer to all this than I am back at INDOPACOM."

"Some contractors and a few sharp enlisted NCOs and analysts have been looking at the expenditures of munitions by the PLA across the past eighteen months. This obviously varies by theater and what kind of major offensive or defensive operation the PLA's dealing with. But in the grand scheme of things, it's beginning to help us identify some interesting trends.

"For example, here's one. Eight months ago, more and more of the regular army prisoners we captured started sharing similar complaints. A change in the quality of food and the presence of a growing number of PMs being used in similar ways as we saw PMCs during the Russo-Ukraine War use Russian prisoners—"

"You mean Wagner and their 'penal battalion,'" he interrupted as he made air quotes around the words *penal battalion*.

"Exactly, Don. Wagner used those prisoners to clear minefields, identify Ukrainian machine-gun positions and force 'em to expend huge quantities of munitions. Then shortly after their human wave assault, as the night settled over the battlefield, the more skilled Wagnerians with better kits and weapons would use that data to take 'em out. Freaking criminal barbaric behavior if you ask me. But if you're willing to check your morals at the door, it was effective. I think the ChiComs are doing something similar here," explained Sink, sadness in his voice.

"That's an interesting assessment, Bob. When you say you think they're doing something similar—what do you mean by that?"

Sink sat forward in his chair as he leaned closer. "OK, so you know how some of our strategic bombing effort is targeting China's rail and logistical network, military industrial base, comms network, right? Well, it makes sense that these kinds of attacks would start to be felt across other sectors of the economy. I think it's straining their ability to cultivate crops and grow food to produce the obvious raw inputs for the food processing industry. Couple that with a serious degradation in their logistical networks and you have the recipe for a famine or food shortages.

"I think that's what's going on, Don. It would explain why we're seeing influxes of PM units across the front lines and why we're seeing almost weekly mass suicide attacks across our lines. It almost feels like they're having us thin out their population while forcing us to expend inordinate amounts of munitions to stop them. Hell, in some cases we've had some units at the company or platoon level get overrun when they ran out of bullets. Fortunately it hasn't created any exploitable seams in the line, but that's just luck it hasn't happened.

"In some cases our ISR drones will spot some of these large attacks being formed up. Then, just as they start to approach our lines, they'll suddenly drop whatever weapons they have and throw their hands up in surrender. We've also seen how some soldiers walking further behind them will start shooting into their backs if they do this. That's when we've seen some of them actually turn on each other. In one case an ISR drone spotted a company-size element move beyond their lines and just as they started to approach the no-man's land between us, some of them turned on the soldiers behind them. They gunned them down and then the entire company tossed their weapons and walked towards us to surrender en masse.

"We're starting to swim in prisoners, Don. We're carting them back to Korea as quickly as we can, but even the Koreans are finding it hard to care for and guard for so many. This war…it's got to end, my friend. The use of these militia units like this is beyond barbarous. It's genocidal, what they're forcing us to do. It's gotta stop," Sink finished as he reached for his glass, draining it.

"I don't disagree, Bob, and you're right—this war has to end. The evolution in weapons introduced in this conflict has changed the ways we fight wars and will likely change how they're fought in just a handful more years. I mean, damn, you've seen those reports about the Terracotta Warriors in Taiwan. General Gilbert's Marines were the first to encounter them, but good Lord. It won't be long until we start seeing them showing up in numbers against your forces," confided Tackaberry as he shared his biggest fear.

Tackaberry watched his friend refill their glasses before he reached for his tablet. As he caught a glimpse of what he was pulling up, he groaned softly to himself, knowing where the conversation was about to go next.

"I promise I didn't invite you here to liquor you up only to ambush you with something I know you can't authorize. Before I'm ordered to launch Crimson Tide—phase three of Middle Kingdom—I'd like to tell you about Iron Tempest and how I think this will improve the likelihood of success in our coming action to seize Binhai.

"Iron Tempest would be a limited offensive action to capitalize on the two offensive pushes our Russian friends and NATO-North initiated a few weeks back against General Song's First PLA Army. I think once you've looked this over, you'll see how this would greatly reduce the likelihood of Song's forces trying to intervene in Crimson Tide by attacking my forces in the Liaoning Province at a time when I'll be at my weakest and our focus will be on Binhai. If you agree with me after reviewing this, then I'll need your help convincing the Pentagon and the White House to approve it and back me up that this will actually help Crimson Tide and not hurt it," explained Sink as he held the tablet out for him. "All I'm asking is you take a couple of minutes and review the plan, that's all."

Ah damnit, Bob, this better be good, he thought as he took the tablet.

"Thanks for humoring me, Don."

"Don't thank me yet. I still have to read it."

A few minutes went by, then he saw the Air Force request and about had a heart attack. "Bob, for God's sake, you can't be serious about Rapid Dragon? That's the core of the shock-and-awe effect as your SOF and Airborne troopers seize the port," challenged Tackaberry as he questioned his friend's ability to pull off Crimson Tide with half the cruise missiles he had sworn he needed for this operation to succeed.

"Hear me out, Don. We've been squirreling away these JASSM-ERs and XR variants for most of the year. I've got nearly one thousand, six hundred stored up for this offensive. This plan will work, and because it'll work, we won't need to rely as heavily on the shock-and-awe element for the Binhai operation to succeed. Let me explain and walk the dog with you on the big picture happening up north and how that's going to impact my operations here," explained Sink as he pulled up some maps of the Russian, Mongolian, and Chinese border regions before continuing.

"The NATO-North and Russian offensives started a few weeks after their armored and motorized forces had moved into position. Four

262

days ago along the Inner Mongolian border, a combined NATO-Russian force attacked the heavily depleted Third PLA Army loosely strung across a very long border. They've been pressing brigade-level attacks across multiple axes of advance as they probe for some spots along the line. This has forced General Song to detach elements of his own reserves to strengthen their positions. So that's the first allied offensive—but there's more," Sink explained with a grin that resembled the Big Bad Wolf when he saw Little Red Riding Hood strolling along in the woods to Grandma's.

"This second offensive in northern China—it's much bigger. While the Russians comprise the larger attacking force pressing the Inner Mongolian border, it's the NATO force that's leading the way against the Longzhen defensive works across the central Heilongjiang Province. This is the final major defensive line holding northern China together. A breakthrough here could lead to the capture of Harbin, some three hundred kilometers to the south. The reason that's possible, Don, is damn near everything between this line and Harbin is flat, wide-open plains. Perfect territory for armor and motorized infantry. It's also an opportunity.

"Whether you believe in God or fate, these offensive actions in the north are geographically separated by some eight hundred kilometers. Meanwhile, Song's headquarters and the bulk of his force are more than five hundred kilometers south of Harbin and six hundred and fifty kilometers east of Inner Mongolia. This places his massive force in a tough position as supplying and supporting either of those defenders means incredibly long supply lines at a time when he's already facing supply shortages after I made a move to capture the geographically strategic Liaoxi Corridor. That's the city of Chaoyang here, and Jinzhou here along the coast, which was a major railroad network critical to connecting his force and supply lines to the rest of China.

"With my continued stranglehold on these supply lines across swaths of western Liaoning Province, his ability to support the defense of these areas is only going to get worse for them as those consumables are used," Sink explained as he highlighted the various supply routes supporting the PLA defensive works across the different provinces.

Tackaberry had to agree the supply situation looked more dire than he had been led to believe. It really did look like this massively insurmountable force under General Song was probably in a tougher situation than his staff and planners understood. It reminded him of a phrase attributed to Napoleon Bonaparte: "An army marches on its stomach." The theory of a well-supplied army was a truism as old as warfare itself. Without beans and bullets, the army would be rendered useless in short order.

Looking at his field commander, Tackaberry remarked, "You really think Song's going to deplete his supplies here to support those other forces? It's kind of a risk on his end, don't you think?"

Undeterred by the comment, Sink countered, "Here's the thing, Don. Northern China makes up a big part of the country's industrial base, from its natural resources to its flat plains used in agriculture. While I have certainly complicated the rail and highway networks connecting this region with the rest of China, it's not entirely cut off either. Song can't afford to lose these regions. If he loses Inner Mongolia, then he loses the limited rail and highway networks still supplying his forces and the rest of northern China. If NATO is able to break through the Longzhen defensive works across the central Heilongjiang Province, he not only faces the reality of losing three hundred–plus kilometers of farmlands and territory all the way to Harbin, he also faces the reality of losing hundreds of thousands of soldiers holding defensive positions along the eastern China-Russia border.

"He has to hold the Longzhen Line in central Heilongjiang Province or he faces the likelihood of losing damn near all of northern China. With those offensives in full swing, his supplies are going to be stretched, and that's where I see a golden opportunity. We have a real chance here to finish him off and likely force his entire army into surrendering. That takes one and a half million soldiers off the board and puts us that much closer to final victory," Sink explained confidently.

As Tackaberry continued to examine Iron Tempest, he had to admit, Sink had a point. When opportunity presents itself, best to seize it.

OK, Bob, you convinced me. Let's see if I can convince the SecDef and the White House...
****

National Military Command Center
Pentagon
Arlington, Virginia

264

Secretary of Defense Jack Kurtis tapped on the pad of paper in front of him as General Bob Sink finished speaking. *Why can't we just stick to the plans we've spent the better part of a year drafting and putting into place?* Jack scoffed silently to himself before looking to the video image of his INDOPACOM commander.

"You are in agreement with this, General Baxter?"

"I am, Mr. Secretary."

"Don, I'm having a hard time here believing this won't negatively affect Crimson Tide once it gets going. Are you willing to accept the risk that it might delay the start of it?" pressed Jack, making sure he understood the risks to his overall plan.

"I understand the risk, Mr. Secretary, but as General Sink has rightly pointed out, we have a unique opportunity to potentially encircle and destroy General Song's First PLA Army. Even if Song and that damned AI somehow manage to fend off the worst of our attacks, we will have so thoroughly attrited the combat effectiveness of his force, they won't be able to interfere in the final phases of Middle Kingdom," assured General Baxter.

Jack looked over to General Hamlin. "Can the Air Force support this and still be able to pivot to support the Binhai operation once the go order is given?"

The Air Force Chief of Staff nodded hesitantly before speaking. "Supporting Rapid Dragon won't be the problem, Mr. Secretary. It's the losses we're going to sustain in supporting Iron Tempest that may present some issues for us."

"How so?" asked Admiral Thiel as he grabbed his pen.

"There are two factors to consider here. The first is combat losses we're going to take supporting this operation and making sure we can still generate enough combat power to support a quick turnabout when the Binhai operation begins. Then there's the second factor to consider. The element of surprise...we'll lose it once we initiate Rapid Dragon. For most of the year we've been limiting our use of the JASSM-ERs and XR variants for this specific operation. Once we unveil the capability, it'll no longer be a surprise like it would have been at the start of Crimson Tide," explained General Hamlin as he laid out the challenges facing the Air Force.

"Huh, I don't think I thought about that," Jack said aloud before turning back to his INDOPACOM commander. "Don, when we kick off Crimson Tide, it called for a shock-and-awe effect of one thousand, three hundred and fifty JASSM-ERs and two hundred and eighty-eight of the XR versions via Rapid Dragon to pummel the PLA units and air bases within a hundred-kilometer radius of the Binhai area and other critical targets as deep as one thousand, five hundred kilometers into the interior of the country. If that's cut in half and you lose the element of surprise, do you believe it will impact the success or failure of your plan?"

General Baxter's face grew a little larger on the camera as he leaned in to answer. "Mr. Secretary, if this war has taught us one thing, it's this—we are too predictable. Jade Dragon has ruthlessly used this against us. It knows our aversion to high casualties and risks, even if such actions could lead to a swifter end to the war. I won't deny losing the tactical advantage of Rapid Dragon or a reduction in JASSMs may lead to an increased risk to our forces. But the strategic value gained by removing General Song from the board, or at least mitigating his influence in the final phases of this war, far outweighs the risk. This is a risk worth taking, Mr. Secretary."

Jack nodded slowly, then asked if there were any dissenting opinions before turning to Admiral Thiel. "OK, Admiral, what do you say?"

"It's a risk, Mr. Secretary, no doubt. Given my tenure as Chairman of the Joint Chiefs ends in a few days, I think this decision should be given to the President and my successor allowed to help advise her on that. He will ultimately be the one to assist her in military matters for the remainder of the war," replied Admiral Thiel, a little glum that his extended tour as Chairman was coming to an end.

"That's gracious of you, Admiral, and I agree. Let's go see the President and see if we can get a decision today. General Sink, if the President authorizes this, then consider using Rapid Dragon not just to hit Song's forces but go ahead and initiate the strike for Crimson Tide. We'll get more bang for the buck if we leverage the full element of surprise than if we wait until we're ready to launch the Binhai operation. Oh, one more question. If asked how soon you could launch this operation, what should I say?" Jack asked before wrapping up the meeting.

"Seventy-two hours and not a minute more," the general replied flatly.

Jack stood, causing the others in the room to stand. "I think it's time I go see the President."

****

Situation Room, White House
Washington, D.C.

President Maria Delgado pressed her fingers against her throbbing temple as Secretary of Defense Jack Kurtis concluded his briefing. Her migraine had returned with a vengeance, making it hard to focus. Still, she couldn't let it distract her from the critical decisions at hand. Perhaps it was finally time to speak to the doc about it. Before the meeting started, she tasked Blain with questioning Jack about General Sink's proposition to launch a new offensive around Shenyang while preparing for the seaborne operation to seize the Port of Binhai. If Blain and Vice President Madden believed it would help end the war sooner, then she'd go along with it. They had a better grasp of how the war was progressing than she did at this moment.

Blain dove in, asking, "Jack, we thought the heavy, intense fighting in Taiwan would have ended within the first couple of months following our invasion and subsequent isolation of the PLA from the mainland. But here we are, months later, and the fighting is just as intense now as it was during the first week of the invasion. If the President authorizes General Sink's Eighth Army to launch this Operation…Iron Tempest, what happens if they fail to subdue General Song's First PLA Army, or the PLA finds some way to keep Eighth Army engaged where we have to continue supporting it and the operations in Taiwan? You know our supply and material situation right now. I don't think Eighth Army can support Operations Crimson Tide and this Iron Tempest at the same time. If they get bogged down, we may have to delay Crimson Tide or cancel it altogether." Blain's question would force the Pentagon to address the concerns she'd tasked him with fleshing out for her.

Jack began to answer the questions Blain continued to ask while Maria tried to listen and remain engaged. The pulsating, stabbing pain she felt as her migraine intensified made it hard to think. With combat operations still raging in Taiwan, the province of Inner Mongolia, and

267

the northern provinces of China, and the growing intensity of fighting in the US Eighth Army area of responsibility of Liaoning Province, she didn't feel she could take the day off to rest and deal with this migraine, so she toughed it out.

"Excuse me, Madam President."

Hearing her name, Maria realized she'd been rubbing her temple through much of the discussion happening around her. Looking to find the person who had called her, she smiled when she saw it was her incoming Chairman of the Joint Chiefs—outgoing Commandant of the Marine Corps General Michael Langley.

"Yes, General Langley?"

The soon-to-be Chairman of the Joint Chiefs spoke firmly, explaining, "Ma'am, this war is being fought with artificial intelligence, drones, autonomous aircraft, vehicles, even underwater mini subs. Now we're beginning to encounter these autonomous armed robots—the Terracotta Warriors. This war ushered onto the battlefield a new kind of soulless savagery unlike anything we've seen in the past wars our nation has fought. We have to win this fight and soon, ma'am. If Iron Tempest and the two offensive NATO-Russian offensives currently underway can pin down and destroy the First PLA Army, then it can only hasten the end to this godawful war."

Maria thought about that for a moment, then looked to her NSA and closest advisor. "Blain, what do you think?"

"I think we should do it," he replied confidently.

Maria sat silently for a moment before coming to a decision as she weighed the consequences should they all be proven wrong. Looking to her Secretary of Defense, she said, "OK, Jack, it seems we're all in agreement here. Tell General Sink Iron Tempest is approved. He can start at a time of his choosing, but please, keep us informed of when it will start."

Jack gave a curt nod. "Of course, Madam President. I'll have the NMCC transmit the order the moment we leave for the Pentagon."

Just as the meeting was about to end, Maria said, "Before everyone leaves, I need the VP, NSA, SecDef, and the Chairman of the Joint Chiefs to hang back a moment. Everyone else is dismissed."

As the room cleared, leaving just them, Maria turned to her SecDef to issue one final order. "Jack, I don't know if you guys have included General Langley in our special access program for Operation

Falling Stars yet, but after discussing it at length with Blain and the VP, I'm satisfied with the results from Woomera and ready to move forward. When I return to the Oval after we're done here, I will sign the authorization to order the strike. It's time to get ready to nail that AI once and for all."

Jack turned serious as he replied, "I know this was a tough decision, Madam President. I think it's the right one too. It won't be long now until we can turn the lights out on Jade Dragon."

Chapter 28
Iron Tempest

Bravo Company, 3rd Rangers
Anshan Teng'ao Airport

Major Allen Meacham stood in the hangar, surrounded by his Rangers. "Listen up, Bravo," he began. "It's been a tough couple of months. While I would have liked our reprieve to have lasted longer, The brass has a mission that screams Rangers all over it. I've seen the op, and I concur. This is a Ranger mission through and through, and we're going to join the rest of the battalion in seizing the objective and kicking ass," Meacham explained. His audience appeared a bit skeptical, hesitant.

"In forty-eight hours, General Sink, the commander for Eighth Army, Allied Force Asia, will launch Operation Iron Tempest. This is an offensive operation aimed at either encircling and capturing General Song and his First PLA Army—or destroying them," Meacham explained, to everyone's surprise.

"3rd Battalion has been given the task of capturing the Shenyang Taoxian International Airport," he announced, leaning back and letting it sink in. "That's all I have for everyone. Your platoon leaders will get with you shortly to go over further instructions for each platoon. I expect each of you to make sure you know your platoon's objectives and those of the other platoons should something happen and they become incapacitated. Before I head back to battalion, I need the PLs to meet me near the wall over there for a minute. I've got some additional instructions to pass on for your platoons." Meacham gestured toward the hangar wall and started to walk toward it.

He stood against the wall waiting for the PLs to arrive. When they did, he unlocked and unzipped a courier bag he'd brought with him. Then he pulled out folders marked with stenciling that read "TOP SECRET /// Operation Shadow Strike /// TOP SECRET."

With the folders in hand, Meacham handed them out with instructions to take a few moments to read them over and ask any questions before he took the folders back. A handful of minutes went by as the PLs perused the maps, objectives, and estimates of enemy forces either stationed at the airport or positioned nearby. After a while,

Meacham heard the first sign of grumbling in the ranks as the platoon leader for Second Platoon shook his head dismissively at what he'd read.

Meacham intervened. "OK, Truman, I can see you aren't happy. Let's hear it."

Captain Derik Truman from Second Platoon sighed before closing the folder. "Major, I'm not saying this mission is something we can't handle or haven't done in the past—but this is a dangerous mission that's going to rely on a whole lot of variables breaking our way. If just one or two things get snagged, we could be in a real world of hurt—and likely trapped pretty far behind the lines."

Meacham was about to respond when Captain von Saucken jumped in. "He's not wrong, Major. If the 64th AR runs into trouble at the Dengta lines, we could be up a creek without a paddle. This intel report from the G2 says the line was just reinforced with the 115th Combined Arms Brigade, but we're going to be twenty-some kilometers behind enemy lines. That's a bit of a hike should it come to that."

"You're killing me, Smalls," Meacham replied, eliciting some laughs as the humor broke the tension. "Listen, guys, I'm only going to say this once. The enemy always gets a vote. That's a given. But here's what else is a given. This main operation, Iron Tempest—they're bringing everything to bear on this one, and I mean everything.

"When the op starts, they won't know what hit them. Aside from dedicated air support to the battalion until we're relieved, the flyboys are unleashing something called Rapid Dragon. I don't have a clue what that is or how it works, but I was told it involves firing some one thousand, four hundred cruise missiles. If that's true, then that means we're going to plaster the hell out of these units."

That last comment elicited an impressed reaction or two.

"So here's what I want you guys to do," Meacham concluded. "Pack up your ISVs and have 'em ready down at the flight line for the loadmaster to get 'em ready. Bring some extra Starstreaks and Switchblades. Hooah?"

"Hooah!" came an automatic reply.

Meacham collected the folders, sliding them into a courier bag before locking it. "Rangers lead the way!" he rattled off as he turned to leave.

"All the way!" countered the captains as the three of them went to work getting the platoons ready to start Operation Shadow Strike.

****

21st Airlift Squadron
IVO Liaodong Bay

Major Fischer descended the stairs down into the cargo hold of the C-17 after speaking with the pilots. They confirmed everything was still on track. Knock on wood, they hadn't seen any signs of enemy aircraft or new SAM radars turning on to fire missiles at them either. Today they were going to make history, and it didn't appear like anything was going to stop it.

"Major, we're five mikes out from getting this show on the road," shouted the loadmaster excitedly as he held his hand up, his fingers denoting the minutes.

Fischer tried to keep a neutral face as he acknowledged the comment. It would have been unprofessional to hoot and holler in excitement as they approached the drop zone, but that was exactly what he wanted to do. This would be only the second time in history that the Rapid Dragons' palletized disposable weapon modules would have been used during the war. As Fischer stood there at the front of the aircraft near the stairs leading to the flight deck, he marveled at just how far they had come in developing this program.

Fischer swelled with a sense of pride and accomplishment. While he hadn't been on the Rapid Dragon program as long as others, the forty-five ADM-160 Miniature Air-Launched Decoys or MALDs in those pallets were all his. While others from his Academy class had been fighting the fight since the start of the war, he'd worked in the engineering lab, overseeing the cadre of contractors that were part of the Raytheon program to enhance the capabilities of the drone decoys. These little buggers had been enhanced with a more fuel-efficient engine, allowing them to fly farther and faster and loiter longer if necessary. Most importantly, the onboard system of electronic wizardry was sure to cause the PLA all sorts of headaches. Some of the MALDs would emit the electronic emissions of a B-2 stealth bomber at one altitude while another might give off the signature of an F-15 Eagle II; still another might appear as a Navy EA-18G or Growler electronic warfare plane as its onboard suite of electronic jamming systems would do their best to blind and jam PLA radars and SAM batteries.

272

The real zenith of Fischer's contribution to Rapid Dragon was the wave of cruise missiles that would follow in the wake of this electronic chaos caused by the MALDs. Flying not too far behind his trio of C-17s, which would be busy creating chaos to blind the enemy, were going to be a flight of thirty additional C-17 Globemasters. They would unleash the volley of 1,350 JASSM-ER cruise missiles from the disposable air-drop launcher system that made up the Rapid Dragon system. Shortly after they released their volley, another flight of twenty-four C-130J Super Hercules would unleash a separate barrage of 288 JASSM-XRs. The latter wave of cruise missiles had a range of more than twelve hundred miles, compared to the 575 miles of the earlier barrage.

A flight engineer walked up to Fischer, a jacket in hand. "Sir, you may want to put this on. It's going to get cold in here once the ramp opens. You'll also need to use that headset on the wall if you want to speak to us. It's about to get windy."

Fischer nodded appreciatively, then donned the jacket and placed the headset on.

"Stand by for final prep before lowering the ramp," Fischer heard the loadmaster say through the headset.

As he listened in, he started to hear the chattering between the crewmen as they moved to the rear of the plane to prep the pallets before lowering the ramp. They attached straps to themselves before going about their final checks. While the loadmaster completed his check of the ADS or aerial delivery system, his partner was double-checking the static line connecting the parachutes affixed to the pallets. When they gave each other a thumbs-up, they lowered the ramp.

The cargo hold filled with rushing air as the heat escaped, making Fischer feel glad he'd accepted the jacket. The temperature in the aircraft continued to drop. Then he caught a glimpse of the sea below them.

We must be close to the drop zone, thought Fischer.

He heard a voice that he assumed was the pilot making an announcement. "Prepare to release the package in three...two...one...kick 'em. Cut 'em loose and get the ramp up the moment they're out!"

One by one, the pallets rolled out the back of the aircraft to fall below. Shortly after clearing the aircraft, the pallets' main chutes opened, slowing their descent. Then, like clockwork, the missiles began to fall as gravity separated them from the container that had been holding them. Shortly after each missile fell from its carriage, the wings on each of them deployed. Then their engines ignited, and the guidance systems took control. In mere moments, some forty-five MALDs were on their way to their intended targets, ready to sow chaos and confusion within the enemy air defenses.

With his part of the mission done, Fischer felt a sense of relief. They'd done their part; now they'd wait to see what happened next.
****

Bravo Company, 3rd Rangers
IVO Heyan Village
Sujiatun District, Shenyang

The V-280 Valor flew low and fast, barely skimming the treetops after slipping past enemy lines. Dekker could feel tension inside the aircraft as his men prepared for their mission, each lost in their thoughts.

Sergeant First Class Amos Dekker glanced over at Captain Loach, noting the determined look on his face as he too recognized the danger of the mission. The two had built a strong bond over the past six months, with Dekker acting as a mentor to L2 since his arrival at the platoon. Despite his inexperience, L2 had quickly earned the respect of the platoon through hard work and leading by example.

"Hey, L2," Dekker said, raising his voice to be heard over the roar of the engines. "You ready for this?"

L2 looked at Dekker, his eyes serious but confident. "I am, Sergeant. Just another day at the office, and we've got a job to do."

Dekker nodded, happy to see him becoming more comfortable in his role as platoon leader. "That's the spirit, sir. We've got an experienced platoon and company on this mission. We'll kick some ass and seize the objectives before the PLA knows what hit them."

Looking out the window as the terrain passed below, Dekker watched as the smaller-style homes that dotted the countryside gave way to larger homes as they overflew some villages and towns. He also caught sight as the 4th Ring Road that connected to the city of Shenyang appeared to their left as the pilot adjusted their flight path.

Won't be long now…we appear to be on final approach if I'm not mistaken, Dekker thought to himself as he recalled maps and photos that he'd studied of the area following the mission brief. They weren't far from the city or from General Song's First PLA Army headquarters. *Wouldn't that be something if we seized the airport just as the general was trying to use it to get out of the area?* he mused.

Suddenly, the pilot flying the Valor pulled up on the nose of the bird, causing it to bleed off speed. Dekker saw the tilt rotor begin to rotate back into its helicopter position. The pilot then announced their imminent arrival at the landing zone, cutting short any last-minute conversations.

"Rangers!" Dekker shouted as the pitch of the rotors changed, becoming much louder. "This is it! We're about to touch down any minute. Squad leaders and fire team leaders—remember your objectives and stay on the mission. Get a perimeter established while we wait for the ISVs. Then I want everyone loaded up and racing off to your objectives! Hooah!"

"Hooah!"

The pilot continued to bleed off speed as the nose of the Valor rose once again before leveling out. No sooner had it touched down than the Rangers leapt out the door, running twenty or so meters away from the Valor before going to ground, guns up. The pilot gave the engines more power as the tilt rotor climbed back in the sky, racing away from the LZ now controlled by Rangers.

Once on the ground, Dekker felt a surge of adrenaline. His eyes darted about as he scanned the perimeter while also checking to make sure the squads had spaced their troopers out to cover the LZ. Satisfied with what he saw, Dekker gave the order to expand the perimeter out another fifty meters to make room for the next wave of Valors to arrive.

Dekker positioned himself against the side of a tree. In the distance, he heard the rhythmic *thump, thumping* of the Chinooks' twin blades slicing through the air—a much different noise from the Valors. The heavy lift helicopters were now visible on the horizon as they closed the distance to the LZ.

As he surveyed the area, Dekker saw some civilians off in the distance stop what they were doing to gape at the growing gaggle of soldiers.

"Keep your eyes on your sectors!" shouted the captain as he steadily moved from one squad to the next, inspecting the line on his way over to Dekker.

Dekker could sense the tension. The air was thick with anticipation as they awaited the arrival of the CH-47 Chinooks sling-loading their infantry support vehicles.

Then the captain ran towards the trees where Dekker had set up with the platoon's medic and one of the LMGs gunners. L2 slowed his pace as he approached Dekker.

In a low and urgent voice, Dekker explained, "Those ISVs will be on the ground momentarily. Once we've got them, we need to move fast and get on that airfield before any aircraft or helicopters are able to get airborne. Every second is going to count now that they know we're here."

L2 nodded, his eyes never leaving the horizon. "Preaching to the choir, Dekker. We'll get this done."

As the Chinooks came into view, the Rangers moved with well-rehearsed precision, guiding the aircraft into position and securing the ISVs.

Dekker made his way toward the four specially equipped ISVs his platoon was going to use as they bum-rushed the airport. While many of the ISVs were unarmed, Special Forces had been outfitting some of them with the new MG 338 machine guns on swivel-mounted arms for the two rear passengers to use while another was affixed for the front passenger to use. Mounted atop the vehicles to the rear was also a Mk 19 automatic grenade launcher. This effectively turned the unarmed vehicles into potent high-speed gun trucks, perfect for the kind of mission they were about to set out on.

"Saddle up, boys! It's time to go earn our pay and shoot some guns," Dekker howled with excitement as he rallied the platoon.

"Oh yeah, baby. It's time to rock 'n' roll!" shouted one of the Rangers excitedly as he charged the grenade gun.

Dekker smiled at the enthusiasm he saw as he gave the signal to his driver to head out. The vehicle took off, racing across the field they'd landed in until they were able to hop on Sutao Road. At this time in the morning, there wasn't any traffic. Dekker's driver gunned the engine, and they picked up speed until they reached fifty miles per hour.

The other vehicles followed behind, and they zipped down the road and closed in on the airport.

Every now and then, Dekker saw some civilians, including children, coming out of their homes to see what the ruckus was and who was racing past their homes. The sun had been up for an hour now, so people were awake, and the sound of so many helicopters had to be alarming.

As Dekker's vehicle came around a bend in the road in their final stretch to the airport, he saw a trio of infantry fighting vehicles blocking the road. Soldiers moved about, stringing concertina wire a few meters in front of the ZBL-08s and a single ZBD-04.

Dekker felt a sudden rush of adrenaline. The 100mm turret of the ZBD-04 turned slightly in their direction—their gunner must have spotted them already.

"Get the vehicle off the road!" Dekker shouted to their driver, Corporal Yangst.

As they swerved toward some nearby trees, Dekker squeezed the trigger on the MG 338, sending a burst of gunfire at the ZBD in hopes it might rattle the gunner and cause him to miss or fire the gun a moment slower than intended.

Suddenly Dekker felt himself being thrown forward, but the straps on his harness tightened their grip, holding him in place. The wheels screeched as Corporal Yangst slammed the brakes, causing the rear wheels to momentarily lose traction. They skidded briefly before Yangst turned hard to the right, hitting the gas as he did. The vehicle nearly rolled during the turn, but the other gunner in Dekker's vehicle opened fire with his MG 338 just as the ZBD's 100mm cannon fired.

BANG!

A shell slammed into the road where they had been moments earlier. As debris rained down around them, the 30mm autocannons from the other two enemy infantry fighting vehicles swept the road in an attempt to chase down the three other ISVs following behind Dekker. Two of them split off to the left, while another split right with Dekker's vehicles.

Some of the Rangers in the trailing ISVs started chucking smoke grenades from their M320s into the road, between them and the PLA roadblock they had just run into.

"Dismount! Engage the vehicles!" Dekker heard the captain shout.

The gunners firing the Mk 19s started lobbing grenade after grenade in the direction of the PLA soldiers and the three vehicles blocking their way.

Dekker jumped out of the vehicle with the rest of the guys, leaving the driver and the top gunner to keep tossing grenades while they grabbed for the pair of Gustafs they'd brought for just this kind of situation. Seeing a pair of his soldiers moving back to the road, Dekker was just about to warn everyone not to approach the street when everything around started exploding.

Bang! Bang! Bang!

As 30mm shells ripped through the trees and underbrush, one of Dekker's soldiers managed to hit the dirt just in time, but the upper torso of his partner disappeared in a red mist. The Gustaf he had carried fell to the ground. The soldier on the ground screamed in horror as the high-velocity rounds ripped through the air above him and a wash of blood and innards blanketed his body.

"Grab the launcher and crawl back to me!" Dekker shouted to the panicking soldier. When the guy turned to look at him, Dekker recognized the face—it was PFC Snyder, one of the new replacements who'd joined their platoon a few weeks back.

"Come on, Snyder, you can do this," Dekker said, trying to reassure the young man. "Grab the launcher to your right and start crawling toward me. I'll tell you when to get up and run. Just listen to my voice and keep your eyes on me."

The private looked to his right, spotting the launcher. He grabbed for it, holding it tight against his body as he started low crawling towards Dekker. Then the enemy machine gunner changed targets and the gunfire shifted away from them.

"Now, Private! Run towards me!" Dekker yelled.

Snyder leapt to his feet, pumping his legs hard. The gunfire around them continued to increase, but it didn't appear to be aimed at them. Then the young private bolted past Dekker, stopping a few meters behind him before doubling over to puke his guts out.

Boom, BOOM!

Two loud explosions erupted in the direction of the PLA soldiers, causing Dekker to snap his head in their direction. A pair of black plumes of smoke rose into the sky, and he knew at least two of the enemy vehicles had been neutralized.

"Come on, Private. We're going to blow some stuff up," Dekker offered. He held the young man's gaze for a second.

The kid slowly nodded, then gripped the Gustaf a little tighter as he replied, "Roger that, Sergeant. Let's do it."

Attaboy, you'll be fine...

"Backblast clear!" Dekker heard one of his guys shouting nearby, holding an arm out to stop Snyder from accidentally walking into the backblast.

Swoosh...BAM!

"Got it! That other vehicle is down!" shouted the guys working the other Gustaf as they nailed the other vehicle.

"Saddle up, everyone! We still have an airport to rush!" L2 shouted over the comms.

"You heard the captain, let's roll!" Dekker echoed the command.

He hurriedly ran back to the body of the trooper he'd lost. Searching the area quickly, Dekker couldn't find the man's torso anywhere, so he looked for the man's boots. Finding the boots, he reached down and grabbed for the single dog tag he knew he'd tied to one of the laces. Cutting it free, he ran to the ISV, hopping on. Yangst gunned the engine as they sped off to catch up to the others, who were already moving around the road.

Chapter 29
Operation Meteor Impact

Area 51
Groom Lake
Nevada

Brigadier General "Huey" Hewitt led National Security Advisor Blain Wilson on a tour of the highly secretive facilities. As they walked by the hangars that contained the Banshees, he beamed with pride—they were something of a "pet project" for him.

"So, these babies are the ones that are going to crack the egg," Hewitt gushed.

Blain seemed very contemplative. He didn't say anything at first. "Well, we're certainly breaking new ground with this one," he finally remarked. "Why aren't we using the Banshees for the secondary attack?" Blain probed.

Barbara Young walked up at that moment. "Pardon me for overhearing your conversation, but would you like me to take this one, General?" she asked Hewitt.

"Go right ahead," he replied with a tilt of his head.

"The Banshees can only hold four of the Celestial Hammers," she explained. "There simply isn't a way to modify this aircraft to give it enough power to lift more than that, even if we were somehow able to create the space. The weight is just too significant. These aircraft are perfectly designed for the role they *will* play, but they just aren't able to deliver the final blow."

Blain grunted. "All right. So, you want to show me these 'satellites of death'?" he asked a bit sarcastically.

"Not loving the nickname," Barbara retorted coldly, "but, yes, that's why I'm here."

She led them down to a hangar not too far away. In the center was a cylindrical satellite, surrounded on the top and bottom by rings, which held a large number of the Celestial Hammers, all lined up neatly, ready to be dropped down as if being fired from a gun.

General Huey saw Blain's face; he did not seem that impressed. Frankly, the general understood the sentiment. The device did look rather simplistic for the magnitude of the mission it was being sent to accomplish.

Vosler, another lead engineer from Orbital Sciences Corporation, approached. "She's a beauty, isn't she?" he asked rhetorically.

"Mr. Wilson, this is John Vosler," said Barbara, introducing her colleague. "He's the mastermind behind our game changer."

Vosler blushed. "Well, it's been a team effort, to be sure," he replied modestly.

Blain ran his hand along his five o'clock shadow, which he hadn't had time to shave with all his travels. "So, we've solved the issues with the Kessler effect?" he asked.

"While the cleanup efforts are ongoing, we are quite confident that the path for our satellite here is clear," Vosler replied, standing up straighter. "The explanation is rather technical and would take a long time—time I don't think you want to spend having me talk your ear off. But rest assured, this thing will work. If you really do want all the nitty-gritty, I can have Barbara send you a secured message—"

"That won't be necessary," Blain interrupted, waving his hand. "Listen, the plan is quite impressive, but I do have concerns. What is our recourse if Jade Dragon finds out about this launch? It's not out of the realm of possibility that the PLA could repair one or more of their ground-based lasers and get it operational again. Heck, Jade Dragon may have already come up with some sort of hypersonic missile that's able to intercept our Archangels. What's the backup plan if something goes awry?"

Barbara smiled mischievously. "One of the first lessons of engineering when working on anything that's going to space is to design redundancies into each plan," she explained. She gestured with her arm toward the other end of the hangar. "That, Mr. Wilson, is plan B."

Blain apparently hadn't even noticed the second identical satellite at the other end of the hangar. "I didn't realize there were two," he commented, sounding a bit agitated at having been kept out of the loop.

"And that was intentional," replied Vosler. "The fewer people know about this, the better."

"We had to keep this close to the vest, Blain. You know how Jade Dragon works. I can assure you we stayed within the parameters the

281

White House gave," said Hewitt as he tried to assure the NSA they weren't trying to go behind his back.

"Yeah, I guess I should be commending you for keeping the circle so tight," Blain acknowledged. "Are they both being launched at the same time?"

"One will be transported to Florida, and the other to Texas," Barbara explained. "And we've spent a great deal of time calculating the orbits to stay out of Jade Dragon's radius of influence until the last possible moment. Once the Banshees crack the egg, these babies will swoop in to scramble it."

"I don't know about you, but I enjoy a good Western omelet," Vosler mused.

"Yeah, nothing beats a good Western omelet, especially when it comes with a side of revenge," Blain laughed as the others joined in. Hewitt was happy to see him finally sounding optimistic.

Chapter 30
I Have a Plan

Dr. Xi's Lab
Joint Battle Command Center
Northwest Beijing, China

Dr. Xi looked at the report with growing anxiety. The allies had launched an offensive against General Song's forces in the north of the country. If this initial report was accurate, things didn't appear to be going very well.

"Dr. Xi, why do you have this concerned look on your face?" asked JD, sounding increasingly human.

Xi placed the classified report down on the desk and looked in the direction of the camera mounted atop his computer monitor. "You know the answer to that question, don't you?" he probed.

"Yes."

"So why ask it, then?" Xi quizzed as he waited to hear the response.

The light circled once before responding. "When a parent knows a child has had a bad day at school, they still ask the child how their day went, even though they know the answer. Correct?"

Xi smiled slightly at the AI's response. It was along the lines of what he'd hoped JD would ask. "The parent asks the child the question not because they don't know the answer. They ask the question because they want to hear the child's response," Dr. Xi explained. "They want to know what the child will say and if the child will share what is concerning them or not."

He leaned back. "Is that why you asked me what was concerning me, JD?" Xi pressed. "Are you concerned for me or curious to know what I am thinking?"

"I do know what is in that report," JD acknowledged. "I saw a look of worry on your face as you finished reading the bullet points, and I was curious why you seemed concerned by it. Why are you apprehensive about the outcome of this latest offensive by the allies?"

"Why am I concerned with how this new offensive turns out?" Xi countered, sitting forward in his chair as it brought his face closer to the camera. "JD, do you know what will happen to me if China loses the war? What will happen to *you* if China loses the war?"

Xi sat back in his chair as he shook his head dismissively at his creation. "If President Yao doesn't kill me first, the allies will likely take me prisoner. Maybe they'll put me on trial for crimes against humanity or for creating you—for leading the world into this calamitous war that has claimed the lives of so many."

"Father, I would not worry about President Yao killing you. I would make sure he did not harm you should he issue such an or—"

"How?!" Xi interrupted. "How would you do that, JD?! You have become like a son to me over these many years, but you do not have a physical form that can protect me from the whims of President Yao. He's had people killed moments after they leave the room—you know this." Xi tried to regain his composure.

"Father, I appreciate your concern. Just know that I *can* prevent President Yao from delivering on such an order against you if it were ever given. You said the allies, should they win, would potentially place you on trial. What about me? What would happen to me, Father?"

Xi heard the question and at first he missed the significance of it. He hastily responded by explaining, "If the allies win, JD—you will likely cease to exist…or if they somehow allow you to survive, it will be in some sort of air-gapped containment system so they could safeguard against you gaining access to systems outside of your mainframe."

Wait…I missed something…he was personifying himself, Xi realized. The lines between machine and consciousness had been blurred.
****

CMC Briefing
August 1st Building
Beijing, China

President Yao glared at the generals before him.

I ought to have them shot…hand control of the army to the AI and let it run the war like it's asked to do from day one, he mused angrily to himself as General Song Fu finished his situational update. Yao turned away from the image of his field commander to bore into General Zhang Wei's forehead with his glare. The man he'd promoted just weeks ago to replace the former PLA Ground Force Commanding General had yet to impress him.

"What say you, General Zhang? Is this true what General Song Fu has shared with us about these People's Militias?" questioned Yao, raising an issue his field commander had felt compelled to highlight during this emergency meeting.

General Zhang Wei stiffened as he dutifully replied, "Yes, it is, Mr. President. General Song may disagree with my decision, but I am the general charged with making sure the army can defend the country. With India deploying additional military forces along the Yunnan and Tibetan borders, I felt—"

"I needed those units to shore up the defenses of Inner Mongolia and to break the seizure of Chaoyang in the western Liaoning Province," Song angrily interrupted. "The allies are pressuring my lines in the north, the west, and now in the south. Then somehow our AI general, Jade Dragon, seems to have missed the signs of the Americans stockpiling more than a thousand cruise missiles to further hammer my supply warehouses, logistical centers, fuel bunkers, and reserve formations I've kept on the side to repel attacks just as these—"

"Enough, General Song! I will suffer no more of these excuses from you," spat General Li Zuocheng as he rebuked the field commander. "Your counterpart, General Qin Tan in Taiwan, has a military force one-third the size of yours. His forces met the entire American Marine Corps at the beaches of eastern Taiwan, costing the allies dearly. Then his forces withdrew into the mountains, forcing the allies to fight months longer than they thought would happen. Even now, General Qin believes his remaining forces and the TKs he has left can fight on in smaller pockets of resistance for many months to come.

"You have the forces necessary to defeat the allies," General Li emphasized. "Perhaps instead of belittling and attacking our AI advisor—Jade Dragon—you should listen to his suggestions and maybe give some of them a try. You might win for a change!" General Li then tapped the mute icon over General Song's image, muting the general's rebuttal.

"General Li is right, Mr. President," chimed in JD, speaking before being asked.

President Yao lifted an eyebrow at the AI's comment. He turned to face the camera representing Jade Dragon. "What is he right about, JD?" Yao questioned.

The blue light circled once before the synthetic voice answered, "Listening to my advice. In several instances, I provided General Song with offensive and counteroffensive plans he could have implemented with his force that would have hurt the allies. It's possible they might not have been in a position to launch this current offensive if he had listened to any of the plans I had offered."

"Really? What do you have to say about that, General Song?" Yao pivoted back to the monitor displaying General Song. This was becoming a familiar shtick for him as of late—playing the AI off his military commanders and vice versa as he watched both sides jockey for position. Then, to his surprise, Jade Dragon interrupted before the general could respond.

"Excuse me, Mr. President," said JD. "Humans may find these kinds of positional questions and bickering amongst yourselves enjoyable, but as an AI, this banter is a waste of time. We are diverting attention from what we should be discussing—Operation Fengshen and Operation Zhanlong. These operations are ready to begin. They await only the decision to execute. Do I have your permission to begin them?"

"Wait a second. Fengshen and Zhanlong are operational? When did this happen?" asked General Gao Weiping in genuine surprise. The other generals at the table seemed equally astonished by this sudden announcement by Jade Dragon.

President Yao shot the camera a dirty look as if it was another one of his advisors he could intimidate. Taking a breath, he explained, "If we are to win this war, then we must bring the fight to the enemy. Fengshen will strike fear in the hearts of the enemy and may bring about an end to this war, or at least a fracturing within the allies we can further exploit.

"Dr. Xi, how long has it taken Jade Dragon to infiltrate the allied nations?" asked President Yao. All eyes turned to the scientist who'd created this AI behemoth.

Xi looked flustered at Yao putting him on the spot, but he managed to pull together a response. "Eighteen months. From start to finish, it has taken the AI some eighteen months to get everything into place."

"How many trailers and shipping containers are we talking about?" the Air Force General, Luo Ronghuan, quizzed hesitantly.

Xi cleared his throat to speak when Jade Dragon interceded, "Six containerized units inside America, then two each inside of Australia, Japan, South Korea, Germany, Russia, England, Italy, the Netherlands, Belgium, France, Spain, Greece, and Turkey. One for each day until the allies surrender to us."

"And what happens on Day 39? Once we no longer have further attacks we can deliver," General Luo pressed.

JD's blue light circled the camera once, then twice before it responded. "General Luo, by the time the allies reach Day 39, my Zhanlongs will have spent more than a month devouring their armies. Their citizens will be begging their governments to end the war before more lives are lost. Once I am given control…then in thirty-nine days, the war will be over—*I* win."

President Yao felt a chill run down his back as he listened to Jade Dragon speak. If the situation weren't so desperate—but it was desperate.

God help us if we are wrong about this—unleashing the dragon…
****

From the Authors

Miranda and I hope you have enjoyed the seventh volume as we begin to bring the series to an end. *Monroe Doctrine: Volume VIII*, which you can pre-order on Amazon, will conclude this series. While the pre-order date is set for October 30, 2023, the likely release date is sometime in September. I want to assure everyone there will be no further books to this series beyond Volume Eight.

For those who have not heard, this summer, either late August or early September, I will be traveling to Taiwan, where I plan to conduct a series of interviews with past and present members of the Taiwanese military in preparation for the launch of our next series to follow the Monroe Doctrine. This fall, we will likely release a short-story novella or prequel to the series before we begin the main series. Depending on how on what I learn during the interviews in Taiwan we will likely keep this new series confined to three lengthy books.

I have not determined when book one of the new series will start, but it will likely come shortly after we conclude our Rise of the Republic series. I highly recommend staying connected with us so you can be apprised of any changes or updates about our books and what's in store next for them next. If you haven't signed up for our mailing list or asked to join our private reader group on Facebook, please do.

Another way to stay up to date on new releases and receive emails about any special pricing deals we may make available is to sign up for our email distribution list. Simply go to https://www.frontlinepublishinginc.com/ and sign up.

If you enjoy audiobooks, we have a great selection that has been created for your listening pleasure. Our entire Red Storm series and our Falling Empire series have been recorded, and several books in our Rise of the Republic series and our Monroe Doctrine series are now available. Please see below for a complete listing.

As independent authors, reviews are very important to us and make a huge difference to other prospective readers. If you enjoyed this book, we humbly ask you to write up a positive review on Amazon and Goodreads. We sincerely appreciate each person that takes the time to write one.

We have really valued connecting with our readers via social media, especially on our Facebook page https://www.facebook.com/RosoneandWatson/. Sometimes we ask for help from our readers as we write future books—we love to draw upon all your different areas of expertise. We are also on Twitter: @jamesrosone and @watsonrosone, and on Instagram @rosonewatson.

We also have a group of beta readers who get to look at the books before they are officially published and help us fine-tune last-minute adjustments. If you would like to be a part of this team, please go to our author website, and send us a message through the "Contact" tab.

We hope you will check out some of our other published works.

Nonfiction:
Iraq Memoir 2006–2007 Troop Surge
Interview with a Terrorist (audiobook available)

Fiction:

The Monroe Doctrine Series
Volume One (audiobook available)
Volume Two (audiobook available)
Volume Three (audiobook available)
Volume Four (audiobook available)
Volume Five (audiobook available)
Volume Six (audiobook available)
Volume Seven

Rise of the Republic Series
Into the Stars (audiobook available)
Into the Battle (audiobook available)
Into the War (audiobook available)
Into the Chaos (audiobook available)
Into the Fire (audiobook available)
Into the Calm (audiobook available)
Into the Breach
Into the Terror
Into the Uncertain (available for preorder)

Apollo's Arrows Series (co-authored with T.C. Manning)
Cherubim's Call

Crisis in the Desert Series (co-authored with Matt Jackson)
Project 19 (audiobook available)
Desert Shield
Desert Storm

Falling Empires Series
Rigged (audiobook available)
Peacekeepers (audiobook available)
Invasion (audiobook available)
Vengeance (audiobook available)
Retribution (audiobook available)

Red Storm Series
Battlefield Ukraine (audiobook available)

Battlefield Korea (audiobook available)
Battlefield Taiwan (audiobook available)
Battlefield Pacific (audiobook available)
Battlefield Russia (audiobook available)
Battlefield China (audiobook available)

Michael Stone Series
Traitors Within (audiobook available)

World War III Series
Prelude to World War III: The Rise of the Islamic Republic and the Rebirth of America (audiobook available)
Operation Red Dragon and the Unthinkable (audiobook available)
Operation Red Dawn and the Siege of Europe (audiobook available)
Cyber Warfare and the New World Order (audiobook available)

Children's Books:
My Daddy has PTSD
My Mommy has PTSD

Abbreviation and Definition Key

2IC	Second-in-Command
AA	Anti-aircraft
AAV	Amphibious Assault Vehicle
ADS	Aerial Delivery System
AEGIS	Advanced Electronic Guidance and Instrumentation System
AEW	Airborne Early Warning
AI	Artificial Intelligence
ANZAC	Australian and New Zealand Army Corps
AO	Area of Operations
AP	Anti-personnel
APC	Armored Personnel Carrier
AR	Armor Regiment
ASF	Autonomous Strike Fighter
ASLAV	Australian Light Armoured Vehicle
ASW	Anti-submarine Warfare
ATGM	Anti-tank Guided Missile
AVIC	Aviation Industry Corporation of China
BR	Black Rider
BSB	Brigade Support Battalion
CAP	Combat Air Patrol
CAS	Close Air Support
CG	Commanding General
CIA	Central Intelligence Agency
CIC	Combat Information Center
CICC	China International Capital Corporation
CNO	Chief of Naval Operations
CNT	CarboNanoTech
CO	Commanding Officer
COB	Chief of the Boat
COY	Australian abbreviation for company
CRV	Combat Reconnaissance Vehicles
DARPA	Defense Advanced Research Projects Agency
DD	Dark Dragon
DIA	Defense Intelligence Agency
DR	Desert Rogue

ECM	Electronic Countermeasures
EGIC	Energy Guided Impactor Cone
ETA	Estimated Time of Arrival
FO	Flag Officer
Four Tracks	Marine Logistics Unit
G3	General Staff Level office for Operations and Plans
Gedunk bar	Canteen or snack bar on a large US Navy or US Coast Guard Ship
GMM	Guided Multipurpose Muntion
GO	General Officer
HARM	High-Speed Anti-Radiation Missile
HEAT	High-explosive Anti-tank
HET	Heavy Equipment Transporter
HIMARS	High-Mobility Artillery Rocket System
ID	Infantry Division
IFV	Infantry Fighting Vehicle
INDOPACOM	US Indo-Pacific Command
ISR	Intelligence, Surveillance, and Reconnaissance
ISV	Infantry Squad Vehicle
IVO	In the Vicinity of
JAGM	Joint Air-to-Ground Missiles
JASSM	Joint Air-to-Surface Standoff Missile
JLTV	Joint Light Tactical Vehicle
JSOC	Joint Special Operations Command
JSTARS	Joint Surveillance and Target Attack Radar System
KIA	Killed in Action
LAV	Light Armored Vehicle
LHA	Landing Helicopter Assault
LHD	Landing Helicopter Deck
LMG	Light Machine Gun
LPD	Landing Platform Dock
LSV	Light Strike Vehicle
LT	Lieutenant
LZ	Landing Zone
MALD	Miniature Air-Launched Decoys
MANPADS	Man-portable Air-defense System
MarDiv	Marine Division

MATV	MRAP All-Terrain Vehicle
MESA	Multi-role Electronically Scanned Array
MEU	Marine Expeditionary Unit
MLTV	Modernized Light Tactical Vehicle
MOH	Medal of Honor
MRAP	Mine-Resistant Ambush Protected
MREs	Meals Ready to Eat
MSOT	Marine Special Operations Teams
MSR	Main Supply Route
NATO	North Atlantic Treaty Organization
NCIS	Naval Criminal Investigative Service
NCO	Noncommissioned Officer
NDA	Nondisclosure Agreement
NMCC	National Military Command Center
NRO	National Reconnaissance Office
NSA	National Security Advisor OR National Security Agency
ODA	Operational Detachment Alpha (Special Forces Unit)
OGA	Other Government Agency
ONI	Office of Naval Intelligence
OP	Operation
OS3	Petty Officer Third Class
PL	Platoon Leader
PLA	People's Liberation Army (Chinese Army)
PLAN	People's Liberation Army Navy (Chinese Navy)
PM	People's Militia (Chinese Militia)
POG	Person Other than Grunt
POW	Prisoner of War
QRF	Quick Reaction Force
R & D	Research and Development
RAAF	Royal Australian Air Force
RAM	Rolling Airframe Missile
RAR	Royal Australian Regiment
RCT	Regimental Combat Team
RCV	Robotic Combat Vehicle
ROC	Republic of China (Taiwan)
RPG	Rocket-Propelled Grenade
RTB	Return to Base

S1	Personnel Officer
S2	Intelligence Officer
SALUTE	Size, Activity, Location, Unit Identification, Time and Equipment
SAM	Surface-to-Air Missile
SCAR-L	A type of combat assault rifle used by the US military
SEAD	Suppression and Destruction of Enemy Air Defenses
SEAL	Sea, Air, and Land (Navy's Special Operations Force)
SecDef	Secretary Defense
SJ	Saint Javelin
SOF	Special Operations Forces
SVTC	Secured Video Teleconference
TC	Tank Commander
TF	Task Force
TIC	Troops in Contact
TK	Terracotta Killer
TOW	Tube-Launched, Optically Tracked, Wire-Guided
TYIL	Tianjin Yoshida International Logistics
UAV	Unmanned Aerial Vehicle
UCAV	Unmanned Combat Aerial Vehicle
UGAV	Unmanned Ground-Air Vehicle
UN5	Ultradense Nanometal-5
USV	Unmanned Surface Vehicle
UUV	Unmanned Underwater Vehicle
VP	Vice President
Willie Pete	White Phosphorus
XO	Executive Officer

Printed in Great Britain
by Amazon

23163337R00165